He pulled on the fingertips first to loosen the glove.

Then he reached for her upper arm and encountered silk-smooth skin. As he slowly rolled the long glove down her slender arm, he imagined doing the same with a stocking and kissing the soft flesh he revealed.

Her breathing was a bit faster now and so was his. He pulled on the fingers of the other kid glove to loosen it. Then he began to roll it inch by inch down her arm. As he removed the glove, he met her gaze and almost staggered at the sultry expression in her green eyes. He stood there, powerless to move. The tension was palpable and her rose scent was like a potion swirling inside him with every breath.

Her mouth was so close, and he wanted her too much to hold back. When their lips met, he turned her in his arms and pulled her up on her toes. He leaned over her, supporting her back with his hands. As she wrapped her arms around his neck, he captured her lips, and she opened for his tongue. She made a soft, feminine sound, and all he could think about was eliciting far more from her....

How to Seduce a Scoundrel

"Regency matchmaking, rakes, rogues, innocence, and scandal: oh what fun! Dreiling knows how to combine these ingredients into a delightfully delicious, wickedly witty slice of reading pleasure."

—RT Book Reviews

"5 stars! A fun and witty tale between two very strong characters...Vicky Dreiling has done an excellent job telling a character-driven story, but has kept it light-hearted enough to make it fun...I'm eager to read Book One now and will look forward to Book Three when it is released. I definitely recommend this one to any romance novel fan."

—TheRomanceReader.com

"5 stars! This was an enchanting tale that had me grinning from ear to ear. The chemistry between Marc and Julianne was flammable and only needed a spark to set it off."

—SeducedbyaBook.com

"The scenes between Julianne and Hawk are lots of fun; they have great physical chemistry and razor-sharp dialogue...I hope Ms. Dreiling's next Regency romance features one of Julianne's friends, as I'd like to revisit these characters again. If you like historical romance, I recommend *How to Seduce a Scoundrel*."

—NightOwlRomance.com

How to Marry a Duke

What a
Wicked Earl
Wants

Also by Vicky Dreiling

What a Wicked Earl Wants

Book 1—The Sinful Scoundrels Series

By

VICKY DREILING

FOREVER

NEW YORK   BOSTON

Copyright © 2013 by Vicky Dreiling
Excerpt from *What a Reckless Rogue Needs* © 2013 by Vicky Dreiling
All rights reserved. In accordance with the U.S. Copyright Act of 1976, the scanning, uploading, and electronic sharing of any part of this book without the permission of the publisher is unlawful piracy and theft of the author's intellectual property. If you would like to use material from the book (other than for review purposes), prior written permission must be obtained by contacting the publisher at permissions@hbgusa.com. Thank you for your support of the author's rights.

Forever
Hachette Book Group
237 Park Avenue
New York, NY 10017

www.HachetteBookGroup.com

Printed in the United States of America

First Edition: May 2013
10 9 8 7 6 5 4 3 2 1

OPM

Forever is an imprint of Grand Central Publishing.
The Forever name and logo are trademarks of Hachette Book Group, Inc.

The Hachette Speakers Bureau provides a wide range of authors for speaking events. To find out more, go to www.hachettespeakersbureau.com or call (866) 376-6591.

The publisher is not responsible for websites (or their content) that are not owned by the publisher.

To Daniel, Regina, and Autumn Rose, with all of my love.

Acknowledgments

Michele, I've said it before, but it bears repeating. Your insights are absolutely brilliant and make an incredible difference in my books. Thank you for everything.

Lucienne, thank you so much for all of your advice, for answering questions, and most of all for your enthusiasm. I'm so fortunate to have you for an agent.

Many thanks once again to Kati for being the best personal assistant ever. Thank you so very much!

Also, lots of thanks and hugs to my street team partner Kieran Kramer and to all of the Regency Rockstars. You are all fabulous. xoxoxo

To all of the readers, thank you so much for reading my books and for the kind e-mails letting me know how much you enjoy the stories I create. I wish you all hours of happy reading.

Cheers!
Vicky

What a
Wicked Earl
Wants

Chapter One

Andrew Carrington, the Earl of Bellingham, was on the hunt for a new mistress.

He stepped inside the elegant foyer, having timed his late arrival to avoid the ubiquitous receiving line in the ballroom. As he relinquished his greatcoat, hat, and gloves to the butler, he thought about the type of mistress he wanted. Beauty was a must, but equally important was cleverness. He couldn't abide foolishness in a woman, no matter how comely her appearance. Naturally he avoided married women and virgins. The former could cost him his life, and the latter could cost him his bachelorhood.

He straightened the stickpin in his cravat and strode into the great hall. A statue of Augustus stood at the base of the stairwell. The stone founder of the Roman Empire helpfully pointed the way upstairs.

Bell walked up one side of the U-shaped staircase, with its ornate iron balustrade. A dull roar sounded from the ballroom as a handful of guests spilled out onto the landing, no doubt to escape the heat generated by one too many bodies packed inside.

He gained the landing and entered the ballroom. The orchestra struck up a lively tune, and the voices grew louder. He pressed through the crowd in search of his friends, but he'd taken only a few steps when a stout matron glanced at him, grabbed the arm of a pencil-thin young lady, presumably her daughter, and hurried toward him. Bell turned and strode off in the opposite direction.

Hell. Five minutes into the ball and he was dodging a matchmaking mama and her daughter. The temptation to quit the place gripped him, but as he broke through the worst of the crowd, he saw his friends Harry and Colin standing by the sideboard.

When Bell reached them, he tugged on his cravat and said, "I need a drink."

Harry Norcliffe, Viscount Evermore, handed Bell a brandy. "Narrow escape, old boy."

Colin Brockhurst, Earl of Ravenshire, laughed. "We saw Lady Coburn and her daughter chasing after you."

Bell scowled. "I don't know her."

"She is Sir Harold Coburn's wife," Harry said. "Her daughter is Miss Anne Coburn, first season."

Bell downed the brandy in two swallows. "Intelligence from your girl cousins, no doubt."

"My aunt's drawing room is famous for the best gossip," Harry said.

Bell frowned. "I've had enough already. I say we quit the ball and go to my town house to play billiards."

"Wait," Harry said. "Last night you said you were looking for a mistress."

Bell set his glass on the sideboard. "The only available woman I'm likely to find here is a bored married lady, and I don't poach in other men's territory."

"You're in luck," Harry said. "There's a new widow in town."

Colin snorted. "Right. More news from the drawing room."

Harry nodded. "Yes. She's rumored to be quite mysterious."

Colin poured himself a brandy. "Harry, how can you take them seriously? Your cousins bamboozle you on a regular basis."

"They said she is beautiful and young."

"More likely old and ugly," Bell muttered.

"Always the optimist," Colin said.

Bell shook his head. "I'm a realist."

Harry shrugged. "I've yet to meet her, but she could be right beneath our noses."

"On the floor, you mean?" Colin quipped.

Harry pulled a face. "It's a bloody expression. Must you be so literal?"

Bell rolled his eyes. He'd only met his friends recently, but already he knew they argued over anything ridiculous. "In other words, Harry has no idea what her name is or what she looks like. At this point, I think the odds of meeting her are nonexistent."

"Because she doesn't exist," Colin said.

"Ha." Harry downed the rest of his brandy and poured another glass. "Her name is Lady Chesfield, and she hails from Hampshire. She's new to town and a particular friend of Lady Atherton."

"A close friend of Lady Atherton?" Colin's dark eyes

gleamed in the candlelight. "I daresay Bell will be delighted...despite the thirty-year age difference."

Harry narrowed his eyes. "You're wrong. I wager you a tenner he'll make her his mistress in a fortnight or sooner."

"You don't have ten pounds," Colin said.

Harry shrugged. "I will when you lose the wager."

The orchestra struck up the opening bars of a country dance. Harry and Colin left to find their dance partners. Bell poured himself another brandy and turned to watch the crowd. A circle of guests disbanded, and then he saw his former mistress, Barbara. He set his glass aside and strolled over to her.

"Bellingham, you are as handsome as ever," she said.

He bowed over her hand. "How is married life?"

"You know it was for convenience," she said. A sly smile touched her lips. "I couldn't wait for you."

There was something in her expression that made him suspect she wasn't jesting. "You have security." It was no small thing for a woman.

"Security is dull," she said.

He examined the diamond-studded ruby ring on her finger. "You also gained a title and wealth."

"I made a bad bargain."

He released her hand and didn't bother to mention the obvious. Marriage was forever—until death do them part.

She lifted her frank gaze to him. "I'm doomed to unhappiness in marriage for a second time," she said.

It wasn't the first time she'd revealed her fatalistic outlook on life. Perhaps it had started when her first husband had died in the war. Yet, she'd taken advantage of her freedom as a widow and had more than a few protectors. She'd likely spent every penny of her pensions and accepted Norris's marriage proposal out of desperation.

"I loathe Norris," she said. "I try to pretend it's you, but there is no comparison. I stare at the canopy and—"

"No tales from the boudoir." He remembered how she'd always worn her feelings on her sleeve like a naïve girl.

She twirled a dark curl by her cheek. "I miss you."

It had been nothing more than a short-lived liaison. He'd made the terms clear, but when she'd said she loved him, he'd ended it immediately.

She closed the distance between them and walked her gloved fingers down the front of his waistcoat. "Perhaps we could meet later tonight—for old time's sake."

Bell caught her hand, lifted it for the requisite air kiss, and released her. "Norris would object."

"He doesn't have to know."

"Your husband is staring daggers as we speak."

"I don't care," she said.

"You will if you're not careful," he said. "Don't do something you'll regret."

"I regret letting you get away."

"There is nothing to regret." He gave her a cynical smile. "I never stay."

"I'd almost forgotten what a heartless bastard you are," she said with a brittle laugh.

"You've got the heartless part right," he said, "but I was born on the right side of the blanket." He paused and added, "In all seriousness, you are courting trouble the longer you speak to me."

"Let me come to you tonight," she said.

She was foolish to even consider such a risk, but she seemed determined to enact her own tragedy. "Sorry, I won't be the instrument of your downfall." He walked away, fearing that sooner or later Norris would catch her in an indiscretion. Some men overlooked it, but by law Norris could beat her and sue her lover in civil court. He hoped for her sake that she would be cautious.

Bell returned to the sideboard and thrust Barbara out of his thoughts. He poured two fingers of brandy and turned, only to find a petite blonde looking over her shoulder. She had a flawless, creamy complexion and a button nose. As she met his gaze, her eyes widened.

He expected her to look away, but she seemed almost mesmerized. Bell frowned, wondering if he'd met her before. No, he would have remembered the way her lips turned up slightly at the corners, even though she wasn't really smiling, at least not full on. Any moment now, she would remember herself and avert her eyes.

Her lips parted a bit as she continued to stare. Over the years, more than a few women had given him second glances as they walked past, but this one was ogling him in a rather blatant manner. A wicked grin tugged at his mouth. He decided to see what she would do when he inspected her.

Bell let his gaze slide ever so slowly from her eyes down past her long neck to her plump breasts. He continued in a leisurely fashion to her slim waist and slender hips. As he inspected her skirts, he figured she had slender legs to match her slender arms. Then he slowly reversed his gaze until he lingered over her breasts. Devil that he was, he imagined pale pink nipples. When he met her eyes, his heart beat a bit faster. He was in the middle of a ballroom and had made no effort to hide the fact that he was mentally undressing her. Obviously the blonde was issuing an invitation. Or was she? There was only one way to find out.

He winked at her.

A rosy flush spread over her face. She spun around, her airy overskirt floating a bit. Then she shook out her fan with a hand as diminutive as the rest of her and covered the lower half of her face. He half expected her to peek slyly above the ivory sticks, but instead she pressed through the crowd as if trying to escape. A moment later, Lady Atherton tapped the blonde on the shoulder, startling her.

Could she be the mysterious widow?

Lady Atherton led the blonde a few paces forward, and the two engaged in a tête-à-tête. The blonde woman shook her head vigorously, causing her sapphire earrings to bobble a bit. For some odd reason, he found it alluring.

Obviously she'd never intended to flirt, and somehow that left him feeling a bit deflated, which was ridiculous. He'd been more than a little intrigued, but he should keep his distance. Lady Atherton was a well-known high stickler and would have put a flea in his ear if she'd seen him visually stripping the clothes off the younger woman.

Harry returned and poured himself a brandy. "Did you meet the new widow yet?"

"No." They hadn't met, but she'd intrigued him, and he couldn't recall the last time a woman had done that.

Harry sighed. "I think my cousins are leading me on a merry chase."

"Probably," Bell said.

"I'm to dance the next set with Miss Martindale," Harry said. "I'd better find her."

As Bell made his way through the crowd, he noticed that Lady Atherton was strolling with the petite blonde again. In all likelihood, she was too respectable to be any man's mistress. For all he knew, she was some man's wife.

He'd had enough of the noise and decided to walk out to the gardens to smoke a cheroot. Though he wasn't familiar with the layout of the house, he managed to find his way to the door leading outside. There were lanterns in the trees, but he detected no one about. The wind was a bit chilly as it whipped the tails of his coat, but he welcomed the cold as he used one of the lanterns to light a cheroot. The wind riffled the leaves in the tall trees. He inhaled the smoke from the cheroot and enjoyed the relative silence.

He blew a smoke ring and wondered about the best way to secure a new mistress. The Cyprians were giving another entertainment next week. He would see if anyone caught his fancy there.

For some odd reason, he couldn't get his visual encounter with the blond lady out of his mind. She was obviously Lady Atherton's protégé, but that didn't mean she was a widow available for dalliance. Lord only knew where or how these rumors got started, but he thought a widow might suit him, provided she understood that marriage was not in the offing. It would be a tricky business, trying to figure out whether the widow was amenable to an intimate relationship or not. If he made a mistake, he would cause a grievous insult. His lips curved a bit. Since when had he ever missed an opportunity to persuade a lady to loosen her morals?

He ground out the cheroot and lit up another. The low rumble of masculine laughter made Bell frown. Patches of misty fog made it difficult to see, but three young men emerged on the other side of the path. They halted and passed something around. Bell wagered it was a flask.

When the trio disappeared from his sight, he shrugged. They were safe from thieves and pickpockets in the garden. How they would fare guzzling whatever liquor was in the flask was another matter altogether, but they likely would pay for it with the bottle ache on the morrow.

A few minutes later, he ground out his cheroot. He thought of returning to the house but decided to indulge in one more cheroot first. Periodically, Bell heard the low laughter of the three young bucks. At one point, he was absolutely certain that one of them was pissing in the garden. By now, Bell was weary of the entire ball and the foolish young men. He inhaled from his cheroot one last time and put it out.

Then the door to the back of the house creaked open and shut.

Bell wondered if a pair of lovers meant to sneak out for a few kisses or more when he heard a feminine voice call out.

"Justin?"

The three bucks suddenly grew silent. Bell couldn't decide if he ought to expose them or not. In the end, he kept quiet. They weren't his responsibility.

The unknown lady's slippers crunched on the gravel path. A misty fog settled near the ground, obscuring the objects in the garden.

"Justin? If you're out here, please let me know."

She was nearing Bell, but he wasn't sure if she could see him or not.

Then she stepped out of the shadowy mist, right before him. In the flash of a lantern, he recognized her as the blond lady. God, even in this dim light, she was stunning.

She gazed right at him and gasped.

"Wait," he said. "Allow me to assist you."

"No." She backed up. Then she lifted her skirts, whirled around, and took off running as if she'd seen Lucifer waiting to snatch her.

He started after her, but his footsteps slowed. She'd said the one word every man should respect. *No.*

The low rumble of masculine voices sounded again. Bell released a long sigh as he watched the trio creep back toward the house like thieves in the night. They paused about five feet from the door and passed the flask around. Good Lord, they were brazen.

Eventually they stumbled inside the mansion and made no attempt to hide their laughter.

Bell wiped the dampness off the shoulders of his coat and strolled back to the house. He might as well return home, since he'd struck out on finding a mistress. Tomorrow he would think of a new plan.

He strode through the corridor, noting someone had lit a candle branch. When he emerged, he heard a cacophony of voices coming from the dining room. He had no wish to make himself agreeable to anyone else this evening.

Bell strode toward the foyer but halted beside the stairwell upon hearing a feminine voice from the staircase. "Justin?"

He couldn't see her from this vantage point.

He heard an odd sound beneath the stairwell. Bell looked underneath in time to see a man pushing a flask beneath it with his heel. Then footsteps clipped on the marble floor. "I'm here," the man said, walking to the bottom of the staircase.

Bell noted he was the young man with a shock of wheat-colored hair.

"Where have you been?" a woman said in a stern tone. "I've looked everywhere for you."

"Oh, we just moved about the ballroom and the adjoining rooms," he said.

What an accomplished liar he was, Bell thought.

"Your face is flushed," the woman said as she descended. Now Bell could see her. She was the blond woman he'd seen in the garden.

"I hope you haven't been drinking with your friends again," she said.

"Always suspicious," the young man said.

"It's late, and I wish to return home," the blonde said.

A few minutes later, their voices receded.

Approaching footsteps alerted Bell. He turned as Lady Atherton regarded him with a knowing smile. "Are you in the habit of listening to others' conversations, Bellingham?" she asked.

"Not if I can help it. And you?"

"I'm just the hostess of this grand squeeze," she said.

"Who is she?" he asked.

Lady Atherton took a deep breath and slowly released it. "She's not for the likes of you, Bell."

He recalled the way the blonde had stared at him earlier with parted lips. "I didn't ask if she was for me. I asked for her name."

Lady Atherton shook her head. "Leave her be, Bellingham. She's a widow with a boy to rear. You want no part of her life."

"I'm afraid I am part of it, unwillingly," he said. The blonde must be the widow his friends had mentioned, but he said nothing of that to Lady Atherton. He reached beneath the stairwell and retrieved the flask. "You see, I believe she needs to know her son is lying through his teeth."

"Oh dear. She did say he was at a trying age."

"That, I believe, is an understatement."

Lady Atherton sighed and held out her hand. "Give the flask to me, and I'll see that it's returned."

This was an opportunity to find out if she had meant to issue him an invitation when she'd stared at him earlier. He told himself he only wanted to warn her about her son. He told himself she had every right to know. He told himself that the boy might find himself in serious straits if he didn't alert her. But ultimately, he knew he wouldn't be able to get her out of his head until he spoke to her. "He's taking advantage of her. Someone needs to put the fear of the devil in that boy."

Lady Atherton's eyes widened. "And you think you're the one to do it? Hah!"

"I'm an eyewitness." He paused and added, "I want her name."

"Only if you swear this is about the boy and nothing else," she said.

He felt victorious, but he hid it. "Her name and address, please."

Lady Atherton hesitated again. "Her name is Laura Davenport. That's Lady Chesfield to you," she said, her expression sharp. "Her address is number ten, Grosvenor Square. And, Bellingham, I meant what I said. She's a respectable widow and not for the likes of a rakehell like you."

Perhaps, but he meant to find out. "She's incredibly naïve where that boy is concerned."

Lady Atherton clasped her hands. "Well, I agree he ought to have more respect for his stepmother."

Bell bowed. "Thank you for an interesting evening." Then he strode out the door.

The next afternoon

After dismissing his secretary, Bell opened the desk drawer where he'd stowed the flask last night. After retrieving it, he thought about his plans to return the flask to Lady Chesfield and reconsidered. What the devil did he expect to gain? The last thing he wanted was to become involved in the lady's problems.

She was a stranger to him. They had not been introduced, and yet, he'd pried her name and address from Lady Atherton, who was very strict about the proprieties. He ought to have left well enough alone. Now he was obliged to return the blasted flask.

Out of curiosity, he opened the flask, expecting to find cheap gin, but one sniff proved the liquor was brandy. Bell sipped it and realized it was of top-notch quality. Most likely the young buck had purloined the brandy from a decanter at home.

The wayward young man wasn't his responsibility. He could send a footman to deliver the flask, but Lady Chesfield wouldn't know why he'd sent it. With a sigh, he drew out paper, pen, and ink, thinking he would describe what he'd seen last night. No, that was too much trouble. He would simply state in his message that he'd found her son's flask. Whatever transpired afterward was none of his affair.

Bell started to shut the drawer when he saw the small leather sketchbook inside that had belonged to his mother. His heart drummed in his ears. A new maid had recently found it in the attic. That day, he'd looked at one page and shoved it inside the desk drawer. Bell ought to have told the maid to return it to the attic the day the sketchbook was discovered. Then it would have been out of his sight and mind forever. He walked over to the bell, intending to ring for the housekeeper. He meant to ask her to return the sketchbook to the attic. But he hesitated, because he didn't want her to touch it.

After four years, he ought to have put the past behind him. Most of the time, he managed to shove it to the far corners of his brain, but the periodic nightmares served as a reminder of all that he'd loved and lost.

He returned to the desk, determined to shut the drawer. But something beckoned him. His ears thudded as he retrieved the sketchbook and opened it to a random page. A small boy sat on a sofa with a bundled infant. He gritted his teeth at the inscription near the bottom of the page. *Andrew, age two, holding Steven one month after birth.* His heart thumped at the sketch of him and his younger brother.

Damn it all to hell. He'd known nothing good could come of resurrecting the memories. They were gone forever.

He'd been too late all those years ago.

Bell shut the sketchbook and shoved it back inside the cubbyhole in the desk. The past no longer existed. There was only the here and now.

Gritting his teeth, he strode over to the bell rope and pulled it. When Griffith, the butler, appeared, Bell made arrangements to have his carriage brought round. He would deliver the flask to Lady Chesfield and have done with the matter once and for all.

Laura Davenport, Lady Chesfield, sat with her new lap desk and drew out paper, pen, and ink. She tried to think of what to tell her sister Rachel about her "London adventure," as her sister called it. Thus far, they had attended only one ball—the one last night that her friend Lady Atherton had hosted.

She dared not say a word to Rachel about Justin's rebellion. From the moment they had arrived, Justin had taken up with his friends from school and his attitude had grown surly. Worse, he'd taken to leaving with his friends at night and arriving home after midnight. He'd told her he was attending parties given by his friends' parents, but she didn't know them and was never invited.

Rachel had always been her confidant, but Laura knew Rachel would read the letter to her family. She didn't want to alarm them, but she was worried.

Last night, Justin had disappeared from the ball for a long time. She'd even gone out into the garden to look for him and encountered that rake Bellingham again, but he was the least of her problems.

She'd finally found Justin at the stairwell. After smelling liquor on her son's breath, she'd rebuked him soundly in the carriage for lying and drinking. Of course, he'd sworn never to do it again, but she had a bad feeling about his friends and the influence they had on him.

Laura put away the writing instruments and shoved the drawer closed. She was furious with her son. He'd begged to go to London with his friends, but she'd refused because she didn't know their parents. Justin had pleaded with her day after day, and she'd finally made a compromise by offering to take him so that she could keep a close eye on him.

A knock sounded. "Come in," she said, hoping it was her son.

Reed, the butler, entered. "The mail arrived, my lady."

She took the letters and dismissed Reed. The first few were from the estate manager at Hollwood Abbey. She read them quickly, satisfied that all was running well in her absence. Then she slit the seal on one and looked at the signature. It was from Montclief, her son's guardian. In the past four years, Montclief had never responded to her letters. Her chest tightened as she started reading from the beginning. His tone was so insulting it stunned her.

You ought to have consulted me prior to taking my nephew on a journey. I certainly hope you've the funds to pay for all the expenses, because I refuse to release his quarterly allowance for a trip that I did not approve. In the future, you will consult me before making travel arrangements for my nephew. He is my ward, and your role is only to follow my instructions.

She stood and fisted her hands. How dare he suddenly decide to intervene in their lives when he'd not lifted a hand to help Justin for years? He'd actually told her that he was too busy with his own children to bother with Justin. Now Montclief had suddenly decided to mount a high horse and start issuing commands. He was awfully late in establishing his authority.

Laura started to tear the letter and then thought better of it. Someday she might require it as proof of his neglect to his own nephew, though she doubted any court would side with a woman.

Fortunately, she did have the means to pay for all of their expenses. She had never intended to make use of Justin's quarterly allowance, even though she had every right to use it to pay for his clothing, food, and lodgings.

She took a deep breath and blew it out. Well, she supposed the only reason Montclief had even responded was because she'd felt obliged to inform him about their activities. In the future, she would simply ignore Montclief, the same way he'd ignored Justin and her.

Reed arrived at the door. "Lord Chesfield left a few minutes ago."

"Did he say where he was going?" she asked. He'd been home only twenty minutes.

"No, my lady. He left with his friends in a curricle."

Her temples ached. He'd not bothered to ask her permission. "Thank you, Reed."

After the butler left, she paced the drawing room. She regretted bringing her son to London, but she had not foreseen that Justin's behavior would take a dramatic turn for the worse. He was seventeen years old and thought himself worldly. It frightened her to think of the seedy places he might go with his friends. In this enormous city, any manner of awful things could happen to him. She had to make him understand that he could get hurt if he encountered ruffians.

The moment he returned home, she would confront him again. He needed to know she would not tolerate his insubordination.

She sat on the sofa and picked up her cup. Unfortunately the tea had grown cold. She started to get up and ring the bell when a light tap sounded at the door. Reed entered and said, "My lady, you have a caller."

"Is it Lady Atherton?"

"No, my lady." He held out a silver salver. Laura picked up the card. Upon seeing the name, she dropped it.

Reed retrieved it. "My lady, shall I show Lord Bellingham upstairs?"

Good heavens no. "Reed, please inform the earl that I am not at home," Laura said.

"Yes, my lady."

After her butler quit the drawing room, Laura exhaled. Doubtless she was the only woman in London who had the temerity to refuse admittance to the Earl of Bellingham. Indeed, she suspected even the most genteel of ladies would flutter their fans and flirt outrageously with him. Since she was a vicar's daughter, Laura liked to think she was made of sterner stuff. Unfortunately, she'd discovered last night that she was more than a little susceptible to the uncommonly handsome earl.

She would not think about the way he'd let his gaze travel over her body last evening at the ball. Most certainly she would not dwell on the way her skin had heated while he'd perused her with his astonishingly blue eyes.

Above all, she would banish the naughty fantasies that had danced in her head while she'd tossed and turned in bed last night.

Even if she wanted to dally with the notorious earl, she would not dare, especially after receiving Montclief's scathing letter. Yesterday, she would not have worried a jot about Justin's uncle. Today, his letter had left her fearful that Montclief would take Justin away if he heard there was even a hint of a problem.

Laura inhaled and exhaled slowly to steady her nerves. She would write a short letter to Montclief to reassure him that all was well in London. It would be an outrageous lie, for Justin had turned quite rebellious recently. She must impress upon Justin the necessity of steering clear of trouble. If he did not cooperate, she would have no choice but to remove him from London.

Another knock startled her. "Come in," she said.

"My lady, Lord Bellingham asked me to convey this flask to you," Reed said. "His lordship said it was imperative that he speak to you."

Laura rose and frowned. How had he discovered her name and address? The thought bothered her more than a little. She had no idea why he'd sent up a flask of all things, but regardless, it did not signify. "Reed, I assume this is Lord Bellingham's idea of a jest, but I will not accept his gift nor will I see him."

"Yes, my lady," Reed said. "I will inform him that you are not accepting callers."

"Thank you, Reed."

After her butler left, Laura released a shaky breath. They had not been formally introduced, and Lady Atherton had made it clear last night that Lord Bellingham was a rake. She most certainly did not wish to make his acquaintance.

Laura walked over to the window. The day was gray and cloudy, promising rain. She fingered the gold, silken ropes and tassels that tied the draperies. The wavy glass distorted the view somewhat, but that shiny black carriage below obviously belonged to the Earl of Bellingham. Any moment now, he would emerge from her town house. All she wanted was to see the back of him retreating.

Another carriage drew up along the street. Laura surmised that it was her new friend Lady Atherton, because outside of making the acquaintance of several people last night, she knew no one else. Oh dear, Lady Atherton would likely encounter the earl as she walked to the door. The situation was terribly awkward, but Laura knew she'd done the correct thing by refusing Bellingham.

Footsteps sounded outside the door. Another tap sounded. Certain it was her butler, Laura said, "Come in." She kept her gaze on the street below, expecting to see Lord Bellingham striding toward his vehicle any moment. After the door shut, she said, "Reed, I hope you sent the earl on his way."

"He tried, but I'm not easily dissuaded."

The deep male voice startled her. Laura turned around with a gasp to find the earl standing in her drawing room. She pressed her hand to her fast-beating heart. For some reason he seemed taller than last night. One thing was clear: The man was far too bold. "My lord, are you in the habit of dispensing with the proprieties?"

His mouth curved sideways in a roguish grin. "As a matter of fact, I am."

Her butler arrived huffing and puffing. "My lady," he said.

She glanced at Reed. "I will take care of the matter."

Her butler hesitated, and then he quit the drawing room.

Laura returned her attention to the earl. For a moment, she found herself captivated by his handsome face and artfully disheveled dark hair. In the daylight, his thick black lashes added to the allure of his brilliant blue eyes.

When he arched his brows, Laura recollected her common sense and gave him a withering look. "I made it clear that I am not at home to callers, and yet you persisted, even though we have not been formally introduced."

"Lady Chesfield, I am honored to make your acquaintance." He bowed. "Bellingham, at your service."

Her temper flared. "How did you learn my name and address?"

"I asked Lady Atherton last evening," he said.

The news physically jolted her. Lady Atherton was her friend. "I find it difficult to believe that Lady Atherton would give out that information."

His brows drew together in a fierce manner. "She did not wish to tell me, but I insisted."

"Why?" she said. "We are strangers. You can have no business with me."

He held up a flask. "Actually, my business is with your stepson."

She tensed, and within moments, a chill ran down her spine. Oh God, had Justin stolen it? She would not voice the words, because she couldn't make herself do it. "How do you know him?"

Lord Bellingham shrugged. "I don't know him, but

I have encountered him and his friends loitering on the streets of London more than once. I don't think they understand the potential dangers of footpads."

"Thank you, my lord. I will discuss the matter with Justin."

"Are you aware that he and his friends were drinking in the garden last night?"

"I did not hear or see them." She had smelled spirits on Justin's breath, but the earl did not need to know that.

"After you left the garden, they returned to the house," Bellingham continued. "I followed and saw him push this flask beneath the stairs."

"My lord, thank you for your concern. Now, if you will give me the flask, I will speak to Justin."

He arched his brows. "It's brandy, very fine brandy, in case you are wondering."

Laura glanced at the sideboard. As soon as she got rid of His Haughtiness, she would check the brandy decanter.

He regarded her with an intense expression. "I don't make a habit of intervening in other's affairs, but I heard him lie to you about his whereabouts at the ball. It is clear to me that he's pulling the wool over your eyes."

How dare he insinuate that she was too naïve to parent her own stepson? "My lord, he is my son and my responsibility. I appreciate your concern and will speak to him."

He took a step closer. "How well is that working?"

She drew in a sharp breath. "I owe you no explanations. This is none of your affair. Now please leave."

He looked away for a moment, and then he returned his attention to her. "Call him to the drawing room. When he realizes that I and others have marked his wayward behavior, he will think twice before lying to you again."

She had no intention of following his orders. Justin wasn't even at home, but she would not tell the arrogant earl that. Laura bobbed a curtsy. "Good day, Lord Bellingham," she said in an obvious dismissal.

He set the flask on a side table. "I beg your pardon for interfering. Despite what you may think, it was meant kindly."

She recollected Lady Atherton's advice about him last night. *What he wants, he gets. Be sure it's not you.* No, he'd definitely not intervened out of kindness.

Footsteps and voices sounded outside the drawing room. "Sir, allow me to inform her ladyship that you have come to call," Reed said.

"I do not require an announcement and will see her now."

Laura gasped as she recognized the voice. She snatched the flask and hid it behind one of the rolled sofa cushions.

"What the devil?" Bellingham said.

She entreated him with her eyes. "It is Montclief, Justin's guardian. Please, say nothing of Justin to him," she said in a low tone.

"Why?" he said. "If he is the guardian—"

"Please," she said, aware that her voice shook. "There is no time to explain. I will do anything you ask, but I beg you not to betray me."

He arched his brows. "Anything?"

"Yes, anything," she said, worrying her hands.

He snared her with his blue eyes. "Be careful what you promise."

Oh dear. Perhaps she should have qualified her response, but there was no time for that now. She must gather her scattered wits and pretend to be perfectly at ease. The notion would have been laughable, if she weren't so desperate. Dear God, she had no idea how she would deal with that rakehell, but for now, she must focus solely on her son's guardian. She entreated Bellingham with her eyes once more. "Please, I beg you to concur with whatever I say."

"What will you say?"

A good question, but the door opened and Reed said, "Mr. Montclief, my lady."

Laura clasped her hands hard. What would Montclief think when he saw her with a scoundrel in her drawing room? Somehow she must concoct a story, but her frazzled mind refused to work properly.

Montclief entered with a thunderous expression, and then he stopped short upon seeing Bellingham.

Laura curtsied and noted her brother-in-law's hair had thinned considerably since she'd last seen him at her husband's funeral four years ago. She took a deep breath and said, "Montclief, what a delightful surprise. I just received your letter today but had no idea you meant to visit. Obviously you wish to see for yourself that all is well in London." Heavens, she was babbling like a fool.

Montclief narrowed his eyes. "Laura, you are clearly discomposed." He turned toward Bellingham. "Will you not introduce me to your gentleman caller?"

Doubtless, Montclief had assumed the worst. He probably thought she'd brought Justin here on a pretext so that she could dally with her nonexistent lover. "Lord Bellingham, may I introduce Mr. Montclief? He is my stepson's uncle and guardian."

Montclief bowed. "My lord, of course I know your name from the papers."

Drat. Montclief had probably seen the mention of the Earl of B—ham in the scandal sheets. Oh, this was a disaster in the making.

"That criminal conversation case before parliament must have been quite the sensation," Montclief said.

"It was a dead bore," Bellingham said.

Laura frowned. "Criminal conversation?"

"Pardon me. It is an indelicate subject for a lady," Montclief said.

A devilish expression lit Bellingham's eyes. "It is a euphemism for *adultery*."

She rolled her eyes. "How ridiculous. Why not call a spade a spade?"

"My sentiments exactly," Bellingham said.

No doubt he'd participated in criminal conversation on any number of occasions. "Shall we be seated? I will ring for a tea tray. You must be thirsty after your journey, Montclief."

"I wish to see my nephew."

"He is out," she said. From the corner of her eye, she saw Bellingham lift his brows in a skeptical manner, but she must not lose her focus. "His friend George took him in his curricle to Gunthers for ices." The explanation sounded innocent enough to her. In truth, Justin had slept past noon, and then George had arrived. When Laura asked where they were going, Justin had regarded her with a mulish expression and walked out the door.

"When do you expect him to return?" Montclief said, narrowing his eyes.

"I cannot say for certain. They will probably take a

turn round Rotten Row at the fashionable hour," she said. "I hope you will dine with us." She hoped nothing of the kind, but she must be polite, even to her loathsome brother-in-law.

Montclief's severe expression did not bode well. "We must discuss my nephew." He turned his attention to Bellingham. "Obviously this is a family matter. I'm sure you understand."

Laura's stomach clenched. The last thing she wanted was to be alone with Montclief. When Bellingham opened his mouth as if to speak, Laura knew she must intervene. "Actually, Lord Bellingham has taken an interest in Justin." Oh, heavens, Bellingham would likely deny her claim.

Montclief looked at Bellingham and let out a long sigh. "So you, too, have seen him running wild in the streets."

Oh, no. She was about to refute the statement, but Bellingham spoke before she could. "I saw them in the garden with friends at a ball last night."

At least he'd not given anything away—yet. "Yes, he saw Justin last evening, but there's no need for alarm," Laura said.

Montclief ignored her and returned his attention to Bellingham. "Was he drinking spirits?"

Laura held her breath and entreated Bellingham with her eyes once again.

Bellingham glanced at her and then shrugged. "I cannot say."

Laura clasped her hands. "You see, it was all a misunderstanding."

When Montclief narrowed his eyes, she knew she'd

said the wrong thing. "There is no misunderstanding. I have a letter from a friend in London who saw Justin drinking from a flask on the streets. You should have contacted me about this matter. I demand an explanation."

She must not let her composure slip. "All is well now."

Bellingham gave her a brief, dubious look.

"Laura," Montclief said, "all is not well. You brought my nephew to London without asking my permission and have concealed his inappropriate behavior. I cannot rely on your poor judgment."

She itched to give him the set down he deserved, but she did not dare incur his wrath. "There is no need for alarm. I have matters under control." She'd lied, but what else could she do?

"You are only a woman and incapable of managing a high-spirited boy," Montclief said. "He needs the daily influence of a man."

Desperation gripped her like talons. "You need not worry, Montclief," she said. "Lord Bellingham is helping to turn the tide." She held her breath, fearing Bellingham would deny her claim.

Bellingham kept his expression impassive. "Young men need to understand that it is wrong to take advantage of one's mother."

He'd adeptly avoided lying and had not betrayed her. She could kiss his big boots.

"I appreciate your assistance, Bellingham," Montclief said. "However, I have already made my decision. My nephew needs more than passing male influence." He turned to Laura. "Please see that his trunks are packed. I will take him home with me tomorrow. You may reside in the house in Hampshire until he reaches his majority."

She couldn't breathe. This could not be happening. He was her son. Montclief had never taken any interest in Justin—until now. Oh, God, she would not let Montclief take her son away. "No," she said. "No, please do not take him."

"Laura, this is not negotiable," Montclief said.

Panic rose up in her chest. She was breathing too fast. The fear of losing Justin nearly overwhelmed her, but she must persuade Montclief to change his mind. "You have such a large brood already and are overly tasked. I have looked after Justin all these years." *I love him too much to let you take him away.*

He gave her a patronizing look and shook his head.

She pressed her nails into her palms to keep from blurting out what she really thought of Montclief's negligence these past four years. As much as she despised him, she could not afford to antagonize her brother-in-law. "He's already lost his father. I am his mother, and if you take him away, he will feel that I have abandoned him."

"You are his stepmother," Montclief corrected.

His words stung, for he'd implied that she wasn't a real mother, but she would not allow his slight to deter her. No matter what anyone thought, Justin was her son. She would do whatever it took to keep him with her, including placating Montclief. "I believe Justin deserves another chance. I will emphasize that he must behave—"

"You've already proven you are incapable of it," Montclief said. "I've made my decision, and that is the end of the discussion."

After all this time, Montclief meant to exercise his rights as a guardian. The disbelief started to wear off, and then her hands trembled. She clutched them tightly, because she didn't want Montclief to see her anguish. "He hasn't even seen you for four years. It will be hard on him."

Montclief puffed up. "The material point is that you cannot give my nephew the discipline and guidance that he needs."

She would do anything—anything—to keep Montclief from taking Justin away. But what could she do to convince her brother-in-law? Oh, God, she must think of some way to change his mind. Laura thought back over the entire conversation, and one thing he'd said stood out. *My nephew needs more than passing male influence.*

The answer popped into her head. She met Bellingham's gaze again and prayed he would go along with her scheme. At this point, she had nothing to lose—except her son. And she refused to give him up without a fight.

God forgive me, but I cannot live without my son.

She drew closer to Bellingham and forced herself to smile. "I suppose we should tell Montclief our happy news."

Suspicion flickered in his blue eyes. "I'll allow you to reveal the particulars."

She clasped his arm and faced Montclief. "You mustn't worry about Justin needing a man to guide him." She took a deep breath and said, "I have this day accepted Lord Bellingham's proposal of marriage."

The woman was mad.

Bell had sensed her desperation climbing as she'd tried to persuade Montclief to let her keep the boy, but he'd never guessed she would resort to this witless fabrication.

Montclief folded his arms over his chest. "You have been in London for a very short time, Laura. This engagement is sudden, too sudden."

"Montclief, I said nothing before because I did not know our relationship would take such a romantic turn," Laura said. "Lord Bellingham and I met last fall in Hampshire."

Bell suspected the wayward Justin had learned to lie from his inventive mother.

She regarded Bell with a dazzling smile. "I met him by pure coincidence while visiting one of the shops in the village. Isn't that right, my dear?"

He nodded, hoping she wouldn't get too carried away. The less she said the better.

"It was raining," she said, "and we were stuck in the shop. Having nothing better to do, we struck up a conversation. When the rain stopped, we walked outside and he laid his coat over a puddle for me." She batted her eyes at him. "That was the moment I fell for my Bellingham."

She was the worst liar in the kingdom.

"Laura, this engagement is suspect," Montclief said.

Bellingham agreed, but he didn't like Montclief. From the bits she'd revealed, he gathered Montclief had taken no interest in his nephew until now. Most likely, the only reason he'd intervened was because he'd gotten embarrassed when his friend in London had sent him the letter about his nephew.

Laura looked quite determined as she gazed into Bell's eyes. "I would do anything for my Bellingham. Anything," she added with emphasis.

He most certainly would hold her to that promise.

Montclief addressed him. "Is this true, Bellingham? You have proposed to Laura?"

He almost exposed her as a liar, but he'd seen her hands shake when Montclief had declared he would take her son away. Bell figured the boy's rebellion would grow far worse under Montclief's thumb. On the other hand, Bell didn't want to find himself trapped in a marriage, either. "We are keeping the engagement a secret for the time being." Why not add one more lie to the growing pile?

Laura exhaled in obvious relief. "Yes, we are concealing our engagement in order to give Justin time to get to know Bellingham. We wish Justin to feel at ease with him before we exchange vows. Of course, we shall rely on your discretion, Montclief."

Montclief narrowed his eyes. "Laura, this engagement rings false." He turned his attention to Bellingham. "What I cannot understand is why Bellingham would act as your accomplice?"

Because I despise you for bullying her. Aloud, he said, "Are you implying that our engagement is a criminal act?"

"You know very well what I meant," Montclief said.

Bell had tolerated Montclief long enough. He strode over to the much shorter man and loomed over him. "You dare to question my word?" he said in a low, warning tone.

Montclief lifted his chin and his nostrils flared. "It is my responsibility to see that my nephew is well cared for and made to behave. I am the best person to see it done."

"Really? If your nephew walked in the door, would you recognize him?" Bell asked.

Montclief's face flushed. "You have no say in this, Bellingham. You are no relation to the boy."

"But when we marry, Bellingham will be Justin's stepfather," Laura said. "He will oversee Justin's activities. Montclief, you need not trouble yourself again."

In one fell swoop, Bell had acquired a faux fiancée and a rebellious adolescent. He was beginning to feel as if he'd stepped onstage in one of Shakespeare's comedies.

"Wait," Montclief said. "I did not agree to this plan."

"But you said that Justin needed daily male guidance," Laura said. "With five other boys, your hands are full. You will not be able to give Justin nearly as much attention as Bellingham can. Why, I'm sure he will take the boy under his wing almost immediately," she said.

Wonderful. Now she'd volunteered him to play nursemaid to a seventeen-year-old.

Montclief regarded them both with a scowl. "Fair warning. I will come to London periodically to see how matters are progressing. If I hear that my nephew is running wild again, I will remove him immediately."

The man strutted to the door and set his hand on the knob.

Bell couldn't wait to be rid of him so that he could collect on Laura's promise.

Montclief paused, and then he looked over his shoulder. "One more thing. I expect there will be no illicit liaisons while my nephew is residing under this roof."

"How dare you make such an accusation?" Laura said in shocked tones. "I would never engage in immoral conduct."

She'd conveniently forgotten her promise to him, but he wasn't about to let her off the hook after she'd involved him in this farce.

"See that you remember it, Laura," Montclief said. "I trust I need not repeat the consequences."

When the door shut behind Montclief, Bellingham muttered, "That man is an ass."

She covered her mouth and collapsed on the red striped sofa. When fat tears welled in her green eyes, Bell whipped out his handkerchief. "It's all over."

Her bottom lip quivered as she took the handkerchief, and then she hastily dabbed it at her eyes. "Thank you," she said.

Bell squatted beside her. "The only reason he came here is because his pride took a hit when his friend sent him the letter. His abusive language to you was out of bounds."

She folded the handkerchief in a little square. When she tried to hand it back to him, he waved it off.

"He would have t-taken Justin if you had not been here," she stammered.

If Montclief had insisted, there wouldn't have been a damned thing Bell could have done. She obviously loved the boy, but unless she got her son under control, his guardian would likely remove him.

She inhaled and released a shaky breath. "Thank you. How much do you want?"

He frowned. "I beg your pardon?"

"I'm prepared to pay you. My son means everything to me. Name the price," she said.

"I do not need money," he said.

"I must say your idea to keep the engagement a secret was quite brilliant," she said.

"Frankly, I did it for my own protection. I've no wish to find myself caught in the parson's mousetrap."

She patted his arm. "You need not worry. I do not wish to marry again."

He rose and helped her to stand.

"Are you certain you do not want some form of compensation?" she asked. "Would fifty pounds suffice?"

A slow grin tugged at his mouth. "My fortune is such that I will be unlikely to spend it all in my lifetime."

"You're a lucky man," she said, eyeing the door as if she were contemplating escape.

He stepped right in front of her. "I had something else in mind."

"Oh?" she said.

He gazed at her lush mouth. "Something more pleasurable."

"Brandy?" she said, her voice a bit squeaky.

"Guess again."

"Port?"

He caught her hand. "You."

She gasped and stepped back. "My lord, I am a respectable widow."

"You promised to do anything I asked."

"I was desperate."

Bell noticed her clenching and unclenching her skirts and sighed. He'd never coerced a woman before, and he wasn't about to start now. He drew in breath to tell her that he'd only been teasing, but she spoke beforehand.

"I suppose I ought to honor my promise," she said. "What do you want, my lord?"

He blinked. "What are you willing to give?"

She smoothed her skirts. "Since we are affianced, at least temporarily, and you've no need for money, I suppose I could grant you a...a kiss."

He struggled to keep his amusement from showing. "I don't want to take advantage of you."

She wrinkled her little nose. "I am the one who took advantage, my lord. You were kind enough not to expose me, but if you do not wish to kiss me, I will understand."

"Did you have something else in mind?" He could provide ample suggestions, none of which any respectable lady would agree to do.

Her face flushed. "Oh, no. A kiss would do, if that is acceptable to you."

"Hmmm. A faux engagement is no small thing, but if it's a special kiss, I suppose that would even the score between us." Surely she knew he was jesting.

She lifted her chin. "You may kiss me," she said.

He wasn't about to make it that easy for her. "I thought *you* meant to kiss *me*."

"Oh." She smoothed her skirts. "Well, I suppose that's only fair since I took advantage of you."

Her full lower lip fascinated him. He almost said she could take advantage of him anytime, but he kept that between his teeth.

She set her small hands on his shoulders, lifted on her tiptoes, and quickly kissed him on the lips. Then she smiled as she stepped back. "There now, that wasn't bad."

"I disagree," he said. "It was terrible."

"What?" she said, her voice outraged. "You— How dare you insult me?"

"You would prefer I lie?"

"No doubt you had something lascivious in mind."

A slow smile spread across his face. "I expected a real kiss, but if you're afraid, I'll understand."

Her green eyes flashed. She closed the distance between them, stood on her tiptoes, and looped her hands around his neck. When he wrapped her in his arms, all of her soft, delectable curves pressed against him. His heart ricocheted in his chest.

She leaned in closer. The faint scent of roses bewitched him. Heat flooded his veins. She was soft and luscious, and he could no longer hold back. "Forgive me in advance," he said, aware that his voice was low and rough.

"For what?" she said.

"This." Then he claimed her sweet lips.

Chapter Two

$\mathcal{L}$aura's head was spinning as Lord Bellingham cupped the back of her head and devoured her lips. She clutched his shoulders, needing an anchor.

She shouldn't compare his kiss to her late, elderly husband's gentle, fleeting ones. But how could she not? Bellingham had taken full possession and left no doubt of his mastery.

This was a rake's kiss—confident, provocative, and oh so bone melting.

She must stop him...soon.

She would. She must. She couldn't—not when the faint trace of sandalwood and something else, something elemental, enveloped her senses. With every breath she took, his masculine scent curled inside her like a sinful potion. Her skin heated, making her keenly aware of the fullness of her breasts and of the virile man who so easily led her astray. She wanted his kiss and so much more.

The heat of his body and the strength of his arms

proved as impossible to resist as his kiss. Propriety demanded she stop him. He was not her husband, and a faux fiancé did not count. She knew almost nothing about him—other than he kissed very well. But, of course, she must not let pleasure overrule her morals.

Just a moment longer, she silently promised.

The room had grown dimmer even though it was only early afternoon. Rain pattered the window as he slid one big hand down the curve of her spine just above her hips. Then he pulled her tighter against him. Her breasts and belly were pressed all along the rock-hard contours of his body. The carnal embrace felt all too good as she threaded her fingers through the crisp strands of hair at his nape.

His mouth curved in a lopsided smile. "Oh, yes," he murmured, wrapping his long fingers around the back of her neck. Then he captured her lips again, commanding her to surrender to him once more.

He angled his head, and this time, he touched his tongue to her mouth. Stunned, she parted her lips involuntarily. He made a low sound in his throat, and then his tongue was inside her mouth. Shock held her immobile for a moment, but he angled his head in the other direction and deepened the kiss. Then he plucked at her lips twice and held still as if waiting for her to reciprocate.

If she was going to feel guilty later, she might as well enjoy sinning now. Tentatively, she touched her tongue to his. He made that rumbling sound once more and took the lead. In her dazed state, she slowly became aware that his wicked kisses were an imitation of a far more intimate act. He cupped her bottom and pressed his hips against her. Then she felt the unmistakable hardening of his sex.

The thin layers of muslin and petticoat provided no defense at all. She ought to express horror and push away from him, but long-denied need rose up.

"I want you," he said near her ear.

She gasped. There was no doubt what he asked of her. His vivid blue eyes grew darker, and she could swear he was drawing her in with them. In a distant part of her mind, she knew she ought to look away, but her befuddled brain froze.

Someone tapped on the drawing room doors. Bellingham released her and walked toward the window.

Laura shook her skirts with trembling hands and hurried to the door. Reed held out a small silver tray with a note. "This just arrived for you, my lady."

She took the missive and dismissed Reed. Then she broke the seal.

Bellingham's footsteps thudded as he crossed the room. "Is it bad news?"

"No, it is only a note from Lady Atherton canceling our drive today because of the weather."

She started to step aside, but he caught her arm. "I dislodged one of your curls," he said.

When she reached to find the errant curl, he batted her hand away. "Allow me."

"Are you training to be a lady's maid?" she said, resorting to sarcasm as a defense.

"No, I've plenty of experience," he said.

"I'm not the least bit surprised." She hoped the butler had not seen her disheveled hair. Now that Montclief had threatened to take Justin, she could ill afford gossip below-stairs.

"Chin down," Bellingham said. As he lifted the errant

lock, her scalp tingled. "So soft," he said in an undertone. His breath sighed over her neck, a shivery sensation.

The masculine rumble of his voice called to the forbidden impulses inside her. He knew exactly how to cut through a lady's defenses. Obviously he'd honed his seduction skills in order to get exactly what he wanted. Even though she'd known this, she'd still succumbed to his wicked kisses. All the years of adhering to her father's strict moral teachings had scattered like torn bits of paper in the wind.

Bellingham pushed the pin in. "There now. You're tidied up," he said.

In any other situation, his words might have elicited a laugh from her, but there was nothing funny about the way she'd abandoned herself to him earlier. No doubt he hoped she would allow him additional liberties in the future. If so, she would disabuse him of that notion.

Anxious for him to leave, she cleared her throat. "I appreciate all you've done today, my lord."

His eyes glinted with a wicked expression. "I believe you found it as rewarding as I did."

Her face flushed. Oh, dear God, her morals had gone on holiday.

He took her hand and bowed over it. "I am at your service anytime, Laura."

She snatched her hand back. How dare he use her Christian name? Then again, she'd certainly encouraged the rake to treat her like a trollop. At the moment, however, she didn't have time to dwell on him or his "services."

"Well, I'm sure you're a busy man. I shan't keep you from your important duties."

"Are you trying to get rid of me?"

His grin made him look rather boyish, but she must not allow his striking looks to distract her. She lifted her chin and said, "Let me be clear. What occurred this afternoon was a mistake on both our parts."

"There was no mistake," he said. "You freely gave me a kiss because I kept silent about our supposed engagement."

"Well, you could have been more gentlemanly about it," she said with a sniff.

"If I'd been gentlemanly, you wouldn't have enjoyed it half as much."

"Hush," she said. "This cannot happen again."

"I agree. Your brother-in-law suspects us of an indiscretion. The last thing you need is to give him ammunition."

Knowing that he was a rake, she'd half expected him to attempt to seduce her, but that was ridiculous. This was not one of those horrid novels with a villain snatching a damsel in distress. "I'm sorry for involving you in my troubles," she said. "I couldn't think of another way to stop Montclief."

"He didn't believe we're engaged. If he inquires, you will blame me for abandoning you."

She shook her head. "I cannot allow you to do that. Your reputation—"

"Would not suffer in the least if it came out," he said. "It is unlikely our names will ever be linked after today, but if necessary, you will say you discovered I'm a scoundrel. No one will blame you."

She suspected neither of them would get off so easily, but there was no point in borrowing trouble. "That is very, er, gallant of you, my lord," she said, "but I couldn't allow it."

"Yes, you can, and you will if word of the engagement ever leaks. If you don't do it, then honor will force us to wed. Since we're both reluctant to marry, I think you'll agree."

"I agree that would be...unfortunate." It would be disastrous. She couldn't even imagine her family's reaction.

"Good luck with your son," he said.

She would need more than luck to bring Justin to heel. "I should take him home to Hampshire where there are no temptations to lure him."

"There are temptations everywhere," he said. "There is just more opportunity in London." He bowed. "Good day, Lady Chesfield."

After he quit the drawing room, Laura sank onto the sofa. She was more than a little unnerved by the events. One thing was certain. If not for Bellingham's presence, matters with Montclief would have gone far worse for her and Justin.

Oddly, she felt a bit bereft after his departure, which was absurd. Their association had begun and ended today. She thought of his words. *There are temptations everywhere.*

She wondered if he'd meant her.

"Mr. Montclief inquires if you are at home."

Virginia Holt, known as Lady Atherton to the ton, regarded her butler without a trace of guile, but inside something sparked to life. The dreary, rainy afternoon had suddenly become interesting. "Let Montclief cool his heels for twenty minutes and then show him up," she said.

"Yes, my lady," the butler said.

After the butler left, she walked over to the window and stood slightly behind the green and gold draperies. Montclief had arrived in a hired hack. He was a second son with no hope of inheriting. While his brother, the late Viscount Chesfield, had left his brother property and a substantial fortune, Virginia suspected Montclief had run through it and was now in debt.

She'd met him years ago at a ball and had disliked him upon first acquaintance. Montclief was the essence of a hypocrite, always toadying up to others and pretending to be sympathetic.

His brother had been a good friend to Virginia and her late husband, Alfred, for many years. They had always met during the London seasons, until Chesfield's health took a downward turn shortly after his marriage to Laura. Thereafter, Alfred had kept up a correspondence with Chesfield, and it had become clear that his young wife was devoted to caring for him. Montclief had pretended concern for his brother's health and used his growing family as an excuse for his absence. Phillip, bless him, had wanted to believe the best of his brother, and of course Virginia and Alfred had said nothing of their true feelings for Montclief.

Her poor opinion of Montclief had not altered since those days. If anything, her perception of him had taken a decided turn downward upon discovering he'd ignored his responsibilities to his ward.

But why had Montclief called upon her? Obviously he wanted something. Long ago, she'd discovered that men always had an objective. The subtleties that defined women's conversation escaped all but the cleverest of them.

Montclief was neither subtle nor clever. Unlike his late brother, Montclief possessed only a mean understanding of the world around him. This was an important distinction to Virginia, as it meant that he was malleable and easily persuaded. He was also a damned fool for waiting in the antechamber for twenty minutes. A strong, confident man would never tolerate the delay.

Virginia treaded across the turkey carpet and poured herself a small sherry. When she was younger and foolish, she never would have indulged in spirits in the middle of the afternoon. She ought to have done that and far more when she'd been younger and still attractive, but society looked harshly upon younger women who did not observe the proprieties to the letter. Now that her sixty-fifth birthday had passed, Virginia reckoned that she'd earned the right to do as she pleased.

She glanced at the clock, finished her sherry, and returned to the settee. Moments later, her butler announced Montclief. Virginia rose and smiled serenely, but inwardly she was appalled at his appearance. He'd grown a potbelly and lost much of his hair. When he drew out a handkerchief and patted perspiration from his forehead, she hid her distaste.

"Montclief, this is a surprise. I've not seen you since Phillip's funeral." She'd written to him expressing her sympathies over his brother's death, but he'd never replied.

"Grave matters have led me to London," he said. "We'd best get to the point."

His blunt manners hadn't improved over the course of four years. She perched upon the sofa and indicated a chair with her beringed hand. When he sat, she noted his tight waistcoat gapped and she half expected a button to pop off from the strain. "Is all well with your family?"

"My own family is well, but there is trouble with my nephew."

"Oh?" Virginia recollected Laura saying her son was at a trying age. Her boys were grown now, but they had been rowdy when they were young men.

"Imagine how I felt when friends wrote to inform me that Justin was running wild in London," Montclief continued. "My sister-in-law Laura sent me a letter, rather belatedly I must confess, saying she was bringing him here. I am shocked and wounded that she did not consult me first."

She doubted his sincerity. "Perhaps she did not realize that you expected it of her," Virginia said. She knew Laura wouldn't have thought to inform him, because Montclief had taken no responsibility for his ward.

He tugged on his tight waistcoat to no avail. "I'm the boy's guardian, and she ought not to be making decisions without consulting me. I fear Justin is too difficult for her to manage."

"I have only recently become acquainted in person with Lady Chesfield, though we have corresponded for some time. She appears to be practical and amiable. Did you discuss the situation with her?"

Montclief sighed. "I have something to tell you that will shock you. I never thought Laura capable of such deceit."

"I beg your pardon?"

He pressed his lips together and drew in a breath. "Laura is involved in a liaison."

Virginia's lips parted. Last night, her protégé had

claimed to have no interest in courtship. "Are you certain?" she asked.

"Yes," he said. "I found her alone with that notorious rake Bellingham."

Last night at Virginia's ball, Bellingham had demanded that she give him Laura's address so that he could return a flask that belonged to Justin. Virginia had suspected Bellingham hoped to make a conquest of Laura, but since he'd just seen her last night for the first time, she found the idea of a liaison improbable. "Perhaps you misinterpreted his reason for calling on her," she said.

"I assure you I did not," Montclief said. "Laura claimed that Bellingham was her fiancé, and he corroborated her convoluted story."

Virginia had to restrain herself from gaping. The earl had made it clear as water that he had no intention of ever marrying, even though all of his property would default to the Crown. All the beau monde knew his intention to remain a bachelor, but that had not stopped ambitious mamas from trying to lure him. "This engagement is certainly sudden," Virginia said.

"I'm sorry to inform you, but I feel certain they were lying," Montclief said. "They said it was a secret engagement."

Virginia's thoughts raced. Why would Bellingham do such a thing? He was known for acting in a logical and methodical manner. She concluded there were missing pieces to the puzzle. "Did they indicate why they wished to keep their engagement a secret?"

Montclief mopped his forehead again. "Some foolishness about gradually introducing my nephew to Bellingham. They must have cooked this goose at the spur of the moment to hide their licentious behavior." His nostrils flared. "I never suspected she was a shameless hussy beneath her veneer of respectability."

Virginia knew differently. "Her father is a vicar, you know."

"But what do we really know about her? Of course, my dearly departed brother was smitten when he met her, even though she was far beneath him. Now I fear she came to London with the express purpose of finding a lover."

Virginia was tempted to ask if his knowledge came from firsthand experience, but she would not lower herself. "Of course, you're concerned about your nephew. Are you planning to stay in London for the remainder of the season?"

"I can't," Montclief said. "You know I have a large family, and the expense would beggar me. That is why I need your assistance."

Virginia frowned. Surely he wasn't begging for money. "What precisely are you asking of me?"

"Keep an eye on Laura. I dislike deception, but I believe in this instance we must fight fire with fire."

"I beg your pardon?"

"Gain her confidence. Encourage her to talk and pretend to sympathize with her. Then send me a letter with a report of her actions."

Virginia touched her high collar and shrank back from him.

"Lady Atherton, please forgive me, but I am concerned about my nephew. I would take him to my home, but he wasn't even present when I arrived. I doubt Laura knows or even cares what he is doing. If I am right, and I fear I am, I want proof that she is having a liaison with that rake while my innocent nephew resides with her."

Virginia reached for her silver vinaigrette, flicked it open, and sniffed the restorative. He really was an odious man. "She has cared for the boy these past four years," Virginia said as she set the silver case aside.

"Of course, I hope that I am wrong, but I fear she has pulled the wool over our eyes," he said.

Virginia drew her brows together, wondering why he felt it necessary to gather evidence. "If you are so certain that the engagement is false, why are you seeking proof?"

He sighed. "The last thing I want is to separate her from Justin. She has always said she cares for him, but now I fear she has changed for the worse." He blinked rapidly and took out a handkerchief. "I am glad my poor brother is not here to witness her fall from grace."

Good heavens, he really believed every word he'd spoken. Virginia was tempted to defend Laura, but she reconsidered. Instead, she would warn Laura to be wary of Montclief.

"I must be on my way," Montclief said, shoving his bulk out of the chair. "I trust you will keep me posted."

Virginia rose as Montclief lumbered out of the drawing room. He didn't even realize that she'd not agreed to his disgusting plan.

After the footman closed the door, Virginia slowly lowered herself to the settee. Over the years, she'd dealt with scandalmongers, roués, and scoundrels, but this situation warranted a great deal of thought.

Until Justin gained his majority, his uncle had power over the boy and subsequently Laura. Montclief's deceit was clear. But why after four years of ignoring the boy had he suddenly professed concern about him?

Something odd had happened in Laura's drawing room. Why had Bellingham, a self-proclaimed lifelong bachelor, gone along with the scheme? Granted, she'd seen him openly gazing at Laura's body at the ball last night.

The notorious rake would have to work very hard to win prim-and-proper Laura. But they would make a fiery couple. With a smile, Virginia poured another thimbleful of sherry in her glass and raised it. When the opportunity arose, she would play the matchmaker.

Well into the evening, Bell sat in his study, looking over the last of the journal entries in the estate books. His estate manager, Wilson, had traveled to London to give him an account of all that had transpired in the last quarter.

Wilson leaned forward in his chair. "I commissioned workers to replace rotting boards on the bridge. Otherwise, all else is in good working order at the estate."

"No complaints from the tenants or servants?"

"All went relatively well on rent day," Wilson said. "Mr. Faraday was a bit short but promised to make it up next quarter."

"He came up to scratch last quarter," Bell said. "Forgive the shortage. I don't want his family to suffer, but make sure he's not spending all of his coin at the tavern again. If you find that's the case, inform Mr. Bullock to refuse him on my orders."

"Yes, my lord. I will speak to the tavern owner if necessary."

Bell massaged his aching neck. He'd been bent over the books for hours. "Is there anything else?"

"No, my lord."

He rose. "Well done, Wilson. I've taken care of your hotel accommodations at the Dorset for this evening. Griffith will send you in my carriage." Tomorrow, Wilson would make the long journey back to Devonshire.

Wilson stood. "My lord, I appreciate your confidence in my work." He swallowed. "I am grateful to you. I daresay not many would overlook my prior poor performance."

"You have worked hard and exceeded my expectations."

"Thank you, my lord." Wilson bowed and left.

Bell rolled his stiff shoulders and snuffed out all the candles, save the ones in the candle branch. He carried it to the drawing room, poured a brandy, and sat in his favorite chair. The fire was burning low, and the *tick-tick* of the clock made him feel peaceful.

He thought about Wilson's candid words. Five years ago, Bell had left the estate all behind for his estate manager to run. Bell hadn't allowed himself to think about Thornhill Park while journeying on the Continent, but there was no denying he'd abdicated his responsibilities. Upon his return, he'd found Wilson had allowed repairs and letters to pile up. Many of the tenants were in arrears. Bell had seen the barely concealed terror on Wilson's face, but he'd not blamed him.

How could he sack Wilson when the man had done his best with no direction at all?

Wilson worked harder than necessary and always expressed his gratitude. Ultimately, Bell knew the estate and everyone who worked for him was his responsibility.

His father had taught him that.

He tried to push the thought of his father away, but it had shattered his peace. With a long sigh, he collected the candle branch and went upstairs to bed.

His heart pounded like a thousand hooves on cobblestones. The carriage hurtled on. Every stop to change the horses felt like an eternity. He kept trying to shout for them to hurry, hurry, hurry, but his voice was lost. God in heaven, let them live. Let them live. He would do anything, give up everything, if only they would recover.

Bile rose up in his throat. He grasped the strap and prayed. Fear raced through him like a wildfire as the carriage careened into the square. As soon as the carriage jangled to a halt, he vaulted out, running, running, running. Oh, God, there was straw at the door.

He was too late. Too late.

"No!"

He reared up in bed, breathing like a racehorse. His heart drummed in his chest. He drew his knees up and laid his head on his forearms. Cold beads of perspiration dampened his temples. He gritted his teeth, trying to will away the dream, but the remnants persisted. The tension in his arms and legs was slow to dissipate.

He shoved the covers back and got out of bed. The coals were smoldering, and his skin prickled from the cold. He donned a banyan and lit a candle. Then he added coals to the fire. He poured himself a finger of brandy and downed it in one fiery swallow. The burning sensation helped clear his head. He drew back the drapery and saw that it was still dark. He gritted his teeth. Was he condemned to relive that horrific day for the rest of his life?

After releasing the heavy brocade material, he held

the candle up to see the mantel clock. It was a quarter past three. The worst part was he never knew when the nightmare would strike, but tonight he ought to have been prepared.

One stray thought about his father had brought it on.

The cause wasn't always so clear. Most of the time, he couldn't attribute it to anything, and he never knew when the nightmare would strike. Sometimes weeks and even months would pass. He'd tried to keep a journal of it in hopes of making sense of the nightmare and perhaps taking control, but it hadn't worked.

Something hot sizzled inside him. He was frustrated and furious at his inability to control his own mind while sleeping. He hated it, because there wasn't a damned thing he could do to stop it.

The chill in the room drove him back to bed. He lay there staring up at the canopy, trying his best to forget the awful events that had altered his life forever. It was bad enough to have lost his family once, but to relive it again and again was pure hell.

The chill woke Laura. She'd fallen asleep on the sofa in the drawing room. The fire had died down and the candles she'd lit had guttered. She took a candle to the hearth, moved the screen, and lit the taper. Afterward she found a branch of candles and lit those. A quick check of the mantel clock showed it was four o'clock. She found her shawl and hurried out of the dark drawing room.

She held on to the rail and took the steps with care in the darkness. When she reached the landing, she breathed a sigh of relief. Then she proceeded down the corridor past her own bedchamber to Justin's room. When she knocked, there was no response. With a sigh, Laura opened the door. The empty bed infuriated her. She'd lied to Montclief to protect Justin, and he didn't even know how much trouble he'd caused.

He didn't care that she'd sat up late worried about him. The only thing he cared about was sowing wild oats with his rakish friends. She'd had quite enough of his rebellion. The minute he came home, he would find his trunks packed. She'd brought him to London so that he could be with his friends, and all he'd done was abuse the privilege. Well, he'd pay for his actions, and he'd better appreciate it, because the alternative—staying with his uncle—would be far, far worse.

Laura walked back to her room. Her maid Fran met her at the door. "My lady, did he return?"

She shook her head. "I'm sorry to keep you from your bed, Fran. If you can help me undress quickly, we might as well try to rest. Losing sleep will not help matters."

But after donning her night rail and climbing into bed, Laura stared up at the canopy. Justin was out there in this enormous city, and there was nothing more she could do except wait for him to return home. If something bad happened to him, she would never forgive herself for bringing him to London.

Someone shook her arm. With a gasp, Laura sat up in bed to find Fran hovering over her and sunlight streaming through the window.

"My lady, your son has arrived home," Fran said. "I thought you would wish to know straightaway."

"Yes, of course," Laura said. "I should dress as quickly as possible." Afterward, Fran pinned up her hair in a simple style. Laura drew in her breath and reminded herself to stay composed no matter what transpired.

When Laura walked to Justin's room, she lifted her hand and heard a guttural sound. She opened the door to find her son heaving over a chamber pot his valet held. "My lady," Hinton said, "you do not wish to witness this."

She swept inside. "I've seen worse." Over the course of four years nursing her ill husband, she'd learned to stay unruffled for his sake. Nothing she'd done had spared him the indignities of his wasting disease, but she believed her calm manner had helped to some degree.

Justin rolled over on the mattress, putting his back to her, and Hinton took the pot away.

Laura walked around the other side of the bed. "Justin, you've been out all night and are obviously suffering from the effects of drinking spirits."

"Go away," he muttered, and pulled a pillow over his head.

She yanked the pillow away. "No. You will not hide from me."

"Sick," he said.

She walked over to the drapes and pulled them open.

He shielded his eyes. "Stop."

"No. You are the one who will stop." She clenched her hands. "You have no idea the trouble you've caused."

"I'm sick. Go away," he said, rolling in the other direction.

Laura couldn't reason with him when he was in this condition. She walked over to the china bowl and poured water into it. Then she dipped a cloth into the water, rung it out, and attempted to press it to Justin's forehead, but he batted it away.

"Rest now, but when you're better, we must talk," she said.

After he turned his back to her once more, Laura took the cloth over to the stand. She walked out the door, closed it quietly, and leaned against it. Four short years ago, he'd been thirteen and anxious to play backgammon or cards with her. She'd taught him to dance, but now she needed to teach him something far more difficult to learn—to act responsibly. If she failed, Montclief would take him, and Laura could not bear the thought of losing him. She must take charge, and this time she would not be ignored.

Two hours later, Laura took a deep breath, opened Justin's door, and directed two footmen bearing empty trunks to proceed into her son's room. Behind them, Justin's valet, Hinton, stood stoically until Laura motioned him to enter as well.

Justin bolted upright with the sheet clutched to his chest. "What are you doing?" he croaked.

Laura ignored him and dismissed the footmen. She would ring for them later. "Hinton, please pack all of his belongings with the exception of a change of clothing."

"No," Justin shouted.

"Keep your voice down. I warned you more than once," Laura said, "but you did not take me seriously. You have continued to rebel, so we are returning to Hampshire as soon as the trunks are packed and loaded on the carriage."

Justin shook his head. "I won't go."

Hot anger shot to her temples, but she refused to let him goad her. "You have no choice," she said. "You have no money, and you cannot pay the lease on the town house."

Justin turned his attention to Hinton. "Leave us, please."

When Hinton hesitated in the process of setting a stack of folded neckcloths in one of the trunks, Laura nodded. "You are excused for now, Hinton."

After the door shut, Justin glared at her. "I'll stay with George. You may leave without me."

She clasped her hands at her waist. "A tidy solution, but you're liable to find yourself in much hotter suds once your uncle discovers you have run away."

He scoffed. "Montclief doesn't even remember I exist."

"Oh, he remembers," she said. "He called upon me yesterday while you were out. Apparently some of his friends reported having seen you running wild in the streets. He threatened to remove you to his country house."

"Why the devil does he care? He hasn't seen fit to even write to me."

"He cares because your behavior reflects upon him."

"Too bloody bad," he muttered.

"Watch your language," she said. "If you had used better judgment, your uncle would have left us in peace." She brought her fist to her chest. "I had to answer for you, and believe me, it was unpleasant."

"I haven't done anything wrong," he said.

"Do not lie to me," she said, unable to keep the vehemence from her voice this time. "I had another visitor yesterday who returned your flask."

He scowled. "What? I don't have a flask."

"You might wish to retract that statement. Lord Bellingham saw you push a flask beneath the staircase at Lady Atherton's home. He brought it to me yesterday. It contained brandy." She took a step closer to the bed. "Today, you were sick from imbibing liquor. If you continue with your rowdy ways, you are likely to suffer the consequences. Montclief will not tolerate your behavior and neither will I."

Justin's jaw tightened. "So you paraded the footmen and my valet in here in order to frighten me?"

She strode around the bed and hovered over him. "No, I did it because we are leaving today."

"No," he said, raising his voice.

"You have given me no choice," she said. "I refuse to stand by idly while you ruin your life." She drew his banyan out from the wardrobe and tossed it to him. "Get dressed."

"Laura, I'm sorry," he said.

"That's not good enough," she said. "You have persisted with this willful, wretched behavior, and I can no longer trust you."

"Give me another chance."

"I'm sorry, Justin, but you've gone too far this time." She returned to the wardrobe, drew out a stack of folded shirts, and set them in the empty trunk.

"What if I refuse to go?" he said in a surly tone.

"Then you will likely find yourself under your uncle's management. I daresay he will be harsher than I am."

He punched the pillow behind him and regarded her with a scowl.

She returned to the wardrobe and drew out stockings.

"Stop," he said. "I'm sorry. I just don't feel well."

She halted. "Whose fault is that?"

"I swear to you I won't do it again."

"You've lied to me more than once. The trust is broken. Hinton will finish packing your trunk. Get dressed. We are leaving today."

"No, I won't go."

"I'll send the footmen to your room in two hours. If you do not cooperate, I will have them force-march you out to the carriage, dressed or not."

"Laura, no. Give me a chance, please."

"It's too late, Justin."

Laura directed the maids to pack all of her belongings and walked downstairs to the drawing room. She retrieved her lap desk and drew out paper, ink, and pen in order to write a note to Lady Atherton. Laura would miss her friend, but Justin's welfare came first. Her son would learn a hard lesson today. No doubt he would be humiliated when they returned to Hampshire after such a short time, but she'd given him ample warnings.

She'd only written the salutation when the door opened. Justin walked inside with a guilty expression. "I know you said that an apology isn't good enough, but I wish you would give me another chance."

"Be seated," she said, indicating the chair across from her.

He sat and leaned forward with his elbows on his knees. "I know it's an excuse, but lots of lads sow wild oats."

"Lots of them lose money gambling or get robbed in the streets," Laura said. "I think your friends are a bad influence, but you are responsible for the bad choices you've made. Now you will suffer the consequences."

"Give me another chance," he said, looking at the carpet.

She released a long sigh. "If something bad were to happen to you, I would never forgive myself."

He looked up. "Haven't you ever made a mistake? Didn't Grandfather give you another chance?"

"Yes, but some mistakes can ruin your life," she said. "And that is the path you're on."

"Please," he said.

Prior to their journey to London, Justin had rarely ever misbehaved. He'd always been a sunny boy and eager to please. His reports from school had always been excellent. But she had to remain firm.

"I know you're angry, but I swear I won't do it again," he said.

She shook her head. "I'm sorry, but it's for your own good."

"What can I do to persuade you?" he said. "I'll do anything if you'll give me a second chance."

Perhaps she would give him one more chance, but there would be strict conditions. "If you wish to remain in London, you will have to prove you are trustworthy. That means you will stop running wild."

"I promise I will," he said.

She wanted to believe him, but she mustn't make this easy on him. "You will not escape punishment, Justin. You will have to stay home for the entire week."

"What?" He looked horrified.

"That's not all," she said. "You will employ your time reading." She walked over to the bookshelves and returned. "Read this."

"*Pilgrim's Progress*? You mean to torture me."

"You will also write a report of the book so that I will know you read it."

"Laura, please don't," he said.

"It's either that or we return home." She clasped her hands. "Make your choice."

"I'll take my punishment," he grumbled.

"Listen well. I managed to thwart your uncle yesterday, but he won't hesitate to take you if he hears you have disobeyed again. He is your legal guardian, and there is nothing I can do to stop him if he decides to take you away." She'd barely managed to fob him off and knew there would be no second chances.

"He doesn't care about me," Justin said. "I cannot wait until I'm twenty-one and free of him."

"You will be in four years," she said, "but meanwhile, you must not do anything that will draw his attention. Until you reach your majority, he has power over you. Don't do something foolhardy that will make these four years unbearable."

"I understand."

"You can have fun and be responsible, too," she said. "Isn't that preferable to being under your uncle's thumb?"

He nodded. "Sorry, Laura."

She wished he would call her *Mama*, but three months ago, he'd insisted upon using her Christian name. Laura knew that it was a show of independence and told herself it was a small thing, but it stung a little all the same.

They had come this far today, and in the end, he'd listened to reason. God knew there were far worse things.

"May I be excused?" he said.

She hesitated a moment. The urge to tell him she loved

him burned inside her, but he would likely find it embarrassing. "Yes, you don't look as if you feel well."

He shrugged one shoulder, a gesture so characteristic of him.

"I'll have a tray sent up to you."

As he treaded out the door, she hoped she'd not made a mistake. He'd accepted his punishment, but his lies made it very difficult to believe him. He would have to earn her trust, and she would have to be vigilant.

Chapter Three

*B*ell arrived late at White's club and found his friends sharing a bottle of brandy. Harry signaled the waiter, who brought a snifter for Bell and poured for him.

After the waiter left, Harry raised his glass. "To Lady Luck," he said, sloshing his brandy a little.

Bell exchanged a knowing look with Colin. Clearly, Harry was in his cups.

"He won a wager in the betting book," Colin said.

Harry grinned. "I'm plump in the pocket."

"Oh?" Bell said. Harry notoriously had pockets to let.

"I wagered Prendergast fifty pounds that it would rain three times this week," Harry said.

"A safe bet," Bell said. "Congratulations."

"Harry insisted on buying the brandy tonight," Colin said.

Bell noted Harry's glassy eyes. "Generous of you."

"Mrs. Hawkins is holding a soiree this evening. I

wouldn't mind a tumble with a disreputable lady of the demimonde tonight." Harry hiccoughed. "You might find a mistress there, Bell."

"Perhaps later. I'm hungry." Harry didn't hold his liquor well. Bell figured it would be best if Harry ate something and sobered up a bit.

Bell caught the waiter's eye and ordered beefsteak and potatoes for all of them. While Harry was speaking to Colin, Bell quietly instructed the waiter to put the brandy on his bill as well. He wouldn't take advantage of his inebriated friend. Those fifty pounds were likely Harry's only funds.

"Too bad you never met the widow, Bell." Harry hiccoughed again. "I heard she's pretty."

Colin scoffed. "Is this more false intelligence from your girl cousins?"

"No. They meant to introduce me, but the widow had already left the ball."

"A likely tale," Colin said. "She's probably elderly and rotund."

"She's pretty," Bell said, keeping his expression nonchalant.

"You actually saw her?" Harry's eyes widened.

"I called on her yesterday," Bell said.

Harry and Colin exchanged looks. Then they turned to him.

"Well?" Colin said. "Is she your mistress?"

"No," he said. "She's not that kind of woman." He'd wanted her fiercely during and just after their kiss, but something she'd said had jolted sense back into his head.

This cannot happen again.

Harry hiccoughed once more. "What happened?"

"I saw her son hiding a flask at Lady Atherton's ball, and I returned it to Lady Chesfield yesterday," Bell said. "I thought she ought to know." He didn't tell them that he'd shocked her when he'd kissed her.

Colin snorted. "Righto. I suppose you managed a bit of flirting while you were at it."

His hands had roamed all over her, even though he'd known she wasn't one of those women who casually flitted from bed to bed. Lady Atherton had said it all. She was a respectable widow and not for the likes of a rakehell like him.

"Her son's guardian called while I was there." He told his friends the entire story but left out the kiss. "Obviously we're not really engaged. Keep that under your hats for her sake and mine."

Colin frowned. "No one really knows her, with the exception of Lady Atherton. What if the widow expects you to make the engagement real?"

"She won't," Bell said.

"How can you be so sure?" Harry asked.

Bell topped up their drinks. "She made it clear she wished to be rid of me, and I politely made it clear that our brief acquaintance was over. That's the end of it."

Harry sipped his drink. "You're giving up?"

Bell set the bottle aside. She wasn't a challenge; she was a lady. "I can't give up what I never had."

"So you're saying she's the sort who expects a wedding ring before a toss in the sheets," Harry said.

"She's a respectable lady," he said in a terse tone.

"Right," Colin said. "Might as well enjoy your freedom for a few more years."

"I've no intention of giving up my bachelorhood."

Harry snorted. "Hah! Cupid will fell you with his arrow one day."

"Not a chance," Bell said.

"Lifelong bachelorhood appeals to me," Colin muttered.

Bell downed his brandy. "Is your family pressing you to marry Angeline?"

Colin shuddered. "My mother made a list of potential names for the shrew's spawn."

"Well, it would be your spawn as well," Bell said.

Colin pulled a face. "I just lost my appetite."

"Angeline can't be that bad," Bell said.

"She's all yours," Colin said.

"No, thank you," Bell said, laughing.

Harry scoffed. "Mark my words, Bell. You'll be the first of us to wed. I wager fifty pounds on it."

"You'll lose."

Colin frowned as he traced the rim of his snifter. "You're serious about staying single."

"Yes." There was nothing else to say. His friends would draw their own conclusions. They knew a bit about his history, but no one knew all of the particulars. He never spoke about the past. There was no point in dredging up bad memories.

"What about your property?" Harry said.

Bell shrugged. "There's no one to inherit."

Harry's eyes widened momentarily, and then he shuttered his expression. Colin said nothing and became engrossed with the condensation on the table. They'd come to the obvious conclusion. The property would revert to the Crown when he died.

An awkward silence ensued. Bell hated when the past

intruded. All he wanted was to forget, but reminders cropped up from time to time, leaving a hollow feeling in his chest. The only way to deal with it was to shove it all back into the farthest recesses of his brain, but sometimes even that didn't work. The bloody nightmares were proof.

"Ah, here come the waiters," Colin said.

The tension in Bell's shoulders slowly dissipated, and the aroma of the sizzling beefsteaks made Bell's stomach growl. He was hungrier than he'd realized. All three tucked into their meal. Colin entertained them with stories of his weird twin sisters, who sometimes spoke in a language they'd made up years ago.

Bell laughed. "You're jesting."

"No, I'm not," Colin said. "Bianca and Bernadette have an alphabet, too, but it looks like tiny pictures of trees, skirts, hair, milk jugs, and other nonsense."

"That's odd." Bell privately wondered if the parents had dropped the twins on their heads early on in life. "Harry, what about your girl cousins? Do they have strange habits?"

"No, but they begged for an introduction to you. I said no."

"Why? Surely you don't think I would seduce your cousins?" Bell said.

"No, I took pity on you. They like to match-make."

Bell shuddered. "You have my eternal thanks."

The waiter appeared. "Would you care for dessert? Chef made a cheesecake."

Bell looked inquiringly at his friends, who quickly assented.

"Bring cheesecake and coffee for all of us," Bell said to the waiter.

Not long afterward, the coffee and cheesecake arrived. Harry finished with a groan. "I think I died and went to heaven."

Colin pulled a face. "Harry, get that stupid look off your face."

"Can't help it," Harry said. "It's been so long since I've had a woman. Food is my only comfort."

"Maybe we should take him to Mrs. Hawkins's establishment after all," Colin said. "He's been irritable."

Bell leaned forward. "Harry, do you have a French letter?"

Harry scowled. "No."

"Forget it," Bell said.

"What? Do you know how long it's been?" Harry said. "I can't even recall."

Bell shook his head. "You'll end up with the French pox."

Harry's forlorn expression brightened when Bell took out a gold case and offered him a cheroot. Colin lit one as well from the candle on the table.

They sat smoking in silence for a while. All around them masculine voices rumbled.

Harry blew a smoke ring. "Bell, if the widow is off-limits, you must still be in the market for a mistress."

"Finding the right mistress is a pain in the arse." Last night, he'd fantasized about Laura while pleasuring himself. He'd gotten the distinct impression that her sexual experiences were limited. Ordinarily, that would put him off, but for some reason, he'd gotten hot just thinking about introducing her to new sensual horizons.

Harry flicked an ash. "I figure the right amount of coin could buy you anyone you wanted."

"They all start out biddable," Bell said. "Then the demands start."

"What demands?" Colin asked.

"Jewels, gowns, perfume, and flowers. They always want more."

"They can't be that bad," Harry said.

"The last one transformed the love nest into a pagoda museum. Then she burned the sheets, and the fire brigade had to come," Bell said.

His friends burst out laughing.

"Bell, you are no romantic," Colin said.

"No wonder he can't find a mistress," Harry said.

"I have good qualities," Bell muttered.

"True. You're generous with cheroots, brandy, and beefsteak, but I don't think that helps your case with the ladybirds," Harry said. "You need to treat them with a little tenderness."

"I begin to see why the widow was anxious to be rid of him," Colin said, laughing.

Bell rolled his eyes and blew out a smoke ring. "Enough about women. Let's go to my town house and play billiards."

"Brilliant idea," Harry said.

Fifteen minutes later, they quit White's and stood on the pavement waiting for Bell's carriage. A block away, a curricle with huge yellow wheels jangled to a halt. Three young men stumbled out, laughing. In the gaslight, Bell recognized the one with wheat-colored hair. It was Lady Chesfield's son.

"What are you staring at?" Colin asked.

"See the young buck with the lighter hair?" Bell said. "He's the widow's son."

"Appears he and his friends are looking for trouble," Harry said.

When Justin drank from a flask, Bell said, "Apparently they've already found it."

The next afternoon

Laura opened a letter from her sister Rachel. They were only one year apart in age and had always been close. Naturally, Rachel chided her for not writing sooner and begged to hear all about London. Laura knew that Rachel would share her letter with all the family, so she decided not to burden them with her son's troublesome behavior. She would describe Lady Atherton's ball and the fancy gowns, because her sisters would enjoy that. Her mother and father would be pleased to know that she had become acquainted in person with Lady Atherton at long last. She thought of mentioning Montclief's call, but she decided against it. Her family knew that Montclief had neglected Justin, and she did not wish to cause them concern.

She most certainly would not include any news about the Earl of Bellingham. If she happened to see him again, she would greet him in a formal, distant manner. When he realized that she would not fall for his abundant charms, he would quickly lose interest and turn his eyes to more willing women. No doubt he'd already forgotten her.

The rest of Rachel's letter was filled with amusing incidents about their neighbors and the local village assembly that had recently taken place. Their sister Judith had played the pianoforte badly, and as usual, she'd beamed at all the compliments she'd received. No one had the heart to inform her that her playing was awful, but that did not matter at a country assembly. Thinking of her family produced a slight ache in her chest. With a sigh, she admitted she'd had such high hopes for her London adventure, as Rachel had called it, but the reality was far different.

Papa would smile gently and tell her not to waste one of the Lord's wonderful days feeling sorry for herself. He was right as always. Laura knew that writing to Rachel would bring her cheer. She rose and retrieved the new wooden lap desk and smoothed her hand over the beautifully painted floral border. The center featured flowers and fruit. She'd bought a similar one for Rachel, who loved corresponding with family and friends.

After she finished the letter, she sanded and sealed it, knowing that Rachel would scold her for using two sheets of paper when she could easily cross it. Laura reflected on how much her world had changed since marrying Phillip. Perhaps she'd grown a bit complacent about the luxuries she'd once never dreamed of having, but mostly she enjoyed the ability to give fine gifts to her family. They were only possessions, but she bought them keeping in mind the interests of her brothers, sisters, nieces, nephews, and parents. With a smile, she decided to send a missive to Lady Atherton inquiring if she wished to accompany her on a shopping expedition. She had just lifted the lid of her lap desk and drew out another sheet of paper when a knock sounded. "Enter," she said.

Reed stepped inside. "My lady, Lord Bellingham has called."

Laura frowned. She recalled the earl's torrid kiss and decided it would be best to steer clear of him. "Please tell him that I am not at home."

Reed cleared his throat. "His lordship anticipated that might be your answer and suggested you had better receive him, as he has an important topic to discuss with you."

Laura suspected a trick. But what if there was a problem? She couldn't afford to ignore the earl, but if he'd lied, she most certainly would call him on the carpet. "Very well, please admit him."

Reed's usual stoic expression slipped a notch, but he nodded and exited. Laura assumed the butler found the earl too bold. She certainly did.

A few minutes later, Reed entered. "The Earl of Bellingham, my lady."

"Thank you, Reed." She rose and maintained her poise until Bellingham sauntered inside her drawing room. He wore a hunter-green coat and shiny black Hessians. Though he was clean-shaven, she detected a faint shadow above his lips and along his sharply defined square jaw. When she met his intense gaze, she found herself mesmerized by his sapphire eyes. Her thoughts scattered, and she felt unaccountably tongue-tied. *Breathe.*

"My lord." His pristine cravat was expertly tied, his coat fit him like a glove, and his fawn-colored trousers were so tight she could discern his rather long male organ. Her face grew warm, and she averted her gaze. Laura could almost hear her mother's voice. *Recall your manners. You're no school miss.* In all fairness, no man should be that incredibly…endowed—or handsome. Doubtless he was well aware of the effect he had on countless women. Well, she certainly did not wish to be one of them. "Please be seated. My butler indicated you had an important matter to discuss."

She expected him to take the chair, but he flustered her by picking up her lap desk and sitting next to her on the sofa. The scent of starch drifted to her.

To her consternation, he pushed up the narrow flap at the top of the lap desk to examine the inkwell and pen. Then he opened the main compartment. "Ah, you have an unfinished letter."

"Are you in the habit of reading other's correspondence?" she said in exasperation.

He lifted the box and looked at the underside. "I'm only interested in the make of the box."

She reminded herself not to roll her eyes. "My lord, when you finish playing with my lap desk, perhaps you would be good enough to tell me the reason you called."

A sly smile tugged at the corners of his mouth as he set the lap desk on a side table. "I like to play. Do you, Laura?"

For a moment, the merriment in his blue eyes captivated her, but she mustn't allow him to draw her in with his games. "You will address me properly," she said.

"Lady Chesfield," he said in a rumbling voice.

"I'm not a child and neither are you."

"I wasn't referring to child's play."

He was much too close, so she moved over. "I assume you called for a reason."

"Yes, I called regarding your son."

"He is my responsibility, not yours," she said.

"Then you're not interested in his whereabouts last night."

"He spent the evening reading, not that it is any of your concern."

"Really? What is he reading?"

"*Pilgrim's Progress*. It was his punishment for being disobedient."

He shook his head. "He may have been at home early in the evening, but I left White's after midnight and saw your son a block away. He and his friends were drinking from a flask again."

Denial rose up inside her. Justin had promised to stop rebelling. "Are you certain it was my son? You saw him only the one time."

"I'm certain. I recognized his friends and the curricle."

She covered her mouth. Justin had lied. He'd broken his promises again.

Bellingham frowned. "I regret having to inform you, but given Montclief's threats, I felt it was the right thing to do."

She lowered her hand slowly and laced her nerveless fingers. "It is not news that I welcome, but thank you for telling me."

"What will you do?" he asked.

"Take him home to Hampshire immediately. He's left me no choice."

Bellingham leaned forward with his elbows on his thighs. His silence made her uncomfortable, but she suspected he was the type to think things through before speaking.

At last he sat back. "It isn't wise to leave town suddenly. Montclief's friends are acting as his spies. They're certain to mark your son's absence, and then your brother-in-law will know you encountered trouble again."

"If I stay and Justin continues to rebel, Montclief is sure to hear about it," she said. "I have two choices, and neither is appealing."

"There are always more alternatives."

"By all means tell me, because my vexation is growing by the moment."

He stood and walked over to the window. She turned sideways to watch him. He was tall and lean. Remembering the hard contours of his body, she assumed he was fitter than most men. His angular jaw and cheekbones seemed sharper in the patch of sunlight bathing him. When he faced her, his blue eyes held a fierce expression. "I never intended to become involved beyond returning that flask."

She frowned. "You are under no obligation."

He paced back and forth in front of the window. His restlessness puzzled her. It was as if he were waging some inner battle with himself. "Yes, I am."

She shook her head. "How so?"

He halted. "You told Montclief that I would oversee your son's activities, and I did not refute you."

"I would have promised anything to keep my son, as you are well aware. Believe me, I appreciate what you did the day Montclief called, but you are not obliged."

"After I left that day, I'd intended to walk away and never return here. Then I saw your son last night." He clenched his jaw.

"You did it for my benefit, and I thank you for it, but I will not hold you to a promise that was born of coercion on my part."

"I was not coerced. My agreement was implied."

"Then I release you from any obligation, implicit or otherwise."

He fisted his hands on his hips. "If something happens to the boy, I'll feel that I failed him."

"But—"

"It's a matter of honor," he said. "To be honest, I have a low opinion of Montclief. He would make a terrible guardian for your son."

"I agree. He's done nothing to help Justin, but given his nasty temperament, I've always figured it was for the best."

"If you take your son home, will your family defend you if Montclief comes for him?"

She hesitated. "I…I don't think Montclief really wants him."

"You didn't answer my question."

He'd spoken in a severe manner. "My father is a vicar. He would not prevent his legal guardian from taking Justin. Papa would consider that breaking the law and therefore a sin."

"Then don't take your son home."

"We must return eventually," she said.

"If you leave now, Montclief will know something is wrong. Wait a few more weeks."

She pressed her nails into her palms. "I fear that would give Justin more opportunity to find trouble."

"Where is he?"

"I checked on him earlier. He was sleeping."

He glanced at the mantel clock. "It's two o'clock. Why haven't you awakened him?"

"I tried, but it was fruitless. It isn't unusual for adolescents to sleep late."

Bellingham's eyes narrowed. "You're making excuses for him."

"I am not," she said. "How dare you?" Of course, she'd made an excuse because she didn't appreciate his arrogance.

Bellingham crossed the room and loomed over her. "Then why is your son still in bed?"

She shot off the sofa. "Leave this instant."

"You're only angry because you don't want to admit I'm right."

"I want you to quit my drawing room, and I do not want you involved in my affairs ever again," she said.

He released a long sigh. "I am a blunt man. It is not my nature to soften the truth, because it never helps."

She smoothed her skirt. "Perhaps the truth is more helpful when it does not humiliate the other person."

"Laura, look at me."

She lifted her gaze to him. "Lady Chesfield," she insisted. "And I do not like your methods."

"Make no mistake. That boy has the upper hand, and he knows it. If you do not get control over him, he will find trouble, and Montclief will take him."

"I'm well aware of the consequences," she said. "Justin, however, doesn't seem to take his uncle's threats seriously."

"Your son needs a jolt, immediately."

"What are you planning?" she asked.

"Leave it to me. He'll learn his lesson."

"He is my son. This is none of your affair."

"Frankly, I'm tired of encountering him on the street. He needs to be curbed."

"I will not allow you to use physical punishment," she said.

Bellingham scoffed. "No doubt Justin would prefer having his knuckles rapped, as it's temporary, whereas my idea of punishment requires him to change his behavior—if he wishes to leave the town house."

"He will just walk out the door," she said.

"Please excuse me. I will return shortly."

She hurried after Bellingham. "What are you doing? You cannot just take over without consulting me."

He ignored her and started down the stairs. She followed close behind until they crossed the great hall and entered the foyer.

"Reed, Lady Chesfield is in need your assistance," Bellingham said.

Reed lifted his chin. "Of course, my lord." He bowed to her. "My lady."

Laura fumed. Oh, she would blister Bellingham's ears for giving orders to *her* butler.

Bellingham smiled at her. "Do not worry. I have matters under control." Then he returned his attention to Reed. "It cannot have escaped your notice that the young master keeps late hours—or early ones depending on one's perspective."

"No, my lord," he said. "I definitely noticed."

"In the way of most young men, he is sowing wild oats," Bellingham continued. "However, his mother finds this distressful, and of course, I am concerned for Lord Chesfield as well. So, I have devised a plan to ensure that Lady Chesfield's son must consult her prior to leaving the town house. What I ask of you is to keep the door locked at all times. You may not unlock the door for him until he receives his mother's permission. The only exception is in case of fire or some other emergency. Do you have any questions?"

To Laura's astonishment, Reed smiled just a little. "No, my lord. You were quite clear."

"His friends will probably call upon him. Install them

in the anteroom and tell his lordship that you are under strict orders not to unlock the door without Lady Chesfield's permission."

"Yes, my lord," Reed said.

"Thank you, Reed." Bellingham offered his arm to Laura. For an instant, she was tempted to march off, but she would not show her anger in front of the servants. She allowed him to escort her, but she was breathing faster because of her ire.

After they stepped inside the drawing room, she turned on him. "How dare you give orders to my servant? You are not lord and master in this house, and you had better not forget it or I will never allow you in my home again."

"It was my idea, so I felt it best to relay the message. Why are you overset?"

She gave him an incredulous look. "Because you did not consult me first. I do not appreciate you managing my servants—or . . . or anything else."

"You will appreciate it when my plan works."

He was the most exasperating man she'd ever met. "I shan't detain you. You most likely have important places to go." He couldn't ignore that blatant hint.

"Actually, I do have plans, but first, I have to wait for your son to wake up. On the other hand, that might take too long. Where is his room? I'll oust him out of bed."

She fisted her hands. "You will do no such thing."

"Well, the other option is to allow him to sleep the rest of the day so that he's refreshed enough to stay out all night again. I don't recommend it, since Montclief's spies are watching."

She pointed at the chair. "Sit and don't move. I will wake him."

He folded his arms over his chest. "Do I look like a dog?"

"You lack a tail." She whirled around and marched out the door.

Bell grinned as he watched the sway of Laura's slim hips until she disappeared from his sight. Then he walked about the drawing room. Next to the sofa, there was the usual basket of sewing accoutrements that was de rigueur for all ladies. Pastoral paintings adorned the walls. On the opposite wall, he came across a portrait of a man and a woman holding an infant. The old-fashioned clothing indicated the portrait was painted many years ago.

He turned to a chair and fingered the silk paisley shawl draped there. Bell liked the feel of things: the lushness of velvet, the softness of silk, and most of all, a woman's soft skin. He pictured Laura lying on rumpled sheets. The image of long, slender thighs arose in his mind. When his groin tightened, he realized he'd better turn his thoughts elsewhere.

He crossed the room to admire a game table and ran his fingers over the polished mahogany surface. Bell examined the checkerboard and removed it. A backgammon board was inside. He examined the draughts and remembered playing the game with his father when he was about Justin's age on a summer's evening.

Unbidden, a sharp memory crept upon him. He'd been playing backgammon with his father. All of his focus had been on the game. He'd moved a draught and sat back. Out of the corner of his eye, he'd seen envy on his younger brother's face. Steven had quickly turned his attention away.

Bell had realized that Steven felt left out. He'd stood and asked Steven if he wished to take his place. His brother had jumped up, excited for the chance to play against his father for the first time. But what he'd remembered most was the silent approval in his father's eyes.

His chest tightened. Damn it all, why had the thought entered his head? He shoved the checkerboard top into place as if he were containing the memory.

The swish of skirts alerted him. He turned around to find Laura treading into the drawing room. "Well?"

She crossed the room and halted a foot away. "He's bathing and dressing. I'm having a tray sent up to him."

"He's putting the servants to extra trouble."

"I know, but sometimes it's best to choose one's battles. He's cooperative. I asked him to join us in the drawing room afterward so that I may introduce you."

"Was he surprised when you told him I'm here?"

"Yes. He looked a bit chagrined, since you caught him with the flask." She paused and added, "I will confront him later about sneaking out of the house."

She looked past him. "Did you see the game table?"

He nodded and drew closer to her. A light rose scent enveloped her. Probably soap. An image of her in a bath, her breasts bobbing in the water, popped into his mind. He'd better shove that out of his head.

She lifted the checkerboard top. "I suspect you have already investigated it."

"Of course."

When she smiled at him, he felt as if the sun had come out.

"Justin and I used to play backgammon."

"You speak in the past tense," Bell said.

"He lost interest after we came to London." She sighed. "I suppose it's not the thing to while away the hours with one's mother."

Bell said nothing, but despite her matter-of-fact tone, disappointment registered in her eyes.

"We could play if you wish," he said.

She hesitated and then gave him a sassy look. "Very well, but I will trounce you."

He pulled out one of the chairs. "Please be seated, my cocky opponent."

When she took the chair, he leaned over her and said, "I fear you are in for disappointment."

She turned toward him, and their gazes met. He breathed in the scent of her, and desire made his skin tingle. For the life of him, he couldn't look away. When her eyes widened like an artless schoolgirl, the urge to kiss her gripped him. He drew closer, but she averted her face.

He took the other chair and realized his heart was beating a bit faster. She must have sensed him looking at her, because she returned his gaze. A rosy blush crept into her cheeks as she lowered her lashes.

To put her at ease, he handed her the dice. His fingers accidentally brushed her soft palm. She stilled but did not look at him. After a pause, she said, "Please roll to see who wins the first turn."

"Ladies first," he said.

She rolled a three. "Drat."

He laughed and scooped up the dice. Then he rolled a six. "I win the first turn."

"Hah! You were lucky once," she said, grinning.

"I was lucky once before and hope to be again," he said, hinting at their kiss.

She frowned. "I beg your pardon?"

Obviously she'd not caught on. "It's nothing." He rolled a six and a three. Then he positioned the draughts accordingly on the pips. When he handed her the dice, she glanced at him and then quickly closed her small fist. She rolled two sixes and clapped her hands. "Doubles."

While she moved the draughts, he asked, "Did you find it difficult becoming a stepmother? I would imagine there must have been some adjustment for both you and Justin."

She finished her moves and handed him the dice. "Justin's mother died when he was only a year old. He had a succession of nannies. When my husband told Justin that I was to be his mother, he was elated. Until very recently, we were close." She sighed. "I know becoming independent is part of his growth, but it's not easy."

He rolled the dice. "You never had any other children."

"No."

He moved his draughts and then looked at her, the question unspoken.

"My husband grew very ill five months after we married," she said, taking the dice from him.

"How long ago did he die?" Bell asked.

"Four years have passed."

He watched her roll. "Did he know he was ailing when he asked you to marry him?"

She made her move. "He believed his health was returning."

Good Lord. "He was older than you?"

She dropped the dice into his outstretched hand. "Yes, by twenty-seven years."

He rolled. "Forgive me, but why would you marry an elderly man?"

"I married the man I loved," she said.

Her tone sounded defensive. He probably wasn't the first to suspect she'd married the elderly viscount for his fortune. "How did your family react to the news?" he said, moving the draughts.

She held out her hand for the dice and rolled them. "My father was a bit concerned at first, but he came around. My mother was happy that I made such a great match."

So there was an element of ambition about her marriage. "You have a large family?" he asked.

She smiled and pushed her draughts into place. "Yes, I have ten siblings."

Her father was a vicar. With such a large brood, he likely struggled to make ends meet. "You probably missed them after you married," he said.

"No, they live in the nearby village and visit often," she said, handing him the dice.

He gazed at her. Blond ringlets caressed her cheeks. Her complexion was flawless. She had a sweet, wholesome look about her and pretty green eyes. He noticed that her fingers and wrists were very slender. She was far more petite than his previous lovers. The thought brought him up short. Laura wasn't his lover...and never would be.

She lifted her lashes. "Your turn."

Recollecting himself, he rolled the dice. He started to move one of the draughts when her voice arrested him.

"Lady Atherton told me that you lost all of your family," she said.

He hated talking about it and made his move. "It happened a long time ago."

"You have no other relatives?"

"No," he said.

"Well, it is my turn to ask for forgiveness in advance," she said, "but under the circumstances, I would think you would wish to marry."

He looked at her coldly. "I don't." Then he handed her the dice.

She rolled. "You are angry at me for asking you about your family, but you must allow the question was natural since you asked about my own."

"You were under no obligation to answer and neither am I," he said.

Her eyes narrowed. "You are not unaware of the conventions of polite conversation."

"I break rules to suit me," he said.

"You are a nonconformist."

"I conform when it suits my purposes."

"Even in parliament?" she asked, tilting her head slightly.

"Yes," he said. He was only now aware of the tension in his shoulders. Now that the conversation had moved in a different direction, he felt easier. "I attend balls in order to mingle with my allies. I learn important information that I need to make political decisions."

She circled her finger round one of the draughts. "Surely you must negotiate sometimes?"

"Yes, but only—"

"When it suits your purposes," she said, smiling.

He grinned. "Exactly."

Something in her expression changed.

"What are you thinking?" he asked.

She hesitated and looked at the board. "I have no idea whose turn it is."

Her hesitation spoke volumes. Too many people had given him the "you shouldn't be alone" lecture. He never explained his reasons. They were his, and that was the end of it.

She shrugged and said, "Shall we call it a draw?"

"Very well." He returned the dice to the cup.

"I shall let you off the hook this time," she said.

Ah, she'd intimated he was welcome to call again. Of course, she wouldn't have admitted him today if not for her son, but that was the reason he'd called.

She looked up at the clock. "I fear my son is keeping you waiting much too long. If you must go, I will explain to Justin."

"No, I'll wait. I wish to meet him."

She moistened her lips and rose.

He stood.

"I-I'll just ring for a tea tray," she said.

He shook his head. "That's not necessary."

She started straightening the game. When he reached to help her replace the checkerboard top, their hands brushed again. He heard her quick indrawn breath and met her gaze once more. The tension drew out. There was no use denying his attraction to her. It was an invisible force, one they were both trying to ignore. But he recalled the feel of her in his arms and the taste of her lips. Everything inside him wanted to pull her flush against him, but he'd silently sworn not to touch her again.

There were multiple reasons he should steer clear of a woman like her, but at the moment, they flew out of his head. Damn it all to hell, she tempted him. He'd called to warn her about her son, but he ought to have ignored what he'd seen last night. Yet, it would have been dishonorable not to alert her.

He mustn't fool himself. There was something about her that made him want to be closer. He'd felt the sparks each time their hands had brushed. He wanted her, and the fact that he couldn't have her—or shouldn't want her—made matters much harder, figuratively and literally. Bell gritted his teeth. He would meet the boy and then have done with him and his mother. Bell's very presence should make Justin nervous.

But would it stop him?

Bell knew he ought to leave. He'd told Laura what he'd seen. Now he must bid her adieu and forget them both. Neither she nor her son was his responsibility.

Rapid footsteps sounded outside the door. Laura smoothed her skirts and turned.

The drawing room door flew open. Bell recognized the lanky young man with wheat-colored hair. Justin's flushed face and clenched fists stunned Bell.

"Justin, may I introduce—"

He loomed over his mother. "How dare you lock me in like a prisoner?"

Bell didn't shock easily, but the young man's rude response stunned him. "How dare you shout at your mother," he said.

Justin turned toward him. "Get out."

"Calm down," Laura said.

Justin pointed at the door. "Get out or I'll throw you out."

Bell folded his arms over his chest. "You can try, but you won't succeed."

Justin strode across the carpet. When he stepped too close, Bell grabbed his arm, turned him around, and pinned the boy's arms behind his back.

When Justin yelped, Bell said, "I warned you."

Laura cried out, "You're hurting him."

"No, I'm not. He's only crying out for your benefit. Aren't you?" he said.

"Let me go," Justin gritted out as he tried to pull away.

"Apologize," Bell said in a harsh tone.

Justin struggled. "Never."

"Since you neither care for nor respect your mother, she might as well send you to your uncle."

"What?"

"In fact, I can arrange to send you first thing on the morrow," Bell said.

"No," Laura said. "Please stop this."

Lord, did she not know that he meant to scare the boy enough to get him to behave? "So what will it be, Justin? An apology or your uncle?"

Justin was breathing hard. "Sorry," he muttered.

"Make it a proper apology."

"I'm sorry, Laura," Justin muttered.

"Speak in a sincere tone, and address your mother properly," Bell said.

"What?" Justin said too loud.

"She's your mother. Address her properly."

Justin was breathing heavily with obvious anger. "I apologize, Mama," he said.

Bell let him go. The young man whirled around with his hands fisted.

"Stand down," Bell said. "You know you were in the wrong."

Justin scowled and rubbed his arms.

"Lesson one," Bell said. "Never insult a lady, especially your mother. Lesson two. Never underestimate your opponent."

"I hate you," Justin said.

"You don't know me." Bell turned to Laura. "Lady Chesfield, I suggest we all sit and discuss this rationally."

Justin slouched in a chair and folded his arms over his chest.

Bell took the other armchair and leaned his elbows on his knees. He realized that this was an opportunity for Laura to enforce her authority. "Your mother wishes to explain to you about the locked door," Bell said. When he glanced at her, he saw approval in her eyes.

Laura drew in her breath. "Justin, you failed in your promise to me again. I could not sit still, knowing that your uncle will take you if he hears you're rebelling again. His friends are spying on you. So I took this measure for your own good. Reed will only open the door for you if you have obtained my permission. And even then, you must be truthful with me about your whereabouts."

Her son pulled a face. "I could just leave via the servant's entrance."

Bell gave Laura a knowing look. "He doesn't seem to care that he'll have to spend the next four years with his uncle."

Justin shoved out of his chair. "No!"

"Be seated," Laura said, "or I'll send you today."

When Bell started to rise, Justin winced and flounced back in the chair. Lord, he was a handful.

"I cannot wait for the day I turn twenty-one," Justin muttered.

"Ah, yes, you will inherit a great estate, along with all the troublesome paperwork, repairs, tenants, and servants," Bell said. "You will be required to make dozens of decisions every single day, and then when spring rolls around, you will spend hours listening to boring windbags drone on for hours in parliament. I bet you're thrilled at the prospect."

Justin snorted. "You left out some of your more pleasurable pursuits."

Bell noted the satisfaction on Justin's face and gave him a warning look. Then he took out his watch. "I'd better be on my way."

A knock sounded. Reed announced Lady Atherton.

Everyone rose as the grand dame entered the room. "Oh, dear, I've interrupted," she said.

"You are very welcome," Laura said.

Bell bowed to her. "Lady Atherton."

She regarded him with an enigmatic smile and then turned to Justin. "It is such a pleasure to see you again, Lord Chesfield. Are you enjoying the season?"

"Yes, ma'am," he said in a wooden voice.

At least he'd remembered his manners, Bell thought.

"Please be seated," Laura said. "I'll ring for a tea tray."

Lady Atherton perched on the sofa beside Laura. "Do not bother, dear. I have news." She smiled at Justin. "Although I fear Justin would find it all rather dull."

Bell figured Lady Atherton did not wish to discuss the news in Justin's presence. He looked at Laura, but her attention was focused on her son. "Justin, you may be excused," she said.

He stood, bowed, and strode out of the drawing room.

After the door shut, Lady Atherton exhaled. "I'm

glad you're here, Bellingham. Montclief called on me with the most astounding story. Well, of course I could not believe it. Perhaps he'd been nipping from the brandy decanter."

Laura moistened her lips. "What did Montclief say?"

"He said the two of you were secretly engaged. Can you imagine that? On one day's acquaintance, no less." Lady Atherton shook her head. "He must have lost his wits."

Bell exchanged a look with Laura.

Laura sighed. "Montclief meant to take Justin away. I tried to persuade him against it, but he refused to budge. He said that Justin needed male influence."

Lady Atherton touched her high purple collar. "It's true?"

"It was a necessary invention," Bell said.

"I assure you that we are not really engaged," Laura said. "It was Bellingham's idea to tell Montclief that we were keeping it a secret. For obvious reasons, we do not wish anyone to know about it."

Lady Atherton looked at Bellingham and then at Laura. "But he will expect you to marry."

"Montclief is only concerned about Justin's wild behavior," Laura said. "Once that is resolved, he won't care. He never wanted responsibility for his nephew."

"I'm doubly glad I called," Lady Atherton said. "Montclief is very suspicious of your engagement and believes that you are involved in a liaison with Bellingham."

"He warned us against it," she said. "There is no need for alarm on that count."

Lady Atherton patted Laura's hand and looked at Bell. "Of course, I know that you are a lady of strong moral principles. How Montclief could even assume otherwise is beyond my imagination."

Bell bit back a smile. Underneath Laura's prim exterior lay a hot-blooded woman.

"There is more," Lady Atherton said. Then she told them about his feigned concerns about Laura's conduct. "He arrived in a hired hack and claimed he was unable to remain in London because of the expense."

"But my husband left him property and a tidy fortune," Laura said.

"Does he release your son's allowance in a timely manner?" Bellingham asked.

"Yes, he's always been prompt," she said.

"His financial problems may be recent," Bellingham said.

"Montclief may despise me, but I know he doesn't want Justin," Laura said. "If he'd really wanted him, he would have waited for Justin to come home that day he called."

The fine hairs on the back of Bell's neck stiffened. He would say nothing to Laura, but privately he wondered if he'd underestimated Montclief. Bell resolved to make quiet inquiries about the man. He would hire someone to visit the village near Montclief's property and see what he could dig up.

Bell looked at Laura. "Out of curiosity, where does Montclief live?"

"Sussex," Laura said, "near the village of Goatham Green. Why do you ask?"

"I just wanted to know how far away he lives from Hampshire."

"He never comes to Hollwood Abbey anymore," Laura said.

Long ago, Bell had learned to trust his gut feelings. He would rather err on the side of caution than discover he'd waited too late. But once again, he was getting more involved in her life. He told himself it was only an investigation, one that he would use to reassure her—and himself. The clock struck the hour, reminding him of an appointment. "I must leave," he said.

As the two women rose, Bell found himself gazing into Laura's eyes. Belatedly, he realized that Lady Atherton was observing the exchange. He bowed and quit the drawing room. As he strode down the stairs, he vowed that this would be the last time he called on her.

After Bellingham left, Laura sighed. "I am glad for his assistance with Justin, but Bellingham is very high-handed."

Lady Atherton smiled. "He is accustomed to ruling over everyone and everything in his sphere. It is second nature to a man like him."

"Phillip was never so willfully authoritative," Laura said.

"Your late husband was a different sort of man, but Phillip acted swiftly when he encountered injustice or cruelty." Lady Atherton paused and said, "Speaking of the earl, you do realize that you're both in a precarious situation."

"You are such a dear, but you must not be concerned. As much as I dislike the way Bellingham takes over, I admit he managed to curb Justin's outrageous impulses today. You will shudder when I tell you that Bellingham actually held Justin's arms behind his back to control him."

"Oh, my." Lady Atherton unfurled her fan. "Alfred told me Bellingham takes after his ruthless forebears."

Laura thought that an exaggeration but said nothing.

"It's unfortunate that he lost all of his family when he was so young. He used to be carefree and sunny-natured."

Chill bumps erupted on Laura's arms. "You told me they died. What happened?"

"They succumbed to consumption. He'd been away at university and rushed home only to find they had already passed."

"How awful," Laura said.

"I heard he was in a very bad way, completely distraught. His friends took him away to the Continent." She released a long sigh. "When he returned two years ago, it was clear to everyone that he had completely changed." Lady Atherton put her fist to her heart. "I think he is damaged inside. Many think it is irrevocable."

Laura shook her head. "No, you must not say that."

"My dear, you were shocked when I told you he refuses to marry, even though all of his property will go to the Crown upon his death."

"It's foolish," she said. "Surely he believes his father would wish him to carry on the earldom."

"I do not know the answer," Lady Atherton said. "No one has ever broken through his defenses."

Laura thought him entirely too bold and imposing, but without Bell's help, Montclief would have taken Justin away from her.

"His willingness to guide Justin is a hopeful sign," Lady Atherton said. "It was very gallant of him."

Laura recalled the way he'd looked at her and the supposedly accidental touches today. Bellingham's motives were not as pure as Lady Atherton believed.

"He clearly doesn't believe he needs anyone," Lady Atherton said, "but perhaps the right woman will open his heart."

Laura said nothing, but she didn't think his intentions involved hearts and declarations of love. He was the sort of man who kept a mistress. The sort of man a woman like her should avoid.

Bell sat at his desk reviewing a letter from his banker. At the sound of a knock, he folded the letter and said, "Enter."

Griffith, his butler, stepped inside. "My lord, a man named Smyth has called." He produced the card.

"Please show him in," Bell said, rising.

Smyth entered and bowed. "My lord, I understand you are in need of my investigative services."

"I am. Please be seated."

Smyth sat on the edge of his seat. "My lord, how may I assist you?"

"I wish to conduct an investigation into a man by the name of Montclief. He is the guardian of a minor who will formally take control of the title of Viscount Chesfield in four years. For obvious reasons, I wish to conceal the investigation. I wish to gain insight into Montclief's financial situation, the state of his property at Goatham Green, and to learn how he is perceived among the general populace. I need information about his friends and any other pertinent facts. Are you able to take on this investigation?"

"Yes, my lord. I have conducted similar investigations

numerous times and will provide both a verbal and written report upon conclusion of my findings."

Bell unlocked a desk drawer and produced a hefty purse. "This is for your expenses. Upon satisfactory conclusion, you will receive four hundred pounds. I might add that you should spare no detail in your report, however mundane it might at first appear. Send me preliminary reports as they become available. Do you have any questions?"

"No, my lord. Your instructions are clear."

After Smyth left, Bell locked the desk drawer. He wanted to be prepared in the event Montclief became a threat to Laura and her son. Long ago, Bell had learned to trust his instincts, and the information he'd gleaned from Lady Atherton had made him doubly suspicious. The investigation might yield nothing of significance, but he'd rather be safe than sorry.

Chapter Four

The next evening

$\mathscr{B}$ell met Colin and Harry at White's and ordered a bottle of brandy for the table. After Bell opened a gold case, he offered his friends a cheroot. They sat smoking in silence for a while. Bell's thoughts turned to a fantasy of Laura in a bath. His blood heated as he imagined parting her thighs and exploring between the plump folds of her sex. He would make her come and then he'd lift her out and apply a towel while he licked water droplets off strategic areas of her slim body. That would require getting her naked and in a bath.

The devil, what was he thinking? She was a proper widow and a vicar's daughter, not his type at all. His type of woman was improper. She was willing to do anything as long as he showered her with jewels and ball gowns. She was skilled in the sensual arts and completely predictable. Just like his last mistress, Marguerite—boring.

Laura was not boring. In fact, she wasn't predictable at all. Granted, she was proper, but he couldn't anticipate what she would say or do. She most certainly did not like it when he took control over matters, but he was accustomed to taking care of problems. And her son was a problem.

But her son was not *his* problem. So why did Bell keep thinking about the young buck? Why the devil was he so obsessed with Laura and her son? She'd released him from any obligation. It was past time he pushed them both out of his mind.

Unfortunately, the harder he tried to forget her, the more he thought about her. He kept remembering the lush kisses he'd shared with Laura. Usually he could walk away from a woman without a care, but for some reason, he couldn't get the feel and taste of her out of his head.

He inhaled from his cheroot and recalled her shock when he'd slid his tongue home. He rather liked that he'd taught her a few things and that she'd responded with such abandon. When he thought about the feel of her soft body pressed against him, his groin tightened again. The devil, he couldn't remember the last time he'd wanted a woman this badly.

"Are you sickening?" Harry said.

His voice interrupted Bell's pleasurable musings. "No, I'm thinking."

Colin smirked. "Looks like he's in lust. What say you, Harry?"

"Cupid has definitely struck," Harry said.

"Cupid is about love, not lust," Bell muttered.

"You're wrong," Colin said. "The Romans said a shot from the arrow caused uncontrollable desire."

Bell blew out a smoke ring. "Uncontrollable? What if there is no ladylove available? What does the poor sot do?"

Harry fisted his hand and made an up-and-down motion. The officious waiter returned. "Sir, did you need something else?"

Colin choked on his brandy. Bell's shoulders shook with laughter.

"No, thank you," Harry said to the waiter.

When the waiter left, Bell guffawed.

"Gad, Harry," Colin said. "Try to control yourself."

Harry pulled a face. "And you don't do it? Ha!"

Colin regarded Bell with disgust. "Look what you started."

"Me?" Bell said. "I'm not the one demonstrating hand relief in the damned club."

Harry grinned. "I could give lessons."

"No," Bell and Colin said simultaneously.

"It was a jest," Harry said.

Bell blew out another smoke ring and looked at Colin. "Harry is good for something. I just can't remember what."

"I am indeed," Harry said. "By the by, I met up with Pembroke. He danced with Lady Chesfield at Lady Atherton's ball and said he plans to call on her."

Bell suspended his glass halfway to his mouth and scowled. "What?"

His friends stared at him.

Colin set his glass down. "Why do you care if he calls on her? You said she was proper. What would you do with a proper woman?"

"I'm not doing anything with her," he grumbled. But he'd like to do something with her, something hot and sweaty.

"Right," Colin said, winking at Harry.

"I ought to have known," Harry said. "Women always fall for brooding men."

"I don't brood," Bell said.

Colin shrugged. "You look like you brood."

"My girl cousins said ladies find brooding men dangerous and romantic," Harry said. "Maybe I should practice it."

"By all means," Bell said. "We'll judge how well you display brooding tendencies."

Harry curled his lip and looked up from beneath his thick brows.

Bell snorted. "I need another drink after that horrid demonstration." He put out his cheroot and refilled the glasses.

"So have you seen the widow's wild son again?" Colin asked.

He nodded. "Today I called on Lady Chesfield. I thought she should know her son was out carousing again."

His friends stared at him as if he'd grown horns.

"He's getting into trouble. His mother is having difficulty managing him, and his guardian is a prize ass," Bell said.

Colin eyed Harry. "He's trying to get in the widow's good graces."

"No, he's trying to get under her skirts," Harry said.

"Don't start. I already told you she's a lady," Bell said with a warning in his voice.

"You're leaving out more than a few details," Colin said.

"Watch out," Harry said. "Pembroke is bearing down on you, Bell. He looks quite determined."

"Thanks for the forewarning," Bell said, and sipped his brandy.

"Bellingham."

He heard Pembroke's voice and slowly raised his bored gaze to the short, balding man.

Pembroke took the chair next to him and regarded him sternly. "I understand your carriage was seen at Lady Chesfield's home yesterday."

"Your point?" Bell said.

He inhaled as if to say something. Then he exhaled. "She's a respectable widow."

"I'm aware of that." He swirled his brandy. "Is that all?"

"No," he said with vehemence in his voice. "If you must know, I have conceived a partiality for her."

"Does she know?"

He huffed. "I danced with her and plan to call."

Bell sipped his drink. "Good luck getting admittance to her drawing room."

"What do you mean?"

"She's not interested in suitors. In fact, she told me she doesn't wish to marry. We share that in common," he said.

"See here," Pembroke said. "She's not one of your light skirts. I plan to court her, and I won't allow you to seduce her."

"Maybe they should fight," Harry said.

Colin shook his head. "It wouldn't be sporting. Bell is twice his size."

Pembroke's face turned crimson. "Are you insulting my manhood?"

Harry looked at Colin. "Would we do that?"

"Never," Colin said.

"You're taunting me," Pembroke said.

Bell groaned. "You're annoying me." He made a shooing motion with his hand. "Go on, now."

Pembroke's nostrils flared. "I claimed her first."

"I'll be sure to inform her," he said.

Pembroke stood. "Well, I plan to warn her about your rakehell past."

"Feel free to tattle," Bell drawled. "I'm sure she'll be impressed."

Pembroke glared at him. "Always cool as a cucumber, but this time you won't win."

"If you were so sure of that, you wouldn't have bothered to warn me," Bell said.

"This isn't the last of it," Pembroke said.

Bell yawned. "Pembroke, go bore someone else."

After the man strode off, Colin said, "Good Lord, he's smitten."

"Who?" Harry said.

"Don't be a nodcock," Colin said. "Pembroke."

"I thought you meant Bell. He doesn't look smitten," Harry said.

"Of course he's not," Colin said in exasperation.

Bell rolled his eyes. "Wonderful. I have a jealous rival."

"So there *is* something between you and Lady Chesfield," Harry said.

"Oh, yes," Bell said. "Her son." The boy's anger yesterday was out of bounds. Bell had never imagined he'd have to physically restrain Justin. "I've hired someone to investigate the uncle. I hope to find some dirt in the event he tries to take the boy away from her."

Colin whistled. "Sounds serious."

"I may not find anything, but Montclief strikes me as the type to have secrets."

"You'll use the investigation to help out Lady Chesfield?" Harry said.

"If I find something, yes. I didn't like the way he browbeat her. He's a nasty sort."

Colin scowled. "The devil. Here comes Lord Gossip."

Bell glanced up to see Lindmoore hurrying toward them. "Why is everyone so bent on intruding tonight?"

"It's the widow," Harry said. "Everyone is curious about her, and your carriage was spotted at her town house."

For some odd reason, Bell didn't like all the speculation about Laura. Damnation, was he actually feeling protective of her? Maybe he was sickening after all.

"Well, well," Lindmoore said as he approached. "I heard an interesting tale about you, Bellingham."

Bell yawned. "The queue is a long one, but feel free to join it."

Lindmoore tittered. "You always have a clever retort, but I have to ask if the rumor is true."

"Which one?" he said.

"There's more?" Lindmoore said, his eyes gleaming.

"Usually, yes," Bell said.

"This one concerns you and the lovely widow, Lady Chesfield," he said, pitching his voice louder. "I've heard you've already made a conquest."

Other men at nearby tables turned to stare.

When Lindmoore leaned his hand on the table, Bell rose. "Surely you do not mean to slander a respectable lady's reputation?"

Lindmoore's face turned ashen. "No, of course I—"

Bell drew closer. "You will apologize for the mistake."

"Begging your pardon," he said, his face suddenly gone pasty. "I meant no insult to the lady."

"I'm not fond of dawn meetings," Bell said. "It interferes with my sleep. I trust you will refrain from speaking about her in the future?"

Lindmoore held up his hands. "Of course. My apologies for the, er, misunderstanding."

Bell regarded him in disgust. "Go."

Lindmoore hurried off.

"I was worried there for a bit," Colin said. "Thought he'd piss himself."

"Maybe we should enter a pissing contest in the betting book," Harry said.

"No," Bell and Colin said simultaneously.

"You're no fun," Harry said.

Colin pulled a face. "I can't believe you bother to read the betting book."

"It's entertaining," Harry said.

"Never mind," Bell said. "I'm weary of this place. Let's repair to my town house."

After they reached Bell's town house, he led his friends to the billiards room. "Your choice of cue sticks," he said.

"I want one of these," Harry said, patting the table.

"You have no money," Colin said.

"I can dream," Harry said. "Who knows? If I inherit my uncle's pig farm, maybe I'll be rich one day."

"You can live in the lap of luxury and black sows," Colin said.

Bell poured drinks and handed them round to his friends. "The two of you play a game. I'll watch." He indicated a mahogany side table. "You can set your glasses on the pewter dish."

Harry set up the balls while Colin chose a cue stick. Bell sat in a black armchair with gold trim, stretched out his legs, and sipped his brandy. "When you finish the game, we can take a smoke break in the garden."

Harry sighted a ball, gave it a smooth tap, and sent it straight into the pocket.

"You're accomplished," Bell said, admiring Harry's skill.

"My third cousin twice removed owns a billiards table. He's richer than Croesus."

"Maybe you have a chance at the dukedom," Colin said.

"No, there are two other relatives ahead of me," Harry said. "Truthfully, I like the old duke. He tells hysterical stories of his youthful years wearing striped breeches and the ladies with vermin in their tall wigs."

Colin sighted a ball. When he tapped it, the ball narrowly missed the pocket. "Damn."

While his friends continued to play and heckle one another, Bell's thoughts returned to that moment in White's when Lindmoore had said he'd heard Bell had made a conquest of Laura. He'd never worried about anyone following him before, but then he'd never had to use care with the reputations of his mistresses. They were sophisticated women who had a string of past lovers as long as his own. They were not devoted mothers who fought to keep their sons safe from wild friends and uncaring guardians.

The first time he'd called on Laura, he'd relished the prospect of chasing her until she surrendered. But there was a great deal at stake. Even if Laura was willing, there was no way to conduct a discreet liaison when she was the latest *on dit*. Pursuing her wasn't a mere challenge; it was nigh impossible when she had a son and others had marked his carriage at her town house. If news of an *affaire de coeur* leaked, it would destroy her reputation and possibly end in the loss of her son. He couldn't ruin her life for a temporary love affair.

The *clack, clack, clack* of balls scattering on the green baize table brought Bell back to the present. He had been brooding, damn it.

Harry crowed as the balls sank into the pockets.

"Rematch," Colin said, slinging his arm around Harry's neck.

A huff of laughter escaped Bell. Somehow the pair always managed to lighten his gloomy moods. "Let's go to the garden. I need a cheroot."

His friends followed him.

"You don't smoke inside the house?" Harry said.

"Lord, no. It makes my eyes water," Bell said.

"You could just open a window," Colin said.

"And let in all that stinky coal smell?" Bell said. "Have you lost your wits?"

For some bizarre reason, his friends guffawed.

Bell found the tinderbox he kept on the stone garden bench. After he managed a spark, he lit one of the lanterns in the trees and then lit his cheroot. His friends joined him and said nothing for a while. Bell appreciated their silence.

Colin blew a smoke ring. "About the widow. Why did you call on her again if you don't intend to make her your mistress?"

For a moment, he was stunned speechless, but he had to say something. "She's alone. I wanted to make sure there were no problems."

"Right," Harry said. "You only want to help her."

Colin snorted. "To what?"

"She's a lady," he said through gritted teeth.

"No offense intended." Colin inhaled from the cheroot and exhaled. "We're only needling you."

Harry ground out his cheroot. "Seriously, Bell, it sounds as if Lady Chesfield needs help with her son."

He frowned. "I've gotten too tangled up in her life already. This is the end of it. If I discover the uncle is involved in nefarious deeds, then I'll make the information available to her."

One week later

After receiving an invitation from Mrs. Norcliffe, Bell felt obliged to put in a brief appearance at her Venetian breakfast for Harry's sake. Generally he avoided these sorts of afternoon garden parties, unless he intended to discuss politics with some of his allies. Even then, he usually left early and certainly intended to do so today.

A cool breeze stirred the leaves of the beech trees as he strolled out onto the grounds. Ladies with parasols walked along the garden paths where a riot of bright-colored flowers he couldn't name blossomed. One path led to a bridge overlooking a pond. Just ahead, a large tent shaded the tables and chairs where guests were enjoying refreshments.

Harry and Colin strolled outside the tent. Then Harry shaded his eyes and waved.

Glad to have found his friends quickly, Bell strode in that direction.

When he reached them, Harry clapped his hand on Bell's shoulder. "I thought you might have decided to bow out of this tepid entertainment."

Bell grinned. "I figured the pair of you would fall in the pond and need to be rescued."

"Careful. We're liable to dunk you," Colin said.

"It would certainly liven things up," Harry grumbled. "My mother refused to serve anything stronger than lemonade and small beer."

"God save us. We might perish of sobriety," Bell muttered.

"This way," Harry said. "My mother insisted upon meeting you."

Once inside the tent, Harry introduced his mother, Mrs. Norcliffe, and two of his female cousins, Agnes and Helen, who whispered to each other as if they were silly schoolgirls. The entire time they regarded him with scheming expressions.

Agnes, a redhead with a flat bosom, curtsied. "Have you seen the pond and the goldfish, my lord?"

He sensed she meant to trap him into escorting her there. "Only from a distance."

Agnes tittered. "You simply must see it."

He'd always found that nervous sort of laugh irritating. The last thing he wanted was to squire her anywhere. He remained silent, a move he'd used many times to discourage either a determined lady or her conniving mama.

"I would be happy to show you," Agnes said.

Apparently she was not easily deterred. "I do not wish to trouble you."

"It is no trouble at all," she said.

He despised women who tried to manipulate him. Unfortunately, he couldn't escape, because she was Harry's cousin. He was on the verge of offering his escort when he saw Laura following Lady Atherton. The grand dame cut a swath through the crowd and greeted Mrs. Norcliffe.

"What a lovely party." Lady Atherton kissed the air by Mrs. Norcliffe's cheeks. After Harry's mother made all of the introductions, Bell turned his attention to Laura. He was struck anew by her sweet smile and pretty green eyes. Today she wore a white gown with a blue sash and blue ribbons trimming the puffed sleeves along with a white shawl. He knew next to nothing about women's clothing, other than how to strip it off, but he liked her simple style.

Bell took the opportunity to go greet Laura. "My friends wish to meet you, if you are amenable."

"Very well," she said. Her expression turned a bit wary, but she accepted his proffered arm.

He leaned down. "Is something wrong?"

"I'm a bit flustered. Miss Agnes Norcliffe glared at me."

A flowery scent drifted toward him. For a moment, his brain froze as he focused on her lips. Her very kissable lips. He reminded himself she was off-limits and forced himself to concentrate. "I suppose she's jealous."

"Of me?"

"Probably. She was rather determined to show me about the grounds, and I was determined not to go."

"You were not interested in seeing them?"

He met her gaze. "I wasn't interested in her."

Her eyes widened. "Oh."

"I prefer you."

Her smile faded. "Your rakish charms will not work on me."

"I'm being truthful," he said. "I prefer you because I'm safe from you."

She pointed at herself. "You, safe from me?"

"You forget we have something in common. You share my disinclination to marry, so I'm in no danger of getting caught in the parson's mousetrap."

"Even if I were inclined to wed, you would be quite safe from me," she muttered.

"I don't know whether to be relieved or insulted."

"I admit you have some positive attributes. You are an earl, extremely rich, and far too handsome for your own good."

"But…"

She put her chin up. "You are an infamous rake and therefore completely unsuitable to be a husband to anyone, let alone to a lady of principles."

He lifted his brows. "Meaning a woman with high moral standards like you."

"Given my father's vocation, you shouldn't be surprised."

"So you never sin."

"Do not be absurd. No one is free of sin," she said.

"Tell me one of your sins… if you're brave enough."

"Very well, it occurred in my drawing room." She glanced at him. "With you."

"It was only a kiss." It was more than a mere kiss. He'd not been able to forget the feel of her in his arms, and that only made him want more from her.

"You see, we are completely different," she said. "To

you a kiss is practically meaningless. To me, it is a momentous step in a relationship."

She was probably thinking of her late husband. "A kiss can mean many things," he said, "but it is never devoid of meaning."

"Are we really debating the meaning of a kiss?"

"I cede the point to you on one condition," he said.

She narrowed her eyes. "What is it?"

"You allow me to introduce you to those two gentlemen just ahead."

"Let me guess. They are friends of yours."

"Yes. They're anxious to meet the mysterious widow."

She huffed. "There is no mystery. I'm exactly who I appear to be."

There was a hidden side to her, a sensual one, but he said nothing as he led her to his friends. "Lady Chesfield, may I introduce you to my disreputable friends, Colin Brockhurst, Earl of Ravenshire, and Harry Norcliffe, Viscount Evermore. I met them when I fished them out of the Thames one night."

"It's a pleasure to meet you, in spite of your watery origins," she said.

"Our friend Bell exaggerates a bit," Colin said. "Harry fell in the river and Bell helped me drag him to shore."

"Well, you appear to have survived," she said.

Harry lifted her hand. "*Enchanté*, Lady Chesfield. Bell neglected to mention your beauty."

She lowered her lashes, and her face flushed. Most of the women Bell knew reacted with affected boredom when complimented, as if it were their due. But he'd realized from the beginning that Laura was different.

"Bell, take her to the bridge," Harry said. "There's a pond with goldfish—my mother's idea of pets."

Bell offered his arm once more and led her out of the tent.

"I left my parasol," she said.

"Where did you leave it?" he said. "I'll fetch it for you."

"Never mind. My bonnet will provide sufficient shade," she said.

"You surprise me," he said as they walked along the path. "Most women wouldn't risk even a bit of sun."

"There are worse things than sunshine."

He wondered what she meant. Not that he could hazard a guess when he knew only a few essentials about her life. It was probably for the best. He didn't appreciate it when people were overly inquisitive about him.

The breeze stirred the leaves of the beech trees overhead. She said nothing more as they walked along.

He looked at her. "How are matters with your son?"

"Justin has improved a great deal since he is no longer associating with his rowdy friends."

"I'm surprised it was that easy," he said.

"It wasn't. George and Paul called earlier this week. Apparently they were intimidated when they realized I would not let Justin leave until I knew their destination and the time they meant to return. They have not called since then."

"Your son wasn't angry?"

"He was furious, but there was nothing he could do. I ignored his shouts. When he threw a vase, I told him that I was deducting the cost from his quarterly allowance. He threw another one, and I refused to release any more funds until he stopped acting like a heathen. Yesterday he finally apologized for his behavior."

"It must have been difficult, but you stood firm," he said.

"I thought parenting would be easier after he grew older."

"Is he here?" Bell asked.

"Yes. I persuaded him to come along and promised to leave if he didn't meet anyone. We weren't here more than fifteen minutes when a group of young people invited him to join in a sack race."

Bell nodded. "Excellent." He paused. "It looks as if everyone is returning to the tent."

"They're serving luncheon. If you're hungry, please go ahead," she said.

He shook his head. "I'd prefer to wait until the crowd thins."

When they reached the bridge, his boots clomped on the wood. He stopped in the center and removed his hat to prevent it from falling into the pond. "There's one," he said, pointing. "Do you see the tail?"

She leaned over the rail. "Oh, it looks orange. I expected it to appear gold."

"There are more," he said. "There is a golden one. Do you see its tail wiggling?"

"Oh, yes, there are quite a few. I wonder what they eat."

He shrugged. "What do any fish eat?"

She wrinkled her nose. "Worms."

"Have you ever gone fishing?" he asked.

"No. My brothers used to chase my sister and me with the worms."

He laughed. "So you weren't a hoyden?"

She shook her head. "I helped my mother with the younger children."

There wouldn't have been funds for a nurse. "How old were you when you started helping?"

She shrugged. "Eight or nine. I can't recall for certain."

Their lives had been very different growing up, and that only made him curious. "You probably had a number of beaux before you married."

She kept her gaze on the wiggling fish below. "Not really."

"I suspect you are being modest."

"I danced at local assemblies and spoke to gentlemen, but I knew that my charms were insufficient to overcome my small dowry." She smiled at him. "Then one day I met Phillip in the shop where we were both caught because of the rain."

He returned her smile. "So your story wasn't a complete fabrication."

"Well, he didn't lay his coat over a puddle," she said, "but we got on famously from the start."

"What of your sisters? Are they married?"

She nodded.

He gave her a questioning look. "They had no trouble finding husbands?"

She smoothed her skirt. "My late husband wished to help my family."

Her husband had made sure the girls had dowries, a good thing because the only acceptable professions available to women were to be a governess or a companion to an older woman. Otherwise, single women of little fortune became dependents on their relatives. "I assume he provided well for you in his will."

"Yes, he was generous with everyone, including his brother."

He shuttered his expression, but inside he was appalled that her late husband would give his brother anything. "Having met Montclief, I'm surprised."

"My brother-in-law reserved his underhanded remarks for moments when Phillip was out of earshot." Her fleeting smile spoke volumes. "He would say things that were supposed to be complimentary but were not."

"Such as?"

"He would say how devoted I was to Phillip, and of course he was grateful for the care I gave him." She continued to speak in a sarcastic voice. "Naturally, he would not treat me in a condescending manner, even though I was *far beneath* my husband."

"Did you not tell your husband that he was treating you in this abominable manner?"

She shook her head. "At first I wanted to keep the peace. I was a little intimidated by the change in my circumstances when I first married. Then later, I said nothing to Phillip, because I did not wish to burden him."

"If your husband had known, he might have used better judgment in naming his son's guardian," Bell said.

She arched her brows. "In hindsight, perhaps I should have told Phillip, but in the early days of our marriage, I didn't know my husband would die."

He sighed. "I beg your pardon for misjudging you and your late husband."

"Phillip grew very ill with a wasting disease five months after our marriage," she said. "He was bedridden and nearly as helpless as a babe. I could not confess his brother's ill treatment when Phillip's spirits were so low. It might have hastened his decline."

"Obviously you did what you felt was best for your husband."

"After Phillip died, Montclief washed his hands of Justin and me. Frankly, I was glad he stayed away."

Another couple approached the bridge. Bell offered his arm to Laura again and strolled across with her. "You said you've no intention of marrying again. Is there a reason?"

"Yes, my son."

"Why would your son preclude you from marrying?"

"If I were to remarry, Montclief might decide to take Justin. I am not his blood relative," she said.

"He could take him at anytime," Bell said, "but then again, your son will be of age in four years. You could marry then."

"In four years, I will be thirty-two. Most men prefer younger wives."

He suspected she was dissembling. "Any man with eyes in his head can see that you are beautiful. Either you do not give yourself enough credit," he said, "or you are afraid that another man may not measure up to your late husband."

"You give your opinion rather decidedly for one who refuses to marry," she said.

"There is a difference," he said. "I do not have to marry in order to enjoy a lover, whereas you are determined to follow a moral code that impedes intimacy outside of marriage."

"My morals are none of your concern," she said. "And you have no right to speak to me in this manner."

"I merely stated the truth. You were married for several

years, and now you mean to remain celibate for the rest of your life?"

Her face heated, and she halted. "You go too far."

Two ladies on the opposite side of the path stared at them. "Let's continue our conversation in private," he said. Before she could object, he turned down a path surrounded by tall hedges.

He walked halfway down the path and joined her on a wrought-iron bench. "Your face is red. Why are you perturbed?"

She had her reasons for her decision, but she owed him no explanation. "You should not speak of immodest topics in my presence."

His lopsided smile made him look boyish. She averted her gaze, refusing to let him lure her with his charm. "It may have escaped your notice, but I am a lady, not one of your mistresses."

"I meant no disrespect," he said. "You were married, and I know that you're not unresponsive. Given what you've told me, I find it odd that you would dismiss marriage."

"Unlike you, pleasures of the flesh are not my first priority."

"Ah, but I've kissed you, and I know you enjoyed it as much as I did."

In truth, she'd lain awake remembering the way he'd touched and kissed her, but she would not, could not tell him. "I beg your pardon. This conversation is unsuitable. I am leaving."

He rose with her. She turned, but he caught her arm and brought her round to face him. "If you're angry, confront me. Don't just walk away."

She averted her gaze. "I do not like it when you speak of indelicate subjects."

"Sit with me for a while."

She met his gaze, and the hungry look in his eyes made her pulse race. "If someone were to find us—"

"We would hear their footsteps long before that happened, and we're not doing anything wrong."

"We should not be alone." Because she wanted him to kiss and touch her again, and once that door opened, she feared she would not be able to close it.

"You are afraid."

Up went her chin. "I'm not afraid of you. You may be a rake, but you are not stupid."

His chest shook with laughter as he led her back to the bench. After they were seated, he said, "I think you are afraid of yourself."

"That's ridiculous." She would never admit it.

"Let me amend that," he said. "I suspect you are afraid you will succumb to desire."

"Hah! You're just hoping I will," she said. "I assure you that will not happen." Why had she said that? He would take it as a challenge, and even though he exasperated her, she knew she would not be able to resist him.

"I won't lie to you," he said, his voice a little rough. "I am attracted to you, but I swore to keep my distance. Even though you don't approve of me, I suspect you feel the same way."

She moistened her lips and looked at her lap. "I was taught that those feelings can be expressed only within marriage. My beliefs are ingrained. Even if I believed differently, I would not risk an *affaire de coeur*, because if I were ever found out, my son and my family would share in my censure."

His blue eyes filled with cynicism. "They would never know, and neither would anyone else."

"You're not listening," she said. "It is a sin outside of marriage."

"So you will live the rest of your life alone—"

"I will not be alone. I will have my family and my son."

"All of whom you will put ahead of your own needs. Why is that, Laura?"

Her temper flared. "You know very little about me, and yet you have the audacity to judge me."

"I know that you accepted a marriage proposal from an old man who knew he was ill, but you were willing to sacrifice because he needed you. You're doing it again with your son, and I suspect it's the same with your family."

She turned to him and put her fist to her heart. "I loved my husband, and my family means everything to me." She'd become defensive, but deep down, she wondered if it was because there was some truth in what he'd said. "Whatever choices I make are mine and mine alone. I'm sure in your world I would be considered provincial for my beliefs. In my world, a man like you is considered a libertine."

"I am well aware that you are a lady of strict moral principles."

"Yes, and I am only just now realizing that I willingly followed you into a deserted area."

He lifted his brows. "Do you think I would pounce on you?"

"Of course not, but I imagine there are plenty of

women who would welcome you into their beds." The moment she uttered the words, she winced. "Oh, how do you manage to bring out the worst in me?"

His mouth curved in the slightest of smiles. "The first time I caught you watching me at Lady Atherton's ball, I thought you were issuing an invitation."

"Oh, do not remind me of that night. I do not even know why I stared at you." She'd been completely mesmerized by his uncommonly handsome face.

"When I asked Lady Atherton for your address that night, she told me that you were not for the likes of a rakehell like me," he said. "You are not the sort of woman I was seeking. I wanted a mistress, a temporary lover. Instead, I discovered a widow with strict moral scruples and a son in need of discipline." He paused a moment. "I know you are a lady and that you will not go against your beliefs. But I won't lie. I am more attracted to you than I've ever been to any woman."

"I find that difficult to believe."

"It is illogical but true. You will never allow me the liberties I crave, and so I desire you all the more because you are forbidden—and incredibly beautiful."

"Forgive me, but I suspect you say those words to any woman you find desirable."

"Most of the women I've known expect compliments. You, on the other hand, have trouble accepting them."

"Only because I distrust your sincerity."

"I have nothing to gain." He grinned. "Unless, of course, you change your mind and beg me to make a dishonest woman of you."

She couldn't help laughing. "I imagine you have disarmed many women with your charm."

"But not you?"

She looked at him beneath her lashes. "Perhaps a little."

"Ah, there is hope for me yet."

"Lady Atherton warned me about you at her ball."

"What did she say?"

"'What he wants, he gets. Be sure it's not you.'"

He laughed. "I have a proposition for you."

Her smile faded.

"Perhaps we could be friends," he said.

She hesitated. It would be rude to refuse him, but she worried where a friendship might lead.

"I don't have an ulterior motive."

She knit her brows. "Very well, as long as it is only friendship."

"For a moment, I thought you would refuse," he said.

"I didn't care for some of the things you said today, but I don't dislike you."

He clutched his hands to his chest. "Faint praise, indeed."

"If I had my fan handy, I would swat you."

"Laura—"

She lifted her chin. "Lady Chesfield."

"If we're to be friends, can we dispense with Lady this, Lord that, when it's just the two of us? It's rather tiresome."

"You are too bold," she said.

He leaned over her, pinning his hands against the bench on either side of her. "You tempt me," he said, "but I will restrain myself . . . if or until you are willing."

"I ought to reprimand you, but I see the mischief in your eyes."

He stood and helped her to rise. "We had better return before someone spreads the rumor that I've had my wicked way with you."

She took his arm. "I hate to disappoint you, but there's no chance of that misapprehension."

"Why is that?" he said, leading her back down the path.

"There's nary a wrinkle in my skirts."

He laughed as they emerged onto the main path.

Male voices drew her attention. She looked to her right and saw Justin stop on the path. Her son's face and ears turned crimson. The two boys with him darted amused glances at him and walked off, leaving him behind.

Laura's stomach roiled. "I have to go to my son."

"Do you need assistance?" Bellingham asked.

"No, I will take care of this." She started off toward Justin, but he turned his back and strode off.

"Justin, wait," she called.

He halted and faced her. His jaw tightened as she approached.

"What is wrong?" she asked.

He scowled. "Are you oblivious?"

"Lower your voice, please," she said in as neutral a tone as she could manage.

Justin's nostrils flared. "What were you doing walking down a secluded path with that rake?"

A couple on the other side of the path glanced at them as they walked past. "We had better leave," she said.

He started striding off. She hurried to catch up with him. "Every passerby is witnessing your anger."

"Yes, and my friends saw you hanging on to that rake-hell."

"You will not address me in an insulting manner. I was only walking with him."

"In the bushes," he gritted out.

"I will not put up with your insolence."

"I don't care."

"We will discuss this when we are in the carriage," she said.

Justin said nothing else, but the rigid set of his jaw spoke volumes.

Once they entered Mrs. Norcliffe's house, the butler showed them to the anteroom to wait until the carriage arrived. She perched upon a sofa, noted the time on the mantel clock, and clasped her hands. Given the number of carriages in the square, she figured they would have to wait a bit.

Justin slouched in a cross-framed armchair and glared at her. "How could you?"

"Hush. I said we will discuss the matter in the carriage and not beforehand," she said in an undertone. His insufferable attitude grated on her nerves, but she would reprimand him when they could speak alone.

Justin kept getting up to look out the window, and then he would start pacing. Laura said nothing, because she didn't trust her son to keep a cool head. But after alternately tapping her toes and fingers for forty minutes, Laura began to wonder if the butler had forgotten them. "I will check on the progress of the carriage," she said.

Laura walked into the foyer and approached the butler. "I've been waiting for some time now. Is there any word on the carriage?"

The butler winced. "My lady, I apologize. I summoned

it but forgot to check again. Allow me to send a footman to inquire for you." He motioned to a footman, and Laura described the carriage to him.

After the footman left, the butler cleared his throat. "My lady, you may return to the anteroom. I will summon you when there is word."

She sighed. "Please inform me the moment the footman returns."

"Yes, my lady. I'm very sorry for the delay," he said.

A dull ache started in her temples. She did her best to conceal her frustration and returned to the anteroom.

Justin turned away from the window. "Is the carriage ready?"

She shook her head. "The butler summoned the carriage, but when it didn't arrive, he apparently forgot to check again."

"We've been waiting almost an hour," Justin said.

"The butler sent a footman after the carriage. It shouldn't be long now."

When another twenty minutes passed, Laura gritted her teeth and returned to the foyer where she found the footman speaking to the butler. "Is the carriage ready?" she asked.

"My lady, your driver apparently left the premises," the butler said. "Evidently there was a miscommunication of some sort."

She rubbed her temple. "Will you please summon a hackney?"

Footsteps clipped on the marble floor behind her. She looked over her shoulder and saw Bellingham.

"I couldn't help overhearing. Since I'm leaving, I will take you in my carriage," he said.

"I do not want to put you to any trouble."

"How long have you been waiting?"

"More than an hour," she said.

Bellingham narrowed his eyes at the butler and then returned his attention to her. "You've waited far too long as it is. I insist."

"Thank you. Let me inform Justin."

When she returned to the anteroom, Justin frowned. "Surely the carriage is ready by now."

"The driver apparently left. Lord Bellingham offered to take us in his carriage. Come along."

"No," he said. "You will have nothing to do with him."

"Justin, we have been waiting for an age. Please do not argue with me."

"Don't you understand? He wants to seduce you."

A deep male voice sounded behind her. "I have no intention of accosting your mother, but if riding in my carriage offends you, feel free to walk home."

Laura dug her nails into her palms. Why had he goaded her son?

"I'm not leaving her alone with you," Justin said.

Bellingham shrugged. "Suit yourself." Then he offered his arm to her. Laura took it and imagined Justin seething behind them, which was completely ridiculous.

Bellingham halted in the foyer and addressed the butler. "Please make sure that Lady Chesfield's driver is informed that she found another ride home the minute he arrives."

"Yes, my lord." The butler bowed and rushed to open the door.

No one said a word as they walked out and entered the carriage. Bellingham sat across from them with his back to the horses. The carriage rolled off, and Justin turned his attention to the window.

Bellingham removed his hat and raked his hand through his hair. "The butler shouldn't have left you waiting so long."

"I should have checked sooner," she said. "There were many guests."

Bell's jaw tightened visibly. "The butler was derelict in his duty."

"I hope you didn't leave early on our account," she said.

He shook his head. "No, I put in an appearance for Harry's sake. I never intended to stay long."

"You're missing your friends," she said.

"I'll likely see them at the club tonight and at Angelo's fencing academy on Thursday morning."

Justin swerved his gaze to Bellingham.

"Do you fence?" Bellingham asked.

"No," Justin said.

"Since you're in London, you might give it a go," he said.

Justin shrugged.

Everyone was silent until the carriage slowed and rocked to a halt. Bellingham got out and assisted Laura.

After Justin emerged, Bellingham turned to him. "If you're interested in fencing, I could give you pointers."

Justin stared at him. "Why would you do that?"

"You looked interested when I mentioned fencing. It's your choice."

Justin hesitated. "All right."

"Thursday, ten sharp," Bellingham said. "I'll take you in my carriage."

Laura smoothed her skirt to hide her surprise at both of them. Had Bellingham made the offer because he felt obliged, as he'd said earlier? She wasn't certain his involvement was wise. He certainly didn't strike her as one to make commitments, and Justin had made no secret of his low opinion of Bellingham. Then why had he agreed to the fencing lesson?

She would never understand men. "Thank you for taking us home, Lord Bellingham."

He bowed.

Laura expected Justin to stride up the pavement, but he offered her his arm. She blinked, because he'd never done it before. At first she thought it was sweet of him, until her son sent a triumphant look at Bellingham. Laura winced as her son led her to the door. The last thing she needed was for her son to become overprotective and overbearing.

Chapter Five

The next day

Bellingham paced about Laura's anteroom. He hoped Justin would not prove obstinate about rising from his bed before noon. If he chose to waste the day, there was nothing he could do. He'd made the offer because of the implied promise that he would provide some guidance to the young man. However, he would not spend his every free hour trying to discipline a recalcitrant adolescent. It was just as well, because Laura did not appreciate when he took over.

He halted at the sound of a feminine voice in the foyer. Laura's voice. Whenever she spoke, her words held a soft, breathy quality. The devil. Next thing he knew he'd be writing odes to her soft, breathy voice.

She walked into the anteroom. "Justin will be down directly."

He clasped his hands behind his back. "Good."

She'd draped an enormous blue shawl over her white gown. An elaborate braid was wrapped round her head, leading him to suspect her hair was very long. Granted, he could never really tell until the pins and the hair came down.

He told himself not to think about unraveling the braid, but his fertile imagination conjured a picture of her standing naked with her blond hair flowing over her breasts. He really must stop devising naked scenarios of her. That would only make things harder, figuratively and literally.

"I think Justin is eager for his fencing lesson," she said. "He would never say so, but he rose early for breakfast. A few minutes ago, he ran back upstairs to collect the gloves he forgot."

The clip of boot heels on the marble floor alerted both of them. Justin entered the anteroom with a wary expression.

"Ah, you're ready," Bell said. "Shall we be on our way?"

Justin nodded and followed him outside. After they'd climbed into the carriage, Bell knocked on the ceiling with his cane. The carriage rocked into motion. Bell regarded the young man who sat across from him, but Justin kept his gaze turned to the window. The silence was awkward, but he figured Justin had no idea what to say.

Bell would have to initiate the conversation. "We'll start with the basics today, but once you learn the correct grip and strengthen your muscles, you can face a well-trained opponent."

Justin regarded him with a cynical expression. "Meaning you?"

"Yes. If you practice, your skills will improve over time."

"How long have you been fencing?" Justin asked.

"Since I was nineteen." He thought a moment and decided to stretch the truth a bit to encourage Justin. "I wanted to begin when I was your age, but my father said I was too scrawny."

"You?"

"Yes, I was tall, but I looked like a twig with big feet."

Justin looked amused and huffed.

"Fencing helped build my muscles," Bell said. "Mind you, it didn't happen overnight."

Justin said nothing, but at least he was polite today.

They remained silent until the carriage rolled to a halt at Angelo's. They climbed out and walked inside the academy. The place smelled of sweat, and the clang of blades rang out. Foils hung crossed inside the arched wall niches.

"I'll introduce you to Angelo," Bell said. "Let's consult him about a weapon for you."

After Bell made the introduction, the chevalier regarded him with an inscrutable expression. Then he bowed and bade them to follow him to choose a foil. Bell eyed the blades and made a few suggestions. Angelo concurred that the pistol grip foil was a good choice for a beginner.

"I will leave you to your demonstration for now," Angelo said.

Justin's eyes registered wariness again. Bell wondered if the boy's defensiveness stemmed from a lack of confidence and resolved to make the experience as positive as possible.

After removing their coats, Bell demonstrated the grip with his own foil. "The mistake beginners make is holding the blade too tightly," he said. "In order to attack or parry, your wrist has to be flexible. Grip the weapon as if it is a fragile figurine."

Justin loosened his grip and immediately tightened it.

"It takes practice," Bell said. "Use two or three fingers with your grip."

Justin experimented with three fingers. Eventually, his grip relaxed. Bell noted he had too much bend at the wrist and corrected it. Then he showed Justin how to slightly bend his elbow for the en garde. "Hold the blade aligned with your forearm," Bell said.

Justin's brows furrowed as he tried again.

"It's a bit tedious in the beginning," Bell said, "but mastering the grip is necessary."

"Right." He blew out his breath, a sign of his frustration.

"We'll work on the grip the next time. Let's work on your foot position," Bell said. "The idea is to point your toe in the direction of your challenger. The knee should be vertically aligned with your toe."

When Justin assumed the position, Bell nodded. "You got it right away."

"Feels strange," Justin said.

"Nevertheless, you caught on quickly. Most beginners struggle."

Justin shrugged. "I got one thing right."

Justin's surliness could possibly be a cover for a lack of confidence. If so, he might find a greater measure of his own worth by successfully learning to fence. "The techniques will become second nature to you if you practice on a regular basis," Bell said.

"All I've done is stand around posing," Justin said. "I haven't even broken a sweat."

"I understand," Bell said. "If you wish to fence, you must be patient, but if you're willing to work at it, you will find it rewarding."

Justin shrugged again as if he didn't care.

"Next time we'll add lunges to the practice session," Bell said.

Someone clapped him on the back. Bell turned to find Colin and introduced him to Justin. "Where is Harry?"

"His manservant said he was still abed."

"It's almost eleven o'clock," Bell said.

Colin cleared his throat. "He's having *bachelor fare* for breakfast."

Bell nodded at the euphemism for a woman of the demirep.

Justin snorted. "You mean he's bedding a trollop."

"Apparently there is no need to protect his tender ears." Bell narrowed his eyes. "I'm sure you've heard worse."

"Seen worse, too," Justin said.

Bell narrowed his eyes. "We'll talk soon."

Justin pulled a face.

"We'll talk," Bell reiterated.

Colin grinned at Bell. "Shall we end today's session with an impromptu bout?"

"He just wants to show off," Bell said to Justin.

"What? Are you afraid I'll beat you?" Colin said.

Bell selected a blade. "Prepare to lose."

A crowd gathered round as Bell and Colin saluted one another. Then Bell advanced. Colin parried, and Bell counterparried. Their blades clanged when they engaged. Bell and Colin disengaged momentarily only to advance again. Bell feinted and heard his friend hiss, and when he executed a running attack, Colin bared his teeth as he parried. Sweat ran in rivulets down Bell's face, but his heart raced as the blades clanged, and once more, he ran forward to attack.

Colin parried, but Bell's instinct to fight overruled him, and he attacked again. When the bout ended, Colin saluted him. The crowd applauded.

Colin slapped Bell on the shoulder. "I'll beat you one of these days."

"You can try," Bell said with a cocky grin. He toweled off the perspiration and looked round for Justin. Where the devil had he gone? Bell slung his coat over his shoulder and strode off in search of the young man. Several acquaintances stopped to congratulate him. The whole time, Bell felt uneasy about Laura's son. Blast it all. The last thing he needed was for Justin to find trouble on his watch. When another acquaintance approached, Bell cleared his throat. "Excuse me. I've got to take care of a matter."

Male voices reverberated in the building. Bell's jaw tightened as he searched. Then he spotted Justin walking toward the door with two other boys. He recognized the brawny one he'd seen driving the curricle and wondered if Justin had planned to leave with them.

The brawny boy said something to Justin as he opened the door. Justin looked over his shoulder and halted. Bell arched his brows.

The other two boys quit the place.

Bell said nothing as they stepped outside to wait for his carriage. Justin waved as his friend steered his curricle wildly into traffic, nearly colliding with a man driving a cart.

"Your friend is reckless," Bell said.

Justin shrugged one shoulder.

When Bell's carriage turned the corner, he raised his arm to hail it. After it arrived, Bell gave the driver Laura's address and climbed in after Justin. The boy turned his face to the window. He obviously didn't want to discuss what had happened back there.

Bell waited until the carriage rolled into motion before speaking. "Were you planning to leave with your friends?"

"I was only talking to them," Justin said.

"The one with the curricle, what is his name?"

"George."

Bell narrowed his eyes. "Where was he going?"

"What difference does it make?" Justin said.

"You didn't answer my question."

"A cockfight."

Bell frowned. "The devil. It's disgusting. Surely you didn't want to see it."

"I didn't go," Justin said.

But he would have if Bell had not been there. "I wager he taunted you because you didn't."

Something flickered in Justin's eyes. "You don't know anything."

"I know that if you continue carousing, there will be hell to pay."

"Why do you care?"

He set his hat aside. "This isn't about me. It's about your mother. If something bad happens to you, she will be devastated."

"Stay away from my mother," he said in a threatening tone.

"I'm not the one wounding her."

Justin's nostrils flared. "I know all about you."

"I doubt it," Bell said.

"You're a rake. If you hurt her, you'll answer to me," Justin said.

"While I'm glad you're protective of your mother, you're giving her insufficient credit. She's perfectly capable of making sound judgments."

Justin scowled. "I know your reputation with women."

"Your mother is a lady, and I treat her as one."

"Right," he spat out. "By taking her down a secluded path."

Bell recalled Justin's reaction at the Venetian breakfast. He'd come to the wrong conclusion. He sighed. "You were embarrassed because your friends were there."

Justin returned his attention to the window. He obviously didn't want to talk about it, and Bell decided to let the matter rest.

Neither of them said anything. Bell looked out the window at the bustling, diverse crowd. He'd spent part of every year in London as far back as he could remember. To him, the scenery was so familiar he rarely paid attention unless a cart overturned, impeding traffic. However, this was Justin's first trip to the city. Bell tried to imagine it from the boy's perspective. Compared to a sleepy village, the city must seem chaotic and foreign. The streets were crowded with all manner of pedestrians, wagons, and vehicles. Costermongers hawked their fruits and vegetables in unintelligible lower-class accents. At a corner, a crossing sweeper cleared the refuse and horse droppings for a pair of ladies and nearly got trampled by a man on horseback.

At long last the carriage turned into the square and

rolled to a halt at Laura's town house. Justin moved over on the seat, but Bell held up his hand to stop him. "There is something I wish to say."

Justin released a loud sigh.

"You're not the first young buck to sow wild oats, but if you're not careful, you're likely to get in over your head."

"You're not my guardian."

"No, I'm not, but your mother worries."

"I worry, too—about you."

"What?" Bell said.

"You can't fool me," Justin said. "The fencing lessons were a way to get in my mother's good graces, weren't they?"

"The purpose was to engage you in a healthy activity, rather than drinking yourself sick every night."

"I don't believe you."

"I think you're trying to divert the topic, because we both know you meant to go to that cockfight," Bell said.

"Are you finished?" Justin said.

"Whether you wish to continue the fencing practice is your decision, but know this. I'm not your enemy." Bell opened the carriage door and climbed out.

When Justin emerged, Bell meant to escort him inside, but Justin shook his head. "You're not invited."

"I mean to speak to your mother," he said.

"No," Justin said. "A man like you has only one thing in mind, and I won't let you touch her."

As Justin strode off to the door, Bell muttered, "You're a bit late for that."

Frustrated, he waited until Justin entered the town house. Then he got back in the carriage and knocked his cane on the roof. He'd meant to give Laura a report of the fencing lessons, but he had also wanted to see her. A voice deep inside asked, *To what end?*

She'd made it clear there could never be anything intimate between them.

There were plenty of widows and courtesans he could have with the mere snap of his fingers. Hell, they flirted and dropped blatant hints. He'd taken what they so easily offered more times than he could count and walked away without a backward glance.

He'd asked her if they could be friends. What the devil had he been thinking?

The next evening, White's

Harry patted his stomach. "Excellent dinner."

Bell finished his cheesecake and coffee. "Gentlemen, shall we repair to my town house for a game of billiards?"

"Sounds like an excellent idea to me," Harry said.

"I wager a pony I'll win the first game," Colin said.

"Twenty-five pounds?" Harry said in an outraged voice.

"If you lose, Colin will loan you the money," Bell said.

"What?" Colin said. "You're the one with plump pockets."

Bell pushed back his chair and started to rise, but a waiter hurried to the table, carrying a silver salver.

"My lord, your footman delivered a message," he said.

Frowning, Bell opened it. He caught his breath. Laura had asked him to call about a matter concerning her son. "What the devil has he done now?" Bell muttered.

"Is there a problem?" Colin asked.

"Yes, Laura's stepson is causing trouble again."

"You mean Lady Chesfield?" Harry asked.

Bell looked up and saw his friends grinning at him. "What?"

"You called her by her Christian name," Colin said.

He ignored their smirks. "I've got to go."

Bell donned his hat and gloves, and then he strode out to his waiting carriage. He gave the address to the driver and climbed inside. After the horses started, he realized he was jiggling his leg, an old leftover habit from boyhood when he was anxious about something. Most of the time, he managed to squelch nervous tendencies through the use of logic, but there wasn't much logic behind that young man's rebellion.

The streets were crowded with carriages, carts, and pedestrians. He mastered his impatience by taking deep, even breaths. Bell told himself that Laura had probably found another flask. It would alarm her, but it wouldn't hurt her son, except for the morning-after bottle ache, which Justin richly deserved. Bell rather thought clanging pots would be the thing to awaken Laura's son after a long night of getting foxed.

At long last, the carriage rocked to a halt. Bell didn't wait for the driver. He opened the door and jumped down. Then he strode up the pavement and rang the bell. The door opened immediately and Reed bade him to come inside.

Bell divested himself of his gloves and hat. "Where is she?"

"Upstairs, my lord, in the young master's bedchamber. I will lead you there."

He followed Reed into the great hall, and Laura appeared on the landing. "I'll see myself up, Reed." Then Bell ran up the curving staircase. "What is it?" he said.

"I found something. Follow me," she said.

Her furrowed brows attested to her concern as they ascended the next staircase. He walked beside her down the corridor. She halted before a door and took a deep breath. "I must prepare you."

"Inside," he said under his breath. "You don't want to risk a servant overhearing."

She nodded and turned the knob.

He followed her inside and shut the door. "Where is your son?"

"He attended a card party at his friend Paul's house. I made him take our carriage, and he promised to come home by midnight. I told him that he would be forbidden to leave the house for a week if he was even one minute late."

"What did you find?"

Her face flushed. "It is…disgusting."

Bell frowned. "Can you be more specific?"

She shook her head slowly.

"Perhaps you should show it to me," he said.

Her throat worked. "It is under the mattress."

The moment she said *mattress*, Bell figured out what she'd found.

"The maid turned the mattress and ran out," she said. "It is awful."

Bell squatted beside the mattress. "Don't look."

He lifted his chin and saw her standing at the foot of the bed with her hand covering her eyes. His shoulders shook with suppressed laughter. Then he lifted the mattress and pulled out a dozen engravings.

"Naked women," he said.

"Those are not the worst," she said, peeking between her fingers. "Oh, they are disgusting."

He sifted through them. "I see what you mean. Do you suppose these lovers actually posed?"

"Do not tease me," she said. "What am I to do? My son is depraved."

Bell pushed the engravings back under the mattress. "Your son is a healthy young man with typical male urges."

"Those engravings are filthy," she said. "I will cover my eyes while you feed them into the fire."

He snorted.

"How dare you laugh?" she said.

He rose, walked over to her, and took her by the shoulders. "I won't burn them, because then he'll know you found them, and that will humiliate him."

"But they are dirty."

"Look at me," he said.

When she met his gaze, there were crimson flags on her cheeks.

"He has needs," Bell said. "Believe me, there are far worse things."

"I mean to burn that filth," she said.

"Hush," he said. Something tender unfurled in his chest. "Let's go to the drawing room."

He offered his arm and led her out into the corridor. Then he escorted her down the stairs to the drawing room. She'd been married, but he already knew her sexual experiences were limited.

After they entered the drawing room, he sat beside her on the sofa. "You know that I'm pragmatic. I don't want there to be any misunderstandings, so I will speak frankly. It's in your son's best interest. Will you allow it?"

She nodded. "You must think me foolish."

"No, I think you were shocked, but nothing bad will happen to your son if he looks at those naughty engravings."

"I will not allow that disgusting filth in my house," she said. "You cannot mean for me to sanction this."

He sighed. "Like it or not, he is experiencing urges that are difficult to ignore. It's perfectly natural. I know those plates bother you, but he is far better off looking at them than risking disease in a bawdy house."

She gasped. "He would never do such a thing."

"Did you ever think he would stay out late at night drinking spirits?"

"No," she said, lacing her fingers in that prim way of hers.

"The important thing is that Justin has a safe way of relieving his urges. There is nothing wrong with it. Women pleasure themselves as well."

"I've heard enough," she said, averting her face.

He remembered how hot his face had gotten the day his father had set him down for a man-to-man talk. But his father's frank discussion had kept him from making stupid mistakes. Unfortunately, Justin had no male figure in his life to guide him. He didn't relish the thought of having to do it, because of Justin's hostility toward him, but there was no one else. "Laura, do you wish me to talk to your son? There are things he needs to know."

She wouldn't meet his eyes. "What do you plan to tell him?"

"About diseases and pregnancy."

"I think you will put ideas in his head."

"Those ideas are already there. The bawdy plates are proof."

"I don't know," she said, her voice miserable. "He is not receptive to you."

"I know, but I think it's important that I try."

She rubbed her temple. "I think you had better not say anything. He's likely to become suspicious that I found the engravings."

"Listen to me," he said. "My friend's brother got into a situation when he wasn't much older than Justin. He sired a son that he was forbidden to see. To this day, he must refer to his own son as his cousin to prevent the label of bastard. You don't want your son to suffer the consequences of an accidental pregnancy—or far worse, disease. If you let me, I will tell him to wait before lying with a woman, but I'm also going to tell him how to prevent pregnancy and disease in the event he doesn't wait. Given his recent history, I think it is a good idea."

"Very well," she said.

"There is something else."

Her eyes filled with dread. "What?"

"It's nothing bad," he said. "I've given a great deal of thought to Justin and his friends. When I was their age, my friends and I went through a rebellious period. We got our thrills by courting danger in low places. Mind you, I had a strict father who put an end to my carousing. The point is that Justin and his friends need to learn they can have fun without getting themselves in troublesome situations, and there are plenty of places where fiends would take advantage of them. I'd like to invite Justin and his friends to play billiards at my town house."

"That is very kind of you, but you already offered him fencing lessons. I'm sure you would prefer spending time with your friends," Laura said.

"Harry and Colin can show them how to play. They will delight in ribbing the boys. If you're amenable, I'll call for Justin at nine o'clock on Saturday."

"I will put the matter before Justin and let you know if he is interested."

Bell hesitated and decided to be honest. "Your son believes the reason I offered the fencing lessons was to get in your good graces."

She sighed. "I know. He thinks you mean to seduce me. It is disconcerting to have my own son warning me of the dangers of big, bad rakes."

His shoulders shook with laughter. "It is ironic, but to his credit, he does wish to protect you."

"I suppose I should find his concern endearing, but to be honest, I'm exasperated. Good heavens, I'm his mother, and it is as if he is trying to parent me."

Bell rested his arm over the top of the sofa. "Placate him. He'll soon tire of it, and when he sees that I mean you no harm, he will relent."

"I'm becoming too dependent upon you."

"Why would you object to my help? After all, we're friends."

"It seems so strange and different."

"Did you not consider your husband your friend?"

"Yes, but it was different because he was my husband. I've only known you for a short time."

He winked. "Well, we are unofficially affianced."

"Oh, please don't remind me of that business," she said.

He laughed. "In all seriousness, men and women can be friends."

"To a certain degree," she said.

"What do you mean?" he asked.

"My sister Rachel is my best friend." She looked at him. "There are things I tell my sister that I could never discuss with you."

"Give me an example," he said.

"Women speak of private things among themselves," she said. "There are things I am uncomfortable discussing with you. I imagine the same is true of men."

He regarded her with a lopsided smile. "I could tell you, but I fear you would take a permanent disgust of me."

"Probably," she said.

"That doesn't mean we cannot be friends," he said, "even if there are subjects we do not feel comfortable discussing with each other."

She moistened her lips. "Were you friends with your paramours?"

He sighed. "The answer is a bit complicated."

Her eyes widened. "Well?"

"The relationships were not of a long standing," he said.

"You only wanted them for . . ."

"I believe the polite expression is I bedded them."

She wrinkled her nose.

"I'm nearly thirty years old and a bachelor," he said. "I took mistresses." The mantel clock chimed. "It is late," he said. "I'd better leave before your son arrives and decides to avenge your honor."

She managed a smile as they both rose, and then she noticed something. "Oh, your sapphire pin is coming loose." Without a thought, she removed it from the starched folds of his cravat and secured it. The whole time, she felt him looking at her from beneath his dark lashes. She'd not even stopped to think that her actions were those of a wife. Oh, this was embarrassing. "I ought to have asked your permission."

"I don't mind," he said, looking down at the pin, and then he captured her gaze. They stood so close she could hear the sound of his breathing. Though he'd obviously shaved, she could see the dark growth. He had a heavy beard.

A subtle masculine scent, a mix of soap and something unique to him, invaded her senses. The very air seemed to crackle between them. His eyes darkened with a languorous expression, and she felt the pull of temptation. Every inch of her skin tingled.

"Laura," he said in a rough undertone.

How could one word be so replete with longing? Despite all of her beliefs, she wanted to kiss him one more time, but she dared not cross that line again. She mustn't risk her reputation, because it would hurt everyone she held dear. She took a step back and masked her yearning with a smile. "There now, you're all set."

He tugged on his sleeves and bowed. "Until Saturday."

When the door clicked shut, she sank onto the sofa. She'd not thought about the other women in his life—the mistresses—until tonight. She'd seen him with that scantily clad woman at Lady Atherton's ball. For all she knew, the woman was his current mistress. She told herself that it was none of her affair, but she could not deny that it bothered her.

How could she remain his friend when she knew that seeing him with another woman would make her horribly jealous? And it would happen, because he was a man with needs and would seek a woman who would give him what he wanted.

She had no right to be jealous. There could never be anything more than friendship between them, and he would likely tire of her and Justin long before the season ended.

The next day

"Lady Atherton, I am so glad you called," Laura said. "I hope you have been well. Let me ring for a tea tray."

"Oh, yes, that would be lovely."

After returning to the sofa, Laura said, "What news do you have?"

"Well, one of the reasons I called is to invite you to participate in the Society Devoted to the Care and Feeding of Orphans. Is this something that would interest you?"

"Indeed, it would," Laura said. "I need some occupation that is not frivolous. I would be more than happy to host the meetings at my town house."

"Well, there's nothing wrong with frivolous entertainment. That is what the season is all about, but it is very generous of you to offer to host the meetings. I will definitely pass that information along. Now, tell me how your son fares."

"Some days are better than others. He has taken up fencing. Lord Bellingham offered to instruct him in order to give him some athletic occupation."

Lady Atherton touched her throat. "Bellingham has certainly taken an active interest in your son."

"He feels an obligation, though he should not."

"What do you mean, my dear?"

"I told Montclief that Bellingham would provide male guidance to my son. I never expected him to take the role seriously. I released him from any obligation, but he claims it is a matter of honor."

"Well, I'm not surprised," Lady Atherton said. "His father instilled good principles in him."

Laura frowned. "While I agree he has helped, he is a rake."

Lady Atherton waved her hand. "Well, of course, he's had mistresses, but they all do until they settle down."

"But he has no intention of marrying," she said.

"I know, and it troubles me," Lady Atherton said. "It is such a shame about his family."

"Did you know them?" she asked.

"Oh, yes. His mother and father were madly in love and very proud of their two boys."

Laura swallowed. "He had a brother?"

"Steven was two years younger. Andrew always looked after him."

"Andrew?"

"Oh, I forgot myself," she said. "That is his Christian name, and that's what everyone called him when he was a mere boy. Lord and Lady Bellingham held a house party every summer. My husband and I always attended. The guests brought their children for the annual play."

"A play?" Laura said.

"Yes, it's customary for adults, but Lady Bellingham preferred to let the children put on a play. All of the ladies helped make costumes, and the older children wrote the plays. By the time Andrew was twelve, he proved himself a natural-born leader. He took over all of the plans and delegated tasks to the other children."

Laura laughed. "I'm not surprised he took over."

A faraway look came into Lady Atherton's eyes. "He had an excellent father. It was such a tragedy when his family died." She reached over and patted Laura's hand. "But I think his involvement with your son is a very good sign."

The tea tray arrived. Laura poured and handed a cup to Lady Atherton.

"There is nothing like a spot of tea," Lady Atherton said. "By the way, I heard from friends that you were spotted walking with Bellingham at Mrs. Norcliffe's Venetian breakfast."

"Yes, he took me to see the goldfish."

Lady Atherton smiled and sipped her tea. "He is a very handsome man, like his father before him. I believe you made more than a few ladies jealous."

Laura finished her tea and set it aside on the tray. "His looks are striking, but we are friends, nothing more."

"Friends," Lady Atherton said. "So you're not the least bit attracted to him?"

"He is charming, usually when he wants something, but neither of us wishes to marry, and I simply will not throw my principles to the wind for a fleeting *affaire de coeur*."

Lady Atherton set her dish aside. "What do you mean you've no wish to remarry?"

Laura bit her lip.

"What is it?" Lady Atherton said with concern in her voice.

"There is the problem of Montclief. If I were to remarry, he might take Justin."

"Montclief has too many mouths to feed as it is," Lady

Atherton said. "And I suspect that this isn't the real reason. I know you're the sensible type, but if you're worried that it's somehow wrong because of Phillip, you must know that he would want you to be happy."

She shook her head. "I know he would, but there is another issue."

"My dear, what is it?"

"I...I fear I'm barren."

"My dear, your husband was ill."

She blinked back tears. "No. Unlike my sisters, my monthly cycle has always been irregular. Phillip and I wanted a child together. After four months of marriage, I was almost certain that I had conceived. I swore my sister Rachel to secrecy and planned to tell Phillip by the end of the week. Three days later, all my hopes were shattered."

"My dear, your husband was elderly."

"He was capable." She took a deep breath. "How can I remarry knowing that I might never be able to give my intended a child?"

"In this instance, I recommend you take a leap of faith."

"You do not understand. How can I allow a man to court me, knowing that I might never be able to give him a child? At what point would I tell him something so intimate? And yet, if I kept it from him, it would be deceit."

"The same could hold true of any woman before marriage," Lady Atherton said.

"But I suspect that I am barren," Laura said. "That's different."

Lady Atherton took her hands. "You may not be. Promise me that if the right man comes along, you will not throw away a second chance at love. Promise me."

"I promise to consider your advice," Laura said.

"I've lived a lot of years," Lady Atherton said. "And my biggest regrets were always about the chances I did not take because I was afraid. Don't make that mistake."

After departing Laura's town house, Virginia tapped her fan on the leather seat. Laura's fears were understandable. Given her unreliable cycle, pregnancy might not happen right away, but Virginia was by no means convinced it was impossible. As much as she admired Laura's principles, she believed the young woman was too hasty in taking the blame for not conceiving with her husband. Phillip had been a wonderful man, but he'd known his health wasn't the best when he proposed to Laura. Of course, it had been a brilliant match for her, considering her lack of a marriage portion. But to throw away a second chance at love was damned foolish.

Virginia had not given up her matchmaking plan, but based on what Laura had told her, the pair had spent quite a bit of time together on account of that rascal Justin. Today she had purposely told Laura about Bellingham's parents and the annual children's plays. She'd set the stage with just a touch of drama so that Laura would know that deep down, Bellingham was a good man. He just needed a good woman to help him overcome his fears. Who better than a caring woman like Laura?

Soon she must devise a plan that would put them in an intimate situation. Too bad she couldn't lock them in a boudoir together. She snorted at her preposterous plan. An opportunity would arise. Perhaps a carriage ride to an entertainment, and naturally, she would find some excuse to send them on alone. Oh, she remembered a particularly passionate carriage ride with her Alfred. Yes, that would do the trick. Virginia walked to the sideboard and poured herself a thimble of sherry. Then she raised the glass. "To carriages."

Chapter Six

Saturday evening

"Justin, you will return home in the earl's carriage tonight," Laura said.

He rolled his eyes. "That's ridiculous. George will take me in his curricle."

"No, Bellingham will bring you home. Either you agree or you stay home."

Justin slouched in a chair and rolled his eyes. "Will you stop treating me like an infant?"

"You will go nowhere unless you agree," she said.

"I agree." Then he mumbled something under his breath.

"Lord Bellingham does you a great honor by inviting you to his home."

"You're always defending him, and I know you're not unaware of his reputation."

She bit back the retort on her tongue. Justin had certainly shown his worst side to the earl recently. She would say nothing of it, because she didn't want Bellingham to find them quarreling.

Laura retrieved her sewing. She was embroidering a tiny gown for her third sister, Mary, who was expecting her first child this summer. Laura sighed. She'd experienced more than a little envy upon hearing Mary's wonderful news. It wasn't the first time. Her sister Rachel had two children already, and Deborah had a little girl. Judith, the youngest, was unmarried. Over the years, she'd told herself that she was fortunate to have Justin, but there were times when she found it difficult to accept that she would never know the joy of feeling a child quicken in her womb.

Sometimes she worried about being alone after Justin reached his majority, but she could not worry about what might be. She had a wonderful, caring family, but she missed those days when Phillip would take her for a walk and stop in the shade to kiss her. Wishing for the past would not bring it back, and she must go on.

The bell rang. Laura rose and hurried over to the mirror to pinch her cheeks. She smoothed her skirts, turned, and saw the accusing look on her son's face. "What is wrong?"

"Are you pinching your cheeks for the earl?" Justin said.

She would never admit it. "Of course not. My complexion has been sallow the last few days and I merely wished to bring color to my cheeks."

Justin muttered something under his breath again that she couldn't hear, which was probably just as well.

Footsteps thudded outside the drawing room doors.

"Mark my words," Justin said. "I heard he's had dozens of mistresses."

"Hush," she said, perching on the sofa.

Justin shook his head slowly.

A knock sounded. Reed entered and said, "The Earl of Bellingham."

Laura rose along with her son, and for some odd reason, she felt a bit nervous, though she could not say why. Bellingham strode inside, and for a moment, her breath caught in her throat. It was impossible not to be mesmerized, nay beguiled, by his brilliant blue eyes.

"My lady," he said in that distinctive voice that had haunted her since the day he'd first invaded her drawing room, much like one of his marauding ancestors. He bowed, and when he rose, his mouth slanted sideways as he looked at her from beneath his lashes.

Was that her heart twirling round like a dizzy girl at her first dance? Then her cheeks grew hot as she recollected her manners and dipped a curtsy.

Bellingham turned toward Justin, and Laura dared not look at her son, for he would surely note her foolish reaction to the earl.

"Justin? Or do you prefer Chesfield?" Bellingham asked.

"Chesfield," he said.

Laura fingered her gold cross and bit her lip. She didn't want others to address him as Chesfield, even though he was seventeen. Among the lower orders, he would be considered a grown man. She knew she must begin to let him go in these small increments, but each little snip of the apron strings felt like a sting to her heart.

With a deep breath, she faced Bellingham again. "I hope you both have an enjoyable evening," she said.

Bellingham drew closer. "Actually, I wish to invite you as well."

"I would be the only lady," she said.

His smile slanted to one side once more. "I've never met a rule I didn't want to break."

She laughed. "Are you certain?"

"My friends wish to see you again," he said. "Do you have other plans?"

She moistened her lips. "No, but you should not feel obliged."

"I would be honored if you would join us," he said.

"Very well," she said.

"Do you have a wrap? It's chilly out," he said.

When she lifted her long paisley shawl, he took it from her and draped it over her shoulders. She instinctively lowered her lashes, but when she raised her eyes, she saw the disapproval on Justin's face. Her son had seen her reaction. She almost changed her mind about going, but Bellingham offered his arm, and it was too late. The entire time he led her down the stairs and across the great hall, she wished she'd used better judgment. Wouldn't her son and Bellingham's friends be uncomfortable with her presence? But what was done was done, and she would make the best of things.

She donned a bonnet and gloves while her son collected his own outerwear. Then the earl led them outside. Bellingham helped her up into the carriage, and Justin sat next to her. "I cannot believe you agreed," he said under his breath.

She didn't have an opportunity to reply as Bellingham climbed inside and sat with his back to the horses.

"Are you warm enough?" Bellingham asked. "There are wool rugs beneath the seat if you need one."

"Thank you, but I'm quite warm with the shawl," she said.

He knocked a cane on the ceiling. When the horses started, he sat back.

"My friends will enjoy showing off for you as they demonstrate the finer points of billiards," Bellingham said.

"I shall be delighted to watch, though I'm certain that ladies are usually not allowed in the inner sanctum of the billiards room. But since you've never met a rule you didn't want to break, I will pretend that it is perfectly proper for me to be present."

At some point during their exchange, Justin had turned his face to the window, even though darkness had set in. He was unhappy with her for accepting the earl's invitation. She could almost feel the waves of his resentment rolling over him, but she was weary of tiptoeing around him. Laura wished for probably the hundredth time that he would grow out of this tiresome stage. Yet, there were other times when she worried that there was more than a need for independence, but if that were the case, she didn't have any idea what could be troubling him. Whenever she tried to ask him, he would pull a face and tell her to stop worrying. She would as soon as he acted like a rational person on a regular basis. With an inward sigh, she figured she might as well wish for rainbows and pots of gold.

When the carriage rolled to a halt, Bell descended and held Laura's hand as she negotiated the tricky steps. All he could think after releasing her was how small her hand had felt in his palm. Her son climbed out, and though it was dark, Bell imagined the young man was displeased. No doubt he was embarrassed that his mother had come along, and truthfully, Bell hadn't planned to invite her. But the moment he'd seen her, he'd wanted to spend more time with her.

The voice inside echoed the words again: *To what end?*

He didn't know—or perhaps he didn't want to examine his reasons too closely—but he did know that there was something about her that he found irresistible. She was like the first creamy bite of a slice of cheesecake to savor and the richness of a very fine brandy sliding over his tongue. And all of that served in a demure, petite presentation.

The devil, he was comparing her to desserts and liquor. He needed a drink and a woman, but not just any woman. He wanted the one he couldn't have.

For now, he would let thoughts of what might be or not dissipate into the ever-present fog swirling round them in the cool night.

He led the way past the two tall lamps. They were filled with animal fat and provided more than sufficient illumination. "My friends are already here," Bell said, looking at her. "They're good fellows, if a bit buffle-headed at times."

She smiled. "I liked them when I first met them."

Bell looked over his shoulder at the glum Justin. "I hope you have a keen eye and steady reflexes."

Justin shrugged one shoulder, his typical reaction.

When they entered the foyer, Bell noted the gleam in Laura's eyes as she regarded the gold-framed mirror, the marble hall table, and the marble floor. They continued on to the great hall. She gasped at the sight of the spiral staircase. "Oh, my, I've never seen one before," she said.

"My great-grandfather installed it years ago," Bell said. "It was the centerpiece of the town house."

"Your family lived here for many years," she said.

"In the previous century, my grandmother entertained a great deal during the season." Bell saw Justin looking up at the staircase. "Go up and explore," he said. "Watch your step. It's steep."

Justin ran up the circular stairs and looked over at one point. "It's fantastic," he said, his voice echoing in the hall.

His friend Paul strode out from the billiards room into the great hall.

"When did you get here?" Justin called out.

"Only a few minutes ago. I took a hackney."

"The staircase goes up two more stories," Bellingham said to Paul. "Go on."

Paul raced up the steps to meet Justin and looked up. "It's brilliant."

Laura glanced at Bell. "I think that is high praise."

"I never thought much of it growing up," Bell admitted. "Probably because I couldn't recall a time when it didn't exist." When he offered his arm again, she took it. "Where is the billiards room?" she asked.

"This way," he said, indicating the direction with his hand. As they neared the room, Bell heard his friends heckling one another. He rapped on the door and pushed it open. "Keep it clean, gentlemen," he said. "A lady is entering."

Harry and Colin turned toward them with cue sticks in

hand. They both looked a bit astounded. Laura was the sort of woman who garnered second and third glances from men. A strange, proprietary feeling gripped him, something he'd never experienced before. He told himself that it was just a foolish, momentary notion, and yet, he couldn't quite shed the feeling.

He glanced at her. "I invited Lady Chesfield."

Harry and Colin bowed.

"You are very welcome," Harry said. "Do you play billiards?"

"Oh, no," she said, "but I will try not to disturb you while I watch."

"You may disturb us anytime," Colin said.

Bell rolled his eyes. He might have known they would flirt with her.

"I say, Bell, she is an incomparable," Colin said.

Laura looked at Bellingham. "Is that good or bad?"

"It's a high compliment to you," Bell said.

"Well, since I am the only lady, and therefore unrivaled, I am in no danger of allowing vanity to overcome my good sense," she said.

Harry clapped his fist to his chest. "I think I just fell in love."

"With my good sense?" Laura quipped.

Harry eyed Bell. "Pretty and clever. I'm jealous, you know."

Bell led Laura to a chair and sat beside her.

"Where are Paul and Justin?" Harry asked.

"They're exploring the spiral staircase," Bell said. "They'll tire of it eventually and remember that they're here to play billiards. Carry on with your game."

While his friends resumed their game, Bell leaned toward her. "I meant to tell you that Justin did well at his fencing lesson last Thursday. He showed patience, even though the positions are tedious to learn."

The effect of her full smile was hard to resist. "Thank you for telling me. I hope he will continue. He needs to be occupied."

The *clack, clack* of the balls interrupted them.

"Have you been enjoying London?" he asked.

She clasped her hands tightly. "I enjoy the shopping and have found wonderful gifts for my sisters and brothers."

He noticed that she'd skillfully managed to make no opinion about the city. "Most people either love or hate London on the first visit."

"Justin enjoyed the Tower of London," she said. "I figured such a ghoulish place would appeal to a young man."

"Have you been to the theater or the opera?" he asked.

"Not yet," she said.

"I'm sure my friends and I could get up a party to attend the theater," Bell said. "You would be very welcome."

She smiled. "I would enjoy that very much."

"The devil," Harry cried out.

Bell looked at his friend. "A lady is present, Harry."

Harry's face reddened. "I beg your pardon, Lady Chesfield."

"Don't mind him," Colin said. "This bacon-brained fellow learned his manners at his uncle's pig farm."

"Ha!" Harry said. "You're just smarting because I've beat you two out of three games."

"I gather George hasn't arrived yet," Bell said.

"Haven't seen him," Harry said.

Colin took a shot and the last two balls sank into the pockets. "I won!"

"I'll fetch Justin and Paul," Harry said.

"Thank you," Laura said. "I fear all that running will disturb the servants."

Bell liked that she was considerate of the servants. Far too many aristos treated them thoughtlessly. His father had taught him at a young age to be respectful of all those in his employ. He tightened his jaw at the intrusive thought and shoved it away.

Laura leaned closer. "Is something wrong?"

She was observant, but he refused to let the bleak memory spoil the evening. "It's nothing."

"I'm so sorry. I ought to have forbid my son from running on the stairs."

He shook his head. "That isn't it."

"I don't want to take advantage of your goodwill," she said under her breath.

"I wouldn't mind if you did," he said, his voice a little rough.

She wagged her slender finger. "I fell into that trap once before."

"Then I'd better build a better one," he said.

"Be careful. I might trick you into falling into my trap."

"What will you do to me?" he said in a low voice.

"I shall chain and shackle you until you beg for mercy."

Oh, Lord. He pictured his wrists tied with silk scarves, and Laura kissing her way down his torso until she reached his cock.

"You have a very wicked gleam in your eyes," she said.

His groin tightened. "I have a very wicked imagination."

"I'm not surprised."

He glanced at Colin, who set up the balls in the center. Satisfied his friend was intent on making his shot, Bell closed his hand round her small wrist and gazed into her green eyes. Her lips parted a little, and every instinct he possessed told him she wanted him as much as he wanted her.

The *clack, clack, clack* of the balls on the green baize brought him back to the present. He released her wrist just as Harry walked inside. "Justin and his friend found the backgammon board in the drawing room. I doubt we'll see them anytime soon."

"Another game?" Colin asked.

"Absolutely," Harry said, picking up a cue stick.

Bell returned his attention to Laura. "Can I get you a glass of sherry?"

"Yes, thank you," she said.

Bell strode over to the sideboard and poured her a brimming glass of sherry. He splashed two fingers of brandy into his own glass. When he returned to her, she blinked at the full glass. "You're not trying to get me foxed, are you?"

"Just a little." He swirled the brandy and inhaled the fragrance.

She sipped her sherry. "I've never had brandy before."

"Do you wish to try it?"

"Is it strong?"

He nodded.

"I'll stick to sherry," she said. "I get a bit giddy after only one glass of wine."

He smiled, thinking he'd like to see her giddy. She turned her attention to the game. Bell took the opportunity to study her face. In profile, her lashes were long. The slight fullness of her cheeks made her look sweet and younger than her twenty-eight years.

She must have felt him staring, because she looked at him with a slight frown. "What is it?"

He shook his head.

She returned her attention to the game, and he did as well.

Harry sighted the ball, readjusted his stance, and took the shot. The last two balls sank into the pockets. "Victory," he shouted, shaking his cue stick.

Colin regarded Laura. "Harry is overly modest."

She laughed.

"Bell, show her your trick," Colin said.

"You have a trick?" Laura asked.

"It's not really a trick," Bell said.

"Do not let him fool you," Harry said. "It's quite impressive."

"Then I insist upon a demonstration," Laura said.

Bell set both of their glasses on a side table. Then he held out his hand to her. Once again, he was struck by her small hand. When she stood, the top of her head barely reached his chin. She was far more petite than most women. "I'll do my best," he said, "but occasionally it doesn't work."

"What is it?" she said.

"You'll see," Harry said. "Bell is a man of many talents."

He said nothing as he lined the balls up in a perfect triangle and set the cue ball apart. Then he picked up the cue stick and sighted the white ball. He slid the stick over his hand and kept his eyes on the target. All of his concentration was on getting the right amount of force when he tapped the ball. He aligned his body with the cue ball, focused, and took the shot. The balls scattered over the green baize surface and dropped into the various six pockets.

Laura clapped her hands. "That was amazing."

"Our friend is an amazing fellow," Colin said from the sideboard, where he'd poured himself a brandy.

"However did you learn to do that?" she asked.

"I just experimented," he said.

"You are too modest," she said. "I doubt I could make even one land in a pocket."

"Of course you could if you know what you're doing."

She shook her head. "I'm quite sure I could not."

Bell beckoned her. "I'll show you."

She looked a bit uneasy as she neared him.

"You'll need to remove the gloves," he said.

Her fingers fumbled a bit as she pulled on the tips.

"Harry, let's go into the garden for a cheroot," Colin said.

Bell kept his expression impassive, but inwardly he applauded his friends for their timely exit.

"Here, I'll help you," he said. "If you'll allow it."

She hesitated a moment, and then she nodded.

He pulled on the fingertips first to loosen the glove. Then he reached for her upper arm and encountered silky smooth skin. As he slowly rolled the long glove down her slender arm, he imagined doing the same with a stocking and kissing the soft flesh he revealed.

Her breathing was a bit faster now and so was his. He

pulled on the fingers of the other kid glove to loosen it. Then he began to roll it inch by inch down her arm. As he removed the glove, he met her gaze and almost staggered at the sultry expression in her green eyes. He stood there, powerless to move. The tension was palpable and her rose scent was like a potion swirling inside him with every breath. But he could not just stand here forever. So he cupped her elbow and led her to the billiards table and handed her the cue stick.

"It's heavier than I expected," she said.

He stood behind her. "Put your right foot forward and your left one back."

She followed his instructions. "Now what?" she said, her voice a bit breathless.

"Lay the cue stick atop your hand between your thumb and forefinger."

"This is a bit awkward," she said.

"You'll grow accustomed," he said. "Now, grip the end of the stick, and slide it back and forth over your hand."

She tried and fumbled with the stick.

He drew closer and put his hand over hers. His breath stirred the curl by her ear. "The stick is a bit long for you, but I'm sure you can accommodate it. Relax and keep a steady back-and-forth rhythm." Lord, he was getting hot just thinking of what he was describing.

"Like this?" she said, her voice a bit husky.

"Excellent," he said. "See the blue ball?"

"Yes," she said in a whisper.

"You want to aim squarely for the white cue ball when you take the shot and knock the blue one."

"I doubt I can hit it hard enough," she said.

"I'll show you." Then he wrapped his hand over hers

at the butt of the stick and helped her slide it fluidly over her hand. "On the count of three," he said.

A little huff of laughter escaped her.

"Concentrate," he said near her ear.

"Yes," she said softly.

"One," he whispered.

She inhaled on a ragged breath.

"Two." His groin tightened again.

"Three." He thrust the stick forward. The cue ball smacked the blue one, sending it spinning into the pocket.

He propped the cue stick against the table. "Well done."

She gazed at him over her shoulder. "You made the shot." Her mouth was so close, and he wanted her too much to hold back. When their lips met, he turned her in his arms and pulled her up on her toes. He leaned over her, supporting her back with his hands. As she wrapped her arms around his neck, he captured her lips, and she opened for his tongue. She made a soft feminine sound, and all he could think about was eliciting far more from her. He slid his hand along her slender waist and cupped her breast. When she arched her back, he bent his head and ran his tongue all along the seam of her bodice. A shuddered breath escaped her.

He captured her lips again. She tasted so sweet, and he wanted so much more from her. His cock hardened, and he knew she felt it against her belly. He slid his hand down to her bottom and pressed her closer to him. Frustration gripped him. He yearned to undo the tapes of her gown and unravel every inch of shift, petticoat, stays, and stockings. More than anything, he wanted to carry her into the adjoining room where he could make love to her over and over on the chaise.

The devil take it. He could not remember ever wanting a woman this much before.

Approaching footsteps outside arrested him. He slid her down his body, and she quickly straightened her bodice. Then she covered her mouth.

He took her hand. "The gloves," he said. He slid the first one on as quickly as possible. Then his fingers fumbled as he tried to put the other one on. She took the glove, turned her back, and walked over to the fire while sliding it on.

Male voices sounded. She gasped as she turned round. He winced, knowing he shouldn't have risked kissing her.

Harry and Colin were projecting their voices to alert him. Relief filled him. If her son had walked in, she would have suffered humiliation and probably blamed herself.

Bell fixed a stoic expression on his face when his friends entered.

"Where are the cubs?" Harry said.

"I'll investigate," Bell said. As he strode out into the great hall, he grew suspicious. If those two had escaped, he would personally hunt them down and blister their ears. He ran up the spiral staircase and into the drawing room, but they weren't there. When he descended, he sought his butler, Griffith. "Did you happen to see where the boys went?"

"Yes, my lord. The footman reported they were playing backgammon. I thought they might be hungry, so I asked Cook to offer them some biscuits and milk. They're in the dining room."

"Thank you." Bell sighed in relief and strode off to the dining room. His previous French chef had quit in a stupid row over the breakfast menu. He'd told the housekeeper to promote the undercook to head cook. He was delighted that she was not very ambitious when it came to culinary masterpieces, as he preferred his plain English breakfast, the only meal he ever ate at home.

His cook must be thrilled to have such an easy job, but he figured if she cooked his regular breakfast of baked eggs, toast, and bacon without complaint, he would be a happy man.

When he reached the dining room, Bell found Justin and Paul eating sandwiches and biscuits while Cook poured them both a mug of milk. "Growing boys are always hungry, me mam used to say."

"Do you have more cheese?" Justin asked her.

"Aye, I'll bring it right up," she said. "My lord, would you like a cheese sandwich and some milk?"

"No, thank you," Bell said, watching the pair wolf down food faster than he'd thought possible. "You'd better bring all of the cheese," he said. "They might gnaw on the furniture otherwise."

Paul choked on his milk. Cook banged on his back. "That's all right. I'll bring another jug of milk."

Colin and Harry entered the dining room along with Laura. When he looked at Laura, her gaze skittered away from him. He felt awful, but he would have to wait to apologize.

"Lady Chesfield got concerned when you didn't return right away," Harry said. "Griffith directed us here."

Cook set her plump hand on her hip. "I'll bring up more food since everyone is hungry."

Laura touched her throat. "Oh, please, do not go to any trouble."

"No trouble," Cook said. "My, you are a pretty one, but you could use fattening up. The men like a bit of meat on the bones, if you take my meaning. Everyone take a seat. I'll be right back."

"Chatty cook you have," Harry said, and bit into a biscuit.

"She's never uttered a word in my presence before," Bell said.

Colin snatched a biscuit. "Mmm."

Laura poured milk into a mug and handed it along with a biscuit to Bell. He tried to communicate his apology with his eyes, but she averted her gaze again.

He looked inside the mug.

"What?" Colin said. "You don't like milk with biscuits?"

"I haven't had milk and biscuits since I was a boy."

"Oh, that's a crime," Paul said.

"Nothing better," Harry agreed.

Bell gave Harry an incredulous look.

"I meant when it comes to food," Harry said.

"Keep talking," Colin said. "You're bound to say something you shouldn't."

"Never mind," Harry said, and swigged his milk.

Justin dipped a biscuit in the milk and looked at Bell. "Dunk the biscuit already."

"I don't need instructions on how to eat a biscuit." Bell pulled out a chair for Laura at the bottom of the table.

"Thank you," she said woodenly.

Bell strode to the head of the table and took his customary seat. As he looked at Laura across the length of the table, he had the strangest feeling he'd done this once before. He mumbled something about nonsensical pre-science and dunked his biscuit in the milk.

"Why are you so gruff?" Justin said.

"He made plans, and things changed," Harry said.

"So?" Justin said.

Colin wiped the milk off his mouth. "He likes order."

"Well, he has us for disorderly friends," Harry said.

"That's a bad joke," Justin said.

He didn't give a rat's arse about order. He bit into the soggy biscuit and allowed that it did taste better after soft-ening in milk. Of course, he would not admit it.

Cook sailed inside the dining room bearing a platter of sandwiches. A footman brought an additional tray of fruits, nuts, biscuits, and another jug of milk. Within minutes, everyone was eating with gusto, except Laura, who was gingerly eating a strawberry. Her lips were damp—and red. Mindlessly, he lifted the cup and got a mouthful of crumbs. He set the cup down and decided not to drink it.

"Is something wrong?" Laura asked.

"No." *Yes, there is. I wronged you.*

"I wonder what happened to George," Justin said.

Paul shrugged. "He mentioned he might have other plans."

"So we're second choice?" Justin said, his voice rising.

Paul shrugged. "You know George. He changes his mind on a whim."

"Sounds like a fair-weather friend to me," Harry said.

Colin nodded. "Not the sort of fellow you trust."

Justin pushed his plate aside and said nothing.

After an uncomfortable silence, Laura glanced at Bell.

"Thank you for a delightful evening. I think we should probably leave now. If you could arrange for a hackney, I would appreciate it."

"No, I'll take you in my carriage," he said.

"Harry and I will be shoving off now as well. Paul, we'll give you a ride, if you wish," Colin said.

Bell signaled a footman to make arrangements for his carriage and bade his friends good-bye in the great hall. When the carriage arrived a few minutes later, Bell led Laura and her son along the pavement. She attempted to speak to Justin, but he turned away.

Justin would be far better off if his friendship with George ended, but Bell understood the boy's anger.

An instant later, he realized his own hypocrisy. He'd gotten Laura to agree to be his friend, but tonight he'd seduced her at the billiards table.

She deserved better.

Bell helped her into the carriage. Justin followed. Bell sat with his back to the horses. No one said a word.

He wondered if she would refuse to see him again. She ought to refuse to admit him.

Damn it all. She would feel guilty because her son had been there. He wanted to tell her that it wasn't her fault. He wanted to tell her that he'd never meant to lead her astray, but she knew better. It wasn't the first time he'd coaxed her into his arms. Oh, he'd played a game with her that first day in her drawing room. She'd fallen hook, line, and sinker for his ploy.

Now something twisted in his gut.

The carriage lurched to a halt. Bell descended and assisted her on the steps. After Justin got out, he ran up the walkway.

Reed opened the door, and Justin fled inside.

She flinched. "Thank you for the escort, Lord Bellingham. I can see myself inside."

"Laura, may I come in?"

"If this is about our earlier...indiscretion, I've no wish to discuss it. It should not have happened, but it did. Now I wish to forget it."

"We need to discuss it."

"I don't think that's a good idea," she said, wrapping her shawl tighter around her.

"It's cold, and I don't like to leave things hanging."

She remained silent for a moment. "Very well, but we will make this brief."

He had a good idea of what she meant to say, but he had something to say as well.

Reed greeted them as they stepped into the foyer. "My lady, Lord Bellingham."

"I take it Justin is upstairs," she said.

"Yes, my lady."

"Thank you, Reed," she said.

Bell led Laura toward the staircase and noted the tight set of her mouth.

When they entered the drawing room, he saw the fire had burned low. "I'll stir the coals if you wish."

"Thank you." She sat upon the sofa and rearranged her shawl.

He removed the fire screen and poked at the coals, producing a decent fire. When he replaced the screen, he looked back at her. "Would you like me to light candles?"

"No, it's wasteful, and we've sufficient light from the fire."

Here was more evidence of their differences. He never would have thought twice about lighting a dozen candles, but he'd always lived a privileged life.

Bell sat beside her. "You probably think me a devil. I didn't plan what happened tonight."

"I know."

He blew out his breath. "You are a lady, and I took advantage of you tonight."

She turned toward him. "I am a grown woman, not an innocent girl just out in society. You did not take advantage of me. I knew from the moment you offered to show me how to make a shot at the billiards table that I was playing with fire."

"Laura, I risked your reputation."

"No, *I* risked my reputation. I could have said no at any point, and I didn't because I wanted you to kiss me. If anyone had discovered us, I would have no one to blame but myself. We are both adults, and we both must take responsibility for our actions."

He shook his head. "I cannot allow you to take any of the blame. I am the one with all of the experience—"

"You will not take over this time," she said, her voice vehement. "From the beginning, you have taken the reins and tried to assert your authority. I am grateful to you for your help with my son, but I am not helpless."

"I'm accustomed to taking charge. I've been managing properties and servants for years. It is ingrained in me."

She stood and naturally he came to his feet. "You have no idea what I have had to manage on my own," she said. "Who do you think took care of my ailing husband? I did, because I knew that I could provide better for him.

Who do you think has been managing the servants and making decisions at Hollwood Abbey? It certainly isn't Montclief."

Bell stared. "You're jesting."

"Is it so difficult for you to believe that a woman has the intelligence and ability to do both?"

He stared at her. "I never considered the possibility. After all, it's customary for gentlemen to manage all aspects of property. Women are in charge of domestic affairs."

"Well, you see standing before you a woman who managed both out of necessity. I daresay you cannot claim as much."

"I let the servants take care of domestic matters," he said. "We are straying from the topic."

"I think you had better leave before I say something I regret."

"What have I done wrong now? I tried to apologize, but you wouldn't let me."

"It has been an interesting evening, my lord."

"Laura, you will not cut me off. I'm sorry for underestimating you. I had the best of intentions, but I suppose I have been a little overbearing at times."

"A little?" she huffed. "It's my own fault. I relied too much on you because I was afraid of losing my son."

"It's not wrong to accept help."

"I appreciate your assistance with my son, but I've been taking care of others since I was a child."

"I know," he said. "You're a good mother, Laura."

She met his gaze. "You knew how to manage Justin."

He frowned but said nothing.

"You learned this from someone."

The *tick-tick* of the clock sounded loud. "My father," he said.

She lifted up on her toes and kissed his cheek. "I think he would be proud of you."

He tightened his jaw. "I've kept you too long. Good night."

She donned her nightgown and slid beneath the covers, but sleep evaded her. Earlier, she'd been so angry with him. He wanted to take all of the blame as if she were too mindless to know exactly what was transpiring in the billiards room. He'd spoken to her as if she couldn't manage on her own, but she'd set him straight.

He truly hadn't understood that his treatment demeaned her. She had accepted his help, but he'd taken over one too many times. Perhaps it was some chivalrous instinct on his part, but tonight he'd carried it too far.

Then somehow their discussion had taken a sharp turn. The haunted look in Bell's eyes still troubled her. She wondered what it had cost him to utter those two words. *My father.*

Lady Atherton had said he'd left England to journey on the Continent and had returned a completely changed man. He purportedly had ice in his veins, she'd said. Laura suspected he hid the wounds behind a cynical veneer.

He'd lost his family, but she knew no other details. Quite possibly no one knew the circumstances, with the possible exception of the friend who had traveled with him to the Continent.

Tonight she'd seen the magnificent town house that

had belonged to more than one generation of his family and wondered how he could turn his back on all of it. Surely he must believe his father would have wanted him to carry on the family legacy.

Something niggled at her brain. He refused to marry, even though all of his properties would revert to the Crown when he died. But there could be no entail if he had no one to inherit. He could sell them. Yet he had held on to everything he'd inherited.

Was it because they were all that he had left of his family?

Under the circumstances, it was illogical not to sell, but emotions were illogical.

Grief could tear one's heart to pieces. She remembered sitting by Phillip's side and begging God to let him stay with her just a little longer, even though her dear husband was suffering. After he'd passed, she'd felt guilty, but her father had told her that bargaining was a common reaction to the impending loss of a loved one.

Her family had sustained her during those first difficult weeks when she'd wept after finding the watch that Phillip had misplaced. Often, she'd broken down over mundane items like a comb. But Justin had needed her, and that had helped her to put one foot in front of the other. The worst of the pain had subsided little by little.

She suspected that Bellingham had never mourned, and she knew firsthand the importance of grieving.

He had likely erected barriers to shut the past out and keep the pain at bay. She could not be sure of anything, other than he'd suffered a great shock early in life. He needed her, but how could she reach him?

Part of her wanted to shy away from asking him about his family. He would likely grow angry and refuse to speak of the tragedy. But tonight he'd opened up just a little. She must not let fear deter her. He was her friend, and she cared about him. More than a little.

Chapter Seven

White's, the next evening

*B*ell was nursing a brandy and a bad mood. Laura had felt sorry for him last night. He didn't want her pity. God knew he'd heard enough of that when he'd returned to England last year. Women, young and old, had come up to him with sorrowful expressions and uttered platitudes. *Time heals all wounds. Your family is in a better place. It was God's will.* He'd never responded; he'd just walked away.

Most especially, he didn't like it when others expressed lurid curiosity about his family's death and his decision to leave England for four years.

Last night, Laura had kissed his cheek and said his father would be proud of him. Her presumption had angered him, and when he'd arrived home, he'd wanted to smash something. She of all people ought to know better than to resort to clichés in answer to insensible death.

He picked up his glass and frowned at the amber-colored brandy. Deep down, he knew Laura hadn't tossed off that phrase thoughtlessly. He'd gotten his back up because he hated any kind of weakness in himself, especially the nightmares. He had to be strong both physically and mentally. And always in control.

The waiter arrived and topped up his glass. Bell downed the brandy in two swallows.

"The devil," he muttered just as Harry and Colin took chairs at his table.

Harry frowned. "What did you say?"

"I cursed," Bell said, and topped up his glass again.

"Oh, no," Colin said. "Look at him. He's sickening from love."

"You mean lust," Harry said, "for the widow."

"Of course it's the widow," Colin said. "She's pretty and sweet."

"I'm not sickening from love."

"They must've had a lover's quarrel last night," Harry said. "Don't worry, old boy. The making up is the best part, right?"

Bell tossed down his brandy and burned his throat in the process. He cleared his throat twice. "I am not sickening." He'd thought she was different, but he'd seen the look in her eyes. She wanted to fix him. By God, he didn't want her to coddle him. He didn't want her to kiss his cheek. And he damned sure didn't want her to console him.

The waiter stopped and topped up his brandy again. He swallowed a mouthful and looked at his friends. Something was wrong. He looked at Harry's and Colin's faces. "You're silent," Bell said.

"We are gaping at you," Harry said.

"Why?" Bell asked.

"Because you are heartbroken," Colin said.

"I don't have a heart to break."

"Of course you do or you would be dead," Harry said.

Bell scowled. "Do you have to be so literal?"

Colin stiffened.

"What is wrong now?" Bell said.

"Nothing," Colin said.

"Right, everything is perfectly fine," Harry said. "Your heart is not broken."

"Why are you acting stranger than usual?" Bell asked.

"I think you'd better tell him," Colin said.

"Me? No, you tell him," Harry said.

"Tell me what?" Bell said.

"It's about your rival," Colin said.

"I have no rival," Bell said.

"The one with the bald spot," Harry said.

"Pembroke," Colin added. "He's crowing over having called upon Lady Chesfield earlier today."

"Hah! She probably told her butler to say she was away from home," Bell said.

Harry and Colin looked at each other.

"You tell him," Colin said.

"No, it's your turn," Harry said.

"I distinctly recall telling him the last time," Colin said.

Bell banged his fist on the table. "Spill it."

"She received Lady Atherton," Harry said.

"So? They are friends."

"And Pembroke," Colin said. "You have a rival for Lady Chesfield's affections."

"No need to worry," Harry said. "She'll choose you over Baldy."

"She doesn't want a suitor—or a husband." He drained the remainder of his brandy.

"Tell that to Pembroke," Colin said.

Bell scowled. "Why? She doesn't want him."

"No, I meant Pembroke is coming this way."

Bell looked over his shoulder.

Pembroke strutted to their table. "Bellingham, I heard your carriage was seen at Lady Chesfield's residence last evening."

Bell covered a yawn.

"I thought you ought to know that I expressed my concern to the lady when I called upon her today. She reassured me that you merely conveyed her and her son home in your carriage."

"Are you done?" Bell asked.

"No, I am not," he said. "I informed Lady Chesfield of your notorious reputation with women, and she assured me that she is in no danger from you."

Bell narrowed his eyes at the odd way Pembroke had combed his hair. "Is that a new hairstyle you're sporting?"

Pembroke's face reddened. "I've no idea what you mean."

Bell lifted his chin. "I see. You combed a few hairs over the bald spot. Ingenious."

"You may enjoy insulting me, but she will choose me."

"Why are you telling me?"

"I wished to give you fair warning. I mean to make her an honorable proposal."

He snorted at the idea of Laura being affianced to two men at once, although their engagement wasn't real.

Pembroke tugged on his waistcoat. "You will not laugh when we announce our engagement."

"You're bloody sure of yourself," Bell said, "but let me give you a tip. She doesn't want a husband."

"How do you know?"

"She told me."

"Hah! You proposed and she declined," Pembroke said, raising his voice.

A hush fell over the nearby tables. Other men were staring at him.

Bell glared at Pembroke. "I did not propose to her."

"She wouldn't have you," Pembroke said.

Bell stood and loomed over Pembroke. "My ancestors were fiendish marauders. They raided castles, plundered the treasures, and kidnapped the women. Their blood runs through my veins."

Pembroke lifted his chin, causing his collar point to poke into his cheek. He brushed at it as if it were an insect and said, "Mark my words. She will be my bride." With that final sally, Pembroke walked off.

Naturally, Lindmoore, better known as Lord Gossip, hurried over. "I heard that you were courting Lady Chesfield."

"You heard wrong," he said.

Lindmoore's eyes gleamed. "Is it true her husband left her a fortune?"

"Stay away from her," he said through gritted teeth.

"Just asking," Lindmoore said. "Of course, many will be delighted to know you have not spoken for her."

The voices in the room dwindled in volume. Every male in the place was listening.

Damnation. He'd better warn Laura that the wolves were about to descend.

* * *

The next day, Laura attended Lady Atherton's at-home. She made the acquaintance of several ladies, and while she was glad for the introductions, Laura felt somewhat on display as the other ladies gave her piercing looks. Many of them spoke of people and events that she had no knowledge about, but she listened politely. One lady interested her, George's mother, and so she made a point of taking the empty chair next to her. "Lady Rentworth, I'm so glad to finally meet you. Our boys are friends."

Lady Rentworth's brows creased. "How interesting."

She'd spoken in a bored tone, making her meaning quite the opposite.

Laura tried again. "George has called for my son in the past, but we have not seen him lately."

"Well, he's somewhere."

Lady Rentworth's friends shook out their fans and exchanged amused glances. Laura maintained her composure, because she didn't want others, especially Lady Atherton, to know that Lady Rentworth and her friends had mocked her.

Doubtless they had formed an opinion before ever meeting her. They would have discovered her past and looked down their patrician noses, because despite her title, she was not one of them. Laura told herself she didn't care, but it was easier to deal with in the abstract as opposed to the reality. Unfortunately, Lady Atherton had asked her to stay afterward so that they could talk, and now Laura regretted having agreed.

All she wanted was to leave this drawing room and these haughty women. She wanted to go home to Hampshire and take gifts to her brothers and sisters. She wanted to walk through the garden and cut flowers for the drawing room. Most of all, she·wished she could turn back time and spend an afternoon with Phillip.

But there was no use wishing for things that could never be. She ought to count her blessings instead. She had a wonderful, large family and her son, all of whom she loved. Laura smiled at Lady Atherton and was very grateful for her friendship. Lady Atherton's many letters had helped sustain the link to Phillip, something that grew increasingly important to Laura over the years. In some ways, it seemed as if only a year had gone by since his death, and other times it seemed an age since he'd passed. Despite his illness, he'd been a wonderful husband, and her only regret was that they'd not had more time together.

When the last caller departed, Lady Atherton rang for a tea tray. "These at-homes are so hectic," she said. "Everyone is determined to hear or spread the latest tittle-tattle. Did you hear anything interesting?"

"No," she said, lowering her eyes.

"I noted your discomfort while speaking to Lady Rentworth earlier," Lady Atherton said.

Laura cleared her throat. "I mentioned that our sons were friends but that we had not seen George recently."

"What did she say to that?"

"She said he's somewhere."

Lady Atherton waved her hand. "She has the mothering instincts of a stray cat. If you ask my opinion, there are far too many aristocratic parents who fob off their children to nurses and live as if their offspring do not even exist. It's really quite horrid." Lady Atherton paused. "But you are genuinely overset by your brief conversation with her."

She explained the way that Justin had learned about George's defection.

Lady Atherton's eyes widened. "You called at Lord Bellingham's town house."

Laura's face heated as she told Lady Atherton the circumstances. "Perhaps I should not have gone, but he persuaded me."

The maid entered with the tea tray. Lady Atherton poured and handed a dish to Laura. "He was very persuasive, was he?" Lady Atherton said.

"Oh, yes."

"Do tell," Lady Atherton said.

"I don't know what you mean," she said.

"Of course you do," she said.

"There can never be anything more than friendship between us." She would not reveal what had happened in the billiards room.

"Really? A platonic friendship. How intriguing." Lady Atherton gave her a sly smile. "Most women would jump at the chance to join him in the boudoir."

"I'm not most women," Laura said.

"No, you are not, and that is precisely why he is attracted to you."

"I will not shame myself or my family for a fleeting liaison. And I most certainly will not disgrace Phillip's memory."

"Excuse me a moment," Lady Atherton said.

Laura watched her cross over to the sideboard, where she poured some type of liquor into two glasses. When she returned to the sofa, Lady Atherton handed a glass to Laura. "When I was younger, I would not have dreamed of taking a glass of sherry in the afternoon. But as the years went on, I realized that all of my regrets were for opportunities that I did not take. In fact, when I was a mere girl, I almost succumbed to my parents' pressure to marry a marquis. Of course, he was much older, and it would have proven to be a brilliant match in the eyes of society. But I was in love with Alfred. At the time, he was a younger son with no prospects. I took a chance and waited for him. As it turned out, he did inherit an earldom."

"You must have been very much in love," Laura said.

"The point of my story is this: Do not allow rules to hem you in. You only get one turn in life. Make the most of it."

"Thank you for the advice," Laura said.

Lady Atherton regarded her intently. "You could do far worse than Bellingham."

"I do not seek better, Lady Atherton."

"What would tempt you? True love?"

"I assure you the earl is not offering that."

"A clever woman knows how to lead a man to the altar."

"He is not the sort of man who will allow anyone to lead him."

"Drink your sherry," Lady Atherton said. "And if you're smart, you'll let Bellingham catch you."

Laura had let that happen twice, and she saw nothing smart about it at all.

Two hours later, Laura was replying to a letter from Rachel when a light tap sounded at the door. "Come in," she said.

"Lord Bellingham wishes to call on you, my lady."

"Very well. Show him up."

After Reed left, she hurried over to the mirror and pinched her cheeks. The curls by her ears were a bit limp, but there was no help for that now. She told herself that she would check her appearance when anyone called, but he was not just anyone. He was her friend.

She smoothed her skirts and wondered why he'd called. After her conversation with Lady Atherton, Laura had grown increasingly curious about his family. Since they were friends, she ought to feel free to ask about his life. He certainly had inquired about hers. But his situation was complicated, and she knew from her years nursing Phillip that men disliked showing any sort of vulnerability. She must be patient and wait for a natural opportunity to broach the topic.

A knock sounded and Bell walked inside. "I told Reed not to bother since I know my way upstairs."

She curtsied. "Please, take a seat. I'll ring for a tea tray."

"Don't trouble the servants. I won't stay long." He joined her on the sofa and cleared his throat. "Where is Justin?"

"Upstairs, writing a letter to his grandparents."

"You made him write the letter?"

"He wouldn't think of it unless I reminded him," she said.

"I understand that Pembroke called on you."

She blinked. "Yes, two days ago. Lady Atherton was here as well. Why do you ask?"

Bell drew in a breath. "He announced at White's in a rather conspicuous fashion that he meant to propose to you."

"What?" She placed her hand over her heart. "I am

stunned. Why would he make a spectacle of himself? I've only met him twice before. How dare he bandy my name around in conjunction with his own?" When she rose, he did as well. Laura started pacing. "Oh, this is mortifying. He has made me the center of attention in your club." She fisted her hands. "I will blister his ears if he ever comes near me again."

"There is more," he said.

"Oh, no."

"This was bound to come out," he said. "It is now common knowledge that you are wealthy. That means fortune hunters will target you."

"They can jolly well target someone else," she said.

He shrugged. "You are a beautiful, rich widow."

"I am a lady, not a prize to be won."

He caught her by the shoulders. "Laura, I know you're overset, but you're too clever to let a bounder fool you."

"I don't like the idea of all those men talking about me." It seemed sordid to her.

His mouth curved in that lopsided smile she knew so well. "Well, they can look, but they cannot touch."

"I don't want them ogling me, either," she said.

He'd done that the first time he'd seen her, but then again, she'd done her share of looking as well. "Did you accept Lady Norcliffe's invitation to her ball?"

"Yes, Lady Atherton sent a note. She will take Justin and me in her carriage."

"If I stay near you at the ball, that will warn the jackals off," he said.

"No offense, but given your reputation, that will send a different message, one that is likely to set tongues wagging."

"You mean, because I'm a rake? I haven't been a very good one lately, you know."

She frowned. "What?"

"Well, except for drinking a bit too much brandy at the club and smoking a few cheroots."

"Eww!"

He laughed. "Men aren't as fastidious as women."

"I know," she said. "I have brothers."

"And I never replaced my last mistress. I definitely get a deduction in raking for that."

She tried to wriggle away from him, but he held her fast. "How dare you speak of such a subject in my presence?"

"The mistress left weeks ago," he said.

"You are outrageous."

"So you've said before, but we're friends, and I've made no secret there have been women in my life."

She pushed on his rock-hard chest to no avail.

"Now you're angry because I told you that I'm failing as a rakehell," he said.

"Next thing you'll be telling me you have needs." That had slipped. She might as well have thrown a door open to perdition.

"A man with needs can find solitary relief," he said, "but wanting what is so near to hand and yet forbidden is like drinking from an empty cup."

"No, you could drink your fill, but without tender feelings the cup would always be empty."

He released her. "You mean love."

"Have you ever been in love?" she asked.

"No."

She felt an overwhelming compulsion to encourage him to open his heart, but her heart was fragile as well.

The budding tender feelings in her chest scared her, because there was no future for them, only a friendship for the season.

"You are a singular woman," he said.

She knit her brows. "How so?"

"You are the only woman who ever said no to me."

"Obviously you were overdue for a lesson in humility," she said.

He put his fist on his hip. "I'm an earl. Haughtiness comes with the title."

"At least you're honest," she said. "By the by, you will not try to protect me from fortune hunters at the ball. I am quite capable of discouraging all manner of rogues."

"Including me," he said.

"You proved quite determined, but I've always been up to the challenge."

He winked. "If I see you flirting, I'll be mortally jealous."

"I suspect you'll never know."

"Oh, why is that?" he asked.

"Because you will be surrounded by a dozen women all vying for your favors."

"But they won't be you," he said.

"Bellingham, go find a snake to charm."

"I would rather charm you...into a kiss."

Bell had teased her, but the intense expression in his eyes was meant to draw her to him. She felt the pull of his will, and a wicked part of her wanted to walk into his arms. But she only wagged her finger. "I am impervious to temptation." It was a bouncer, of course.

"Are you sure you won't reconsider?"

Dear God, he would tempt a saint, and she most certainly was not one. But she shook back her curls as she looked up at him, amazed anew by his beautiful blue eyes. "You know the answer to that."

"Woe is me," he said, "but now we're friends, so you can't get rid of me so easily. I'm quite fond of you."

Her heart beat a little faster. It was an admission, but what did it mean? She couldn't think properly when he was so close, and the heady scent of him swirled all around her.

He tugged on the curl by her ear. "I'd better go."

She felt a little giddy as she walked with him to the door.

"I will see you at the ball," he said.

After she closed the door, Laura leaned her hands against it. *I'm quite fond of you.* Her heart continued to thump as she tried to discern whether he'd intimated deeper feelings. He'd said he would be jealous if other men flirted with her, but they had both reverted to banter and teasing. Yet somehow it hadn't felt like teasing at all. He'd looked at her as if he didn't want to let her go.

She turned round and hurried to the window, wanting to see him again. Perhaps he would look up and wave at her. She laid her hand against the cool glass, and not long afterward, he strode down the pavement. "Look back," she whispered.

He climbed inside without a backward glance, and reality washed over her. She leaned her forehead against the glass. How could she be so foolish? She wasn't a giddy young girl with her first beau. She knew better, and still she'd stupidly tried to make more of his confession that he was fond of her. He'd meant as a *friend*.

How could she let herself look for meaning in his words when she knew better? He'd mastered the art of seduction; it was like breathing to him. The flirting, the banter, the jests were all a part of his charm. Oh, she'd wanted his deep, wet kisses, but one kiss would lead to another, and another. The next time, and there would be one, she would tell herself it was over, but she would fail, because he'd begun to mean more to her than he should. Eventually, the kisses would lead to touches, and the craving would intensify until she abandoned all of her principles and gave herself completely to him.

If she allowed it to happen, she would no longer be singular; she would only be another woman he bedded and forgot. And while he moved on to his next conquest, she would be left to pick up the shattered pieces of her heart.

Bell knocked on the roof of the carriage. When it rolled off, he pinched the bridge of his nose. He'd gone to her house with one purpose: to warn her about fortune hunters. Then he'd proceeded to tease and flirt with her. Damned if he hadn't tried to coax her into a kiss.

They had both danced all around what was between them, and the banter had been a way to keep it light. If it were only flirtation, they could simply laugh and be just friends. But each time they touched or came close to each other, the tension grew and grew until it felt unbearably like an impending thunderstorm.

He'd not been jesting when he'd said she was the first to tell him no.

At the ripe age of twenty, his scrawny frame had filled out. His muscles developed, due in part to the fencing lessons, but also it seemed he was destined to grow as broad and tall as his father. Women had taken notice of his athletic build and commented on his bright blue eyes.

He'd always thought it made him look odd, but he wasn't about to argue with the countless women who coaxed him into their beds.

In all the years of journeying on the Continent and the past year here in England, he'd never met any woman he couldn't walk away from.

He'd intended to walk away from Laura, but he hadn't. It was strange how one decision to call on her with that flask had changed so much. He'd thought to make her his mistress, but he'd realized almost immediately that she was not that kind of woman.

All this time, he'd told himself that he'd wanted her because she wouldn't go to bed with him, and he'd thought it was like the proverbial forbidden fruit. If it were that simple, he would never have gotten so involved in her life. He would have found another woman who would give him what he wanted. But something inside of him had shifted. He didn't understand it completely, but he knew it was because of Laura.

In hindsight, the part that astounded him was that he hadn't even attempted to find a new mistress. He wanted Laura, but he knew he couldn't have her, not in the way he wanted.

He couldn't go on this way or he'd end up a madman.

He would find a new mistress, right after Mrs. Norcliffe's ball.

Three days later

Laura considered wearing the pretty gown with lace round the hem, but she knew why it tempted her. She wanted to impress Bellingham, and she would not do it.

After their last encounter, she'd taken herself in hand. She'd become a bit infatuated with him. What woman wouldn't be flattered by his teasing and flirting? As long as she remembered that this was nothing more than a friendship for the season, there was nothing to worry about. Having made up her mind, she donned a simple white day dress and checked her reflection in the cheval mirror. "Fran, is this neckline too low for daytime?"

"Perhaps you could tuck a fichu into the bodice." The maid went to the wardrobe and produced a rather sheer one. After Fran helped her insert the fichu, Laura looked in the mirror again. It provided only marginal modesty, but any heavier fabric would look out of place.

She pinched her cheeks and walked downstairs to the drawing room to find her son slouching in a chair. Laura perched on the sofa. "Justin, your surly expression troubles me. Lord Bellingham will arrive soon for your fencing lesson. You ought to be grateful for the opportunity, but if you cannot, tell me now. I will explain to Lord Bellingham that you no longer wish to fence."

"It's not the fencing that provokes me," he said. "It's the way he speaks to me as if he has some right to tell me what to do. He's not my guardian."

She sighed. "Is that such a hardship? He could easily ignore you, but he hasn't. And do you know why?"

He huffed. "Yes, because his real interest is in you."

"No, Justin. He was here the day your uncle called, and he told me that your uncle would make a terrible guardian to you. I did not expect him to return after that, but he did because he was concerned."

"What does he have to gain from it? You."

"He is a friend, nothing more. I think you could learn

a great deal from Lord Bellingham's wisdom," she said.

"How can you say that when you know his reputation?" Justin said.

"You view him from one side only," she said. "People are far more complex. I've gotten to know him fairly well, and he is a very honorable man."

"You defend him because he's turned your head."

"He doesn't need my defense. I'm only stating what I know about him firsthand and from what Lady Atherton has told me. But if you cannot be respectful in his presence, then do not attend the fencing practice. I will leave that decision to you."

A knock sounded. Bellingham opened the door. "I told Reed I'd see myself up," he said.

Laura rose and looked at Justin with raised brows.

Justin stood as well. "So, will I be posing again?"

Bellingham huffed. "No, today you'll practice lunges. In a fortnight, you can try your hand at a real fencing bout with me."

"That will be no contest," Justin said.

"I have years of experience, but that's how I learned. Are you ready?"

Justin nodded.

Laura smiled. Justin might resent Bellingham, but he'd agreed to a second lesson. The exercise would do him good. He needed some occupation that didn't involve carousing with his friends.

Bell acknowledged a few acquaintances as he walked inside Angelo's with Justin. The fencing master greeted them and stood aside to watch.

"You remember the position from the last lesson," Bell

said. "The reason you 'posed' was to get accustomed to moving forward with the front foot first. Then you follow with the back one. I want you to practice with your sword arm fully extended. When you've mastered that, you'll practice the lunge with a blade."

"Understood," Justin said.

"Watch me first," Bell said. Then he demonstrated the forward movement. "Your turn."

Justin executed it perfectly.

Angelo clapped. "Well done."

Justin blew out his breath and practiced again. Four times out of five, he got it right.

"I believe he's a natural," Angelo said. "Now it's time to try it with a blade. Allow me to select one."

Bell worked with Justin on the grip again. "This part takes time, as you will recall."

Justin tried the lunge with a blade, but he had trouble.

"I know it's a bit frustrating, but with practice, you will catch on," Bell said.

Justin's mouth thinned as he tried again and again. When he was obviously tiring, Bell halted him. "You've done well today, but you're getting frustrated. We'll return next week and practice again."

"All right," Justin said. He toweled off the perspiration, picked up his coat, and slung it over his shoulder.

They walked out of the building, and Bell hailed his carriage. When it arrived, he instructed the driver to take them to Hyde Park.

After entering the carriage, Justin looked at Bell with suspicion. "Why are we going to the park?"

The carriage rolled into motion. "I mean to have a man-to-man talk with you."

Justin scowled. "I don't want to listen to your lectures. You are not my guardian."

"No, but be grateful it's me and not your ass of an uncle. I won't apologize for my words, either. The man has neglected you and treated your mother disrespectfully."

"Bloody hell," Justin said.

Bell ignored the boy's curse. As Laura had said, it was best to pick one's battles, especially with Justin.

When the carriage rolled into the park, Bell knocked his cane in a signal to stop. Justin followed him out of the carriage with slumped shoulders. Bell took him to a bench beneath a shady oak. The sky was a bit overcast, but the breeze was comfortable.

Justin leaned forward with his elbows on his knees. "Well?"

He'd planned to give him impersonal advice and leave out his own history, mostly because he didn't like to talk about his lost family to anyone. But Justin's father had died, and in effect, the boy had no male figure to guide him. Bell knew that just telling him that he shouldn't do this or that wouldn't have sufficient impact on the boy. It would be difficult to talk about his father, but he also knew that it was something he had to do if he were to have any influence on Justin.

He took a deep breath and released it. "Ideally, your father would be sitting here and giving you the advice that every young man needs. He's not here, but I am. My father had this talk with me when I was a year younger than you. I know he didn't plan it, because my actions precipitated the talk."

Justin frowned at him. "What did you do?"

"When I was sixteen, I met a tavern wench. All I could think about was how to get under her skirts."

Justin snorted.

"Naturally, my father found out. He was livid. My ears burned while he proceeded to give me a blistering lecture. Of course, I would only admit to kissing her, but there was more than a little touching going on. Then my father proceeded to scare the breeches off of me. He told me the tavern wench was taking coin from dozens of men in exchange for a toss in the sheets. He told me she likely carried diseases from her many lovers, and the only cure was hideous mercury treatments that don't always work."

"Did he punish you?" Justin asked.

"Oh, yes. He made me muck out the barn every day for a fortnight. I've hated flies ever since."

Justin laughed. "I figured he'd taken a switch to you."

"Oh, no. The switch would have ended too quickly. He wanted to make sure I was humbled and never forgot a word he'd said."

"My father didn't believe in physical punishment," Justin said.

Bell nodded. "Good for him."

Justin eyed him. "So did you ever get in trouble again?"

"Of course I did. When I was eighteen, my friends and I were in London for the season. We decided to visit a bawdy house. My eyes almost fell out from all the flesh displayed, but on closer inspection, the whores wore a lot of cheap perfume and it didn't disguise the unpleasant smells."

Justin looked at him. "Did you bed one?"

He shook his head. "Unbeknownst to us, my friend's

older brother saw us go inside. He and his friend jerked us out of there by our collars. To be honest, I was relieved because I worried my friends would poke fun at me if I didn't go upstairs with one of the whores."

Justin looked at the ground. "George claimed he'd been to a bawdy house, but I think he was lying."

"The ones who boast generally are," Bell said. "The thing is you're too damned young to lie with a woman, but when you get older, use a French letter. It will prevent disease and pregnancy. And stay away from prostitutes. They don't enter the profession because they're eaten up with lust. They are women and sometimes just girls who are down on their luck. They sell their bodies because they don't have any other choice." He looked at Justin. "Do you have any questions?"

"How old were you…the first time?"

"Twenty," he said. "She was five years older. I was scared and humiliated myself, but she taught me a few things." He paused and then said, "For me it was pure lust, but she was widowed, and I think a little lonely. One day, I just didn't go back." He'd felt bad about it, but he'd been young and didn't know what to say.

Justin scuffed his boot on the gravel.

"All I ask is that you remember what I told you today for your own protection," Bell said. "And trust me, you won't go blind using your hand."

When Justin pulled a face, Bell laughed. "Come along. I'll take you home."

Bell had meant to stay in the carriage while Justin climbed out, but Laura emerged from the town house and hurried toward them. He stepped out to greet her, but he would not linger or follow her inside. He was spending too much time with her. Even his friends had taken to teasing him about her, and his name was publicly linked with hers. They had agreed to friendship, but he wondered if he hadn't waded in a little too deep.

"Justin, did you enjoy your fencing lesson?" she asked.

"I'm progressing," he said.

"He is being modest," Bell said. "Your son is a quick study."

Justin gave him an enigmatic look. "Thank you."

Bell wondered if he'd meant more than the fencing lesson, but he'd never know.

"I need a bath. I stink," Justin said.

"Go on," Laura said, laughing. She shaded her eyes and watched her son stride inside the house.

He was reluctant to leave her, but that only spurred him to do so. "I'll be off, then," Bell said.

She turned and smiled at him, and something unfurled inside of his chest, though he couldn't identify the feelings. All he understood was a persistent urge to be near her.

"You were gone a long time," she said. "I worried something had gone awry."

"I took him to Hyde Park and had a man-to-man talk with him, as I promised you."

"Oh." Her cheeks flushed pink.

"He listened, and even asked a few questions." Bell drew in a breath. "It went much better than I expected."

"I am grateful to you," she said.

He shook his head. "Laura, I *wanted* to help him."

Her eyes misted. She blinked rapidly and averted her face.

He touched her arm. "What is it?"

She brushed her fingers at the corners of her eyes. "You've been so kind and given so much to us. And you have gotten nothing in return."

"Friendship shouldn't have strings attached," he said.

She smiled a little. "Yes, I agree." She moistened her lips, drawing his attention. He vividly remembered the way she'd felt in his arms as he'd kissed her that night in the billiards room. Since then, he'd fantasized about making love to her slowly, savoring each thrust into her body and looking into her eyes. He was torturing himself, but he couldn't help wanting her.

"Will you come in for a cup of tea?"

He wanted to accept, but he thought it would be in both of their best interests to put a little distance between them. Because he feared that he was inadvertently creating expectations. A woman like Laura needed a husband to make her happy, and a man like him could only give her a temporary liaison. "Thank you, but I have a mountain of paperwork awaiting me."

Chapter Eight

Lady Norcliffe's ball

As she moved through the receiving line, Laura was very glad that Lady Atherton had insisted upon taking her and Justin to Lady Norcliffe's ball. After her last encounter with the ladies of the ton, Laura was none too keen on mingling with them. If they snubbed her, she would simply ignore them. After the season ended, she and her son would return to Hampshire, where her family and friends would welcome her. She had seen a bit of the booming metropolis and could safely say she preferred the country.

They had not progressed far when Harry, Viscount Evermore, came to greet her, Justin, and Lady Atherton. Justin's wary expression troubled Laura somewhat, but hopefully he would not be too bored this evening.

"You must meet my cousins, Justin," Harry said, and proceeded to introduce all six. "My youngest cousin, Sarah, is out for the first time this season."

The dark-haired Sarah blushed and lowered her lashes.

Laura noticed her son watching her, transfixed. Someone came to stand beside Laura. She turned to find Lord Bellingham.

"My lady," he said, bowing much lower than necessary.

She wondered if he meant to send a message of some sort, but this was neither the place nor the time to ask. Perhaps she would be better off not asking at all.

Then Bellingham strode over to her son. The two were conversing. Laura had no idea what they were discussing, but a moment later Justin took a deep breath and walked over to Sarah. She blushed and curtsied and then looked at him as if he were the moon and the stars. Not long afterward, Justin led her toward the dance floor.

Bellingham looked at Laura over his shoulder and smiled. Her heart turned over. He'd planned to encourage Justin to dance tonight. She lifted her white satin skirt and joined him. "I think you just did something wonderful for my son."

He met her gaze. "I remember the first time I attended a ball. It took me three tries before I got the courage to ask a girl to dance."

"I hope she accepted."

He nodded.

"You must know what that meant to me." She'd thought her heart well guarded. If it had been something for her, she could have resisted. But how could she contain her tender feelings when he'd demonstrated his thoughtfulness for her son? She would, because she must conceal it from everyone, especially Bellingham.

He looked out at the dance floor. "I wanted to do something special for you. I turned to my friends for advice. They asked me what meant the most to you." He returned his burning gaze to her, and he did not have to say a word.

She blinked back the moisture in her eyes as he escorted her closer to the dance floor so that she could watch. Justin led Sarah to the bottom of the line and turned with her.

"Oh, he's so much taller than Sarah," she said.

"Watch how he makes the adjustment to her lack of height." Bellingham met her gaze. "Someone taught him well."

His words made her feel a little breathless, and everything inside of her bubbled up until she really was in fear of losing her heart to him. But she knew there were limitations on what he was willing to give. Most of all, she knew he shielded his own heart, and that alone should douse her ardor.

Tonight she would allow herself to bask in his attentions, but tomorrow in the light of day, she would remember that it was only friendship and nothing more.

"The dance will end soon," Bellingham said. "Let's walk away so they don't realize we're spying."

She took his arm and immediately noticed others staring at them. Laura suspected that he was a much-hunted prize among the single ladies, and quite probably the married ones, too. Doubtless they resented her for usurping him, but she would not worry about them tonight. A year from now, she would remember this special night he'd given her.

He led her to the punch bowl and poured her a cup. At that moment, Lady Norcliffe rushed forward. "Do not drink it. I caught Harry dumping brandy in it."

While Lady Norcliffe directed the servants to cart off the strong brew, Colin joined them. "It's Harry's annual tradition to spike the punch bowl at his mother's ball. He insists the strong punch is the only reason anyone attends."

"You never know quite what to expect with Harry except the unexpected," Bellingham said.

Tonight that applied to Bellingham as well.

An older man approached them. Bellingham introduced him as one of his political allies. When the gentleman mentioned a bill in parliament, Laura knew she must mingle with others or there would most certainly be rumors about her and Bellingham. She craned her head and saw Lady Atherton. "Please excuse me. I see my friend."

Bellingham caught her hand. "Before you go, will you promise the first waltz to me?"

Oh, dear. This would definitely be a night to remember. "How could I say no?"

He kissed her glove and let her go.

Laura joined Lady Atherton in one of the chairs near the wall and unfurled her fan.

"What are you doing here?" Lady Atherton said, holding her own fan up to shield her words. "You were making a conquest of Bellingham and walked away."

Laura wafted her fan. "You know we are only friends." Oh, if only she weren't such a terrible liar.

Lady Atherton snorted. "I saw what he did for your son, and I also saw the look on your face. You're in love with him."

"There is no future for us, but tonight I confess I'm a

little infatuated." She gave her friend a wry smile. "How could any woman resist such thoughtfulness?"

"I daresay you have a flair for making gentlemen long for your company," Lady Atherton said. "Pembroke is hunting for you as we speak."

"Oh," she said. "Bellingham forewarned me."

"Did he? That is very interesting."

"I'm grateful he told me. Apparently word has spread that my husband left me a fortune."

"Do you think Pembroke is a fortune hunter?"

"No. He is a very nice man, but he is almost too obliging."

"The bald spot is unfortunate, I'll give you that," Lady Atherton said.

Laura shook her head. "I am not so shallow as to judge a man by his hair."

"Well, you are a better woman than me."

Laura clapped her hand over her mouth to stifle her laughter.

"Pembroke is coming this way," Lady Atherton said. "My, my, he is eager."

Laura released a long sigh. Pembroke had called upon her twice. The first time, he'd regaled her with Bellingham's lengthy list of conquests, which had ended up sounding like childish tattling to her. The second time, however, he'd concentrated on himself and listed all of the excellent qualities he possessed. By the time he'd finished, she'd been tempted to ask him if he were a candidate for sainthood.

"Lady Chesfield, how fortunate to meet with you again so soon," Pembroke said.

"Good evening, Lord Pembroke," she said.

"I hoped to secure the first waltz," he said.

"I beg your pardon, but I have already promised that to another gentleman."

"Who?" he demanded.

Lady Atherton snapped her fan closed. "Pembroke, have you forgotten your manners? How dare you ask such a question? If you had wanted that dance, you should have asked earlier."

He bowed and his hair flopped over his bald spot. "Please forgive me." When he rose, he hurriedly adjusted the thin strands of hair. "I just cannot bear to think of another man enjoying a minute of your wonderful company when I might possess you."

"My lord, I am not a possession."

He put his hand over his heart. "Of course you are not. I only meant for the length of the midnight supper. Do say you will do me the great honor of accompanying me?"

Laura desperately tried to think of an excuse, but he was a nice man, even if he was a bit too eager. "Very well," she said.

"I shall count the minutes," he said. Then he walked away with a jaunty air.

"If I had known he was so foolish, I never would have insisted you dance with him at my ball," Lady Atherton said.

"Granted, he does carry things a bit too far sometimes, but overall, he does wish to please."

"A bit too much, if you ask me," Lady Atherton said.

"Oh, look, there is Justin and Sarah," Laura said. "Doesn't he look debonair leaning against the pillar?"

"He is a handsome young man and likely to be a favorite with all the young ladies," Lady Atherton said.

"I hope so," Laura said. "I always thought I saw a bit of Phillip in him."

"Look, there are late arrivals," Lady Atherton said. "The Duke and Duchess of Shelbourne."

"Oh, yes, you introduced me to her recently," Laura said. "What a dashing couple they are."

"Their love story is most unusual," Lady Atherton said. "I would venture to say that it was the most romantic proposal that anyone can remember."

"They look very happy," Laura said wistfully.

Lady Atherton sighed. "Some couples are meant to be together." She regarded Laura with a knowing smile.

Bellingham saw Laura speaking to Harry's numerous female cousins. There was something infectious about her laughter, and when she smiled, she lit up from within like a candle flame. He'd made her happy tonight, and now at last he would claim her for the waltz.

As he threaded his way through the crowd, Laura turned round. Bell kept his eyes on her as he strolled toward her. A moment later, Pembroke dashed through the crowd and accosted her.

Bell gritted his teeth and strode over to her in time to hear Pembroke attempting to usurp his dance with Laura.

"Well, I see you are still waiting for your partner," Pembroke was saying. "You mustn't worry about the earl's negligence. It is one of the signs of a rake. Now, I will gladly take his place."

Bell tapped Pembroke on the shoulder. Harry's female cousins hid their smiles behind their fans as Pembroke turned.

"Oh, you're late, Bellingham," Pembroke said. "I have already offered to partner Lady Chesfield."

"She promised the waltz to me earlier."

"I'm sure she did not know how to refuse you." Pembroke turned toward her. "Lady Chesfield, allow me to escort you."

"You must wait your turn," she said. "Now please excuse me."

Bell offered his arm. She took it, and they strolled away.

"I thought Pembroke a sensible man, but he certainly forgot his manners," Laura said.

Bell leaned his head toward her. "He has the notion that we're in competition for you."

"What? That's silly," she said.

"Every time I go to White's, he makes a point of telling me that he called on you or plans to call on you."

"He stayed overly long yesterday," she said. "Today I informed Reed to say that I was not at home."

Bell grinned. "I'm happy to hear it."

She gave him a pointed look. "You will not compete over me."

"Very well. May I try to impress you?" he said.

"You know that you did tonight," she said.

They reached the dance floor, and he leaned closer. "I want to please you."

She lowered her lashes, because his words held a sensual meaning. "You confuse me sometimes."

"Can it just be enough for tonight?" he asked.

The orchestra played the opening bars. "For tonight," she said.

He clasped her waist and her hand. As they turned to the one-two-three rhythm, he thought they danced well together, despite the differences in height. He imagined he could sweep her up in his arms so easily.

When he turned in ever-widening circles three times, she laughed. "You're making me dizzy," she said.

He shortened his steps. "Who taught you to waltz?"

"Phillip," she said, averting her gaze.

He'd asked the wrong question. "Sorry."

"Don't be," she said. "Who taught you?"

All the muscles in his arms tightened. "My mother." He'd stupidly opened up the topic, but he didn't want to talk about her.

She looked up at him. "I taught Justin."

"He's lucky." That was all he could manage.

"I'm the lucky one," she said. "If not for you, I would be dancing with Pembroke."

He smiled a little. It struck him that she knew how to lighten the mood at the right time. She'd probably had to do it on a daily basis for her late husband.

He turned her in a wide circle until they reached the end of the dance floor, and then he offered his arm. Bell caught Pembroke staring daggers as he escorted her off the dance floor. "I'll take you to the refreshment table for a cup of punch."

"I think we should separate," she said. "If we spend too much time together, we might stir gossip."

"Of course," he said. Then he reluctantly let her go, because it was the sensible thing to do. But for once, logic held no appeal.

Laura needed to be alone to sort out her feelings for Bellingham. "Lady Atherton, I must go to the ladies' retiring room. I need to freshen up a bit."

"Go on, dear. You're smart to do so. These balls can be exhausting if you do not take a bit of time to rest."

"Thank you. I will return shortly," she said. Perhaps one day soon, she would ask her friend's advice. Tonight her emotions were bouncing up and down. She needed time alone to reflect on everything that had happened with Bellingham in the last fortnight. Laura was a little frightened of her feelings and very unsure of Bell's intentions. But that was the problem. He likely had no intentions, other than friendship. Then why would he encourage her? There was no mistaking that he had done so.

When she stepped out onto the landing, Pembroke was waiting. He was the last man she wished to see right now, but he made a beeline for her. "There you are," he said. "I grew concerned when I saw you leave Bellingham's side. I hope he did not say anything to vex you."

She had no intention of explaining to him. "I beg your pardon," she said. "I am on my way to the ladies' retiring room."

He started walking on the stairs with her. "Tell me what he did, and I will have a word with him."

"I do not need you to interfere," she said.

"Of course, I did not mean to pry. I was only concerned, given his reputation." Pembroke continued to natter on, but she ignored him. When she reached the next landing, he kept walking alongside her down the corridor. Finally she halted. "Lord Pembroke, you cannot follow me to the ladies' retiring room."

"Oh, how silly of me. Really, I was taken with your beauty, and I only wanted to remind you about the midnight supper."

She continued down the corridor. "I have not forgotten," she said.

"Very good. Oh, I shall count the minutes," he said. "Just hearing your sweet voice—"

"Lord Pembroke, I am for the ladies' retiring room. You should return to the ballroom," she said.

"Oh, yes, of course. How remiss of me," he said.

As she opened the door, he called out, "Don't forget."

Laura winced. She wished she'd never agreed, but what was done was done. After entering the retiring room, she sat upon a settee. A maid offered her sweetmeats, but Laura declined. At last, she was able to think about all that had occurred during the waltz.

They had been teasing one another, and then he'd swept her into a dizzying waltz. All had been lightness and amusement until that moment she'd asked him who had taught him how to waltz. She'd felt the tension in his arms when he'd spoken two words: *My mother.*

His wounds were deep. Lady Atherton had told her that much. Others knew of the tragedy and probably speculated. Quite possibly no one really knew him. Or perhaps he was simpler than she thought. He spoke plainly and made no attempt to soften his words just because she was a female. Heavens, she would never forget his words about sexual needs.

Beyond that, she knew only a few facts about him. He lived alone and took his parliamentary duties seriously. His friends had revealed that he liked order in his life. But there were other aspects of him she could not help noticing. The way Bellingham dealt with Justin seemed ingrained in him. He'd instinctively adopted the discipline and good principles handed down by his late father, but he'd clearly been unwilling to speak about his father that night she'd broached the subject. He knew the sorts of things that boys enjoyed. Most of all, he'd known Justin had been intimidated about asking Sarah to dance and had encouraged him.

He would make a wonderful father.

The thought had popped into her head, and now she wished to chase it out, because that road was destined for heartache. He had many good qualities and a few irritating ones, but one thing was clear. He had no intention of ever marrying and carrying on the earldom. And she had never considered remarrying because of her own fears. He knew that she didn't wish to marry again, and so he was safe from her.

He could tease her, flirt with her, and say things that would make her heart flutter. They were both trying very hard to pretend that what was between them didn't exist. But it did, and she knew she must resist the pull that he exerted on her.

Laura sat in the dining room with Pembroke and toyed with the lobster patties that he'd insisted upon bringing to her. She had no appetite, and yet he kept bringing her fruit and cheese. At least his short absence was a reprieve from his nonstop chattering. A few minutes later, Pembroke's voice broke through her thoughts. "There you are, safe and sound," he said. "I feared you would disappear." He laughed as he set more food before her.

Her temples were starting to ache.

"I confess I'm jealous you awarded the waltz to Bellingham," Pembroke continued. "You must promise me the waltz at the next ball."

She was growing weary of him. "A gentleman asks."

"I do apologize," he said. "I do not usually forget myself. Oh, dear, you must think me witless, but surely you will forgive a tiny mistake."

She rose. "Please excuse me."

"Are you unwell?" he asked. "Perhaps I could bring you something else? You barely touched the lobster patties."

"Lord Pembroke, I thank you for escorting me to the midnight supper, but you needn't be so attentive," she said.

"But I wish to be attentive," he said.

"My mother had an old saying: There can be too much of a good thing."

"But—"

"I wish to find my son. Enjoy the supper," she said, and quit the dining room. The man tried too hard to please, and in the process all he did was make himself disagreeable to others. She wished to be kind to him, but she had better not allow him in her drawing room again. He'd stayed far past the usual twenty minutes the last time, and he'd not stopped talking. Poor man. He really didn't know how to get on with others.

Laura climbed the stairs and entered the ballroom. It wasn't as noisy since many of the guests were downstairs partaking of the supper. Admittedly, she was rather surprised that Justin had not joined the throng in the dining room, considering his large appetite. She often joked that he was like a bottomless well.

Then she saw Justin sitting beside Sarah and smiled. She would not interrupt them. The guests were returning to the ballroom in droves. Laura craned her neck, looking for Lady Atherton.

"There you are," Lady Norcliffe said. "I have been looking for you all evening."

A gentleman stood next to her. Laura grew a bit flustered when his gaze dropped to her bosom.

"Lady Chesfield, Lord Lindmoore applied to me for an introduction. May I?"

"Yes, of course," Laura said.

Lindmoore bowed over her hand. "I've heard so much about you, but you are even more beautiful than I was led to believe."

"I hope you are enjoying the ball," Laura said. Something about the man made her more than a little uneasy.

"May I take you to the refreshment table for a cup of punch?"

She scrambled to think of an excuse to evade him when another gentleman appeared.

"See here, Lindmoore, you will not keep her all to yourself."

Laura regarded Lady Norcliffe with raised brows.

"Stovington, you know the rules of conduct. If you wish an introduction, you must apply to me or another lady of her acquaintance first."

"Forgive me. I was overcome by Lady Chesfield's beauty."

Laura was growing weary of their overblown compliments and figured they were more interested in her fortune than anything else. She'd decided to plead weariness and excuse herself when a gentleman by the name of Brodely arrived. Their avid stares disconcerted her. The gentlemen started arguing over who would get the next dance with her. She was on the verge of claiming a sore ankle when Bellingham appeared. "Gentlemen, all of her dances are spoken for."

Laura pressed her lips together. Once again, he'd taken over.

He met her gaze and offered his arm. She took it, because she didn't want to make a scene, although the men had certainly acted foolish.

As Bell led her away, he looked at her. "You may thank me now."

"I intended to make a graceful exit," she said. "Then you had to come along and make things worse."

"I rescued you from that pack of jackals. Every last one of them is a fortune hunter."

"I agree they made a spectacle, but I was perfectly capable of handling the situation."

"You don't know what they were thinking," he said in a gruff voice.

"That is beside the point."

He led her over to a chair near the fireplace. "No, it isn't beside the point. Every last one them are rogues and gamesters."

She raised her brows. "Do you think I didn't guess what sort of men they are?"

"Damn it, Laura, I meant to protect you."

"I can protect myself," she said.

He gave her a look that clearly indicated he disagreed.

"It is a miracle I managed to safely reach twenty-eight years without mishap—until you came along, that is."

His jaw worked. "I did, in fact, protect you and your son from Montclief, but I suppose that no longer counts."

"I am not insensible about all that you have done for us, but I do not need you to step in and rescue me."

"Are you so proud that you will not accept my assistance?"

"I have relied on you, but you do not give me credit. I managed quite well before I ever met you, and I will continue to do so. Understand this—I don't need or want you to rescue me."

He leaned forward with his elbows on his thighs. After a few minutes, he sat back. "You are very independent for a woman."

"Your mistresses were independent, were they not?"

"That topic is off-limits."

"Why?"

"They were not independent. I was their protector. I paid for their keep. I trust you understand what I received in return."

"What happened when you tired of them?" she asked.

"There were contracts. Pensions."

She bit her lip. "Where did they go?"

"They found new protectors," he said.

"So they have to be independent," she said. "They cannot rely on any one man."

"What is your point? I would think you would find the subject inappropriate."

"The point is that men may rule the world, but women have to be self-reliant because a man may not always be there for them."

He was silent for what seemed like an age. "It's true for men as well. The people you depend on will not always be there."

She met his gaze. "Your family."

"I don't want to talk about them, Laura."

"If or when you wish to talk, I will listen," she said.

"They're gone, and that's all."

No, it wasn't all, but a ballroom wasn't the place for such a discussion, and she knew by his responses that he was unwilling to say more on the subject.

One week later

Laura had decided to embroider a handkerchief for Bellingham. She had dithered because she wasn't sure whether to use his formal title or his initials. In the end, she'd decided to make it personal by using his Christian name. While she knew she was taking liberties, she'd decided to make a jest of her indecisiveness.

She wanted the gift to be a special gesture, a thank-you for all that he'd done for her and Justin. But she ought not to even think about his Christian name, let alone use it this way. She would tell him that it was a mark of her respect and gratefulness.

A light tap sounded. "Come in, Reed."

Bellingham opened the door. "I hope I'm not interrupting."

"Oh, no, not at all." She quickly shoved the handkerchief beneath another baby gown she'd been embroidering and hoped she didn't look as flustered as she felt.

He sat beside her on the sofa. "Not long after I first met you, I decided to instigate an investigation into Montclief's affairs."

Laura stared at him. "Why did you not tell me?"

"I didn't want to alarm you and thought it best to wait until I received a report. Given Montclief's disrespectful treatment of you, I suspected something was wrong."

"You have news?" she said.

He nodded. "You said your husband left him a fortune, but something is very wrong. He's bleeding the tenants."

"Oh, dear God."

"He has obviously run through all of his money."

She gasped. "But how? Why?"

"I don't know yet. The investigator noted that Montclief leaves Goatham Green periodically for as long as a fortnight on a regular basis. As you can imagine, the investigator must use great care so as not to tip him off."

"Montclief is a fool," Laura said. "I suppose we'll have to wait to find out more."

"I thought you should know."

"Justin's fortune is in trust," she said. "It is safe."

"But meanwhile, Montclief could take over the property. The real stickler is that if Justin were your natural child, your husband would have named the nearest relative on the mother's side, who could not inherit. But I take it there was no one."

She shook her head.

"He's obviously desperate for money. He may try to oust you from Hollwood Abbey so that he can take advantage of Justin's property. But this is all speculation."

Her heart was beating too fast. "I will try not to borrow trouble, but it is difficult."

"Promise me you won't worry," he said. "I wanted you to be informed, but I'll feel badly if you're overset."

"I'll keep busy with my embroidery, and I have a meeting tomorrow with the society for the orphans." She didn't tell him that her nerves were on edge, because he didn't want her to worry, but she knew already that it would prove futile.

"I must go," he said.

She stood and stumbled over the sewing basket. He caught her with his strong arms and pulled her back. "Oh, my, how clumsy of me."

"I feared you would fall," he said. "You didn't twist your ankle, I hope?"

"No, I'm fine." She saw half the contents of her sewing basket scattered on the floor. She didn't want him to see the handkerchief. She started to bend down, but he stopped her. "Let me."

Her face heated. Oh, God. Why had she ever thought it would be appropriate to embroider his Christian name?

He would know that she'd developed feelings for him. It would be so mortifying.

He bent down on one knee as he placed the items inside. She couldn't stand it any longer. She bent down and picked up the handkerchief while he retrieved the baby gown she was embroidering. Using the sofa arm for support, she rose and trembled a little.

He frowned at the baby gown.

"My sister Mary is expecting her first child this summer," she said, hoping she didn't sound as breathless as she felt.

"Ah, I see." He looked at her quizzically.

"What is it?" she asked.

He shrugged. "It's nothing."

"I insist." She hastily stuffed the half-finished handkerchief beneath the scraps of fabric in the basket.

"You indicated you never plan to marry, but you seem like the sort of woman who likes infants. Then again, you took care of your younger siblings when you were growing up. Perhaps you had your fill."

She kept the smile plastered on her face, but a little

piece of her heart crumbled. Her dream of having her own babe would never come true.

He stood and dusted off his knees. "I will be sure to let you know of any news about Montclief."

After he left, she sank onto the sofa and put her head in her hands. He could not have known that his words about the infant gown would pierce her heart. Worse still, he'd come within inches of seeing that handkerchief.

She must be honest with herself, because she had allowed herself to develop strong feelings for him. The worst part was that she'd begun spinning fantasies. In her mind, she pictured sitting with him and Justin in the drawing room after supper. She imagined calling them her boys and watching them play backgammon while she embroidered. Sometimes she imagined placing her hand over a rounded belly, but that only made her sad.

When the season ended, she and Bellingham would go their separate ways. She knew it would be hard, but she would always remember him.

A footman brought a tray with the mail. "Thank you," Laura said.

She opened the invitations and was delighted to see that Mrs. Woodley, the secretary of the Society to Benefit the Orphans, had accepted her offer to host the meeting. The other four invitations were for balls. She smiled. Perhaps she would make friends in London after all.

Feeling buoyant, she opened a letter. It was from Rachel. Laura smiled as she read about the problem of Mr. Hunmaker's snoring in church. Apparently, he had interrupted Papa's sermon to the point that no one could hear. Mrs. Landon had solved the problem by rapping her parasol on Mr. Hunmaker's prodigious nose.

Smiling, Laura turned the page around in order to read the crossed portion of the letter. Her smile faded as she read Rachel's warning.

Dearest sister, you know how much our mother dotes on reading the doings of the ton in the Daily Tattler. Of course, it is always two weeks late, but rain or shine, Mama rushes to Mr. Jones's shop to purchase it. Imagine if you will her initial excitement upon reading that a certain widow new about town was seen with the Earl of B-ham at a ball. Mama was so over the moon that Papa actually condescended to read what he calls the Daily Rag.

Since he reads every word of the Times, he quickly deduced that the man was none other than the Earl of Bellingham, who is evidently a famous politician. We were all delighted that you had made his acquaintance, until Mama grew very quiet. Papa asked her why she looked so vexatious, and she could not speak for a full minute. Then she admitted that she had read the earl's name in connection with numerous ladies (whose names are not well concealed) over the past two years. Papa's expression turned almost purple, and he was ready to take the stage to London in order to have a "word" with the "notorious rakehell." I then managed to persuade him to let me write to you so that you could reassure all of us.

I am quite sure that there is a reasonable explanation, as I told all of our family. I can almost hear you laughing at our concerns over what was probably a brief introduction to a haughty lord who looked down his patrician nose at you. In light of Papa's concerns, I do urge you to respond as quickly as possible.

Laura inhaled sharply. She retrieved her lap desk and drew out paper, pen, and ink. She was so rattled she blotted the first page and had to start another. With a deep breath, she told herself to slow down and be calm. She would tell her family only as much as she thought they needed to know.

Dear Rachel,

First, I wish to assure you and our parents that there is no cause for alarm. It is true that I am acquainted with the Earl of Bellingham. I met him in a most peculiar set of circumstances that involve Justin. You will no doubt chide me for withholding a behavioral problem that arose with him, but I did not want all of you to worry when we were so far away.

You are aware that the reason I traveled to London was in order to give Justin a chance to see his friends here. I had no idea that his friends were wild. As it turns out, the Earl of Bellingham caught Justin hiding a flask containing spirits. After consulting our mutual friend Lady Atherton, he called upon me to inform me of Justin's transgression. Matters grew worse when Montclief learned of Justin's behavior. I will keep this brief, but essentially, the earl offered to provide guidance to Justin after Montclief threatened to remove him from my care. You can well imagine how terrified I was of losing my son.

To be honest, I was reluctant at first to allow the earl to assist with disciplining Justin, but Bellingham soon proved to be more than capable. He has been an excellent role model for Justin and has introduced him to fencing. I am grateful to him for his kindness and count him as a friend. When I return home, I will tell you all of the details. For now, I trust that you will convey all of my love to everyone and let them know that we are enjoying our London adventure.

Yours etc.
Laura

Her conscience roared at her as she reviewed the letter she had written. She had omitted the sham engagement, and of course, she would never tell her family that she had kissed the earl more than once.

Laura told herself that it would be impossible to explain every circumstance in a letter. It would only cause her family needless concern. When she returned home, she would confess everything to Rachel in private and ask her to forgive her for withholding so much information. By then, all the problems would be resolved, and she would be left with the memories of a man who had gone out of his way to help her son.

She sealed the letter, accepted the invitations, and rang for a footman. A few minutes later, Reed appeared. "My lady, Lord Pembroke has come to call."

Laura did not want to see him, and she most certainly

did not want to encourage him. "Please inform him that I am not at home."

Reed nodded, took her letters, and quit the drawing room.

Laura returned to her embroidery, but voices on the stairs interrupted her.

"My lord, her ladyship is not receiving."

"I must see her immediately," Pembroke said.

Laura groaned. If only the draperies were longer, she might hide behind them. She tucked the embroidery back in the basket and rose.

The door flew open and Pembroke marched inside like a rooster. "I will not take no for an answer."

Reed stood behind him with a harried expression.

"My lord, you are welcome to cool your heels in my drawing room. Good day."

When she took a step, Pembroke grabbed her hand and knelt on one knee. "My lady, allow me to express my ardent—"

"No, I will not allow it," she said, yanking her hand away. "My answer would only create ill feelings. Please abide by the proprieties and leave me in peace."

"But I can no longer contain my admiration and tender feelings for you."

She suspected his tender feelings were the work of a fervid imagination. "My lord, I do not wish to be the cause of any wounds, but I highly recommend you do not utter words that will embarrass both of us."

"I thought you understood how I feel," he said.

She sighed. "Please stand." When he did, she said, "You are a very nice man, but you must find someone who will return your, er, ardent feelings."

"I feared it was thus," Pembroke said. "You are married to the grave."

"In a manner of speaking, I suppose that is correct." She saw the disappointment on his face and sought to make him feel better. "You deserve a woman who will appreciate your enthusiasm, and most of all, you deserve someone who will share your interests and love you heart and soul." She smiled. "Let me know when you find her."

He sighed. "I worried your answer would not be in the affirmative and thought I would be in lowered spirits, but you have managed to reject me in the kindest way possible."

Obviously he had expected her refusal. "I hope so, Lord Pembroke."

"Are you certain you won't change your mind?" he asked.

She laughed at his persistence. "I'm certain. Thank you for the great honor. Now bestow it on someone you know will be thrilled to accept."

Chapter Nine

Laura returned home after a day of shopping with Lady Atherton and invited her to join her for tea. As the servants carried her numerous purchases upstairs, she smiled at her friend. "I fear I'm too free with my spending," she said.

"Nonsense," Lady Atherton said as they climbed the stairs. "What good is money if you don't buy things that make you happy?"

They stepped inside the drawing room, and Laura produced a stool for Lady Atherton.

"Thank you, dear. I fear my feet complain when I use them too much."

Laura laughed and rang the bell. After instructing the maid to bring the tea tray, she sat on the other side of the sofa. "I excuse my shopping habits by making most of the purchases for my family."

"I'm sure they appreciate your gifts," she said.

"Before I married Phillip, I was relegated to looking

in shop windows and dreaming of buying all the pretty shawls and hats I saw. So now I do not have a great deal of self-control. It is probably a good thing that all the pretty temptations in London are not very close to home."

When Lady Atherton set her feet on the carpet, she turned to view Laura and inadvertently upset the sewing basket on the floor. "Oh, dear, I've made a mess."

"It's quite all right," Laura said, starting to rise. "I've overturned it more than once. I always forget to push it out of the way."

"Stay where you are. I'm not an invalid," she said, putting items back inside. When she picked up the handkerchief, she regarded Laura with raised brows. "Andrew? As in Carrington, the Earl of Bellingham?"

Laura winced. "He has been so good to Justin. I honestly do not know what I would have done without his help. I wanted to make a gift for him, but I should not have used his given name. It was silly of me." Her face heated. "I'm so embarrassed."

"My dear, I wondered if you had developed tender feelings for him."

"Only as a friend," she said. Why had she left the handkerchief out in plain sight? What if he had seen it the other day? The humiliation would have been too much to bear.

"You can be honest with me. Anything you say will go no farther." Lady Atherton paused and added, "Sometimes it helps to discuss these things with a friend. I'm guessing you're confused."

"No, I'm not confused," she said. "I've just fantasized like a silly schoolgirl, that's all."

The maid arrived with the tea tray, and Laura was glad for the interruption. She hoped to turn the conversation in a new direction. As she poured the tea, Laura said, "I'm looking forward to my first meeting of the charitable society for the orphans. I admit I was a bit disappointed that we would not actually visit the orphans, but I suppose that isn't acceptable."

"No lady should venture into that part of town," Lady Atherton said, accepting a cup. "Now, you have turned the conversation, but I wish to circle back."

"So much for my attempts to divert you."

Lady Atherton set her cup aside. "The night of my ball, I saw the way Bellingham looked at you."

"Yes, and you warned me not to become one of his conquests."

"Allow me to continue," Lady Atherton said. "Later that evening, he insisted upon personally returning that flask. I knew then that he had conceived a partiality for you."

"We had not even spoken," Laura said.

"My dear, men are visual creatures. He was mesmerized at first glance."

"He soon was caught up in my problems with Montclief. I was desperate and said we were engaged. He was too much of a gentleman to deny my claim."

Lady Atherton snorted. "I know Bellingham. He would not have supported you unless he had some expectation of being rewarded."

Laura tried to control her reaction, but her face heated.

Lady Atherton studied her. "What did he demand in recompense?"

"He made no demands," she said.

"Then you must have promised him something," Lady Atherton said.

"You are as relentless as he is," she said. "If you must know, I told him I would do anything if he did not expose me."

"Dear God, tell me you didn't go to bed with him."

"Of course I didn't!" she cried.

Lady Atherton pressed her hand to her heart. "Thank goodness. No man will buy the cow if he can get the milk for free."

Laura burst out laughing. "I assure you he is not interested in buying the cow."

"Did he kiss you?" Lady Atherton said.

"I refuse to answer that question. In any case, I would never kiss and tell," she said.

"You just answered my question," Lady Atherton said.

"I beg your pardon?"

"If you had not kissed, you would have said so."

"We have formed a friendship. He intimated to Montclief—or rather I did—that he would provide guidance to Justin. He is a gentleman and has kept his word. I've had trouble with Justin, and Bellingham has been of great assistance."

"It's a convenient arrangement," Lady Atherton said. "Before you become defensive again, hear me out."

"Very well."

"I have no doubt that he is good with the boy."

Laura frowned. "To be honest, I think the way he handles Justin is remarkable. More than once I've suspected his methods were learned at his father's side."

"I'm not surprised. He had an excellent father and a loving mother. She drew pictures of her boys and displayed them." She sighed. "Bellingham was away at university when the three of them succumbed to consumption. The doctors warned him to stay away since he was the heir. Near the end, he rushed home, or so I've been told, but he was too late."

Laura covered her mouth.

"I think his interest in guiding your son is a very good sign," Lady Atherton said. "Perhaps there is hope for him to heal."

Laura sipped her tea, remembering his words while they waltzed. *My mother.*

After all these years, he'd probably learned to cope with the grief by going on with life, the way everyone did. She could understand. When Phillip died, she'd gone through the motions, but her son's needs had given her purpose. Concentrating on Justin had helped her to get through the worst part. But Bellingham had been young and had no time to prepare. She'd been fortunate to have those four extra years with her husband, but she'd hated seeing him suffer. No matter how death came, it was always a shock.

Lady Atherton finished her tea. "Did you receive an invitation to the Bonhams' ball? It is in a fortnight."

"Yes, I was very surprised, since we've not met. Did you suggest they send an invitation to me?"

"Of course I did. Will you accompany me?"

"I would be delighted," she said.

Lady Atherton smiled. "Perhaps a certain earl will be there."

"The handkerchief was a mistake—just a passing fancy. I am done with spinning fantasies in my head."

* * *

Five days later

Laura looked out the window once again. She'd told herself that he must be busy. He was a prominent politician, after all, and had many duties with his properties. But another voice, one deep inside, answered that he'd always made time for them before. She shouldn't assume the worst. He'd always kept his word in the past. Tomorrow was Justin's fencing day. Bell would call for him at ten o'clock as he'd always done before.

Her silly worries were for nothing. She returned to the sofa and continued embroidering the handkerchief for him. For reasons she didn't understand, she felt compelled to finish it, even though she didn't have the courage to give it to him.

A tap sounded at the door. Laura's heart leaped. She rose and shook out her skirts, expecting Bell to walk inside and say as he always did that he'd told Reed not to bother, since Bell knew his way upstairs. "Come in," Laura said.

Reed entered and brought her a letter.

"Thank you," she said, trying to mask her disappointment. She must be patient. He would call soon. Something had come up. Perhaps he was gathering information about Montclief and wanted to ensure everything was correct before calling to give her the latest news.

She perched on the sofa and set the handkerchief aside. After breaking the seal, she opened a short missive. She surveyed the page and saw his signature. Then she read the note.

Dear Lady Chesfield,

*Business detains me on Thursday. I have arranged
for Angelo himself to give Justin his fencing lesson.
Please convey my apologies to your son. I hope all
is well with both of you.*

> *Yours truly,
> Bellingham*

The missive was so impersonal that it shocked her.
She told herself that his use of her title was probably
a customary formality for him. Perhaps he was terse
because of his obligations. Perhaps he was mired in a
difficult problem. Perhaps he'd gotten news about Montclief and wished to have all the facts in order before
calling upon her.

She was making excuses for him as she had done all
week. There was no justification for that detached senti-
ment in his note. Even if he was very busy, he could have
apologized in advance for having to sign off so quickly.
But he'd done none of that.

He'd made arrangements for her son, and yet, he'd not
included even one truly personal comment for her. This
was not a note from one friend to another. This was a note
that insinuated he'd tired of her and wished to spend his
time elsewhere.

Pain wrenched her heart. Her eyes welled, and she
swiped at the tears. Part of her still wanted to believe that
she was wrong, that he would have a good explanation
and apologize for the brevity of the note. But she couldn't
fool herself. That letter was curt.

He'd probably found a woman who would give him what he wanted. What had she expected of a notorious rake? He'd shown his true colors with that note. She took a deep breath. It was her own fault. She'd been warned in advance that he was a cold man, but he'd seemed so different. He'd helped her, and now she could almost feel him pushing her away.

She had no idea why he'd done this, but she knew one thing. If he were really her friend, he would not treat her in this distant manner. She told herself she didn't care. Why should she when he clearly did not have enough regard for her to speak to her face-to-face and explain his callous actions?

How dare he treat her in this cold manner? She'd thought he cared about her and Justin. He'd waltzed with her and made her feel special. And now he'd made it clear he wanted nothing more to do with them.

She marched over to the fire and threw the note on the hot coals. She'd let him into her heart, and in a few short words, he'd crushed her. He could go hang for all she cared. If she saw him again, she would give him the cut direct.

Her face crumpled. She didn't want to cry over him, but the tears came anyway.

One week later

Bell strolled into White's and hailed Harry and Colin. When he reached their usual table, he took his chair and said, "Miss me?"

Harry snorted. "Like a bad egg."

"What is that supposed to mean?" Colin said.

"I think he just said I stink," Bell said.

"You've been busy," Harry said.

"I've been mired in letters, invitations, and banker meetings." Bell didn't tell them that he'd put distance between himself and Laura. He'd gotten too caught up in her life. Justin needed a male role model, but he needed a permanent one. All Bell could offer was a few fencing and billiards lessons. He ought to have foreseen the consequences, but somehow in the midst of one crisis after another, he'd lost sight of what was transpiring beneath his nose. In retrospect, he ought to have encouraged Laura to take her son home to Hampshire. He wondered why he hadn't thought of it, but he knew the reason. The same one that had led him to get involved in her life.

He was attracted to her, but there was something else. She was his friend. He liked her—more than a little. And he thought about her far more than he ought. He'd realized he was in a little too deep. In truth, he'd become a bit obsessed with her. No good could come from that.

"So how is Lady Chesfield?" Colin asked.

Bell shrugged. "I don't know."

His friends exchanged glances.

"You haven't called on her?" Harry asked.

"I've been busy."

Colin leaned forward. "So you're giving her the brush-off?"

Bell released a loud sigh. "She's the prim-and-proper sort. I'm not. It's time to take a step back. "

"She's the kind who wants forever," Harry said.

Laura had said she didn't want to remarry, but he'd seen the look on her face when he'd picked up that infant gown, and that had checked him. "It's better to cut the ties now," Bell said. He'd continue with Justin's fencing lessons until the end of the season and let Laura know any news of the investigation.

Colin circled his finger along the rim of his glass. "I like her."

"Me too," Harry said.

"It's best to ease out of the picture before she gets attached," Bell said.

"I think you're a bit late for that," Colin said.

Bell swigged his brandy. It burned going down, and so did the knowledge that he had probably wounded her. He'd never intended to get so deeply involved in her life, but they were too different. She needed things that he couldn't give her: a ring, a promise, and a family.

Twice she'd managed to get him to answer questions about his mother and father. She didn't try to prod him the way others had done, but he'd sensed she wanted to know more.

Laura was a caretaker, a role she'd assumed as a child while helping her mother. He knew she'd genuinely loved her late husband, but she'd chosen a man who was elderly and sick—and who had a motherless son as well. She needed to be needed.

He suspected that Laura wanted to fix him. Knowing her, she probably thought she could heal him with tenderness and love. She didn't understand that some things were broken beyond repair, and other things were better off forgotten and relegated to a dusty attic, both literally and figuratively.

"I heard Pembroke proposed to her," Harry said.

Bell jerked his chin up. "What?"

"My girl cousins told me," Harry said.

"I heard it, too," Colin said.

"She didn't accept Pembroke," he said.

"How do you know?" Colin said. "Maybe she likes Baldy."

"She can't accept him—or rather she wouldn't."

"Why?" Harry asked.

"She's secretly engaged to me."

His friends burst out laughing.

"You mean the faux engagement," Colin said, still laughing.

Harry slapped the table. "I still can't believe that one. What a lark."

"Will you lower your voices? I don't want anyone to know."

Colin snorted. "No one would believe it."

"Stubble it," Bell grumbled. "We agreed to be friends, but I got the idea she wanted more."

"More what?" Colin said.

"I think she wants something permanent."

"You mean marriage," Harry said.

"I'm a lifelong bachelor—not the sort of man she needs."

"Right," Harry said. "You don't want her, so why should you care who calls on her?"

"Wait a minute," Bell said. "Are you saying other men are calling on her?"

"Actually, they called at Lady Atherton's," Harry said. "My mother said it was like a parade. All the gents want to meet her."

"Devil take it," Bell said. "The same thing happened at the ball. She insists upon being independent, but she has no idea what those men are thinking."

"About what?" Harry said.

"You know what," Bell said. "They think a widow is fair game."

Harry shrugged. "Isn't that what you thought?"

Every muscle in Bell's body tightened. "I have to call on her. Now."

Colin pulled out his watch. "It's nearly midnight. Not a good idea."

"Call on her tomorrow," Harry said.

"Damnation," he said. He removed a gold case and offered his friends a cheroot. Bell lit his with the candle. He thought it would make him calmer, but it didn't.

"A piece of advice," Colin said. "Don't go charging into her drawing room like a bull."

"I will clear the room," he growled.

Harry blew a smoke ring. "Wait a minute. I thought you planned to ease out of the picture."

"I can't now," he said. "She needs protection from those horny devils." Except she didn't need his protection. She'd made it clear that she could fend for herself. Blast it all. She'd been taking care of herself nearly all her life. She didn't need him. Why wasn't he rejoicing?

"Right," Harry said. "How will you get rid of the horny devils?"

"I'll throw them downstairs."

"Not a good idea," Colin said. "She will feel sorry for them and blame you."

"Bloody hell. She will be angry because I haven't called on her."

"Probably," Harry said. "You need a plan."

"Tell her the truth but embellish it," Colin said.

"How?" Bell said.

"Explain about the letters and bankers and parliament. Then tell her you thought about her the entire time."

"Good idea," Harry said.

"Bring flowers, too," Colin said. "Try to look abashed."

He pulled a face. "I am not an actor."

Harry stubbed out his cheroot. "Tell her you're sorry."

Bell stiffened. "No."

"You have to if you want to get back in her good graces," Colin said.

Harry nodded. "Women like it when you admit you're in the wrong. She will feel sorry for you."

"I don't want her to feel sorry for me," he said.

"Yes, you do," Colin said. "She will forget her anger when she sees you looking miserable."

"I think you are giving me bad advice," Bell said.

Colin leaned back in his chair and blew a smoke ring. "Tell her you're sorry and then tell her you missed her."

"Damnation," Bell said. He'd gotten cold feet that day he'd seen the infant gown. Then he'd started thinking about the fact that he'd not made any efforts to find a new mistress. And how much he thought about Laura. Often he'd find himself grinning as he remembered something she'd said or the way she would light up like a dozen candles when she smiled. And every night in bed, he would imagine what it would be like to make slow love to her.

Then he'd seen that tiny infant gown for her sister, and his long-dormant conscience had roared at him, because he could never give her what she deserved. And she would never understand that he could never go back to the young man he'd been and that there would never be any resolution for him.

The next afternoon

Bell was furious as he walked past a long line of carriages before Laura's town house. He imagined all those men forming naked images of her in their minds. They would smile at her as they mentally threw her skirts over her head.

He had to get rid of them. Perhaps he should run into the drawing room and yell "Fire!" No, that probably wouldn't work. The horny devils would be so besotted they would burn before leaving her side.

Reed opened the door, and Bell entered the foyer holding a bouquet of roses. He'd bought three dozen, thinking that might impress her. But he knew she was probably angry with him. He couldn't blame her. He should have called on her. Bloody hell, he would have to say he was sorry.

"I'll just see myself upstairs, Reed," Bell said.

"I beg your pardon, my lord, but Lady Chesfield is unavailable to callers."

Bell tapped his boot. "There are multiple carriages in the square. She obviously has callers. One more will make no difference."

"My lord, I am under strict instructions not to allow callers."

"I am not just any caller," he said. "I am here to give her a report about her son."

"I beg your pardon, my lord, but I have my orders. However, I will be happy to have a maid put the flowers in a vase for Lady Chesfield."

Bell had no intention of leaving. He strode across the marble floor and ignored Reed's pleas to stop. Thoughts of the horny devils spurred him to run up the stairs. He threw open the drawing room door and blinked.

Nine ladies smiled at him.

Laura did not smile. She rose and said, "Lord Bellingham, you surprise me yet again."

Something warm crept up his neck. By God, he was blushing.

"You are just in time for the Society Devoted to the Care and Feeding of Orphans," Laura said as if gritting her teeth.

"Yes, the orphans," he said. "I wish to make a contribution."

"Oh, that is wonderful," one lady dressed in yellow said.

A maid entered, took the bouquet, and set it in a vase.

"Oh, how sweet," a pregnant lady said. "He brought you roses."

In the corner chair, Lady Atherton regarded him with an amused expression. "I am impressed that one of our premier politicians is personally taking time out of his busy schedule for the orphans."

"Yes, the orphans are a great concern," Bell said. "They probably need shoes."

The pregnant lady smiled. "They need parents, too."

"Right," Bell said. "I'm a bachelor, so I'm unqualified."

One lady dressed in pink made a notation with a pencil in a little book. "My lord, how much are you willing to contribute?"

"How much do you need?" Bell asked.

"Oh, what a wonderful gentleman you are," the pregnant lady said. "Can we count on you for at least fifty pounds?"

Laura narrowed her eyes. "He is very wealthy and very generous, are you not, Lord Bellingham?"

"I am now," he said. Then he decided to impress her. "Put me down for one thousand pounds."

All the ladies, save Laura, clapped their hands. They continued to chatter about his timely entrance and generosity. When he saw Laura's lips thin, he realized his bribe had not worked.

He was doomed to make an apology.

The lady with the pencil moved that the meeting should end. Lady Atherton seconded the motion. He bowed as the ladies filed out.

Lady Atherton was the last to depart. She halted before him. "A piece of advice," she said. "Grovel."

He had not groveled since the day his father caught him kissing the local tavern wench.

After Lady Atherton left, Bell closed the door, put his hands behind his back, and walked over to her. "You have every right to be angry with me."

"You promised to give my son fencing lessons. Instead, you delegated the task to someone else. You said he needed a role model and you felt honor bound to take on that role."

He took a deep breath. "I'm sorry."

"You expect me to forgive you when you have given no explanation?" Her eyes welled, but she blinked back the threatening tears. "He is my son, and you of all people know how much he means to me."

"It was stupid and selfish of me," he said.

"That is your explanation?" she said.

It had started to feel like a family.

"I have not always agreed with you," she said, "but I admired and respected you until you sent that curt note."

His head came up. No one had ever questioned his honor.

"I was getting deeper and deeper into your lives," he said. "I took on responsibility for your son, and I realized I had encouraged him to become attached."

"You were a good influence on him," she said.

"But it is temporary. I realized that he was bound to be disappointed, because you and I will go our separate ways at the end of the season."

"This is not just about Justin," she said.

"I know. You cannot give me what I want, and I cannot give you what you need."

"You make it sound so simple, but it is not," she said.

"Please sit with me," he said quietly.

She joined him on the sofa, and he clasped her hand. "From the day Montclief threatened you, I somehow found myself playing the part of Sir Lancelot. I have never taken on an obligation like this before. I didn't anticipate the consequences."

She withdrew her hand. "Perhaps it would be better if we severed our friendship now. I will invent an explanation to Justin."

"Laura, I made a mistake. I will not fail him," he said. "My honor demands that I fulfill my obligations to your son."

"I don't give a damn about your honor." She raised her small fist to her heart. "Justin is not an obligation. He is my son."

He took her by the shoulders. "That is not what I meant. I do care about the boy or I would never have taken the time to help. I made a mistake, and I owned up to it. Now I humbly ask you to forgive me."

There was a suspicious sheen in her eyes. "You wounded me."

"I know." He put his arms around her and held her tightly.

A few minutes later, she lifted her head. "I made your coat damp."

"It will dry," he said, handing her a handkerchief.

After she blotted her eyes, he remembered something. "Oh, hell."

She elbowed him. "Watch your language."

"I forgot something." He slid to the floor on his knees."

She looked alarmed. "Oh, no, please don't say the words."

"Lady Atherton told me to grovel. I'm groveling."

She released her breath. "Oh, thank goodness. I thought . . . well, never mind."

He pointed. "Both knees. I didn't want there to be a misunderstanding."

"Get up now," she said. "You look ridiculous."

They both stood. "Can we be friends?" he said.

She smiled a little. "I suppose that's allowed between secret faux fiancés."

"I heard you turned down Pembroke."

"He's a very nice man. I believe he anticipated my answer."

"He has a bald spot," Bell said.

She patted his arm. "Don't be jealous. You'll probably acquire one someday."

Bell looked at his boots. "Will you attend the Bonhams' ball?"

"Yes," she said.

"I would be honored to escort you and Lady Atherton if you will consent."

"I will ask her, but I'm sure she will accept," Laura said. "I think she likes you."

"I think she has a strong opinion of me, not all of it favorable."

"Probably justified," Laura said, "but you have a few good qualities."

He grinned. "Such as?"

"I think you know." She lifted up on her toes and kissed his cheek.

"Your aim needs work," he said, grinning.

She wagged her finger. "You are not a real fiancé. No more kisses on the mouth."

He bowed and as he quit the drawing room, his chest no longer felt tight. Because she'd forgiven him.

Chapter Ten

The Bonhams' ball

𝓑ellingham had insisted upon taking Laura and Lady Atherton in his carriage to the ball. He tried to offer his arm to Lady Atherton, but she insisted he escort Laura. As they climbed the stairs, Laura was all too aware of the bulging muscle in his arm. She was a bit afraid of her feelings for him, but her mother had long ago counseled her to be wary of having a long memory. He was her friend, and he'd admitted he'd been wrong. She would let go of any lingering doubts about him.

Justin had attended Vauxhall tonight with Sarah, Paul, and some of his new friends. Lady Norcliffe and a few of her friends had agreed to chaperone the young people tonight. She was glad that Justin had remained friends with Paul. Obviously George had been the ringleader, probably because he owned that fancy curricle.

Laura smiled at Bellingham as they entered the receiving line. Lady Atherton was ahead of them in the queue.

After they finally emerged into the ballroom, she saw Lady Atherton waiting. When they reached her, she had a crafty smile on her face.

"I am going to the chairs by the wall to gossip," she said. "It is the best part of a ball. I will leave you in the care of Bellingham."

"But I should mingle," Laura said.

"You will mingle with me," he said.

Lady Atherton laughed and walked away.

"Would you care for punch?" he asked.

"Yes, that would be nice."

He led her along the perimeter of the room.

"People are staring because I am walking with a notorious rake," she said.

"They are staring because I am with the most beautiful woman in the ballroom."

"There are many beautiful women here, I'm sure," she said.

"Every man in this ballroom envies me because you are mine."

"I am not a possession."

He gave her a sultry look. "You are mine tonight."

Was that her heart twirling in her chest? She told herself to be sensible. Honeyed compliments rolled off his tongue. They were friends, nothing more.

When they reached the refreshment table, Laura looked about her. The cacophony of voices grew louder.

Lady Bonham rushed over to the table. "Do not drink the punch," she said. "I heard that Harry poured half a bottle of rum into it."

Bell tasted it. "No, it is tepid."

Lady Bonham clapped her hand to her chest. "Oh,

thank goodness. If you see Harry, tell him I will take a switch to him if he pours spirits in the punch."

Bell raised his brows. "That would be akin to waving a red flag at a bull." He handed a cup to Laura and she looked out at the crowd. "Harry and Colin are coming this way.

"I will tell Harry you poured rum in the punch," he said.

She waved at Bell's friends. "He will be so disappointed."

"Do not worry," he said. "My friends will not ogle you."

"How can you be so sure?"

"Because I claimed you."

She turned on him. "What did you say?"

"I beg your pardon. It is the blood of my marauding ancestors talking."

"Are you feverish or do you really hear voices?"

He leaned closer to her. "I like to hear your voice."

She drew in her breath. He knew exactly what to say to make her a little breathless.

"There you are," Harry said. "How is the punch?"

"Lady Chesfield poured rum in it," Bell said.

"Ah, she is a vixen," Colin said.

Laura let out an exasperated sigh. "I did not pour spirits in the punch."

Lady Atherton brought Lord Lindmoore to Laura. "Lord Lindmoore insists he will be up in the boughs if you do not dance with him."

His eyes kept dipping from Laura's face to her bosom, making her skin crawl.

"May I have the honor of the next dance?" Lord Lindmoore said.

"No, I have already claimed it," Bellingham said.

Oh, dear, he was being possessive tonight.

"Well, perhaps the next one," Lindmoore said.

Harry's eyes gleamed. "I have claimed the second dance."

Lindmoore regarded Bell with suspicion. "Then I will wait for the third set."

"Sorry," Colin said. "I have already spoken for that one."

"That is perfectly fine," Lord Lindmoore said. "I will gladly waltz with Lady Chesfield."

Laura thought Lindmoore had a mean expression. She did not want to dance with him. "I am sorry to disappoint you, Lord Lindmoore, but I promised the waltz to Lord Bellingham."

"And the midnight supper," Bell said.

Lady Atherton addressed Lindmoore. "You cannot say I didn't warn you."

Lindmoore sniffed. "Good evening, Lady Chesfield, Lady Atherton."

After he left, Laura turned to Lady Atherton. "What warning did you give him?"

She unfurled her fan. "I told him Bellingham wouldn't let him within a foot of you. Enjoy your dances," she said, and walked away.

"I think this is a conspiracy," Laura said.

The musicians struck up the opening bars of the first country dance.

Colin's shoulders slumped. "I've been dreading this."

"Why?" Laura asked. "Do you not like to dance?"

"He doesn't like to dance with Lady Angeline," Harry said.

"Then why ask her?" Laura said.

"I have no choice," Colin said. "Our mothers insisted we dance."

"They were promised to each other in the cradle," Harry said. "Their families have been planning the wedding since their birth."

"Colin and Angeline hate each other," Bell said.

"Surely not," Laura said.

"She is evil," Colin said. "The last time I was forced to dance with her, she kicked me in the shin."

Harry leaned closer to Laura. "Angeline has not forgiven Colin for kissing her under the mistletoe."

"She actually wiped her mouth," Colin said. "She is a shrew."

Bell pointed at a beautiful, tall brunette who stood near the dance floor. "Look, her hands are fisted."

"She will probably plant you a facer, Colin," Harry said.

"I will trip her if she does."

"You will do no such thing," Laura said in an outraged voice. "I'm sure she's a perfectly amiable young lady."

"To everyone but Colin," Harry said.

Colin muttered under his breath and strode toward the brunette.

Bellingham offered his arm, and as they walked toward the dance floor, Laura said, "What did Colin do to make her despise him so much?"

"I don't know. He won't talk about it."

They reached the dance floor and stood across from each other. When the music started, they crossed each other to the other side. A few minutes later, they joined hands with another couple and turned in a circle and crossed back to their original places. Laura glanced at the bottom of the queue. Angeline glared at Colin as they met in the middle, turned, and started up toward the top of the queue. Bellingham winked at Laura.

Colin and Angeline took their places at the top of the queue. Angeline bared her teeth. When Colin blew her a kiss, Angeline rolled her eyes. Laura looked at Bellingham and he held his palms up.

Then it was their turn to meet in the middle. He met her gaze, and she felt breathless at the seductive expression in his eyes. He set his hand on her back as they walked up the line. She told herself not to fall under his spell, but when they turned in a circle, she could not look away. In that moment, she understood that the desire between them could flare out of control if she wasn't careful. She had to be strong, because there was something powerful between them.

At long last, the dance ended. She took his arm, but as they strolled away, she knew that others would talk if she continued to stay by his side. "I think we should mingle—separately."

He grinned at her. "I have never met a rule I didn't wish to break."

"If we spend the entire evening together, it will cause talk."

He leaned down. "I wish we could spend the entire night together."

She met his gaze and everything inside of her yearned to throw caution to the wind. "We are taking a risk at this moment," she said. "I must go before we stir up gossip." She walked away before he could say another word, because she didn't trust herself. He was too persuasive, and he wasn't the only one who burned.

Laura enjoyed speaking to her new friends from the charity organization. They were all friendly and genuinely concerned for the vast number of children languishing in orphanages. She was especially taken with Mrs. Faraday, who was expecting her first child in two months' time. But she was also gratified to learn that Mrs. Whitmeyer also had an adolescent son whom she jokingly said regularly turned into a monster for no reason whatsoever. Now Laura didn't feel quite so bad about failing her son, knowing that other mothers faced similar challenges.

Afterward, she went to the ladies' retiring room to get away from the roar of the crowd and rest a bit. She found a chair, and one of the maids brought her a glass of sherry. Laura sipped the sherry and felt a bit restored. Her dealings with Bellingham were often intense. She thought of his words: *I wish we could spend the entire night together.*

Despite everything that she believed in, she couldn't help longing for his kisses and touches again. Sometimes in bed, she imagined what it would be like to make love with him. She wanted him desperately, but she was also afraid that she could never measure up to all of the women who knew how to please a man like him.

The door opened to the sound of feminine laughter. Lady Rentworth, George's mother, entered along with two other women. Laura studiously avoided looking at the woman. In her previous encounter with Lady Rentworth, Laura had quickly surmised that the woman thought Laura unworthy of her regard.

Lady Rentworth's avid gaze lit on Laura. "Well, well, if it isn't the sweet little widow. I heard you made a conquest of Bellingham."

"You heard incorrectly," Laura said. "Lord Bellingham agreed to provide guidance for my son while his guardian had duties elsewhere."

"I bet he did," Lady Rentworth said. Her two friends laughed.

Laura set her sherry aside and rose. She started past when Lady Rentworth raised her voice. "Aren't you the lucky one? Is it true he is a superb lover?"

"You will have to ask someone who knows." Laura held her head high as she walked out. She could not control what others said about her, and she would not let a spiteful woman like Lady Rentworth ruin her evening.

By the time she returned to the ballroom, Laura realized she was walking against the throng of guests. She was supposed to meet Bellingham for the midnight supper, but finding him in this crowd would prove difficult, especially from her vantage point. Yet, she didn't want to get swept along with the crowd. She pressed past the other guests. Once, someone stepped on her foot. While it smarted, she knew it was nothing serious. All she wanted was to find a chair and wait until the crowd thinned.

She managed to inch along the perimeter of the room and saw Bellingham. He pressed through the crowd and reached her. "I looked for you."

"I went to the ladies' retiring room to rest for a bit."

They waited in a corner until the crowd in the ballroom emptied, save for the footmen clearing the punch bowl and glasses on the refreshment table. "Do you wish to go to the dining room?" he asked.

"No, I just want to relax and be away from all the noise," she said.

He led her to a chair and sat beside her. "Better?"

"Yes, I'm glad I found you," she said. Then she told him what had occurred in the retiring room.

"People will always gossip," he said. "But I should not have pressed you again. It was selfish of me, but I want you to know that I do respect you." He leaned forward with his elbows on his thighs. "I want you to know that it is not just desire on my part. I care about you and enjoy your friendship. Be assured that I will be available for you and Justin until the end of the season."

He made it sound so final. "Are we to part ways forever?" she said.

He sat back. "I will return to Devonshire this summer, and you will go home to Hampshire."

Her heart seemed to fall to her feet.

"I don't wish to mislead you or your son."

You already have misled us.

"Your son needs permanence. He needs to know that my involvement is only temporary."

She gripped her hands hard. He meant her as well. But she couldn't deny the truth of what he'd said. He'd never promised beyond the season. She knew it was unreasonable of her to expect more, because he'd always been clear that their relationship was based on friendship only. She'd accepted that, but now it stung her, because she didn't want to lose him.

"I don't mean to sound cold," he said. "I've spent far too many seasons in London surrounded by sycophants. I've gotten cynical about all of it: the politics, the pretentions, and the hypocrites. You encountered it tonight."

He looked at her. "You are genuine. It's rare in the world of the ton. I sincerely want to spend time with you and Justin. I only want to make sure that I don't inadvertently set the wrong expectations."

"You've selflessly given of your time to Justin and me," she said in a wooden voice.

"It's not enough, but it's all I'm capable of giving," he said.

"I think you are capable of far more." Her voice had cracked. He'd tired of her and was ready to move on to a woman who would do anything he wanted in bed.

"You see only what you wish to see," he said. "Some things are irreparable."

She wanted to encourage him to talk about the irreparable things, but a ballroom was a poor place for a discussion of what had happened to him all those years ago when he'd lost his family. And truthfully, she didn't want to think about the ending when she must tell him good-bye forever. If this season was all that she would ever have of him, then she must not waste it on the time that remained.

"Perhaps we should go downstairs," he said.

"Yes, we should see how Colin and Angeline are faring." She'd tried to infuse gaiety in her voice, but it sounded forced.

"She is probably kicking his shin under the table."

"We do not want to miss the fun." She didn't let on that she felt as if a candle had guttered inside her.

He rose and held out his hand. "Let us join the party. If we're lucky, Harry will have poured spirits in the punch bowl, and everyone will be foxed."

For a moment, she considered pleading a headache and

requesting a hackney to take her home. But she would ruin the evening for Lady Atherton and Bellingham. "Lady Bonham will be delighted when her ball is the most talked-about event of the season so far."

She took his arm, determined to pretend to enjoy the festivities, and no matter how much she wanted to make the most of her time with him, she couldn't forget that it was nearing the end.

As they approached the dining room, Bell frowned at the uproar inside. "Something is amiss."

"We will find out soon enough." She released his arm. "We had better sit apart to avoid the gossips."

He nodded. "Yes, it's probably a wise move." He'd noticed her crestfallen expression when he'd made it clear that his involvement with her and Justin would last only until the end of the season. It was for the best, because he'd already gotten in deep with them. She needed a forever kind of man, and he never would be.

When they walked inside, all the voices hushed. A fork clattered on a plate. The fine hairs on Bell's neck stiffened. He searched the crowd and saw Lady Atherton lift her brows.

Lady Bonham hurried forward. "There they are at last. We have a special announcement tonight. How remiss of both of you to keep such a secret."

His heart stampeded. He looked at Laura. Her face was pale. She looked as if she would swoon.

How the devil had word gotten out about their engagement? Was Montclief here?

Bell drew closer to Laura and took her arm. "Be calm," he murmured. "I will explain." He had no idea what he would say, but he couldn't deny the engagement, even if it wasn't real. To do so would ruin her reputation.

Lady Bonham cleared her throat. "Lord Bellingham, you are known for your brilliant politics, but we had no idea of your generous philanthropic efforts." Lady Bonham turned to Mrs. Faraday. "I will let you tell the particulars."

Bell blinked. Philanthropy? For the past few minutes his gut had twisted over...philanthropy?

Laura's breath whooshed out. "Dear God, my prayers are answered," she whispered.

Mrs. Faraday stepped forward. "On behalf of the Society Devoted to the Care and Feeding of the Orphans, I wish to thank Lord Bellingham for his substantial donation of one thousand pounds."

Applause rang out.

The orphans, he thought. He was being lauded for his contribution to the orphans. Dizzying relief filled him.

Mrs. Faraday waited for silence, and then she continued. "We are also grateful to Lady Chesfield for taking on the role of president of our organization."

Bell grinned at Laura and said, "I must give credit to Lady Chesfield for informing me of the great need for the unfortunate, forgotten children. I'm sure Mrs. Faraday would welcome additional contributions this evening."

Applause rang out again.

Mrs. Faraday fished out her book and pencil from her reticule. Guests gathered in a queue. Harry emerged from the back of the dining room and clapped Bell on the back. "I poured brandy in the punch bowl. No doubt that will loosen the purses tonight."

"Where is Colin?" Bell asked.

"Over there in the donation queue."

Laura clasped her hands. "How wonderful of Colin, but why does he look so glum?"

Harry grinned. "Angeline volunteered him for five hundred pounds."

Soon after the donation announcement, Laura and Bellingham escaped the ball. Lady Atherton had insisted that Bellingham take Laura home because her complexion had looked a bit wan. They were both laughing as they hurried to Bellingham's carriage.

When the carriage rolled away from the Bonhams' mansion, Laura placed her hand over her heart. "I thought for certain we had been found out."

"I know," he said. "I was racking my brain, trying to think of some explanation that didn't include a faux engagement and me laying my coat over a puddle."

"Don't remind me," she said. "That had to be the worst lie I ever told."

"I'm shocked," he said. "A vicar's daughter lying through her teeth. You ought to be ashamed," he said.

"I was desperate, and you know it."

"True, you promised me anything. I ought to have demanded far more. My marauding ancestors would be appalled."

"Honestly, I was frightened half to death in the dining room," she said.

"We're safe," he said.

"For now." Laura blew out her breath. "Sooner or later, Montclief will raise his head and cause trouble."

A tealike scent enveloped her. It took him a minute to identify it. "Roses," he said.

"I beg your pardon?"

"The perfume," he said.

"Actually, it's soap," she said. "I know it is an extravagance, but I cannot resist."

Her words marked another difference between them. He never would have thought of soap as an extravagance. Her father was genteelly impoverished. She probably had never had small luxuries until she married.

"I went shopping recently to buy presents for my family," she said. "I enjoyed finding gifts that I knew they would appreciate. Then I tried to think of something for my son and realized I no longer knew what would please him."

"Well, believe it or not, I was an adolescent cub once and could probably make suggestions."

She looked at him. "It is not the gift so much as the knowledge that I no longer know his preferences. I couldn't think of a single gift for my own son."

"Your son is changing rapidly," Bell said. "Making his own choices is part of his independence. Granted, he's made bad ones recently. But in a mere four years, he will reach his majority, and he will be required to make dozens of decisions every single day."

"But I've been managing most of it, with the help of estate managers and others. I can assist my son."

"Laura, you miss the point. He doesn't want his mother assisting him. He needs to be independent in order to take over his legacy. If you cling too tightly, he will push you away."

"Is that what I do?"

He chose his words carefully. "I think you and your son are dealing with changes in your relationship. That can prove difficult when you've accustomed yourself to the years when he was younger."

"I focused all my energy on Justin after Phillip's death. My son needed comfort. We had each other." She missed their close relationship.

"It was natural for you and your son to become closer after your husband died, but those days are gone," he said. "He has matured quite a bit in the last few weeks."

"Yes, he was unduly influenced by George."

They were silent for a while, and then she spoke. "It will sound so foolish when I have such a large family close by, but when Justin was in school after Phillip's death, I felt so alone. I'd hoped to spend time with Justin in London, and then he rebelled. I had such grand expectations, and then I found myself in a huge city where I knew no one, except Lady Atherton." She looked at him. "And you."

"You fear being alone," he said.

"Doesn't it ever bother you to live alone?" she asked.

"I have friends and political allies." His old friends had married and now lived in the country. He had found the changes in their lives disconcerting until he'd met Harry and Colin.

"You are right," she said. "I think I try to smother Justin, and so he pushes me away."

Bell looked at her, but she was staring straight ahead. Then she shivered.

"Are you cold?"

"A little."

He scooped her onto his lap and wrapped his arms around her.

"Oh," she said with a nervous laugh.

"I'll keep you warm." He liked the feel of her bottom on his lap and wished there were no layers of clothing. He imagined holding her naked in his arms. Heat traveled through his veins, and his groin tightened. He would make himself mad if he continued on like this, all desire but no satisfaction. Yet, he still wanted her, even though she'd made her objections clear. At first it had been the thrill of the chase, but she didn't play those sorts of games. She was nothing like the sophisticated women of the ton who thought nothing of taking a lover. In Laura's world, men and women did not enter into casual liaisons for mutual pleasure, because it was considered a sin.

"If I confess my secret, will you promise not to rebuke me?" he said.

"I think you mean to trick me."

"Tricks are allowed," he said. "Remember, I'm a rake."

"Oh, do you have a book of rake tricks?"

He tapped his temple. "It's stored in my brain box. I have a trick for every occasion."

"Such as?"

"Luring pretty widows onto my lap."

She burst out laughing.

He smiled.

"Your charm is very hard to resist," she said.

"Then don't."

The carriage rocked to a halt at her house. He didn't want to let her go this night, but no matter how much he desired her, he was a gentleman to the core, and he'd promised not to press her to act against her conscience. "I will escort you to the door."

She moistened her lips, and he was so tempted to kiss

her senseless and soften her objections with his hands. But she wasn't that kind of lady.

Laura looked out the window where two tall lamps burned animal fat to light the way. "I'm the oldest of ten children," she said. "I was expected to be the model child, the one who set the example for my siblings." She turned to him. "It was so easy back then to distinguish between right and wrong. Now I find myself questioning my beliefs for the first time."

"What do you mean?" he asked.

"I devoted myself to caring for my husband and my child. I felt needed, but my husband is gone, and my son will soon be grown. I am at a crossroads in my life. Nothing will ever be the same. I will always cherish the years with my husband and son, but I cannot go back as you said."

He said nothing, but she seemed to be struggling with a decision.

"I have always taken the straight path. I was always sure of right and wrong, but now I see it is not so simple."

"Few things in life are," he said.

"When the season ends, I will return to my home where I will be the proper widow and devote my time to my family and helping those who are less fortunate. But I realized tonight that in trying to make others happy, I have often neglected myself. This will be my last London season. Years from now, I will look back and remember you."

"I will remember you, too," he said.

She took a deep breath. "I fear I will regret that I made the wrong choice."

"What choice is that?" he said.

"One night with you," she whispered.

Oh, God. "Are you certain?" He was an idiot for asking, but he was a gentleman. "I don't want you to have regrets in the morning."

"I am afraid," she said.

"Of what?"

"That I will disappoint you."

"No, you won't." He framed her face with his hands. "I will make sure that this will be a night we will both always remember."

He slid her off his lap, got out of the carriage, and gave the driver new directions. When he climbed back inside, he considered that in the interval she might have changed her mind, but she laid her hand in his and held it until the carriage rolled to a stop at the modest little town house where he'd kept mistresses. This time would be different, because Laura was unique. He'd set out to win her as his mistress, and then she became his friend. This night was not about a conquest. It was about a woman who had chosen to make love to him.

Chapter Eleven

$\mathcal{L}$aura trembled as Bell turned the key and opened the door. All was shrouded inside. "The butler isn't expecting me," he said. "He and the maid are likely sleeping."

She surmised he had not recently had a woman here. For some reason, that reassured her.

He fumbled with a flint box and produced a flame. After he lit a candle branch, he offered his arm. As they approached the stairs, she knew a moment of doubt. He had said she would not disappoint him, but she feared she would.

A memory of her wedding night flashed in her mind. She'd been frightened half to death, and yet she'd yearned to hold Phillip close. She'd wanted to please him because she'd loved him.

Bell took her up the stairs. She told herself not to think of her late husband. Yet, the first time she'd kissed Bellingham, she had compared him to Phillip. She couldn't help it, because the kisses and sensations

Bellingham had aroused in her were completely out of her experience. Now she worried that she would feel that she had somehow betrayed Phillip.

Bellingham stopped before a door. She released his arm, and he opened it. He took her hand and led her inside. A huge canopied bed dwarfed the rest of the room.

He set the candle branch on a bedside table and turned to her. "You're nervous. It's understandable."

Laura questioned the decision she'd made. It wasn't because of Bellingham. It was because she feared that she could not live up to the countless women who undoubtedly had known sophisticated ways of pleasing a man.

Bellingham caught her by the waist and hoisted her onto the edge of the mattress. He sat beside her and took her hand again. "I want to say something first, because I imagine that you are remembering your husband right now."

"How did you know?" she whispered.

"Because I know you, and it would only be natural for you to think of him. I know that you loved him and cared for him when he was ill. I will not pry into your marriage, because I want you to preserve your happy memories of your husband."

And just like that she fell in love for the second time in her life. "He was a wonderful man, and so are you."

He smiled. "I was a bit worried I couldn't live up to your sainted husband."

"He had his faults. You are very different men, but I think I chose well both times."

He stood and removed his coat. Her nerves jangled as he stripped off the cravat. He cocked his head and looked at her. "I think you need to relax a bit. I'll pour us both a glass of wine."

She turned sideways on the bed and watched him walk over to a chest. He lifted a decanter and poured wine. Then he returned and handed her a glass. "To this night," he said, and clinked her glass.

She sipped the wine. "It's claret."

"Yes, do you like it?"

She nodded and kicked off her slippers.

He sat beside her. "You have very small feet and hands."

"They match my very small height."

He smiled. "Drink up now."

"Are you in a rush?" she asked.

"I won't rush you," he said. "Much."

She laughed and felt a bit anxious again. "I don't really know how this will proceed."

"Now, now. You know I've never met a rule I didn't want to break."

"Are there rules?" she asked.

"Oh, yes. Dozens of them. Rule number one. Do not throw a lady's skirt over her head."

She burst out laughing. "You are bad."

"Rule number two. Ladies first."

She frowned.

"That goes along with rule number three. Do not race to the finish line."

"Oh."

"Rule number four. Do not crush her with your weight."

"Oh, dear. That would be unfortunate," she said.

"Rule number five. Look her in the eyes."

She sipped her wine and regarded him over her glass.

"Rule number six. Kiss her senseless on the mouth and on every inch of her skin."

Her breathing grew ragged.

"Rule number seven. Have a gentle touch."

She was feeling a bit giddy from the wine and his rules.

"Rule number eight. Pay attention to how she responds and ask if she likes it."

"Very gentlemanly," she said, and sipped wine again.

"Rule number nine. Tell her she's beautiful."

Oh, dear, he really did know how to seduce a lady with words.

"Rule number ten. Let her lead occasionally."

She nodded, even though she wasn't sure what he meant.

"Rule number eleven, the most important rule of all. Do not snore afterward."

She laughed again. "You are charming."

"I'll skip back to rule nine. You are beautiful." He kissed her cheek. "Now give me the wineglass because I don't want you foxed."

"I am a bit giddy."

He took her glass and set it aside with his own. "Giddy is good. Foxed is not."

"Is that rule number eleven?"

"I lost count," he said. Then he pulled the pins from her hair and sifted his fingers through the long locks as he gazed at her. "Now you get to choose. I can undress you first or you can undress me first."

She blinked. "Oh."

"So what will it be?"

"Do you have dice? We could roll to see who goes first," she said.

"I'm too impatient to hunt for dice. Let's go with ladies first."

"I've never done this before," she admitted.

"Well, let's see. I have three buttons on my shirt. Buttons on the falls of my trousers. Oops, forgot about the boots. I'll do those first. Then there is a ribbon on my drawers. Do you have any questions?"

"I think your clothing is less complicated than mine," she said.

He stood and shucked off his boots. "I'll take the stockings off, too. Bad form to keep those on."

She fell back on the bed, laughing.

He grabbed her hands and pulled her to a sitting position. "No reclining. You have a job to do."

She unbuttoned his shirt and grew brave enough to pull the voluminous fabric out of his trousers. He slid the braces off and pulled his shirt over his head. She reached for the button on one side of his falls and brushed her hand against his erection. When he sucked in his breath, she continued slowly, teasing him with her fingers occasionally. After she finished, the fall opened, and she saw the bulge in his drawers.

"You're very good at this," he said, his voice low and a little rough. Then he pulled off the trousers and stockings quickly.

She took his hand and drew him closer. Then she untied the ribbon of his drawers. She looked up at him and heard his fast breathing. She pushed the drawers past his hips and he sprang out. Laura swallowed. She'd sworn not to compare, but good heavens, he was huge.

He shucked off the drawers and just stood there waiting.

"Do you know what I want?" he asked.

She touched him. Then he wrapped her hand around him. She squeezed him gently, and he was definitely breathing as if he'd run a race. "My turn," he said.

He lifted her off the bed and went to work quickly, untying tapes. She knew he had vast experience, and at the moment it showed. When he encountered the front-lacing stays, he grinned. "Oh, I approve."

Moments later, the dress, shift, and petticoats slid to a heap on the carpet. "Keep the stockings on—I like it that way."

"Very well," she said.

Then he held her hands and looked at her. "Oh my God. I had better ask forgiveness in advance. I may forget a rule."

"You are forgiven," she said.

He picked her up by the waist and dropped her onto the bed. She scrambled back, and he followed. "Come here, pretty lady."

She hesitated, and he grabbed her. "My marauding ancestors are applauding," he said.

Laura couldn't stop laughing. She'd not expected his playfulness, but she loved him for it, because it eased her anxiety. Well, that and the wine.

He pressed her back onto the mattress and hovered over her. Then he cupped her cheek and kissed her. The sweep of his tongue thrilled her. She cupped the back of his head and fingered the short layers of his thick hair. Then she tangled her tongue with his, and all of the playfulness dissolved into heat and desire. She ran her hand over the sparse hair on his chest. His arms bulged with muscles. His ribs and hips were sculpted as well. He was strong and big, but when he touched her breast, he was so gentle.

He nudged her thighs apart and set her feet on the bed. Then he took her nipple in his mouth and sucked. Her back bowed as the indescribable pleasure sizzled through her veins. He switched to her other breast, and she realized she was wet between her thighs. Then his hand feathered down her abdomen, and he touched the folds of her sex. She jerked, but he whispered near her ear, "Shhh. I'll be gentle." He parted her and slipped his finger inside her. "You're wet," he said. Then he did something with his thumb and a spurt of pleasure stunned her. She lost all sense of everything except the way he rubbed her. "Oh, yes, sweetheart. Move with the rhythm."

She reached for the pleasure beckoning her, and then he inserted another finger inside her. "I'm stretching you," he said.

Mindlessly, she kept moving and she could hear the wet sounds as he continued. She dug her nails into his shoulders and then ecstasy wracked her. Her inner muscles contracted again and again. Then he positioned himself and slowly slid inside her. She couldn't help but cry out.

Bell kissed her on the mouth and bent her knees to her chest. Her eyes looked dazed and her mouth was kiss swollen. He got even harder as he held still inside her. Then he gave into the urge to thrust. She was hot, wet, and tight. He watched her face as little feminine sounds escaped her. "Come for me again," he said, reaching between their bodies, and she gasped as her back bowed again. As her rhythmic contractions gripped his cock, he came and barely managed to withdraw in time.

He collapsed atop her, still breathing hard, and then remembering himself, he rolled to his back. His eyes grew unfocused and then he gave in to the little death.

She pulled the sheet over them both and turned on her side to watch him sleep. His lips were slightly parted and his breathing was slow and even. His lashes were thick, and she detected a slight bristle along his jawline. She wanted to touch him, but she didn't want to wake him. "I love you," she whispered, knowing that she dared not tell him when he was awake. She knew he did not return her feelings. He liked her, and he desired her, but he kept a part of himself hidden. She suspected there were demons inside of him that he'd closed off long ago when he'd lost his family. She wished that she could heal his inner wounds, but she knew that it would prove as impossible as her attempts to heal Phillip.

It wasn't that she thought he was incapable of tender feelings; it was that he refused to confront the tragedy that had changed his life forever. He would not speak of his family, except for a few terse words, but there had been that moment during their waltz when his face grew grim as he uttered, *My mother.*

Laura wished with all her heart that they could forge a life together. He would be a good father to Justin, but he'd made it clear that their time would end with the approach of summer. She would never regret this night, even though she'd been taught that lovemaking was sanctioned only in marriage. But tonight she could not think of their lovemaking as sin. To her, it had been beautiful, playful, and erotic. He was a special man, and she knew that in years to come, she would be glad that she'd shared her body with him. No one but the two of them would ever know.

His eyes opened, and he gave her a sleepy smile. "Thank you for the birthday gift."

She was taken aback. "Is it your birthday?"

He stretched his arms. "I'm thirty years old."

"Practically ancient," she said.

He rolled over her, holding himself up on his elbows, and she spread her legs to accommodate him.

"I can prove my youthful vitality," he said.

"Oh, my," she said, looking down at the long length of him.

"Hold on," he said.

"What?"

He rolled to his back and pulled her atop him. "Straddle me."

Her eyes widened as she did his bidding.

He reached between them and inserted two fingers. "Mmm. Still hot and wet."

She inhaled on a constricted breath.

"Put my cock inside you."

Desire flooded her at his words. She reached for him and slowly pressed down his hard, long length.

He put his hands on her hips. "Ride me."

She began to move, and he pulled her forward. When he took her nipple in his mouth, she cried out again. She looked into his eyes and saw his glazed expression. He moved with her in a slow rocking back and forth. Then he cupped her breasts and circled his thumbs around her sensitive nipples. She bit her lip and concentrated on the exquisite pleasure. It was as if she were enveloped in an erotic fog. Then suddenly, without warning, she came apart and collapsed on his chest.

He rolled her over and entered her again. Laura wrapped her arms around him and held on tightly. She loved watching him. The expression in his eyes was fierce and determined. "You feel so good," he said. He kissed her lips and eased inside her. "I want to savor you," he said, and continued the slow tempo. She caressed his chest, amazed anew by his muscular body. His eyes looked a bit glazed in the candlelight. His breathing was a bit rough. Then he started moving quicker and soon he was thrusting faster. She watched his face as he closed his eyes and suddenly he stilled. With an exhalation, he withdrew and collapsed atop her. Laura ran her hands over his slightly damp back. He lifted up on his elbows and rolled to his side, bringing her back up against his chest. His arm came around her and he cupped her breast. "Sleep," he said.

She lay there, loving the way his body curled behind her. His deep, even breathing indicated he was sleeping. Lethargy claimed her and soon she could no longer stay awake.

He awoke disoriented. His hand was cupping Laura's breast and his erection was hard as a rock. Three of the candles still burned, though two had guttered. "Laura," he whispered.

She opened her eyes and gave him a sleepy smile.

He pushed her hair back and sucked on her neck. Her shattered breathing let him know she enjoyed it. Then he pressed her to her back and pinned one of her wrists above her head. This was how he'd imagined her that day on the wrought-iron bench. "Guide me," he said.

Her lips parted and her eyes held a lethargic, sated look, but he meant to awaken desire in her again. As she guided him inside her body, he hissed in a breath. At first he took his time, but the lust took over and he rocked into her faster and faster. She locked her legs around him and cried out. Her rhythmic contractions felt so damned good and then wave after wave of pleasure shook him. He strained and spilled his seed inside her. Then he wrapped Laura in his arms.

He awoke to the sound of birds chirping. A crack in the drapes showed it was dim outside, but dawn was not far off. He turned to face Laura. Her lips were slightly parted. Ribbons of her blond hair fanned out on the pillow. She looked younger and a little vulnerable to him, but he knew that was an illusion. Laura was a strong woman, and even though he knew she could manage on her own, he still felt protective of her.

He'd never felt that way about a woman before, but then, he'd never known a woman like Laura.

He wanted to make love to her again, but he would be considerate and let her sleep a little longer. It was a new experience for him. He'd never stayed all night with a woman, because he'd feared the blasted nightmare would return. Yet, he'd not even thought of it when he'd brought her here. All of his thoughts had been centered on her.

She'd been anxious and unsure what to do, but she'd laughed at his silly rules. He'd worried a bit about her nervousness, but the moment she'd opened her arms to him, she'd let go of all her inhibitions.

He'd let go of his own inhibitions about the nightmares, and deep down, he knew it was because of her. A peaceful feeling settled over him as he watched her sleep. He wished they could stay abed all day, but the light filtering in from the crack in the drapes was growing brighter. "Laura," he said, and kissed her cheek.

Laura rolled over and blinked at him as if she couldn't remember where she was. "Andrew?" she said.

She had never used his given name before.

"Your beard is scratchy."

"Sorry. I have to take you home soon," he said.

She gasped as she clung to the sheet. "What time is it?"

"Let me check." He fumbled with the flint box, managed a spark, and lit a candle and squinted at the clock on the bedside table. "It's five-fifteen."

"It's early," she said, holding out her arms for him.

Of course he couldn't resist. "How are you?"

She blushed. "Wonderful."

"I watched you sleep."

She gave him a sleepy smile. "You didn't snore."

He couldn't resist teasing her. "You did."

"I did not." She sat up and the sheet fell, exposing her beautiful breasts.

He cupped her breasts and circled his thumbs around her nipples.

She inhaled.

"I want you again."

"I don't want to leave you," she said. "But I must return home before Justin awakens and finds me gone."

"I will let you go on one condition," he said.

"What condition?" she said with a slight frown.

"That you will come back again," he said.

"I want to, but I must be careful."

"We'll be discreet," he said. "Don't say no yet. We'll figure out a way."

"I won't be able to resist you," she said.

He grinned. "Good."

She pulled the sheet over her breasts. "I should dress."

He cupped her cheek. "There is something we have to discuss."

Alarm flitted in her eyes.

"I don't want you to worry too much, but I accidentally spilled my seed inside you once. I hope there are no consequences." If there were, they would be in a tight spot.

"I doubt there will be," she said. "I'm...irregular and I never conceived during my marriage."

She pleated the sheet with her fingers and looked a little sad.

He remembered the baby gown she'd been embroidering for her sister. And because he didn't know what to say, he kissed her cheek. He was relieved that they didn't have to worry about pregnancy, but he knew that her inability to conceive must have devastated her.

"I'm reluctant to let you go, but I don't want you to be late arriving home. I'll have a servant bring up hot water so we can wash."

"There is no time for that," she said. "My butler will wonder if something has happened to me."

"He is a servant. He won't question anything."

"But my maid will know as soon as she sees last night's ball gown."

"Shhh," he said. "Another half hour will make no difference. As for your maid, she'll guess you were with a lover, but she will say nothing because she needs her position."

He walked naked over to the bell and rang it. Then he donned his drawers, trousers, and a banyan. "Wrap this around you," he said, handing her one of his banyans.

She pulled it on. He rolled up the sleeves for her. "It swallows you."

"I do not want your servants to see me."

"You could hide under the covers."

She swatted him.

"Just turn on your side when the servant brings it up," he said. He didn't tell her that the servants had seen a number of women pass through the doors here.

The hot water took twenty minutes to arrive. He managed to shave without cutting himself. She looked uncomfortable as she faced the washstand. He found her shyness a bit endearing. "I'll slip downstairs for a cup of tea and give you privacy." She looked grateful as he closed the door.

After he left, Laura hunted for her hairpins, then washed and twisted her long hair in a simple roll in the back. She slipped her shift on and knew she would be embarrassed when her maid saw her. Now she would have to wait for him to help her dress. Restless, she walked over to the bed where she had lain with him. Deep inside, she could feel where he'd joined with her last night. She wanted to experience his lovemaking again, but she had to be cautious, because she could not risk discovery.

A light tap sounded at the door. He opened it and smiled at her. "We'd better dress you."

Her one night was over, and she wasn't ready for it to end. The servants would know no matter what time she arrived home. Dear God, was she really thinking of love-making again?

"Laura?" he said, closing the distance between them. He looked into her eyes and smiled. "What are you thinking?"

"Wanton thoughts," she whispered.

"Well, then." He shrugged off the banyan. Then he lifted her onto the mattress. She started to scoot back, but he pulled her hips to the edge of the bed and lifted her shift up to her waist. "I've become shameless," she said.

"I'm glad to hear it." He caressed the folds of her sex. Her breathing grew labored as he inserted two fingers. "You're hot and wet again."

She watched as he unbuttoned the falls on his trousers and untied the ribbon on his drawers. When he sprang out, she grasped the sheets.

"Wrap your legs around me," he said.

When she did, he took his cock in his hand and teased her all along the damp folds.

"Do you want it?" he said in a rough voice.

"Yes," she said.

"How badly?" he said.

"Please," she said.

He inched inside her. "Slow or fast?"

"Fast," she said.

He held her hips and thrust inside her over, and over, and over again. His blue eyes were intent on her as he moved faster and faster. "You like it like this?"

"Yes."

His eyes lowered. He was watching as he pushed in and out of her. Then he reached between them, caressing her, and she arched up to his touch, seeking the peak, and suddenly she was contracting all around him. He stilled and she could feel him throbbing. Then he suddenly withdrew, spilling his seed on the sheets.

She lay there bared to him and breathing hard. He leaned over and kissed her. "I wish I could keep you here all day and night."

"I can't believe I did that," she said faintly.

He laughed. "Stay there." A moment later, he returned with a damp cloth. When she tried to protest, he laughed. "Sweetheart, it's a bit late to go shy on me. Come along, we've got to dress you and take you home."

He helped her dress and donned his own clothing. By the time they were ready to leave, more than an hour had passed.

Her guilt set in as soon as his carriage rolled off. Laura worried her hands. He finally grabbed them in his palms. "Be nonchalant."

"My maid will see me in last night's ball gown."

"She is a maid and will perform her duties with an impassive expression. What she thinks is of no importance."

"But servants gossip, and what about Justin? Oh, never mind my son. He will sleep until noon."

Bell laughed. Then he kissed her deeply. "You were wonderful."

"Really?" she asked.

"Really. I cannot wait for tomorrow night."

"We shouldn't. I worry that we'll be seen."

"I'm not letting you go now," he said. "All we have to do is be discreet."

"Walking into my town house in a rumpled ball gown is not discreet."

"The sun is not up yet."

"It's getting lighter by the moment," she said.

"We'll be more careful with tonight's gown," he said. "Speaking of tonight, what are your plans?"

"I'm attending the theater with Lady Atherton," she said.

"I will visit her box," he said.

"Bellingham, I don't want her to know about us."

"Andrew, when it's just us. As for Lady Atherton, she may suspect, but she'll say nothing. You can leave the theater with me."

"In front of all those people?" she said.

"Laura, we'll arrange to meet separately in the foyer. It's done all the time."

"I fear one of Montclief's friends will report that we were seen together."

"First of all, I won't let Montclief rule our lives. He has no proof about us. Don't forget I've been seen giving your son fencing lessons. Lady Atherton can vouch for the interest I've taken in Justin. Do stop worrying."

"I shall try," she said.

"Good girl." He gazed into her eyes. "Do you know I've never stayed all night with a woman before? I never wanted to. In case I forgot to say it, you were magnificent."

She blushed. "I don't know what came over me."

His blue eyes glinted with mischief. "Me."

"Oh, my stars," she said. "You are incorrigible."

"Admit it. You like it."

"I think my morals took a boat to America."

He laughed.

When the carriage slowed to a halt before her town house, he kissed her on the lips quickly. "Come now. I'll escort you to the door."

"No, that is not a good idea," she said. "The neighbors might see us."

"I imagine they've seen me before."

"Not with me in a wrinkled ball gown. I had better go now." She looked into his eyes and wrapped her arms around his neck. Then she kissed him deeply. "I already miss you."

He opened the carriage door and helped her negotiate the steps. She blew him a kiss and hurried to the door.

Chapter Twelve

*L*aura felt conspicuous as she joined Lady Atherton in the theater box. Justin had plans to play cards at Lady Norcliffe's home. Of course, Sarah was the chief attraction.

She had hoped for one of Shakespeare's plays, but this play was not one she'd ever heard of. "Do you know what it is about?" she asked Lady Atherton.

"Nobody pays attention to the play, my dear," Lady Atherton said. "It's all about seeing and being seen."

"I had just convinced myself that I was imagining others staring at me," she said.

"Curiosity about you remains rampant," Lady Atherton said. "You look radiant tonight."

"It must be the gown," she said, smoothing the sheer lavender overskirt.

"Last night, I thought your strange engagement had somehow leaked to the scandal sheets," Lady Atherton said.

"I was terrified," Laura said, "but then it all turned out to be about the charity."

"Well, you do look in much better health tonight. I hope Bellingham was a gentleman when he escorted you home. A scamp like him would not waste a golden opportunity all alone in a dark carriage with a beautiful lady."

She had to deflect her friend. "We talked about Justin," she said.

"I might have known," Lady Atherton said as if she were disappointed.

"Bellingham is a good role model for my son."

Lady Atherton lifted her quizzing glass to look about the other boxes. "I've heard others say that he is too blunt, but I think he has an ability to see through a person's veneer, if you get my meaning. That talent has served him well in his political career."

They remained silent for a few moments, and then Lady Atherton spoke again. "What do *you* think of Bellingham?"

He is a superb lover. She told herself not to think of her wanton behavior last night or her face would give her away. "When he wishes, he can be quite charming."

Lady Atherton lowered her quizzing glass. "I think he pours on the charm for a certain pretty widow."

Laura grew uncomfortable and changed the subject. "Most of the ladies are wearing tall feathers in their hair. I never cared much for the fashion."

"Fashions come and go," Lady Atherton said. "Now it is my turn to change the subject. You've said nothing of Montclief. Has he written?"

"No," Laura said. "I rather hope he never does, but that is wishful thinking on my part."

"What will you do about the secret engagement?" Lady Atherton asked. "It seems to me that you and Bellingham could easily find yourselves in hot suds if that information ever came to light."

"I sometimes fear that Montclief might reveal the engagement out of spite. It would be a disaster."

"The worst that can happen is that you and Bellingham must marry," Lady Atherton said.

Laura couldn't breathe for a moment. "How can you say that in such a detached manner? You forget he is a determined lifelong bachelor. An enforced marriage would only create resentments on both sides."

"Well, if you are found out, he would have no choice. His honor and yours would be at stake."

"No, that cannot happen," Laura said. She had fallen in love with Bellingham, but she knew that if he was pushed into marriage, it would breed acrimony. And she feared that Bellingham would refuse. She thought of his words: *I never met a rule I didn't wish to break.*

Laura felt anxious and decided she'd better discuss the situation with Bell. They had to prepare in the event that Montclief threatened to expose them.

Footsteps sounded. Laura turned around and her heart beat faster. "Lord Bellingham."

Lady Atherton rose, and Laura only then remembered her manners. She stood and a dizzying feeling rushed through her as she dipped a curtsy.

He smiled. "I saw you from across the theater."

"Do join us," Lady Atherton said.

"Thank you, I will."

He took the chair next to Laura. "You look ravishing tonight."

Laura felt the blush rising to her cheeks. She wasn't adept at concealing her thoughts and worried Lady Atherton would somehow guess that she and Bellingham had become lovers.

Sure enough, Lady Atherton regarded her with a knowing expression.

"It is a pleasure to see you again," Laura said to him.

His blue eyes gleamed. "And you as well, Lady Chesfield."

"Your visit is timely," Lady Atherton said. "We were just discussing your dilemma."

Laura regarded Lady Atherton with a warning look.

"There's no point in avoiding the issue," Lady Atherton said.

"What issue is that?" Bellingham asked.

"Your secret engagement, of course. What will you do if Montclief threatens to expose you? He may very well try to use your secret to take the boy."

"I made plans in the event he does," he said.

Laura looked at him, the question unspoken.

"If he tries to blackmail us, I will counter with my own information, which I hope to get soon."

"But what if you do not find anything?" Laura said.

"I will," he said. "Whatever happens, I won't let him take your son. He's shown no inclination to do his duty to the boy, and I will not hesitate to make that known if necessary."

"But Montclief is his guardian. Legally, you can do nothing to stop him," Lady Atherton said.

"If, as I believe, he is in serious debt, his creditors are probably hounding him. I can put word out that Montclief is on the verge of fleeing the country. The creditors will descend on him like locusts. The last thing he'll want is another mouth to feed."

"But then he will be desperate," Laura said. "He's likely to demand money in exchange for Justin."

"I'll bribe him if necessary," Bellingham said.

"I cannot allow you to do that," Laura said.

He gazed at her intently. "I was under the impression you would do anything to keep your son."

"I don't like this," she said. "I have a terrible feeling it will all blow up in an awful scandal. You should not have to bear the consequences."

"He treats you and Justin abysmally," Bell said. "I will not allow him to ruin your lives. But we speak of worst-case scenarios. My instincts tell me that Montclief has some dirty dealings he doesn't want anyone to know about. The only reason he threatened you in the first place is because his friends discovered he was shirking his duty to the boy. My guess is Montclief is nervous about his own reputation, because he likely has something to hide. Once I have all of the information, I will use it to keep him from ever bullying you again."

Lady Atherton regarded Bellingham with a satisfied smile. "I might have known you had planned for any contingency."

"It is the way of politicians," he said. "Lady Chesfield, I beg you not to worry. I know you are vexed, understandably so, but I believe we will resolve this matter before the season ends."

"I am appreciative," she said. "But you made all of these plans without consulting me."

"I wanted to plan it all carefully before presenting it to you. It's the way that I work, nothing more," he said.

She didn't really believe him, but she didn't want to argue the point in front of Lady Atherton any longer. "We will have to take it one step at a time," Laura said.

"Your main concern is keeping the secret engagement a secret," Lady Atherton said. "But you must both prepare yourselves for the possibility that it may be divulged. Then you'll have no choice."

"There are always choices," Bellingham said.

"Well, we are here for entertainment," Laura said. "And we will not resolve the issue of Montclief tonight."

Bellingham gazed into her eyes. "Yes, I weary of him when there are more pleasurable diversions to be had."

A warm flush spread to her cheeks. She busied herself by smoothing her skirt to conceal her blush from Lady Atherton. But his words were like a seductive potion making her yearn for more of his touch. She remembered the heady sensation of making love to him and squeezed her thighs. The spurt of pleasure made her eager to join him tonight.

Voices sounded outside the box. Laura unfurled her fan to cool her face. Dear heaven, she must learn to hide her feelings for him, but it wasn't easy when he was so near.

"Ah, there they are."

Laura rose with everyone else at the sound of Harry's voice and saw Colin as well.

"We wanted to greet you, Princess," Harry said.

Colin elbowed him. "And you as well, Lady Atherton."

Lady Atherton snorted. "What mischief have the pair of you planned tonight?"

"Colin's father threatened to cut off his allowance if he

didn't make himself agreeable to Angeline this evening," Harry said, grinning.

"It's impossible," Colin said. "If I try to compliment her, she pinches me."

"Oh, dear," Laura said. "But, Colin, why does she dislike you so much?"

"She doesn't," Colin said. "She loathes me, and I loathe her. Our families are blind to it all. When they see us quarreling, they call it a lover's spat."

"Surely the two of you can be civil to one another," Lady Atherton said.

"I beg your pardon, Lady Atherton," Colin said, "but in all honesty, it's hard to be civil to a lady who threatens to stab her fork in your leg under the table."

Everyone laughed. As the conversation continued, Bellingham leaned down and said to her, "Meet me in the foyer after the intermission."

"I will," she whispered.

Bell left with his friends. As he walked away, Laura found herself anxious for the intermission.

When she returned to her chair, Lady Atherton remarked, "You look very much like a woman in the first blush of love."

"He is a friend," Laura said.

"He looks at you as if he's already made the conquest."

Laura fanned her face. "I would have to be inhuman not to find him handsome."

"You're lovers," Lady Atherton said.

"We are friends," Laura insisted.

"My dear, you know my thoughts about grabbing life's opportunities. I do not disapprove, but you must learn to conceal your feelings for him. From the moment he walked in this box, you lit up like the lanterns at Vauxhall. For the sake of your reputation, you must learn to adopt a cool façade in his presence."

Laura lowered her fan and toyed with it. "I don't know how to do this."

"No need to worry with a man like him. I'm sure he knows a dozen ways to Sunday how to pleasure a lady."

Laura gasped. "Oh, my stars."

"You'll get over the shy stage."

Laura wafted her fan. Lady Atherton was certainly blunt about intimate matters.

Lady Atherton shook out her own fan. "He made arrangements to meet you, I assume."

"Yes," she said. "After intermission."

"I will leave the box at the same time to visit friends. To those in the theater, it will appear we are leaving together."

"I'm sorry to involve you," Laura said.

"There is no reason to apologize. You've been alone for many years and put all of your energy into your son. You will not regret this *affaire de coeur*." She sighed. "I would add that you should guard your heart, but I see very well that I am too late."

"How could I not love him when he has done so much for Justin and me?"

"He is a fool if he doesn't make an offer for you," Lady Atherton said.

"You know as well as I do that he will never marry. I cannot allow myself to even contemplate it, because then I might hope."

"Then live in the whirlwind and do not let guilt interfere. You've given to everyone else but yourself. In years to come, you will be glad that you lived in this moment."

Laura's nerves jittered a bit as she descended the stairs to the foyer. There were still a few people walking about, but she didn't recognize them. When she stepped onto the marble floor, she looked around for Bellingham and saw him talking to an older gentleman. She walked over to a painting, pretending to admire it. As much as she wanted to be with him, this secretiveness troubled her, and yet it was very necessary to guard her reputation.

"Lady Chesfield, I thought I saw you in Lady Atherton's box."

Laura's hands trembled upon hearing Lady Rentworth's voice. She turned and said, "Hello, Lady Rentworth."

"Are you waiting for someone?" Lady Rentworth looked past Laura. "Is that Bellingham?"

She looked over her shoulder. "Yes."

Lady Rentworth's smile spoke volumes. "I have heard your name in connection with his on several occasions. He's reportedly been at your town house many times."

Laura's heart felt as if it had fallen to her stomach, but she had to remain calm. "He gives my son fencing lessons." If Montclief heard similar rumors, he would take Justin.

Lady Rentworth laughed. "He is an expert with a sword, is he?"

No one could miss the obvious double entendre, but Laura refused to let the nasty woman engage her in a prurient discussion. "Please excuse me." Laura felt nauseous as she walked over to the ticket desk. "Can you please hail a hackney for me?"

"Yes, madam. Do you have a wrap stored?"

She had kept her shawl, thank goodness. "No."

"Please wait here. I will call for you when it arrives."

Her mouth was dry. "Thank you."

She didn't look at Bellingham. Instead, she stood near the door waiting. Humiliation made her chest burn. This was her punishment for daring to enter into a liaison with him. Behind her, she heard Lady Rentworth greeting Bellingham. At least he would know the reason she'd left. But it did not matter. She was done with this illicit business. Shame overcame her as she thought of her son and all that she'd intended to risk for a man who would only offer his bed.

Lady Rentworth had obviously guessed her intention. Now all Laura wanted to do was flee this place, but she must wait until a hackney arrived. The minutes ticked by and still Lady Rentworth chattered on. The other man with Bellingham said something she couldn't hear.

The clerk entered. "Your hackney is here, madam."

She rushed out into the night. The driver opened the door, and she almost fell in her haste to board the hackney.

"Careful, madam," the driver said as he handed her up.

When he closed the door, Laura covered her mouth. *Never again*, she silently swore. She had violated her own beliefs, and now she knew Lady Rentworth had ammunition to gossip about her.

She had willfully lain with a man who only offered his bed temporarily. Lady Atherton had been wrong. She already regretted living in the moment.

Bell gave Lady Rentworth a bored look as she continued to chatter about his generous contribution to the orphan charity. He knew damn well she'd been watching Laura and him in the box. She'd probably followed Laura downstairs. He was glad Laura had told him about her encounter with Lady Rentworth last night. Now he was stuck, listening to this woman who had obviously been waiting to pounce.

"Well, I suppose I had better return to my husband, not that he will notice." She gave him a sultry look. "Of course, I could be persuaded to something more agreeable."

The devil, she was propositioning him. "I hope you find it," he said. Then he strode over to the clerk to collect his greatcoat, hat, and gloves. When he turned toward the door, he noticed that Lady Rentworth had disappeared.

The wind whipped his greatcoat, chilling him. Laura was overset, and now he had to reassure her that she'd played her hand well. When his carriage finally arrived, he gave the driver directions and climbed inside. The horses started, but the streets were crammed with vehicles and carts. He planned what he would say to Laura and guessed her response. She would likely tell him that it was over, but he wouldn't allow it. Their plan had gone awry, but Laura had done well by leaving.

An interminable time later, his carriage arrived at Laura's town house. Reed opened the door. "My lord."

"Thank you, Reed."

"Lady Chesfield is not at home," Reed said woodenly.

"Reed, let us do away with the formalities. I know she is at home, and it is imperative that I speak to her."

"I will consult her, my lord."

Bell paced the great hall while he waited.

A few minutes later, Reed descended. He feared she'd refused to admit him.

"Lady Chesfield will see you in the drawing room, my lord."

"I'll see myself up." He ran up the stairs and knocked lightly on the door. When she didn't answer immediately, he opened it and walked in.

Her face was pale as she rose from the sofa. "I will make this brief," she said. "I am grateful for all that you have done for my son, but I made a mistake last night. A grievous one."

"Laura, you did well tonight. I'm sorry for the circumstances."

"Let me finish," she said. "I was humiliated, but it is my own fault. I willingly entered into this clandestine liaison. I selfishly pushed my son and my family to the back of my mind to lie with you. It was wrong, and what happened tonight opened up my eyes. I am sufficiently punished by my shame."

"Laura, you believe that you're being punished? That is nonsensical. I know that it was embarrassing for you, but we'll use more care in the future."

"No, there will not be another time."

"I don't want to lose you," he said.

"As you said, we will go our separate ways when the season ends. You are welcome to give my son fencing lessons, if you are still interested."

"Of course I wish to give him the lessons," he said. "But I don't want to end our friendship."

She wrapped her shawl tighter around her as if it were a shield. "Even if it means only friendship? Because I will not come to your bed again."

She was testing him. He knew it. "Yes, even if it means only friendship."

"Very well." She curtsied as if to dismiss him.

"Laura, may I stay awhile so that we can talk? I feel awful about this." He swallowed. "I wanted to go to you tonight, but I didn't because Lady Rentworth was there."

"She knew what we were doing," Laura said. "I went against all of my beliefs for selfish, foolish reasons. I risked my son's welfare. For all we know, Lady Rentworth is one of Montclief's spies, but that doesn't matter. Because Lady Rentworth is a horrid gossip, and by now, everyone in London probably knows that I went to bed with you."

He took her by the shoulders. "You made the decision to make love with me. Now you're feeling guilty and looking to blame someone. The truth is Lady Rentworth might have made that assumption whether we had done something or not."

Something hot rushed up her throat.

"Don't cry," he said. "I didn't want to hurt you."

She shook her head. "I lashed out at you because it was easier than to face my own guilt. That's unfair to you."

"You feel guilty for lying with me?"

"I felt guilty when I was confronted with the possibility of exposure and knowing it could cost me my son."

He wrapped his arms around her. "I'm still working to get information on Montclief, and all we have to do is ensure that Justin stays out of trouble. And I do believe he is past that." He handed her his handkerchief.

"We also have to be careful with our relationship," Laura said, "because Montclief will use it against me, and if rumors spread, it will hurt my family. My father is a vicar. I cannot bring shame on my family."

"First of all, never show your guilt. It's like playing cards and inadvertently showing your hand. If rumors spread, ignore them if possible and deny them if necessary."

"You make it sound so easy," she said.

"Laura, let's sit for a while."

She joined him on the sofa. "I had intended to tell you how wonderful you were last night to acknowledge my late husband. You must know how much that meant to me."

"I know that you loved him, and I also know that it couldn't have been easy to watch him grow ill."

"It occurs to me that you may have firsthand knowledge of it."

His jaw worked. "No."

She looked into his eyes, her question unspoken.

"I was at university when they grew ill, and I wasn't allowed to see them because I was the heir."

Chill bumps erupted on her arms. She did her best to control her reaction for his sake. She had no words to describe how much she ached for his sorrow. Instead, she took his hand and held it. He squeezed her hand, letting her know without words that he understood the way she'd meant to convey her sympathy for him.

He looked at her. "I'm sorry for what happened at the theater, but I'm not sorry for last night. Most of all, I'm glad I met you and Justin. You may not wish to hear this, but I will say it anyway. I will never forget last night."

"Given your rakehell reputation, I find that a bit difficult to believe."

"Do you think I don't care about you? I wouldn't be here if I didn't. And, yes, I care about your son as well."

"You say that, but you insist that our relationship must end with the season. That sounds like a fair-weather friend to me."

He let out a loud sigh. "It has nothing to do with you. I know what I'm capable of and what I'm not." He inhaled, knowing that his next words would be hard to admit. "I think a long-forgotten part of me has...come back since I met you and Justin. That's as much as I can explain."

Her eyes softened. She took his hand. "It might help if you talk about it."

He shook his head. "I can't."

"You have given us so much already. I am glad to hear that you have found a part of you that was lost. I will not pry, but if ever you wish to talk about the past, you do have a friend who is willing to listen without judgment."

"Thank you."

"You are a good man. Well, you have your faults."

He laughed.

"You are entirely too authoritative and think that you are the only one who can resolve a problem."

"I can't help it. I see a problem, and I fix it."

She laughed. "But you don't let others do for themselves. You are constantly giving orders to Reed when he is my servant."

"Ah, but you are equally guilty of trying to do for your son."

"Well, then, I suppose it is a draw," she said. "We are both flawed like the rest of the world."

"I had better go."

They both rose. He kissed her hand and quit the drawing room. As he walked down the stairs, that hollow feeling in his chest returned. He'd managed to control the bleakness by shoving everything so far back into his mind that he couldn't retrieve it. But he'd done something stupid, something he ought to have known would bring it all back.

He had re-created a family.

Chapter Thirteen

One week later

Early in the afternoon, Laura took the mail upstairs to the drawing room and settled on the sofa. While she imagined Lady Rentworth had spread gossip after seeing her in the foyer, Laura had decided to take Bell's advice and act as if nothing was amiss. It was the best way to counteract it.

She felt restored after her conversation with Bellingham, but she had not seen him since that night. He'd sent a note saying he had urgent business out of London. He'd told her to contact Harry or Colin in the event of an emergency, but all had gone well.

She would not dwell on people who wished her ill. Instead, she would focus on her new friends from the society for the orphans. They would call today in order to discuss the total amount of the donations. She was gratified that so many had made contributions, and she also looked forward to seeing her friends. They were genuine people with no artifice or malice, unlike Lady Rentworth, whom Laura decided was beneath her notice.

Justin walked into the drawing room. "Mama, I got a missive from Sarah. All of our friends decided to brave the rain and play cards at Lady Norcliffe's home. May I take the carriage?"

"I don't suppose you'll melt in the rain," Laura said. "You have my permission."

"Thank you," he said.

"Sarah seems like a very nice young lady."

"She is," Justin said. "I like her very much."

"I'm very glad for you, and it seems you've made new friends."

"Real friends," he said.

"Whatever happened to George?" Laura asked.

Justin shrugged. "I heard that he banged up his curricle badly one night."

Laura figured he probably had been drinking.

"Paul is done with George, too," Justin said.

"I'm glad to hear that he is no longer under George's influence."

"Well, I'm off now."

"Enjoy the card party," Laura said.

"I'll be home for supper," he said.

Twenty minutes later, the rain came down hard. Laura walked to the window where it sheeted against the wavy glass. The gloomy weather dampened her already-low spirits. She missed Andrew. His absence reminded her that in the not-so-distant future they would part forever. She ached just thinking about the day that she would have to tell him good-bye. With all of her heart, she wished that he would not make that break permanent. The distance between their homes was formidable, but there was no reason they couldn't write to one another.

But she knew what would happen if he agreed to correspond. At first, the letters would come regularly, but over time, they would arrive less frequently. She would wait anxiously for them, and then one day, he would stop writing altogether. He would move on with his life and take a new lover. Her life in Hampshire would resume as if this season had never happened.

She turned away from the window, determined to shed her melancholy thoughts, but the dreary weather made it a little difficult. The ladies of the orphan society were supposed to meet at her town house today, but the rain was gusting now. Laura wouldn't blame them if they chose to remain indoors.

She needed to occupy herself, so she retrieved her sewing basket. When she saw the handkerchief she'd embroidered for Andrew, she decided to give it to him the day they said good-bye. For now, she would resume embroidering the gown for the infant Mary would give birth to this summer.

Thirty minutes later, the thunder and gusting rain subsided quite a bit. Laura looked out the window and saw carriages arriving. Her heart gladdened because her friends weren't letting a bit of English rain keep them at home. She rang the bell and requested a tea tray. Her spirits rose. She was fortunate to have made wonderful new friends and to make a difference in the lives of the orphan children.

Two hours and many cups of tea later, Laura thanked all of the members of their society for their efforts. The donations had been exceedingly generous. She thanked the ladies again as they drifted out of her drawing room, and then she turned to Lady Atherton. "Will you stay for a little while?"

"Of course," she said.

They sat on the sofa and Laura turned to her friend. "I am gratified to know that we've accomplished something worthwhile for the orphans. Unfortunately, we cannot give them parents."

"Dear, every philanthropic effort starts somewhere. We may not be able to provide the children with mothers, but the donations should make a real difference in their lives."

"Very true," Laura said.

"How is Justin?" Lady Atherton said.

"He's fond of Sarah, and he's made other friends as well."

"Well, it's a good thing he's no longer under the influence of George."

"I agree to a point, but Justin is old enough to make the right decisions. Like all of us, he has to take responsibility for his actions." She smiled at Lady Atherton. "When the season ends, I would be honored if you would consent to visit my home in Hampshire. I'm quite sure that my mother and father would be delighted to make your acquaintance. And, of course, all my siblings. Do say you will consider it."

"Well, I would be delighted."

"Good. We have a plan for the summer, but meanwhile we must take advantage of the shopping. I had my doubts about London when first I came here, but as soon as I saw the shops, I fell in love."

Lady Atherton laughed. "But what of Bellingham?"

"What do you mean?" Laura asked.

"You know very well what I mean."

She mustn't let on how much she dreaded the day they parted. "We will go our separate ways, and I will hold wonderful memories of him."

"What of Justin? He has benefited from Bellingham's influence. Surely you do not wish to disappoint him. He does need a role model."

"My father and brothers can provide that for him as needed when we return home. It will also eliminate Montclief's threats. Once we're home, Montclief will leave us in peace, the same way he has done for several years. He has his own brood to worry about and will not trouble us any longer."

Lady Atherton stared at her as if horrified. "You will leave Bellingham even though it is clear that you are in love with him?"

Laura laced her fingers. "He likes me as a friend, but he does not return those feelings." The admission left her with a hollow feeling in her chest. She loved him with all of her heart, but there was no future for them.

"Have you lost your mind?" Lady Atherton said. "Don't let him slip away."

She met her friend's gaze. "He made it clear that our friendship would end with the close of the season."

Lady Atherton raised her brows. "And you think there is nothing you can do to change his mind? I assure you it can be done."

"You know his history. Nothing has changed. I do not know why he is so adamant about remaining a bachelor, but it is his decision. And even if he decided to marry, I can't give him children."

"You do not know that for certain, and furthermore, since he has said he doesn't want a family, you have no reason for concern."

"He made his wishes very clear to me."

"You would give up so easily on a man who dotes on you and your son? He does, you know, whether he says so or not. No man spends that much time with a woman unless he is halfway to falling in love."

Drat it all, she didn't want to tear up. "Halfway isn't enough."

"Oh, my dear. Here is a handkerchief."

"I've turned into a watering pot," she said.

"It's understandable when you're crossed in love," she said, "but truly if you love him, do what you must to make this work."

"A one-sided love would be miserable. When Phillip declared his love, I had no doubts about his feelings for me, and he knew that I loved him dearly," Laura said. "Early in our marriage, he told me that I had made a bad bargain with an old man. I told him never to utter those words again. They were an insult to me. He apologized afterward. Phillip felt guilty and frustrated." She drew in a breath. "I would never say this to anyone except you, my dear friend, but he felt unmanned in the latter part of our marriage."

"Well, you were young and never conceived. I assumed he became impotent when his illness progressed."

Laura bit her lip.

"I do not believe you are barren," Lady Atherton said. "And you must not let that dictate your future. You don't know that to be the case. Frankly, I suspect your poor husband was responsible. It makes more sense."

She wanted a child with all of her heart, but the likelihood seemed very remote.

Lady Atherton remained silent for a moment. Then she looked at Laura. "I know you loved Phillip, but he would want you to find happiness with a good husband. The second love of your life is within your grasp. Do not walk away from Bellingham. I truly believe he loves you, even if he is too pigheaded to admit it."

"He promised that he would be available to Justin and me until the season ended. I heard the finality in his voice."

Lady Atherton had listened with her finger over her lips as if to stifle the urge to respond. She set her hand on her lap and said, "You are the first woman Bellingham has seriously expressed interest in. He needs you, Laura. If there is any woman who can break through to him, it is you."

"I will consider what you've said, since you have asked, but at this point, I have no expectation that anything will change."

"Foolishness," Lady Atherton said. "The young make mistakes because they think only in terms of the present. You are not looking down the road where you will be gray and kicking yourself for not taking a chance because you are afraid. Pride will not comfort you when you are alone. I have plenty of regrets, and every last one of them involved my unwillingness to take a risk, because I let fear overrule me. But the one thing I did not do was let the love of my life slip away. I was a mere girl when I refused to marry a marquis. You can imagine the pressure my parents exerted over me, but I would not do it. I waited for the man I loved, and he was worth the wait. You will only be this young once. Don't let love pass you by."

"I will remember your advice," Laura said.

"But will you take it?" Lady Atherton said.

"I think it is in his hands, not mine."

"Mark my words. It is in your power. You may have to swallow your pride, but the worst that can happen is that you try and fail." Lady Atherton paused. "I have spoken my mind. Promise me you will give what I have said serious thought."

"I promise," she said.

"Now, we had better put on our party smiles."

Laura frowned. "What?"

"You forgot," Lady Atherton said. "Little wonder after all the turmoil. The Duchess of Wycoff is holding a card party. I know you accepted, because we discussed it and you sent an affirmative."

"Oh, dear," Laura said. "I don't feel up to entertainment this evening."

"Well, I don't wish to go alone," Lady Atherton said. "I think you should attend, as it will take your mind off your problems."

"I daresay I will be poor company," she said, "but I will not let you down. To be honest, I am concerned that Lady Rentworth's gossip will make me the subject of avid stares."

"Staying home will make it worse," Lady Atherton said. "The trick is to act as if nothing is awry. That way you put doubts upon the tittle-tattle. At any rate, no one cares for Lady Rentworth."

Her advice was essentially the same as Bellingham's. "Well, I shall not be a coward, and you are right. If I say home, I will only dwell on things that will not be resolved tonight."

"That's the spirit," Lady Atherton said. "The cards will not be the amusement. Everyone will be on pins and needles to see what mischief will brew between Colin and Angeline, but I have heard they are both always on their best behavior when their family is watching."

"Oh, I forgot that Angeline is the daughter of the Duke and Duchess of Wycoff. I will play cards and enjoy the company." She sounded braver than she felt.

Lady Atherton touched her hand. "My dear, I know you well. You have listened to my advice, but I suspect pride will keep you from taking it."

"You are a dear friend, and so is he."

Lady Atherton rolled her eyes. "I will say nothing on that score, as I'm sure you will refute it. I will take you in my carriage tonight. Wear something especially pretty. It will make you feel confident, although I daresay you would look elegant in a sack."

"I certainly would turn heads if I wore a sack," Laura said.

"It is too bad Bellingham is out of town. If he attended, you could flirt and make him jealous."

She laughed. "I would never do such a thing," she said. "At any rate, if he truly wishes to win my affections, he will have to work at it."

Lady Atherton clapped her hands. "Brava."

Laura took a deep breath and told herself that no one at the card party would stand up and point an accusing finger at her. She would take the advice that Bellingham and Lady Atherton had given her. She would pretend that nothing had ever occurred at the theater. After all, Lady Rentworth had no proof of anything, but Laura remembered Bellingham telling her that what mattered in society was the perception, not the truth. While that worried her to a degree, she allowed that anyone would be a little apprehensive. Once she arrived and mingled with the other guests, she would be able to relax. If Lady Rentworth happened to attend, Laura would ignore her.

When her maid set the silver bandeau with the sapphire in her hair, Laura wondered if it was too much for a card party. But it was a beautiful hairpiece, and she knew she would never have an occasion to wear it in Hampshire. Her friends and family would think she had become haughty and full of herself if she wore it at a village assembly.

She padded over to the long, cheval mirror and regarded her reflection. The blue gown with the sheer overskirt looked very well in the candlelight. The blond lace on the bodice and hem was lovely and did not overwhelm the gown. She was glad that she would attend with Lady Atherton. In a very short time, she'd benefited from her friend's wisdom. The one point of divergence pertained to Bellingham, but she did not resent Lady Atherton for making her appeal.

With one last deep breath, she walked downstairs, where she encountered Justin.

"You look very pretty tonight, Mama," he said.

She found it endearing when he offered his arm to her. "Will Sarah be attending the party?"

He smiled. "Yes, she will. Sarah promised to play backgammon with me if there is a board there."

Laura remembered the day she and Bellingham had played. He'd flustered her with the accidental brush of his fingers when he handed her the dice. It seemed like an age since that day. Justin had been so difficult during that period. Now, looking at her son's smile, she couldn't help but think he was a very handsome young man. Phillip would have been very proud of him.

When Justin opened the door, Laura's lips parted. Lady Atherton sat on the sofa with a glass of sherry, and Bellingham stood at the sideboard with a glass of brandy.

Laura's breath caught as she met his blue gaze. "I didn't know you had returned to London."

A slow smile spread across his face, and then he regarded her with that slanted grin of his. "You are stunning," he said.

Lady Atherton regarded Laura with a crafty expression. "He insisted upon the escort, and I could not persuade him otherwise. You know he is quite determined when he wishes to have his way."

Laura suspected Lady Atherton's hand in this arrangement, but she kept that to herself.

"I think Justin and I shall be the most envied men this evening, as we will be escorting the two most beautiful women to the party," Bellingham said.

"Ha!" Lady Atherton said. "I am old and wrinkled, you scamp."

"You are elegant and wise," Laura said. "And few ladies of your years have maintained their youthful figure as you have done."

"Lady Atherton, I have heard that you were the most sought after belle in your youth," Bellingham said.

"Well, I admit I was popular with the gentlemen. I never lacked for a dance partner, but I only had eyes for Alfred."

Laura noted the faraway look in her friend's eyes. In

spite of the difficulties, she had married the man she loved.

Laura's confidence waned as soon as they entered the large drawing room set up with card tables. She kept a serene smile on her face. After surveying the room, Laura did not see Lady Rentworth. That meant nothing, however, since a late arrival was considered de rigueur among the ton. Her nerves jangled as she imagined that woman glancing at her while making accusations. Laura worried that somehow the gossip would make its way back home and cause problems for her family.

"Oh, there is my friend Mrs. Berrington," Lady Atherton said. "I must consult with her about her dear Oscar."

"Is her husband ill?" Laura said.

"Oh, no, it's her pug. He's off his food. Mrs. Berrington is beside herself. She dotes on Oscar, even though he has a nasty tendency to chew the legs on her furniture."

Laura and Bellingham exchanged amused glances.

"May I get you a sherry or a cup of punch?" Bellingham asked.

"Sherry, I think. Lady Atherton has persuaded me that a thimble of sherry in the afternoon is an excellent restorative."

He led her to the sideboard and poured her a sherry and two fingers of brandy for himself. Laura looked about the room again. She would be jumpy all evening, wondering when Lady Rentworth would appear.

"Lady Rentworth sent late regrets," he said.

Laura looked at him. "How did you know?"

He smiled a little. "I have friends and considerable influence."

"What specifically do you mean?" she said under her breath.

"My allies informed Rentworth that his wife was engaged in an adulterous liaison with a younger man. He knew about it, but he only cared when others expressed concern that he was being cuckolded."

"I don't know whether to be frightened or impressed," she said.

"Don't feel sorry for her. She's smeared other ladies in the past. I've heard she will soon be languishing in Scotland. She deserves her banishment."

"Why would she set out to wound others?"

He shrugged. "Misery loves company, I suppose."

"It's little wonder that George's bad character is fixed."

The card party progressed well, mostly because the Duchess of Wycoff forbade Colin and Angeline to compete in any games together. Angeline did make a nuisance of herself by peering over Colin's shoulder to see his cards.

Laura played whist for a while, but she found it difficult to concentrate. She was a bit weary and her back ached a bit. She must have bent over too much while embroidering this afternoon. She was probably about to start her monthly cycle.

She found a comfortable spot on a sofa and felt a bit better.

"May I join you?" Bellingham asked.

She nodded. "Your journey went well?"

"Yes, I went to Devonshire to meet with the land steward. He instituted a new drainage system, and I wished to inspect it." He smiled at her. "Did you miss me?"

She met his gaze. "Did you miss *me*?"

"Yes." He leaned down. "Will you stay with me tonight?"

Despite her fatigue, she was tempted, but she had to resist. Going to his bed would only make matters harder on her. "I think I had better not." She yawned. "Oh, dear, I'm undone."

"You are very tired. I hope you are not ill."

"No, I'll be fine after a night's rest," she said.

"Allow me to take you home. I'll ask Colin to escort Lady Atherton and your son in his carriage."

"You will miss the entertainment."

"I insist," he said.

She was too weary to resist any longer.

Laura rearranged her shawl for more warmth in the carriage. Bell followed her inside and knocked his cane on the roof.

"It's chilly," he said. "You must be cold."

"A little," she said.

"I'm shameless and beyond redemption," he said. "Pretend to be outraged as you crawl onto my lap."

"What?" she said.

He picked her up and sat her on his lap.

"Bellingham."

"Andrew," he said, wrapping his greatcoat around them. "Think of this as a survival measure. We're sharing our warmth."

"You are ridiculous. I am pretending that one of your marauding ancestors kidnapped me. Help, help."

"I captured the castle, and you are my reward. By the by, that was a very weak cry for help."

"You got a bad bargain with this wench."

He laughed. "No, but I fear you did."

She placed her hand on his chest. *What are you afraid of, Andrew?* She would not voice the words. He was a man, and men almost never admitted their flaws and fears. They were supposedly the stronger sex, but only in brawn. Women discussed their flaws and fears, because by confronting them, they could understand them.

He tightened his hold on her as the carriage rolled along. "I wish you would stay with me tonight, but I know you're tired."

Even if she weren't tired, she wouldn't go back to his bed again, because it would only make things harder for her. She had to adjust her mind now to the fact that he meant to leave her. He had made the decision, and she had to accept it.

"You seem preoccupied," he said. "Is something wrong?"

"No." She couldn't tell him and that made her sad. He would never know that she loved him, and it hurt to know that she was only a temporary lover. But she'd known all along that he would never offer marriage and happily-ever-after.

"You are so quiet and seem dispirited."

"It's nothing but a little fatigue. I will be myself to-morrow." But she would never be the same, because of him. Little by little, he'd captured pieces of her heart. It hurt because she loved him, and she could never tell him, would never put that burden on him.

She had no doubt that he cared about her and Justin, but they would never see him again when the season ended. He wasn't a cruel man; he was simply a man who would never commit beyond a season. When he pressed her head to his shoulder, she gave in to the fatigue and closed her eyes.

Disoriented, she lifted her head and realized she was alone in the carriage. She wrapped her shawl around her and moved over on the seat when the door opened.

"Bell," she said, still groggy from sleep.

He climbed inside, sat beside her, and knocked his cane on the roof.

The carriage jerked and rolled into motion.

"What is happening?" she said.

He took her hands. "Montclief gained entrance to your town house. He ransacked Justin's room and yours. Thank God neither of you were there."

"You think he was looking for valuables?"

He nodded. "I'm sorry, Laura. Reed said he took a box of your jewels."

"I don't care. All I want is to ensure Justin's safety."

"Montclief is obviously desperate, but Reed reported he is very angry that Justin wasn't there. I don't want you alone in the town house tonight. We're going back to the Duke of Wycoff's house. I'll send Justin with Harry and Colin to Thornhill Park in Devonshire, tonight if possible. Then I'm taking you and Lady Atherton to my town house for your protection. I instructed Reed to have the maids pack trunks for you and your son. We'll leave at dawn."

"I feel hunted," she said.

"We'll be safe on the roads and most especially at Thornhill Park. As long as Justin is on my property, Montclief cannot touch him."

* * *

Laura sat in the Duke of Wycoff's study with Lady Atherton and the gentlemen as they made plans.

"I'm sending outriders with you for extra security," the duke said to Bell. "You are too important of a statesman for us to take any chances, and we must be vigilant for the ladies."

Bell looked at his friends. "Harry and Colin have the letter from me to show the butler. Our journey at dawn will be slower with the addition of the trunks. With good roads and hopefully decent weather, we can make the journey in three days. Is there anything I've forgotten?" he asked.

"I'll have to bring Brutus," Harry said.

Lady Atherton squinted at him. "Who, might I ask, is Brutus?"

"My collie," Harry said. "Can't leave him all alone."

"The dog stays outside," Bell said. Then he turned to Laura. "Is there anything you wish to say?"

"Thank you," she said.

Bell turned to Justin and said something to him.

Laura rose from the chair, feeling wearier than she could ever remember. Even though she had confidence in all of the plans, her spirits were depressed. Then her son wrapped his arms around her and her heart welled. "I love you," she whispered.

"It will be an adventure, Mama," he said. "All will turn out well. Bellingham will see to that."

Bell climbed the stairs. As he passed by one of the guest chambers, he heard snoring. Then he eased the next door open to check on Laura. He'd been concerned about her, because she'd seemed unusually fatigued. She lay curled on her side with her hands beneath her cheek.

He stood there for a moment, tempted to cross to the bed and kiss her forehead, but he didn't want to chance waking her. She needed to rest as much as possible for their dawn departure. He pulled the door closed and continued on to his room.

Bell reared up in bed with a gasp. His heart pounded and cold beads of sweat trickled along his temples. He shoved his hands through his damp hair. The terror still gripped him. He remained still, waiting for his harsh breathing to slow.

"Fuck." He hated the loss of control, the sheer stupidity of the fear when he knew it wasn't real.

He pushed the covers aside and stood. His skin prickled from the cold. He walked over to the ewer and poured cold water into the basin. Then he splashed cold water over his face, shivered, and fumbled for the towel. Bell walked over to the glowing coals, moved the screen, and raked them. He lit a candle and checked the clock. It was three in the morning. He held his cold hands out, seeking warmth from the fire.

Bell was loath to get into bed again, but the nightmare had left him depleted. He crawled back into bed and stared at the canopy. The nightmares had started four years ago, after he'd left England. He never knew when they would come back, but they always did.

He knew it was because Laura and Justin had come too close to harm tonight. If they had not been at that card party, Montclief would have taken Justin. God only knew what the man might have done to Laura.

Bell would not rest easy until they were well away from London and out of Montclief's reach.

Chapter Fourteen

Dawn

*S*he wanted her sewing basket.

"I must have some occupation or I shall grow mad," Laura said.

Bell stood on the pavement with Laura and Lady Atherton. The servants were riding in a separate carriage with the trunks piled on the roof. "Everything is ready, Laura," he said. "We have a long journey, and I don't wish to delay."

"Please, I need something to keep me busy."

"Surely it won't take more than a quarter of an hour, probably less at this ungodly hour," Lady Atherton said.

He sighed. "Very well." Bell strode over to the other driver with instructions to meet them outside the square where Laura lived. Then he returned to the ladies and helped them negotiate the carriage steps.

Bell sat with his back to the horses and knocked his cane on the roof. The carriage rolled off. The outriders would meet them at the Swan's Inn twelve miles outside of London, where they would change horses. Bell had a pistol hidden in a secret compartment beneath the seat in the event they met up with brigands.

When the carriage rolled to a stop, Bell turned to Laura. "I remember seeing the sewing basket near the sofa. I'll fetch it."

"No, I can—"

"Stay put. I'll be right back." He climbed out of the carriage and strode up the walk. He didn't know the extent of the damage from Montclief's thievery last night, but he didn't want her to see it. He'd thought of having Montclief brought up on charges for thievery, but Montclief might counter by charging Bell and Laura with kidnapping. The last thing he wanted was for Laura's name to be smeared in the papers.

He met Reed in the foyer. "I hope Montclief won't return. Bar the door to him. I recommend you hire a couple of brawny footmen for protection and have one of them posted in the foyer in the event Montclief comes back." He pulled a card out of his coat pocket. "Here is my address at Thornhill Park. You may reach me there."

"Yes, my lord."

"I'm going upstairs to fetch Lady Chesfield's sewing basket."

The front door opened. Laura walked into the foyer.

Bell fisted his hands on his hips. "I asked you to remain in the carriage."

"I wanted to tell Reed good-bye, and while I'm at it, I will retrieve my workbox and sewing basket."

"What is the difference?" he asked.

"The sewing instruments are in the workbox. The fabrics and notions are in the sewing basket."

"Stay here, I'll get them."

"For heaven's sake, you don't even know what you're looking for. She marched off, but he was close on her heels. When they reached the landing, he opened the drawing room door, and she proceeded inside. He strode ahead of her, knelt on one knee by the basket, and accidentally knocked it over. "Sorry," he said.

Oh, God, she didn't want him to see the handkerchief. "Let me."

"I've got it." He piled yarn and fabric swatches inside. She saw the handkerchief and her heart knocked against her chest. When he picked it up, she winced.

He looked at the embroidery. She turned her head away and covered her heated cheeks. Oh, why had she not tucked it safely away? She'd never wanted him to know how she felt about him. He would not welcome her feelings for him. She couldn't look at him.

"You made this for me?" he said.

"Forgive me for the presumption." She was mortified.

"Thank you. I haven't received a gift in a long time."

His words pierced her heart. She turned to face him, her embarrassment fading.

He scowled. "Don't look so stricken. I'm a very rich man and can afford whatever I wish to buy."

"I know." He was proud and didn't want anyone's pity. "You have done so much for Justin and me. So I...I wanted to give you a gift." Her voice trembled. Now she felt so foolish, because he would know that wasn't the reason.

He tucked the handkerchief inside an inner coat pocket, grabbed the workbox, and escorted her down the stairs.

She'd been embarrassed, and he'd gotten a bit gruff after admitting he hadn't received a gift in a long time. Now he wondered if she'd developed tender feelings for him. If it were any other woman, he'd distance himself immediately, but Laura would not expect marriage.

She carried the basket and seemed determined not to look at him. When they reached the marble floor, he stopped, kissed her hand, and looked into her eyes. "Thank you." *I don't mind if you've developed a bit of a tendre for me.*

She looked up at him from beneath her long lashes. "You're welcome."

When they reached the foyer, she addressed Reed. "Thank you for your excellent service above and beyond your normal duties. You were loyal and helpful in even the most trying of circumstances. I will send word when matters are settled."

"Very good, my lady," Reed said. "It has been a pleasure to serve you. I will look forward to your return."

Bell led her down the pavement. Her face was still flushed, so he decided to divert her. "Now you will have some occupation during the journey."

"My mother says that the devil finds work for idle hands."

"That is ridiculous," he said.

"What will you do on the long journey?"

"I will nap. The devil will be delighted to find that for the length of the journey, I will have idle hands."

She smiled a little. "You are bad."

He'd managed to smooth things over. "I have no choice but to behave since we have Lady Atherton as a chaperone."

"You presume I would allow you liberties?" she said with raised brows.

"No, but I would be very tempted to tempt you."

"Put temptation out of your head. We're almost to the carriage."

He helped her climb inside. Then he followed with the intention of sitting on the bench with his back to the horses. But Lady Atherton wrapped a voluminous shawl around her and reclined on the seat with a pillow under her head.

Bell frowned at her. "Your back will be to the horses."

"No, it will be on the leather seat. It's early, and I need my beauty rest."

Bell sat beside Laura and wondered if Lady Atherton had purposely arranged for the two of them to sit together. When the carriage rolled off, she closed her eyes. A few minutes later, her lips parted, and she snored softly.

Laura set the infant gown on her lap and threaded a needle. "She is elderly and probably did not sleep well last night in a strange bed."

"She is having no trouble sleeping on the bench."

"Well, I'm glad she's comfortable," Laura said.

"We will stop at the Swan's Inn to change the horses," he said. "The distance is twelve miles."

"Oh, we can take tea," she said.

"We will wait for the next change. It's only twelve miles."

"Speak softly. We don't want to awaken her." Laura poked the needle into the fabric. "Lady Atherton may wish to freshen up."

"Freshen up what?" he asked.

Laura gave him an exasperated look. "I meant use the facilities...after we have tea."

"I think it would be better to wait. The next change is a better inn."

"I did not suggest we tour every inn on the king's road. I meant we might have some refreshment to sustain us for the long journey."

"A quick cup of tea," he said. "We will stop for luncheon at the Boar's Inn. The food is plain but edible. They have excellent ale."

"You chose to stop there because of the ale?"

"Yes, I always stop there when I travel." He bumped her shoulder. "We won't starve."

"I know." She pulled the needle through the cloth. "Will you stay at Thornhill Park for the summer or return to London?"

"I plan to invite Harry and Colin to travel with me to the Continent."

"Oh, where will you go?"

"Paris, and wherever else the wind blows us," he said.

"How long will you travel?" she asked.

"Only for the summer. And you?" he asked.

"I will return home as soon as things are settled," she said.

"I'll see you next spring in London," he said.

She kept her attention on her embroidery. "I won't be there."

His chest tightened a little, but he told himself that this was bound to happen. When the season ended, they would both resume their old lives. He thought about asking if she would agree to a correspondence, but the question he'd asked himself before popped into his head. *To what end?*

* * *

When the carriage rolled into the inn yard, Laura was anxious to visit the facilities. Perhaps it was that second cup of tea she'd drunk this morning.

Bell was speaking to a man about the horses. "We will meet you inside," she said.

He frowned. "Wait. I'll be just a moment."

Laura took Lady Atherton's arm. "I can't wait."

"Oh, dear, I hope you haven't been uncomfortable too long."

"I am now," she said, hurrying her step. Once inside, she applied to the innkeeper's wife, who showed her to the facility. She relieved herself and splashed her hands in the water in the basin. When she returned to the entrance, Bell was pacing about. Lady Atherton raised her brows in answer.

He strode over to her. "I asked you to wait."

Her face heated. "Obviously I couldn't."

"Oh." He looked a bit abashed and led them into the dining parlor. There were all manner of people inside. They were by far the wealthiest customers. Naturally, the innkeeper was solicitous and focused all of his attention on "his lordship."

A busty woman wearing a stained apron appeared at the table and regarded Bell as if he were a joint of beef she'd like to gnaw. Laura sniffed and lifted her chin. Bell requested tea for her and Lady Atherton. "I'd like a tankard of your good ale," he said.

The tavern wench hurried off, and Laura yawned.

"Tired already?" Bell asked.

"Probably from the motion of the carriage," Lady Atherton said. "Always puts me right to sleep."

"Are you comfortable enough?" Laura asked.

"Oh, yes, but perhaps you would like to lie down on the bench."

She shook her head. "I will be fine."

"You were exhausted last evening," Lady Atherton said. "I hope you are not unwell."

"I think it is all the vexation over the last few days," she said, "but I feel better knowing that my son will be safe."

"We will stop for the night at the Bear and Bull Inn. It is clean and the beds are not too uncomfortable. There is the noise from the yard, but hopefully you will be able to sleep," Bell said.

"That reminds me," Lady Atherton said. "You had better take a second room for me. One of the unfortunate effects of old age is snoring."

"Very well, three rooms it is," Bell said. "The servants can share."

The tavern wench set a tankard in front of Bell and managed to display even more of her large bosom for his inspection. After she left, Laura glared at him.

He sipped the ale. "What is the matter?"

"You ogled that tavern woman's bosom," she said.

"She practically stuck them in my face."

Lady Atherton snorted.

A few minutes later, the tavern wench reappeared with the tea. She put her hamlike hand on her hip and regarded Bell. "Anything else I can do for you, your lordship?"

"I wish to settle up quickly. We must be off soon."

"Well, that's a shame," she said. "We don't often get gents as handsome as you."

After she left, Laura narrowed her eyes.

Bell shrugged his shoulders. "Don't blame me."

Laura sighed and poured tea for herself and Lady Atherton. "Well, it's not the best tea, but I'm grateful for it."

When she poured a second cup, Bell frowned.

"What is it?" she asked.

"Don't drink too much," he said. "I'd like to just do a quick change of horses at the next inn."

Lady Atherton set her cup aside. "Bellingham, I realize you are a bachelor and unaccustomed to traveling long distances with ladies, but may I remind you to act in a gentlemanly manner?"

His ears grew hot. "I beg your pardon."

"It makes little difference what time we arrive at the Bear and Bull Inn," Lady Atherton said.

He thought it would make a big difference if they arrived only to find there were no rooms available, but he kept that to himself. He looked over his shoulder and lifted his hand in a signal for the ticket.

"Please excuse me," Laura said, rising.

He stood and frowned, wondering if it was normal for a female to visit the facilities so often. Perhaps all of his complaining had made her anxious that he wouldn't stop often enough. He cleared his throat. "I will check on the horses. Please take as much time as you need."

He had not traveled with females since boyhood and did not realize that women had to empty their bladders more often. He had deduced their bladders were small, because they frequently had to "freshen up." They might avoid the problem by drinking fewer cups of tea, but he was smart enough not to make that suggestion again.

He thought about his old traveling days with his male companions. No inns were necessary for their large bladders, which truly made no sense at all to him. If a human needed privacy to void their bladders, the bladders ought to be larger in order to accommodate their lack of external organs. Naturally, he did not share such thoughts with his female companions, who would think him coarse and unmannerly. They did not know that all males were coarse and unmannerly when ladies weren't about.

When they returned to the carriage after yet another stop, Bell thought they would be lucky to reach Thornhill Park by Christmas. But when he climbed inside, he saw the fatigue in Laura's eyes and felt like a devil for being so impatient with the ladies. "You look thoroughly exhausted."

"I will be fine," she said.

Lady Atherton sat up. "I insist you lie down, Laura."

"No, I'll curl up on the seat."

He set her sewing basket and workbox in the compartment beneath the seat to make more room. Then he knocked his cane on the roof.

When the carriage rolled off, he beckoned her. "Take off your bonnet and lay your head on my shoulder."

She curled up next to him, and he put his arm around her.

"I'm so tired," she said. Then she closed her eyes and slept.

Her lips parted a little. She twitched once, and he thought she looked a little vulnerable.

"I worried her vexation is making her ill," Lady Atherton said.

The idea that she might be sick made his chest tighten. "We will stay at the inn an extra night if she requires more rest," he said.

"Reassure her that all will turn out well," Lady Atherton said. "Remind her that you will not let anything happen to her son."

He nodded.

"She has had to be strong for a very long time," Lady Atherton said. "I'm glad you were there that day Montclief berated her for taking Justin to London."

"So am I," he said.

Laura awoke with a start.

"Are you all right?" he asked.

"Yes," she said. "Lady Atherton is sleeping?"

"Yes. You must tell me if you are feeling unwell."

"Truly, I will be fine. I think all the worrying caught up with me."

"Let me do the worrying," he said.

"I depend on you too much."

"There is nothing wrong with depending on me."

"I cannot become accustomed to it, because we will soon part ways."

"You may depend upon me during this journey and at my estate."

She covered a yawn. "You step in and take over everything. I suppose you are a natural ruler, due to the blood passed down to you from your marauding ancestors."

"I am an earl. I am supposed to rule over everyone in my domain."

"Did you ever wish that you were not the earl and had to rule?"

"I didn't for four years," he said. "I hired men to do it. I had no intention of returning."

She looked up at him. "Why did you return?"

"My friend Will was called home for his brother's wedding. We thought to travel back to the Continent afterward, but Will was unable to return for financial reasons. And then he married."

"Did he intend to be a lifelong bachelor, too?" she asked.

"He did not plan to marry, but he was caught in a compromising situation."

"Oh, dear, that must have been difficult for them."

"Despite the circumstances, they are happy and expecting a child in the summer." He paused and added, "Another one of my friends recently married as well."

"Do you visit them?"

"Not yet. I try to avoid situations where the hostess decides I must be in need of a wife."

"Do you ever think about what it would be like to have a wife?"

His chest tightened. He'd thought about what it would be like to lose a wife.

She cupped his cheek. "You didn't answer my question."

"You don't want to know."

She hesitated. "Is it the bad memories of your past?"

"No." He paused and said, "The good ones."

She laid her head against his heart. "I understand. After Phillip died, I would encounter some mundane object such as a shaving brush or a comb. It was strange that such things made me weep more than the many letters of condolences."

He placed his hand over her hair and said nothing more. The one admission was more than he'd ever revealed to anyone, except to his friend Will. Laura understood that much because she had lost her husband. But there was more than grief in his case. There was guilt.

After a long, slow journey, Bell was eager to escape the carriage and stretch his legs. A porter appeared, and Bell doled out generous vales in order to hurry things along. They went to the dining parlor and dined on roasted chicken, potatoes, and cauliflower. It was adequate for an inn.

While a maid showed the ladies upstairs, Bell waited in the dining parlor and drank a tankard of ale. When he finished it, he went upstairs. He hoped to sleep undisturbed tonight.

Lady Atherton poked her head out of the room. Her hair was tied in rags. "I told the maid to bang on my door in the morning. I have been known to sleep through thunderstorms. As soon as my head hits the pillow, I am dead to the world."

He frowned, wondering why she felt it necessary to inform him of her sleeping habits.

"Sweet slumbers," she said, and let a maid out. The maid crossed over to Laura's room.

Bell went to his room and removed his coat and cravat. Several minutes later, a door creaked open. He looked out, startling Laura, who opened her door to let out the maid. The maid hurried down the stairs.

"Is something wrong?" Laura asked, clutching a wrapper to her throat.

"No, but Lady Atherton warned me she can sleep through thunderstorms. Why didn't she just inform the maid?"

"Shhhh," Laura said. "She might hear you."

"Good night," he said.

Laura closed her door and he went inside his room. He removed his coat, waistcoat, and cravat. Then he sat on the edge of the bed to remove his boots and stockings. He walked to the basin and splashed water on his face. Gad, his heavy beard made him look like a pirate.

He started to unbutton his trousers when he heard footsteps on the stairs.

Bell opened his door at the same time as Laura. A different maid juggled towels in one arm and knocked on Lady Atherton's room. When there was no answer, she turned, took one look at Bell's bare chest, and fled to the stairs.

He laughed and stepped out into the corridor.

"Shhh," Laura said. "We don't want to wake Lady Atherton."

"I don't hear any snores," he said.

"Keep your voice down. You might awaken other travelers."

"With all that racket out in the inn yard it hardly makes a difference."

A voice sounded from the stairs. "I tell you, there's a half-naked man in the corridor."

"Alice, you got windmills in your head," a woman said.

"I tell you, I seen him with me own eyes. Knock on his door. You'll see."

Laura motioned him with her hand. He shut his door and stepped into her room.

She shut the door behind him and put her finger to her lips.

Footsteps thudded down the corridor. A knock sounded on Bell's door.

"I don't hear anything," a woman said.

"Open the door," Alice said.

"And get sacked for stealin'? Are you mad?"

"He could be ravishing the womenfolk," Alice said.

Laura clapped her hand over her mouth. His shoulders shook with laughter.

Their voices and footsteps faded away.

Laura clutched him. "H-he c-could b-be ravishing the w-womenfolk."

He bent her backward. "Aha, my pretty. Be prepared to be ravished."

"Help, help," she said weakly.

He pulled her upright. "Lord, what a caper."

She pressed a hand to her chest. Belatedly, he realized she wore only a shift. He looked at her breasts and could see her nipples through the thin fabric. His groin tightened. "You are probably tired," he said.

"I'm wide awake," she said. "I slept too long in the carriage, but I'm sure you're tired and wish to go to bed."

"I'm wide awake, too." *And getting hot all over.*

"Perhaps a glass of wine would help us relax."

"It will be poor quality and undrinkable, but I brought a flask with brandy."

"Perhaps we could talk awhile until we are both sleepy."

"I will bring the brandy. You can drink a bit. It will relax both of us."

"That sounds like an excellent idea," she said.

He lit a candle and nudged the door open. Seeing no other travelers, he eased Laura's door closed and stepped into his room. He grabbed the flask and eased the door open again. He felt like a schoolboy sneaking into her room, but he really didn't want to drink alone.

"We have no glasses, so you will have to lower yourself to drinking straight from the flask."

She grinned and patted the bed. "I figure you don't want to sit on a hard chair."

"You figured right," he said. His eyes lowered to the display of her breasts above her shift. Heat traveled to his cock, and he was breathing faster. He bit back the urge to tell her how much he liked what he'd seen and touched. "Have you ever tasted brandy?"

"No, I imagine it is strong."

"Yes, it is. Take a tiny sip and don't cough."

She sniffed it and reared back. "No thank you."

He took the flask and sipped. Then he set it aside.

"Tell me about Thornhill Park," she said.

"It is a huge property, more than a thousand acres." He pictured the circular drive and the formal landscaping. "A landscape artist proposed transforming the formal gardens into the latest fashion for wilderness. I refused."

"You wanted to maintain it as you remembered it from boyhood."

He sipped the brandy. "The cliffs are magnificent." He pictured the jutting rock and the crashing sea below.

"Tell me about them," she said.

He hadn't gone to the cliffs since returning to England, but it all came rushing back. The bizarre rock formations, the cry of birds, and the constant roar of the sea. "When I was a boy, I climbed one by myself."

"Your parents must have worried."

In his mind, he heard the crashing waves and saw himself staring below at the swirling sea. He recalled feeling dizzy by the height.

"What happened?" she asked.

The memory was like a dream. He remembered strong arms snatching him up and a hoarse voice. *My God, oh my God.*

"My father." He hadn't meant to speak the words.

"He found you?" she asked.

He'd forgotten or shoved it back into the dark recesses of his mind. Now the memory flooded his brain. "His arms were shaking."

His father had held him so tightly that it hurt.

"You might have been injured," she said. "Or killed in a fall."

He flinched and sought a little oblivion in the brandy decanter. His father had probably saved his life that day, but years later, he had not been there in his father's final hour. He'd not been there to say good-bye to his mother and brother. His jaw clenched. He'd been too late.

She took his hand. Her palm was soft and warm. "Did your father punish you?"

He shook his head.

"You don't remember?"

"I woke in the night. My father was asleep in a chair next to my bed."

"He needed to be near you," she said. "I imagine he forbade you to go there ever again."

"He took me to the cliffs the next day. My father pointed out the dangerous places and said he would take me there so that…" Something hot rushed up his throat. He gritted his teeth.

She looked at him. "So that…"

He whipped his face away.

"Tell me," she whispered.

He leaned forward with his elbows on his thighs. "He didn't want my mother to worry."

"Did he tell your mother?"

"I don't know."

"It was smart of your father to take you," she said. "He was a wise man."

"Yes and no."

"What do you mean?"

"He used to say the cliffs were shaped from the hand of God." He huffed. "I believed it."

She was silent at first. "You don't believe in miracles?"

"I believe in what I can see, hear, smell, and touch."

"When my sister Rachel's first child was born, I thought it a miracle."

He thought about the hundreds of children born in squalor, but he knew her beliefs and bit back his cynicism.

She turned his palm up and traced one of the lines. "You managed Justin so well from the beginning. I knew you must have learned from your father."

He said nothing. He couldn't.

"Your friends married. Did you ever think about what it would be like to marry?"

"Briefly, after my friend Fordham's wedding." He'd felt adrift and isolated. His friends had moved on with their lives. Damn it, he missed them.

"You will give up your family's legacy?"

His jaw tightened. "I won't be here to care."

"That's not a reason," she said.

"I don't want to talk about it."

"I realized something," she said. "There's no entail, is there?"

"There's no one to inherit." He scowled. "What is your point?"

"You mean to let it revert to the Crown."

"It's none of your affair," he said.

"If you really don't care what happens to the property, why not sell it now?"

He got off the bed. "How dare you poke into my affairs?"

"You've poked into mine, and you're not angry at me."

"Oh, yes, I am."

"You're angry because you lost your family," she said.

"No, I'm angry at your presumption. This is the reason I never speak of the past."

"I know how you feel. I walked around in disbelief after Phillip's funeral, even though I'd known it was coming. A month after Phillip passed, I went into his room and discovered that the valet had disposed of Phillip's shaving brush. I was so angry. It made no sense."

He was breathing harder. "I know it doesn't make sense to you. You think you know me, but you don't. I have my reasons for my decisions. I know what I'm capable of and what I'm not. There will never be a little family. There will never be an heir of my body. There will never be another Lady Bellingham."

"I think you had better leave," she said.

He raked his hand through his hair. "I never misled you, Laura."

"What do you mean?" she asked.

He met her gaze. "The handkerchief."

Humiliation burned her chest. "It was my way of thanking you."

"You don't have to thank me. I had a duty, given what transpired."

She bit her lip, because the last thing she wanted to hear was that he thought of her and Justin as his duty.

"Good night," he said.

When he shut the door, her face crumpled. She'd known all along that there was no future for them. And still she'd held out hope. Tonight he'd opened up a bit of his past to her, and she'd believed that she could help him heal. But he didn't want to be healed.

She'd known all along that even if he could give her the moon, the stars, and his heart, she would be unable to give him children.

She'd known for weeks now that she'd developed tender feelings for him, and she'd allowed them to grow. She loved him, but he didn't love her. He wanted only friendship, and now she wasn't even sure that could exist between them after this night.

With a heavy heart, she walked to the bed and frowned. She reached beneath the bed for the chamber pot, realizing her back ached and her breasts were a little sore. Now, of all times, her irregular cycle would have to come. Oh, this would be a humiliating experience. She prayed she was wrong.

When the maid woke her in the morning, Laura sat up and a wave of nausea gripped her. She thought it must be all of the emotional turmoil from last night. The maid brought a clean chamber pot and promised to bring a cup of tea to settle her stomach.

She was starting to feel better after sitting still when she realized that she needed the chamber pot for the second time this morning. When she pushed the pot under the bed, she nearly retched. She stood, wondering if she was ill. Then her skin prickled all over.

The day she'd gone to Rachel's house and confessed she might be increasing, her sister had asked her if she'd found herself needing the necessary more often than usual. It was the first suspicion she'd had that she might be wrong about a pregnancy.

Laura sat on the edge of the bed and covered her mouth. She told herself it couldn't be true. In the first five months of marriage, she had never conceived. After that, her husband had grown too ill to lie with her.

But how could she be pregnant? There had been only that one night with Bell. Was it possible? Her eyes smarted with tears. She'd wanted a babe so badly and thought it would never happen. Laura set her hands on her flat belly and hope blossomed in her heart.

Her happiness fled quickly as she realized the enormity of what had happened. The night they'd made love, she'd told him that she'd never conceived during her marriage. He'd looked relieved.

Last night, he'd told her in no uncertain terms that there would never be a family or an heir of his body. She couldn't tell him her suspicion, but if it was true, she would have to tell him. The babe would be his child, too.

But if she told him, he would feel trapped.

He didn't love her, and he didn't want a family. He was willing to let his property go back to the Crown because he believed himself incapable of being a husband and father.

She mustn't panic. There was no certainty. But if she was carrying his child, she would be in terrible trouble.

She would be an unwed mother with a bastard child. Her child and her family would all suffer.

"Oh, God, help me."

Bell felt like an ogre. She'd said very little at breakfast and had looked away each time he tried to catch her eyes. Now she focused all of her attention on embroidering that scrap of a gown for her sister's babe. She was probably very sad about her sisters having children while her womb remained empty. Bell wondered if the problem had been with her elderly husband. Then it struck him if that was the case, he might have impregnated Laura. He told himself that was far-fetched. He'd known men whose wives didn't conceive for months after marriage.

A memory jolted him. He could almost feel how hot his face had gotten as his father rebuked him for kissing that tavern girl. *It only takes once, and then you've created a bastard child.*

He silently chided himself for letting his thoughts run to a nonexistent disaster. The only reason he'd thought about it was because she was embroidering that infant gown. What he ought to be worried about was his ill treatment of her last night. He'd gotten his back up because she'd poked and prodded a little too far. He'd known all along that Laura was the sort of woman who doted on others. She probably thought she could patch him up. Perhaps this evening when they stopped at the White Dove, he would ask her to walk with him so that he could make amends.

Chapter Fifteen

The moment they arrived at the White Dove, Laura applied to the innkeeper's wife. She was embarrassed by the number of times she'd had to find the necessary. Now as she emerged into the entrance, she felt conspicuous. She knew it was ridiculous. Bell didn't suspect a thing. She told herself a bachelor wouldn't know the early signs of pregnancy. Of course, she wouldn't be in this dilemma if her courses were regular—or if she'd not gone to his bed. But she didn't want to regret that night or him.

The porter took the bags upstairs as Laura approached Bell and Lady Atherton.

"Well, I'm going upstairs to wash and read my book of poetry now that I'm not in a rocking carriage," Lady Atherton said. "Laura, you were wise to bring embroidery for the journey. Will you accompany me upstairs?"

Bell met her gaze, and Laura realized he wished to speak to her. She turned to Lady Atherton. "Actually, I wish to stretch my legs. Lord Bellingham, would you accompany me?" she asked.

"Yes, a walk would be nice."

"Well, we'll all meet in the dining parlor later," Lady Atherton said.

Laura took Bell's arm. The inn yard was noisy and full of travelers. He led her past a group of children who were playing. When he stopped by an oak tree, he took a deep breath. "Laura, I'm sorry for my harsh words last night. I was uncivil, presumptuous, and unkind—to you, my dear friend."

Her eyes welled. "Forgive me."

He reached for her hand. "You have done nothing wrong. I think I have a fair idea about the kind of woman you are. Your role in life as a caretaker started early, and you're very good at it. You are very aware of others' feelings, and you want to help. Given the decisions I've made, I understand why you want to help me come to terms with the death of my family."

"You never mourned them."

"I failed them," he gritted out.

"I don't understand."

"I don't want to talk about the details. I was tried, and I failed."

Laura thought of the child that might be growing in her belly and wondered how she would fare if she failed with this trial. She squeezed his hand. "You know I'm tempted to offer to help, but I will respect your wishes and privacy."

"I was out of my head when I realized I was too late. I had the perfect family, and I lost them all. If not for my friends, I don't know what would have happened. Those four years that I traveled, I knew that I could never make up for that failure. There is no resolution. I can't bring them back, and I can't make it better by creating another family."

"Are you being too hard on yourself? You were younger and tested in one of the worst possible ways."

"I decided years ago that I would never be a family man. It's not who I am. I'm not going to marry just to pass on an estate and a title. It won't bring back my family, and it won't absolve me."

He was afraid of letting himself love again because he couldn't bear to lose those he loved.

He was relieved by the jovial atmosphere at dinner. Laura was primarily responsible for the lighthearted evening. She told them funny stories about the more interesting people in her father's parish, and she also regaled them with stories of some of the local folks who put on airs.

Bell laughed. "How does your father give a sermon with a straight face when one of the parishioners snores so loud no one can hear him?"

She smiled. "Papa says it saves him time as he can easily repeat any sermon with no fear of anyone having heard the entire thing."

The innkeeper's wife brought a bottle of wine and three glasses. Laura begged off. "I would prefer tea this evening."

"You don't wish to have wine?" Lady Atherton said.

"My tastes must be changing," she said. "At any rate, a cup of hot tea is always invigorating."

Lady Atherton regarded her with an enigmatic expression. Laura knew her friend was too astute not to miss the signs.

Laura sat in a chair in Lady Atherton's room. "Well, we have one more day of the journey, and then I will see Justin again."

Lady Atherton finished her glass of sherry. "I'm certain the boy is enjoying his time gallivanting about Thornhill Park, especially with those scamps Harry and Colin."

"I fear we will not be able to keep Montclief from taking Justin," Laura said.

"Mark my words, Bellingham will not allow that to happen," Lady Atherton said.

"The courts are likely to let Montclief's guardianship stand, unless Lord Bellingham can produce evidence that Montclief is unsuitable. Thus far, the investigator has not uncovered anything substantial, other than my brother-in-law is bleeding his tenants dry."

"Bellingham's influence and his knowledge of the courts will win the day." Lady Atherton patted her hand. "I know that is probably not comforting at this moment, but I urge you to have faith in him."

"I have faith in Bellingham," Laura said, "but I would be lying if I did not admit I'm frightened that the courts will not rule in our favor."

"Be patient," Lady Atherton said. "Bellingham will save the day. Mark my words."

Laura knew he would do everything possible, but unless incontrovertible evidence of Montclief's bad character was found, she stood to lose her son.

* * *

Later that evening

Laura was scared, more scared than she'd ever been in her life. More scared than when her son had caroused with friends on the dangerous streets of London. More scared than when Phillip's doctor had confided his condition was fatal. More scared than when Montclief had threatened to take her son.

She had to make a decision, one that no mother should ever have to face, and she would have to cover up her actions every step of the way to protect all those she loved.

In the near future, she would have to leave Hampshire and invent a story for her absence. She would have to prepare in advance because her family would question her, and she must never, ever let them know.

She would apply to Lady Atherton for assistance. It was imperative that she conceal her secret, and that meant the most heart-wrenching decision any woman could ever make.

She could no longer avoid the truth. There were too many signs.

She was carrying Bell's babe.

Laura's eyes welled as she laid her hand on her flat belly, as if she could protect her unborn child. She had lain awake most of last night, wrestling with a decision that offered nothing but heartache and, worse, a life as an orphan for her child.

How could she do it? How could she give away her own child? What kind of mother would leave her child in an orphanage? The thought alone made her so sick she could hardly eat.

But the babe was Bell's as well. Did he not deserve

to know that he was to be a father? Did he not deserve to have a say in the decision? Yet his words echoed in her mind. *I know what I'm capable of and what I'm not. There will never be a little family. There will never be an heir of my body. There will never be another Lady Bellingham.*

She didn't know what to do. He'd suffered so much already, and he did not want a family. If she told him, he would do his duty and marry her, but she feared it would never be a real marriage. Bellingham was not one to let the proprieties govern his life. He would en- sure that she and the child had every comfort, but she suspected he would live apart from them. There would never be harmony between them, and their child would suffer for it.

If she didn't tell him, their child would suffer in far worse ways. She pictured a little boy with blue eyes ask- ing for his mother, and her face crumpled. She knew with every ounce of her being that she could never leave her baby, but she had to find a way to protect her child and all of her family from ruin.

Laura had no answers, but her father had taught her to trust in prayer. She knelt on the hard wooden floor, bowed her head, and prayed for an answer. "Lord, I can- not do this alone." As she strained to listen, she knew a moment of doubt, but she would not forsake her child. She waited, counseling herself to be patient as her fa- ther had taught her.

Laura waited a long time, and then the answer came. Tears rolled down her face. She wrapped her arms around her belly. "I love you," she said.

* * *

The maid had braided Laura's hair and put a hot brick in the sheets. Laura washed her face and donned a fresh nightgown. Tomorrow she would see her son again. She'd missed him so much and hoped that he'd barely thought of her as he explored Thornhill Park with Harry and Colin.

A measure of peace stole over her. She knew that in the months to come she would face unimaginable difficulties, but she had faced difficulties before, and she knew that no matter what came, she would find a way to do what was best for the baby growing inside of her and for Bell.

She laid the voluminous shawl across the foot of the bed and meant to retire when a knock sounded at the door. She cracked the door open to find Bell. "Come in," she said softly.

"I can hear Lady Atherton's snores through the adjacent wall," he said. "You will not be able to sleep with that racket."

"It's late, and I doubt there are any available rooms left."

"Laura, this is the last night before we arrive at Thornhill Park. We will be surrounded by others." He looked directly into her eyes.

She wasn't surprised. He was a direct sort of man. "You wish for more privacy?" she asked.

"Yes, I wish to talk to you, but you know me well. We need to talk, and there will be more discussions when we arrive at Thornhill Park. But for your sake we must observe the proprieties when we arrive there. The truth is I can no more get you out of my head than I could the day I brought Justin's flask to you."

"What are you saying?" she said.

"I want to discuss what is between us. Will you come to my room? The walls are paper thin, and I want to speak frankly."

She retrieved her shawl and wrapped it around her. Then she followed him across the hall. A tiny spark of hope lit within her, but she mentally chided herself. Nothing had changed for him, and everything had changed for her.

He had made it clear that permanency was not an option.

When she entered his room, they sat on the bed, facing each other.

He captured her hands. "I know we live far apart, but I don't want distance to stand in the way of our friendship. I hope you will agree to correspond."

She studied his face, realizing that for him this was probably a big step. "You will travel this summer. It may be difficult."

"Colin holds an annual hunting party in the fall. You could attend and bring Justin."

By fall, her condition would be difficult to hide. "Perhaps."

"When I return from the Continent, I will send you a letter, and we will make plans. Justin will help me persuade you."

"Let us wait until the time grows closer to tell him. Otherwise he will be constantly asking me about the plans." She looked at their joined hands. He'd invited her to his room, and now she had the opportunity to tell him that he would be a father by next winter. But she had not planned how to tell him, and there would be plenty of opportunities when they reached Thornhill Park. She just needed time to consider the best way to tell him, and she must, no matter how much she dreaded giving him news he would not welcome.

"It occurs to me that you've told me very little about your family," he said. "Is your father stern?"

"Only when he needs to be. My brothers got caned more than once."

"Let me guess. Spare the rod, spoil the child."

"Yes. Phillip did not believe in caning a child. I was glad. What about your father?"

"He knew that a caning would end too quickly. He made us muck out the barn."

"Your brother got in trouble, too?"

He only then realized he'd used the word *us*. "Yes, all boys are bad."

She laughed. "Sometimes girls are bad, too."

"Now this is interesting. Did you do bad things, Laura?" he said in a low voice.

"Yes. I was jealous that my brothers got to swim in the stream, but the girls were forbidden. Adam and Caleb were always lording it over me. One time I stole their breeches. They had to run home naked."

His shoulders shook with laughter. "Tell me about your first kiss," he said.

"Ugh," she said. "I was ten. Robert Bayer caught me by a tree and mashed his mouth to mine. I kicked him in the shin."

"Oh, so you're not so different from Angeline," he said.

She doubted Angeline had taken care of siblings as a child, but she kept that to herself.

"Did your family ever travel?" he asked.

"No, I lived all my life in Hampshire," she said. "London was the first place I ever journeyed to."

His parents had taken Steven and him to Brighton for sea bathing. They had gone to see Stonehenge. Every spring they had gone to London. "I saw the Tower of London when I was a boy. You took Justin, did you not?"

"I did. He liked it because it was ghoulish."

Bell smiled. "You're a good mother to him. It cannot have been easy to be the only parent."

"My parents helped when they could. So did my brothers and sisters. But they all have children of their own. I didn't want to impose on them."

He cupped her cheek. "Laura, you're a special woman. Don't ever forget it."

"I think you are the most remarkable man I've ever met," she said.

He laughed. "We have admired each other and can now declare we are perfect together."

With all of her heart, she wished it could be so.

"Why are you so solemn?" he asked.

"I find myself a little reluctant for tomorrow."

"Why?" he said.

"Because I don't want tonight to end."

"Laura?"

She'd fallen in love with him, and in years to come, she did not want to look back with regrets. "I want one last night with you."

Bell searched her eyes. "Are you sure?"

She answered him with a deep, hungry kiss.

Oh, God. He removed his boots, trousers, and stockings. When he looked at her, she gave him a sultry look. He wrapped his arms around her. When their lips met, he teased his tongue along the seam of her mouth until she opened for him. The kiss was deep and hot. He wanted her so badly, but he would not rush her.

Bell lifted the shift above her hips and pulled it over her head. He cupped her breasts and teased her nipples with his thumbs. She arched her back. He knew what she wanted and suckled her. She placed her hand on the back of his head, and she started breathing faster.

She ran her hand over his chest and down his torso. His cock was straining against his drawers. She reached between them and pulled the ribbon loose. Her hand slid over him. "It's hard," she said.

He was breathing heavily. She slowly pulled his drawers off, teasing him with her fingers, and he watched the whole time until he sprang out. This time, she curled her hand around him, and he groaned.

He cupped Laura's breasts and suckled them. Then he reached between them and encountered wetness. "Oh, yes," he said.

He pushed her thighs apart, reached under her bottom, and lifted her up. When he used his tongue on her sweet spot, she cried out. He paused and met her gaze. She grabbed the extra pillow and bit it.

He looked up at her while he used his tongue to drive her to the edge. Her head had fallen back, and her hair spilled over the pillow. She placed her hand on the back of his head as he spread the folds and laved her faster.

She was writhing on the bed. "I want you," she said.

"Where?" he said, sliding his finger along her wet folds.

"Inside me. Now."

He positioned his cock, and this was no leisurely lovemaking. He pushed inside her and she lifted up to him, her back bowing. Then he pulled her legs over his shoulders and held her hips. He could not ever remember being this lust-crazed in all his life. He watched as he pushed inside her. She was hot and tight inside. He withdrew partway and pressed in as far as he could go. He held still and said, "Squeeze me."

When she did, he nearly spilled his seed because it felt so damned good. He reached between them and rubbed her sweet spot as he thrust faster inside her. Little feminine sounds came out of her throat, making him insane. When she came apart, the powerful contractions gripped him, and ecstasy took over. Afterward, he collapsed atop her, but he didn't want to crush her. He rolled to his back and looked at her. She was still breathing hard. He was losing his focus. His brain shut down, and he remembered nothing.

At some point, he awoke with a start. The candle was still burning, but it would gutter soon. She was watching him with a sleepy smile. He cupped her face. "Are you all right?"

"Yes," she said, smiling.

He leaned over her. "I'm going to have a hard time resisting you at Thornhill Park."

She shook her head. "We cannot when my son is there, and Lady Atherton as well. We cannot be seen sneaking in the night."

He kissed her long and deep. "God, I want you again."

She took his hands and placed them on her breasts. He pushed them together and flicked his tongue back and forth. She arched her back, and her nails bit into him. He kissed his way down her belly, and then he pressed her thighs wider. He used his tongue to give her pleasure, and she threaded her fingers in his hair. When he slid two fingers inside her, she reached between them and wrapped her hand around his cock.

"You want me inside you?"

"Yes," she said.

He slid home and held still, loving the way it felt inside of her. When he set a slow rhythm, she arched up to him, straining her body. He reached for her sweet spot and a moment later, she cried out as her body contracted all around him. Then he thrust inside her without restraint, swearing this would not be the last night. He knew he would not be able to resist her. But his thoughts became unfocused and he came, straining inside her. He kissed her sweet lips and curled behind her on his side. His eyes shut, and the last thing he remembered was her whisper. "I love you."

They changed horses at an inn within twelve miles of Thornhill Park. Laura's eyes held the languorous expression of a woman well loved. Last night, she'd obviously thought him asleep when she'd said she loved him. In the past, he'd hated when women said that to him, because he didn't believe them. But he'd suspected Laura held tender feelings for him. He didn't mind, because unlike all the others, she wasn't looking for a husband.

When he turned to Laura, she regarded him with a sultry expression. He wanted her again, and he could clearly see the desire in her eyes. She'd made it clear that lovemaking was off-limits with her son in residence at Thornhill Park. He must respect her decision, but he didn't think either of them would be able to resist the powerful desire between them.

* * *

As the carriage rounded the bend at Thornhill Park, Laura sucked in her breath. "Oh, the façade of the house is beautiful, and the gardens are magnificent," she said. The conical shrubs lined the path to the door. A riot of colorful flowers attested to a well-kept garden. "You were right to keep the formal landscaping," she said. "I know the fashion is for wilderness, but this is a showpiece."

Lady Atherton stirred herself from her nest of pillows and shawls. "Oh, my, the flowers are delightful. Bellingham, you should entertain more often so that others may enjoy these fabulous gardens."

The carriage slowed along the circular drive. Harry, Colin, and Justin walked out to meet them. Bell descended the carriage and assisted Lady Atherton on the steps. Then he helped Laura.

Her heart leaped at the sight of her son. She greeted him with a hug. "You have grown as brown as a nut."

"Yes, I have been fishing and practicing archery," Justin said.

Bell thought the boy was in especially good spirits.

"Let us all go inside now and have tea." Lady Atherton regarded Bell. "I assume you have more than bachelor fare on hand."

"Yes, we have a variety of foods at Thornhill Park," Bell said, laughing. "Come along, everyone," he said.

"Mama, there's a lake," Justin said. "I didn't catch a fish, but I'll try my hand again. And there's a folly," he said. "You'll like that. The house is enormous. It's been in Bellingham's family for many generations."

Laura raised her brows. "Would that include the marauding ancestors?"

Bell laughed. "We have no portraits of my really ancient ancestors, but according to legend, they were blood-curdling and ruthless."

Harry made a noise that sounded ominous.

Bell looked at him. "You are a bad marauder. Let us go inside."

A collie trotted into the great hall and bumped against Justin's leg. He petted the dog. "Brutus thinks I'm a sheep and tries to herd me."

Bell put his hands on his hips. "Harry, I said no dogs in the house."

"Brutus is accustomed to the life of luxury," Harry said. "He yowled for hours when I tried to put him out."

Justin bent down to ruffle the dog's fur. "You're a good dog, Brutus." Justin grinned at Laura. "Last night there was thunder. Brutus got scared and jumped in bed with me."

"He tried that with me," Colin said. "I showed him the door."

"Wonderful," Bell said. "There will be dog fur everywhere."

After they stepped inside, Laura looked round at the curving staircase and the marble statues on either side of it. "How many rooms are there?" she asked.

"Two hundred," Bell said. "Not that I ever intend to invite that many people to stomp around the gardens. At any rate, I think we should all meet in the red drawing room for tea and then we'll make plans."

Laura had dreaded this journey because of what they faced with Montclief and because of her relationship with Bellingham. Last night they had both been wild with lust, but she'd wanted that night with him. She'd thought of what Lady Atherton had said about grabbing life and knew there would never be an opportunity again.

She loved Bell heart and soul, but she had no illusions about his feelings for her. Yes, he cared about her and Justin, but he wasn't willing to give more. She wanted to believe that he could overcome the demons inside him, but he had to want to do it. She'd always thought that she could make things right for others, but she could see now that he had to want to heal.

"There are maids for the ladies," Bell said as the footmen carried the trunks upstairs. "I'll have hot water sent up for baths. We will meet in the red drawing room in two hours if that is acceptable."

The housekeeper, Mrs. Anders, appeared. The rotund woman led the way. Her keys jangled as she walked upstairs. "This room is for you, Lady Chesfield," she said, opening the door. It was a large room with a canopied bed. The blue bedding and bed curtains were lovely. She found a pretty dressing table in the corner.

"The maid will be up directly," Mrs. Anders said.

"Thank you," Laura said.

"Lady Atherton, your room is farther down the corridor. His lordship specifically assigned it to you. There's a pretty view of the gardens from your window."

"Oh, well, in that case, I suppose I can bestir myself to the exercise." She winked at Laura and followed the housekeeper.

Laura smiled as they turned the corner. She shut her door and walked about the room, admiring the polished furnishings. There was a little settee next to the window. She eyed the door to the right, and curiosity drew her. She opened the door and peeked inside, where she found an enormous masculine bed. It was a connecting door set up for husband and wife. Her stomach clenched, thinking of his poor parents and brother suffering from that cruel disease. The whole time, his mother and father must have worried about their son away at university, and yet, they would have wanted him to stay away from possible contagion.

She closed the door and walked about the dainty room with the rose-colored bedding. The vanity table held no feminine bottles. When she opened the drawer, it was empty. There was not a single item in the room that gave any hints about his mother. It had been four years since their deaths, and he'd indicated the servants had put away all the personal items. She sat on the edge of the bed and her heart filled with sadness for him. The room was pretty, but it felt melancholy. It struck her that the reason he'd planned a journey to the Continent was to escape the house that was no longer a home.

Two hours later, Laura found her way to the red drawing room, thanks to a helpful maid. The tea tray had arrived, and Laura offered to pour. There were fairy cakes and little sandwiches.

Justin had piled sandwiches on his plate and proceeded to wolf them down.

"He eats a lot," Harry said. "Brutus is grateful because he gets the scraps, not that Justin leaves much for poor Brutus."

Bell brushed his trousers. "Dog hair," he said.

"It's dog hair," Justin said. "There are worse things."

"You sound like your mother," Bell said.

"Brutus is a good dog." Justin fed him a bit of roast beef.

"I'm sure Brutus thinks you're a soft touch," Lady Atherton said.

Everyone laughed, including Justin.

"I'm ready to be outdoors," Colin said.

"Justin, there's an enormous crevice," Bell said. "I'll take you there, but you have to promise to be careful climbing it. Your mama would have my head if you cracked yours."

Laura smiled at Bell, remembering his story about his father.

"We saw it," Harry said. "I bet the view is fantastic."

"It is," Bell said. "There's still plenty of light out if anyone is interested in archery."

"Oh, dear me," Lady Atherton said. "I haven't held a bow in more years than I can count, but I did enjoy it when I was younger."

"Then you must try your hand at it again," Bell said. "I'll set up the targets and get the bows for archery."

"I'm anxious to see the folly that Justin spoke about," Laura said.

"There's a bridge that crosses the lake. It's perfect for walking," Bell said.

"Is it far?" Lady Atherton said. "Perhaps I should ride Brutus."

Bell laughed. "By all means. Afterward, we can put Brutus in the stables with the horses."

"He's terrified of their snorts," Justin said.

Bell frowned at Harry. "Your dog is afraid of horses and thunder."

"He's afraid of baths, too," Justin said.

"Great dog," Colin said.

"If the weather holds, we should have a picnic tomorrow," Bell said.

"That's an excellent idea," Colin said. "Food always tastes better outdoors."

The gentlemen went to find the targets, bows, and arrows. Laura suggested that Lady Atherton join her for a walk in the garden. "The garden is beautiful," Laura said. "I confess I'm a bit surprised that he keeps it maintained so well when he spends so little time here."

"I don't believe he ever neglected it in the sense of decay," Lady Atherton said. "It is almost as if the house is a museum, for it is never really used. I believe this may be the first time he has ever invited anybody here."

He'd mentioned his father and referenced his brother at the inn where they had made love. There had been many happy years at Thornhill Park. "Did you like his mother?" Laura asked.

"Indeed I did. Beautiful woman. He gets his eyes from her. She was quite accomplished at drawing, and I already told you about the annual house party. It's such a shame that he has no wife to carry on the tradition."

It sounded like an idyllic life. "His parents were happy together?"

"Oh, yes. Bellingham's father quite doted on Elizabeth—that was her given name. One year, they canceled the house party. I understood from others that she lost a babe. There weren't any more children."

"I imagine that was difficult," Laura said.

"Well, if he was smart, he prevented another pregnancy. Most men are too selfish—the ones with ten or more children. Or they forget themselves in the moment."

Laura's face heated at her friend's frank words. She bent down to admire a daffodil.

"Laura," Lady Atherton said.

She rose and looked at her friend.

"I have been concerned about you," Lady Atherton said. "You have been unusually tired and needed the necessary quite often."

Laura's mouth grew dry.

"Does he know you're increasing?" she said gently.

Her heart felt as if it had dropped to her stomach. She shook her head.

"You must tell him," Lady Atherton said. "The sooner the better."

Laura sat on a wrought-iron bench. "I'm terrified."

Lady Atherton joined her. "You needn't be. You're hardly the first couple to anticipate the wedding. He can get a special license and marry you posthaste."

Her stomach roiled. "There won't be a wedding."

"What? Of course there will be a wedding. You can't have a child out of wedlock, and frankly I think it is probably the best thing for both of you," she said. "It is high time he settled down."

"It's far more complicated than that." She wished with all of her heart that it was not.

Lady Atherton sat beside her. "I don't have to tell you the consequences of being an unwed mother. And if it ever became known, you would be giving Montclief more ammunition."

"He will never know." But she shivered just thinking of Montclief taking her son away.

"In a few months, it will be obvious to anyone that you're with child," Lady Atherton said.

"I've been thinking about what to do," she said.

"Good, now tell him at the first opportunity that he's going to be a father," Lady Atherton said.

"You don't understand. He has no intention of ever marrying."

"He will adjust to the idea," Lady Atherton said. "This is not a choice, Laura. You have to think of the child, your son, and Bellingham. He will live up to his responsibilities, and the two of you will probably end up with half a dozen brats."

Laura shook her head. "He will believe I trapped him."

"He will make an honest woman out of you. Quite frankly, he is responsible."

"He is leaving for the Continent when the season ends."

"Laura, go to him today. I daresay he will be thrilled."

Laura bit her lip to keep from crying. He would not be thrilled.

"Now, now. I know it is a bit frightening, but everything will come out right in the end."

Laura wished she could believe it.

"You mustn't make yourself ill worrying over what can't be changed. It's not good for you or the babe."

"I have a plan, but I need your help," she said.

"Laura, I will do anything for you, provided it is sensible, and the only sensible thing is for you and Bellingham to marry."

"Before my condition becomes obvious, I want to come to you in London. I cannot stay in Hampshire," Laura said. "I will tell my family that I am spending time with you and that the two of us are helping the orphaned children. Then I will bring my own babe home and say that I took in an orphan."

"Laura, that will never work. Your family would be suspicious, and I know you would be heartbroken if you were apart from Justin so long. He would not understand if you leave him. More important, Bellingham has a right to know."

"I'm so vexed that I cannot even think straight," she said. "I see now it was desperation that led me to such a foolish plan. He doesn't want a wife or children. There is something broken in him. You were right about that, but unless he is able to face his demons, he should not marry."

Lady Atherton squeezed her hand. "Promise me that you will tell him. It is his child, too. Will you do that?"

"Of course I will." Her eyes welled. "I love my child, but I wish..."

"There now, all will be well. You'll see. Sometimes the fear is much worse than anything else. Get some rest, and do not suffer in silence. I'll stand by you no matter what comes."

The next afternoon they all set out for a picnic. In deference to Lady Atherton's age, Laura had ridden with her in a carriage to the folly. They had to transport the food at any rate, so she didn't mind missing the walk.

They arrived before the men, and the servants laid out blankets and cushions.

"What?" Lady Atherton said. "Where is the table and awning?"

Laura patted her arm. "We have the trees for the awning and a blanket for a table. It will be great fun."

Lady Atherton frowned. "I am to lower myself to the ground?"

"To the blanket, dear. May I provide assistance?"

"Absolutely not. You are with child."

Laura put her finger to her lips. "We must be careful."

"Humph. It would serve him right if he overheard. I daresay he would...well, never mind, it isn't fit to speak of." She gingerly knelt upon the blanket. "In my day, this would be considered uncivilized. I ought to have expected it from Bellingham. He comes from savages, you know."

Laura laughed. "Yes, he claims his ancestors were marauders."

"I don't doubt it," Lady Atherton said.

After the servants set out the china and silver, Laura arranged the food on the blankets. She poured a glass of lemonade for Lady Atherton and herself.

"Well, this is refreshing. I daresay I haven't sat on the ground since I was a child," Lady Atherton said. "Perhaps not even then."

Laura laughed. "You were probably a hoyden."

"I was indeed. Like you, I had brothers. Well, I do hope there's enough food. Three grown men, your son, and one cowardly dog are about to descend on us like locusts," Lady Atherton said. "Are you feeling well today?"

"I was a little nauseous when I awoke, but sitting still helped."

"I'll instruct a servant girl to send up dry toast and tea early each morning. It helps if you keep a little something in your stomach."

"Thank you for the advice." Laura looked up and saw the gentlemen approaching. Harry said something to Justin. Then both of them were racing to the blanket. Justin barely beat him, and Laura clapped.

Harry put his hands on his thighs, obviously winded.

Colin and Bell strolled over to Harry.

"Looks like he's ready for the pasture," Bell said.

"He might live yet," Colin said, slapping Harry on the back.

"Harry, look at the sprig," Colin said. "He's still dancing around ready to have a go again. Maybe you want a rematch?"

"Stubble it," Harry said, straightening.

Laura rose from the blanket. "Lady Atherton said you would descend on the food like locusts. Will you prove her wrong?"

"Your son has already found the chicken."

Laura's jaw dropped as she saw Justin walking around chewing a chicken leg. "Justin, have you forgotten your manners?"

He swallowed. "I'm hungry."

"You must wait until everyone else is seated."

"Very well," he grumbled.

Everyone laughed. Laura was proud of him. Her heart gladdened to see her son in such good spirits.

The men found places, and Bell sat next to Laura. She would give anything if things could be different.

He leaned down. "You seem preoccupied."

"Forgive me. May I serve you?" she asked him.

A sultry look came into his eyes. "Absolutely."

Oh, dear heavens. He'd made it sound as if...never mind.

Lady Atherton poured lemonade for everyone and passed the glasses around. All of the men piled food upon their plates and ate with gusto. Laura ate a bit of chicken and part of a finger sandwich and salad. Then she set her cutlery aside.

Bell looked at her plate. "You didn't eat. You nibbled."

She knew she had to keep her strength up, but her vexation made eating difficult.

He picked up a strawberry. "Eat it."

When she attempted to take it, he shook his head. "Open for me."

She bit the strawberry from the stem and ate it. He looked into her eyes, and that heady feeling rushed through her chest. Out of the corner of her eye, she spied Justin looking away. He was probably embarrassed. She lowered her lashes and picked up her fork. She moved food around on the plate to make it seem as if she were eating. When an opportunity arose, she must take Bell aside and warn him to be more cautious with the way he looked at her. Justin was observant, and Laura did not want him to be confused.

The servants packed up all of the food and the men walked down to the stream. No doubt they were making plans for an early morning fishing expedition. Lady Atherton declared that the food had made her sleepy. Laura encouraged her to take the carriage back to the house to rest.

When the men returned, Bell asked if she was ready to see the folly. She'd planned on walking with Justin, but Colin was whispering something that made Justin laugh. So she twirled her parasol and walked alongside Bell. "The fresh air is wonderful. I almost forgot what it was like while we were in London."

"How do you like the property so far?"

How could he let it revert to the Crown? "It is beyond words, truly," she said as they crossed over the bridge. She looked at him. "You must be very proud."

"I'm glad you like it." Bell pointed. "There's the folly."

It was a Grecian temple folly with tall columns and a rectangular roof.

When they reached it, Bell took her inside. "It's a building that has no purpose other than to be ornamental."

"Quite an extravagance," she said. "But it is a lovely building and provides shade, so it is not entirely useless."

"Unlike you, scamp," Bell said, messing Justin's hair.

Laura frowned. "Justin, your hair needs trimming."

"You don't want to look like a girl," Harry said.

Justin chased after Harry. "I'll get you for that," her son called good-naturedly. Colin joined the fray and chased Justin.

Someone walked up behind her. "I could rest my chin on your head," Bell said.

She inhaled fresh air and the subtle scent of sandalwood soap. "Why do grown men revert to boyhood when let out of doors?"

"Because we're wild beasts underneath our civil façade," he said.

She wondered if the child would be a boy or a girl. She turned and looked up at him. "There is something I must discuss with you soon." As soon as she uttered the words, her mouth dried.

"What is it?" he asked.

She swallowed. "Not now. Later."

"You leave me in suspense," he said, gazing at her hungrily.

"We must use care around everyone else."

"What do you mean?" he asked.

"At luncheon...the strawberry. Justin was watching."

"Laura, he's a smart boy. He knows that I have feelings for you."

"What feelings?" she said.

He shaded his hand over his hat brim. "Must we define it? I care about you, and I think you care about me."

"He will ask questions that I will have trouble answering." What would she tell Justin when her condition became obvious?

"Keep it simple," Bell said. "Tell him that you and I care about each other."

It was simple and true, though there was nothing simple about their relationship. "For my sake, please be discreet."

"Is this what you meant to tell me later?"

She hesitated and lost her courage. "Yes."

"I'll do better," he said. "It's just that sometimes I look at you and I'm undone."

She looked away. When he said things like that, her heart leaped, but moments later, she would remember that it was all temporary. "Where did the others go?" she asked.

He shrugged. "They'll be back."

She looked at him. "You arranged it."

"No, but my friends know that I'm fond of you."

Fond. It was not enough for a lifetime, but he'd been clear about the limits. Last night, she'd fantasized that she'd told him about the child. In her fantasy, he picked her up and twirled her around. In reality, he would probably be unhappy at first and then resigned. She didn't want to ponder what would happen if he felt he must marry her out of duty.

"I had a letter this morning," he said. "The investigator

is on to something. I hope to get a specific report soon."

"I worry that Montclief will take my son."

"Worrying will change nothing," Bell said. "I know it's difficult to put it out of your mind, but the investigator is close. We will prevail."

"And if we do not?"

He cupped her cheek. "Your son is safe here. He is no longer surly, and you need no longer worry that he will find trouble on the city streets. While he is here, I plan to show him the workings of the property. I'll talk to him about the tenants and how to deal with those in his employ. I know that the circumstances are difficult now, but we have no choice except to be patient. For now, Laura, let it be. Otherwise you will make yourself ill with vexation. That won't help your son."

"I will try," she said. "It is easier said than done."

"I know." He wrapped his arms around her and pulled her up on her toes. She knew she ought to resist, but she was weak where he was concerned, and she kept remembering Lady Atherton telling her that regrets were about what one didn't do.

He kissed her softly at first, and then with more intention. His hand slid down to her bottom, and he pressed her against nim. She could feel his erection against her stomach and desire raced through her veins. In the very near future, they would part forever and probably far sooner than she wished. So she opened her lips for him because this time was all she would have with him. As their tongues tangled, she placed her hand over his heart. *I love you, but it's not enough for both of us and my children.*

Chapter Sixteen

*T*hat evening after an excellent dinner of roast beef, Lady Atherton rose and said, "Gentlemen, enjoy your port."

"Justin, you may come to the drawing room with us," Laura said.

He pulled a face. "I want to stay with the men. Brutus is resting next to me."

Bell had seen the boy feeding bits of roast beef to the dog. Brutus must be the best-fed dog in all of Britain.

Bell ruffled Justin's hair. "You may stay, but no port for you." He looked at Laura. "We'll be along shortly." He retrieved the decanter and poured for his friends.

"Can't I at least try it?" Justin asked.

"I will pour a tiny bit in a glass for you to taste." Bell poured a very small amount. "Sniff it first and then drink."

Justin tasted it. "I like brandy better."

"If that's a request, forget it," Bell said.

"You'll acquire a taste for port," Colin said.

"Not until he turns twenty-one," Bell said.

"That's four years," Justin said. "That's a long time."

"He has no trouble with arithmetic," Harry said.

"Unlike you, Harry, he will not always have pockets to let because he doesn't calculate the costs until it is too late," Colin said.

"I am always low in the water," Harry said. "It grieves me, but fortunately I have generous friends."

"You could marry a lady with pots of money," Justin said.

Harry clutched his cravat and pretended to choke.

"I have to take a piss," Colin said. "Where's the pot?"

"Not at the table," Bell said. "I do not eat where I piss."

Justin burst out laughing.

"Colin, you know where the water closet is," Bell said. "Get off your lazy arse and walk there."

Colin grumbled and strode out of the dining room.

Bell regarded Justin. "We must talk."

Justin narrowed his eyes. "Why?"

"Because you need to learn the man code."

Out of the corner of his eye, Bell saw Harry's shoulders shaking.

"What is the man code?" Justin said, his voice full of suspicion.

"It's what we do when ladies are not present," Bell said. "Once they withdraw, we are free to be our normal beastly selves. Ladies, however, have tender sensibilities. They do not appreciate burping, passing wind, pissing, and all other beastly things that send them running for their smelling salts."

Justin snorted. "I hope you did not take years to learn what I knew at age six."

Harry laughed. "A hit, Bell. You must allow he scored a hit."

"I get a pass because I have been a bachelor for many years and can do as I please at home."

"But you will marry someday," Justin said. "You need some brats to inherit, do you not?"

Bell's stomach clenched. "For tonight, you're the brat," he said.

Bell invited the ladies to observe them play billiards.

Lady Atherton seemed especially thrilled. "Well, it isn't often we ladies get to observe the gentlemen in their manly pursuits."

Colin grinned at her. "Perhaps you wish to join us. Do you play billiards?"

"Oh, heavens, no, but I'll take a glass of sherry."

After Colin brought her the sherry, he pulled out a gold case and flicked it open. "Perhaps you wish to indulge in a cheroot?"

"I don't mind if I do," Lady Atherton said.

Laura looked at her friend in horror. "You aren't serious?"

"At my age, I figure I might as well try a few forbidden experiences." She winked at Colin. "Do bring a candle and light this for me."

Bell took the cheroot out of her hand. "Not in the house."

"Why?" Lady Atherton said.

"They stink," Justin said.

"No wonder men like them," Lady Atherton said.

"Justin, are you ready to try your hand at billiards?" Bell asked.

"I'll give it a go," he said.

Laura watched Bell instruct her son. He was so patient with Justin, and it was clear to her that Justin admired him. Tonight she felt especially emotional, which must be a consequence of her pregnancy. She set her hand on her flat belly, and then she saw Harry look away hastily. Her heart felt as if it were in her throat, but she doubted he would say anything to Andrew. Then again, it was entirely possible that she was just being overly sensitive. Harry probably had not thought twice about it.

Bell's voice drew her attention.

"You have a good eye," Bell said to Justin.

Her son knocked three balls into pockets.

"Glad I didn't wager with him," Harry said.

"You're sadly flat," Justin said. "You have nothing to wager with."

"How else will I get money?" Harry said.

"Bell, show him your trick," Colin said.

"What's that?" Justin asked.

"Just watch," Harry said.

Bell lined up the balls in a triangle. Set the white cue ball in place. Then he sighted the ball and thrust the cue. Every single one rolled into a pocket.

"Brilliant," Justin said. "Show me how to do it?"

Bell looked at the clock. "It's late. Your mother will have my head if you aren't awake by ten for breakfast. Run along now. We'll ride tomorrow."

"Very well," Justin said.

"I confess I'm weary," Laura said.

Lady Atherton exchanged a poignant look with her. "I might as well turn in, too."

After Justin and the ladies left, Bell said, "Let's go outside for a cheroot. I haven't had one in days."

His friends followed him. He found the flint box and when he managed a flame, he lit his cheroot and his friends' as well. The three of them blew smoke rings for a while. Bell kept thinking about what he'd said to Justin. "I shouldn't have said that."

Colin blew out a smoke ring. "Said what?"

"That Justin was the brat tonight."

"It was only a jest," Harry said.

"I fear I've set the wrong expectations," Bell said.

Colin ground out his cheroot. "How so?"

Bell inhaled from the cheroot and blew out a smoke ring. "I'm getting in a bit deep."

Harry flicked an ash. "I'm unsure what you mean, but the boy is safe and happy here."

"It's not just the boy," Colin said. "You've got cold feet. It's understandable, but we've got eyes in our heads. You're mad about Lady Chesfield, and I'm sure she feels the same."

Bell inhaled again. "It's not that simple."

"Well, Montclief is a big hurdle," Harry said. "You could eliminate it if you married her."

Bell's chest felt tight. "He's the boy's guardian. Neither Laura nor I have any blood ties with him."

Colin scuffed his boot on the gravel path. "You have a lot of influence. I'm not saying it would be easy, but the courts can appoint Justin's guardian. Call in your favors and get the courts to appoint you. Whatever dirt you dig up on Montclief will help, but the most damning evidence is his complete neglect these last four years."

"Don't get me wrong. I care about Laura and the boy, but she deserves better."

"Devil take you," Harry said. "You're just reluctant to jump in the parson's mousetrap."

He shook his head. "You don't understand. There are...things I've never reconciled."

Colin sighed. "This is about losing your family."

"I can't explain," he said.

Colin gripped his shoulder hard. "You don't have to explain. You're our friend."

"Right," Harry said. "Whatever it is doesn't matter to us."

His jaw worked. "Thank you."

The next morning, Laura awoke with morning sickness. She stayed very still and nibbled on the bit of toast. She knew the consequences of her pregnancy would be terrible if Montclief ever learned of her condition. Montclief would surely take Justin, and her family would partake of her shame. She might have to leave her home and family forever to protect them.

The alternative—Bell offering to marry her—would be disastrous. No marriage should start off under those circumstances. But she didn't know what to do.

A few minutes later, Lady Atherton stepped inside the bedchamber. "Laura, you are still abed?"

"The morning sickness is worse today."

"Oh, dear."

Laura gripped the sheet. "I have to conceal it from him."

Lady Atherton shook her head slowly. "You know my opinion on all of this. What are you really afraid of?"

"That he will resent being trapped."

"He will have to accept his responsibility."

"That's the problem," Laura said. "It's the fact that he would be forced to marry me. His resentment would come between us. I married Phillip knowing that we loved each other. Bell doesn't love me, and he believes himself incapable of devoting himself to a family."

"I have eyes in my head, and that man adores you. As for his issues with having a family, I cannot agree. Look how well he gets on with Justin. He's been excellent with the boy, and I honestly believe his influence accounted for a good part of Justin's reform."

"Everything you say is true, but Bellingham is adamant."

"Perhaps the reluctance is not all on his part," Lady Atherton said.

"I don't know what you mean," Laura said. "I love him with all of my heart."

"Then I will give you the same advice I gave you previously. When you are my age, you will only regret the opportunities you missed. I am not you, but I daresay if you do not confess everything—and I mean not only the child but also your love for Bellingham—then you will regret this for the rest of your life. Mark my words, for the rest of your life."

Bellingham watched Justin fill his plate for the second time and grinned. Where did the lanky boy put it? A strange feeling entered his chest, not unpleasant at all. Then he realized it was fondness for the young man. He'd gotten in deeper than he realized, but there was no going back now. He'd set the wheels in motion, and now he must fight for the boy's right to stay with his mother.

Justin had turned over the proverbial new leaf, and he was flourishing in the country. All of his rebelliousness had disappeared. He'd just needed guidance, but that brought to mind his promise to Laura. Bell needed to discuss Justin's choice of friends. He had an idea of what had caused it, and he figured he ought to draw Justin out. It had been a long time since Bell had attended Eton and then Oxford, but some things never changed. Bell wanted to make sure that Justin knew how to handle bullies and have the courage to stand by his principles.

A knock sounded at Bell's door. "Come in," he said.

When Justin entered, Bell directed him to take a chair. "We'll wait for your mother."

"Lady Atherton told me Mama would be down directly."

"Very good. I take it you're enjoying your stay here?"

He grinned. "I'm enjoying the archery and riding. Harry and Colin are good sports."

"They're fine fellows, the sort you can depend upon."

"Like you," Justin said.

Bell gave him a wry smile, but Justin's words troubled him. He'd been dependable, perhaps a little too much so. This summer, he'd be leaving for the Continent. He didn't know when or even if he'd see Justin again. That was partly the reason he'd requested this meeting. He wanted to give Justin advice, but he'd felt that Laura should be present. After all, Justin was her son.

Laura appeared at the door. "It was open."

Bell and Justin stood.

"Please, take a seat," Bell said. "I wanted to discuss a few things with Justin, and I wanted you to be here as well, Lady Chesfield."

He turned his attention to Justin. "It's been a long time since I was your age, but I remember the bullying that went on in school. Someone was always the ringleader and harassed any boy who didn't go along with the leader. In your case, I suspect it was George."

Justin stared at the floor. "It wasn't precisely like that when we were in school," he said. "The older boys dunked one of my friends in the cold water. Everyone laughed. George had money and was in good with the older boys. Paul and I stuck with George so the older ones would leave us alone."

"So you felt grateful to George."

"Not really. I just tried to steer clear of bad situations. I figured George was a friend. I liked that he had a curricle, so he could take us places."

"He dared you to drink and stay out all night."

"Yes, I thought it was fun."

"I'm glad that's over," Laura said. "I won't mince words, Justin. I worried myself sick."

"I'm sorry, Mama," he said.

Bell folded his hands on his desk. "In four years, you'll be the lord of your property. You'll have to make hard decisions, and you'll have to be fair to the tenants. I know you understand your duty, and your mother has indicated she has been managing the estate. She will share her knowledge with you, and I think it would be beneficial if you starting taking over some of the responsibilities, gradually. Don't take on too much at first. There's a great deal to learn, so take your time.

"But you must be observant. There are men who will try to cheat you or lie to you. What I'm saying is you need to be a leader now. You need to stand up for yourself and those who depend on you. It's important to make sound decisions and not let others sway you. You will make mistakes, we all do, but the important thing is to find a solution. Of course, you will consult others, and you will sometimes have to make compromises. But don't ever compromise your honor."

"I won't," Justin said.

"Do you have any questions? You can ask me anything."

His chin came up. "Is my uncle going to take me away?"

"I'm doing everything in my power to prevent it. I won't lie to you. Your uncle is not an honorable man. The day I returned that flask to your mother, I saw the way he treated her, and I didn't like it. No man should ever bully a woman, but he did. I know he hasn't lived up to his responsibilities to you. None of that is your fault."

Justin looked at his mother. "I don't want you to be alone, Mama."

Laura's brows furrowed. "Try not to worry, Justin."

"I think we all need to be mentally prepared for the best- and worst-case scenarios," Bell said. "I have money, influence, and powerful friends, all of which I will use to stop your uncle. I will do my best to get the courts to award me legal guardianship over you. I will use evidence to make the case. It will go hard on your uncle when the courts learn that he ignored you for years. But I can't promise that I will succeed. So we have to think about the worst-case scenario, and that is that the courts will not transfer guardianship to me."

"I don't want to live with Uncle," Justin said, fisting his hands.

"I know it would be very hard," Bellingham said, "but no matter what happens, you need to be strong for your mother's sake. It would be a long four years for both of you, but do not let your uncle's behavior take away your honor. If the worst happens, you will know at the end of four years that you are free of him, and you will cut him from your life forever."

"I'm glad you told me the truth," Justin said.

"I'll keep you and your mother informed," Bell said. "I would want to know if it were me."

"It's so unfair," Justin said.

"What is?" Bell said.

"If my father were here, none of this would have happened."

Bell met Laura's gaze. She looked a little sad.

"I understand, Justin, but I have every expectation that you will make your mother proud." He stood. "It's a sunny day. Perhaps the three of us could ride."

Justin's eyes lit up. "I'm up for it. Mama, what about you?"

"I think I shall ask Lady Atherton to walk with me."

"But you're an excellent rider," Justin said. "And you've not had an opportunity since we went to London."

"Yes, but I want to ensure Lady Atherton has company this afternoon. She probably doesn't ride anymore."

"Another day, perhaps," Bell said, noticing she'd laid her hand on her stomach. She'd done it last night as well. He wondered if she wasn't feeling just the thing.

"Justin, let us find you a suitable mount," Bell said. "I'll show you the property. There's a bridge that recently was repaired. I want to inspect it. It's important to keep your property well maintained so that there are no accidents."

Later that afternoon

Laura had asked Bellingham to walk with her. Her stomach clenched as she went downstairs. She'd decided to take Lady Atherton's advice and tell Bell about the child. He deserved to know, and she would rather face it sooner rather than later. She would not sleep well until she had spoken to him. She donned a spencer and bonnet. Then it started to rain.

She placed her hand to her fast-beating heart and decided that his study would be the next best thing. When she reached his study, she found the door open. Harry and Colin were there. "Oh, I'm sorry for interrupting."

"The rain is keeping us all indoors," Bell said. "We plan to play billiards. Would you like to join us?"

She recalled that night the two of them had indulged in that wild kiss. From the beginning, she'd fallen under his spell. "Perhaps another time," she said. As she left the study, Laura felt a moment of relief, but she had to tell him at the next opportunity, no matter how much she dreaded it.

Chapter Seventeen

Thunder sounded as Laura dressed. The toast had helped settle her stomach this morning. Vexation filled her as she walked down the corridor, but she mustn't let fear keep her from doing what was right. Perhaps she could find a moment with Bell after breakfast. She treaded down the curving stairway, crossed the great hall, and stepped into the dining room. Everyone else was already seated.

"Good morning," she said. "Although I fear the weather will keep us indoors when I was so hoping to go out today."

Bell pulled out a chair for her. "May I fill a plate for you?"

"I had a light breakfast earlier, but I'll join you for a cup of tea." She was miserable because of what she was keeping from him.

Brutus barked, and Laura nearly spilled her tea.

"It's all right, Mama," Justin said. "Brutus is anxious for a scrap from my plate."

"Justin," Harry said. "I had a letter today from my cousin Sarah. She asked me to wish you well and hopes to see you in London soon."

Laura turned her gaze to Bell. "Since we must remain indoors, perhaps we could play cards or backgammon today."

Bell looked as if he meant to reply, but Lady Atherton spoke. "We have yet to get the official house tour. Bellingham, will you let us view the fine paintings and sculptures?"

"I think that is an excellent idea," he said. "Perhaps tonight we can play cards or a board game. Shall we gather in the great hall now?" he asked.

"Excellent," Lady Atherton said. "Justin, I would consider it a great honor if you escorted me. I realize that the usual custom would be for Bellingham to lead me, but we will not stand on ceremony."

Justin offered his arm to Lady Atherton "I would be honored."

Laura smiled. She was so glad to have her sweet, courteous son back.

She took Bell's arm, and he led the way upstairs to an enormous room that she had gotten a peek at not long after they arrived. "There is something I need to tell you soon," she said.

"Is something the matter?" he asked.

"I can't speak of it now, but it is important," she said.

"Let us meet in my study after we view the sculptures."

She nodded, and now her anxiety returned in force, but she must conceal her vexation.

After entering the room, her lips parted. "Oh, my," she said, walking past the statues. Everyone walked about and stopped to admire the fantastical art.

"It's stunning," she said to him.

"Thank you. He walked to the other side of the room. "This painting is one of my favorites," Bell said to Laura. "*Trompe L'Oeil of a Violin and Bow hanging on a door.*"

"I can see why," Laura said. "It is an illusion as it appears almost real."

He took her to the next one. "This is *Jacob's Ladder*. You see the foot of the ladder and seven angels climbing up and down?"

"Oh, yes," she said. "My father would like this one, I think."

"Now here is one I think Justin might appreciate." He'd pitched his voice so that Justin would hear.

Her son joined them, and a look of disgust crossed his face.

"It's made of marble and is called *Roman Foot Wearing a Sandal*," Bell said. "Supposedly the sandal would have been worn by a woman in the fifth century BC."

"Ugh," Justin said. "Those Roman women didn't have very attractive feet."

Laura laughed.

Harry clapped Justin on the shoulder. "What did I hear? Are you a foot man?"

"Harry, your jokes are ridiculous," Justin said.

"We keep him around for amusement," Bell said.

The rain sheeted outside the Palladian windows. Laura went to the window and looked out the wavy glass. Bell joined her shortly thereafter.

"Laura, I can't help noticing that you aren't yourself."

Her chest felt tight.

"Where are the family portraits?" Justin said. "I want to see the marauding ancestors."

There was a moment of charged silence. Justin could not know that his question would create such an uncomfortable moment.

Laura hurried over to him. "I believe Lord Bellingham is having them cleaned at this time," she said softly. "It is important to preserve art."

"Very well," he said.

Everyone started speaking again.

She hoped her son did not realize his comment had created a stir. When Laura turned to Bellingham, she saw his disturbed expression. Her heart went out to him. "Perhaps we can adjourn now and gather for games later this evening," she said, pitching her voice a bit louder so that everyone would know that the viewing was over.

Bellingham looked grateful as the others trickled out of the room.

Justin walked over to her and Bellingham. "Mama, did I say something wrong?"

"It wasn't you," Bellingham said. "I just don't like to see the portraits. It reminds me of happier times."

Justin looked at him. "I understand. I always feel a little sad when I see my father's portrait."

Her son had never told her about his feelings. "I think it is only natural," Laura said, "because we miss them and wish that they were still with us."

Lady Atherton looked at Bell. "We have the portraits made to honor our living relatives, because we know that one day we will be parted from them. I treasure my portrait of my husband. Without it, I fear that his features might begin to fade from my memory."

Laura felt the tension in Andrew.

He took a deep breath. "I will ask the servants to remove the sheets in the gallery now. We can assemble there in one hour."

When everyone else trailed out of the sculpture room, he looked at Laura. "What is it you wish to tell me?"

"I think we had better wait until after the tour of the portrait gallery," she said.

"Why?"

"Please trust me that it would be for the best," she said.

"Now you've got me worried."

She met his gaze. "Believe me, you are not the only one."

"Why are you purposely being cryptic?"

"Because what I will tell you will change the course of our lives forever."

"Laura, tell me now," he said.

"You will understand why afterward."

"You give me no choice, Laura, and I don't like it."

Her mouth trembled a little. "Actually, I will be giving you a choice." Then she hurried out of the sculpture room.

"Damn it all to hell," he muttered.

He went to the gallery immediately. The servants stood on ladders and pulled the sheets off. He'd wanted to view the portraits alone first. Four years had passed since he'd seen them. He'd left to attend a house party with Will, and when he'd returned, the doctor had ushered him out of the house due to the risk of contagion.

He walked about as the servants worked. The Elizabethan portraits were interesting. Then he found the one of his grandparents. He smiled a little. His grandpapa used to secretly give him and Steven sweetmeats when Mama wasn't looking.

Footsteps clipped on the wooden floor. He turned to find Laura approaching. She took his arm. "I thought you might come early, and if you are amenable, I would like to view them privately with you."

He grazed his knuckle along her cheek. "Thank you."

He showed her the portrait of his grandparents. "They passed only two years before my parents and brother."

"You had no cousins?"

"My father was the youngest and had no expectation of marrying. He had two living older brothers, who died in a carriage accident. One of them never married, and the other's two sons died in a boating accident. Of course, the entail passes down the male line. My mother's family was beset with tragedy as well. Two of her cousins died in riding accidents, and her brother died of illness."

He led her to the next portrait and took a deep breath. "My family."

"You and your brother look very alike in the portrait," she said.

"Steven...was two years younger. We played together." He inhaled and was a little humiliated by the shakiness of it. "My mother, Elizabeth, and my father, Harold."

"I see your resemblance to your father, but you have your mother's eyes, I think."

"She drew pictures. I have her sketchbook in London."

"I imagine she was very talented," she said.

"Her pictures were all of...Steven and me."

"That tells me she was a devoted mother."

"Like you," he whispered.

She bit her lip and blinked back the tears.

"Laura, they've been gone four years," he said.

He didn't know. She'd thought he could heal if he just faced the past, but looking at the portrait of his lost family made it all very real for her. They had been a vibrant and happy family. She knew what grief was, but unlike her, Andrew had not had an extended family to stand by his side when he'd lost his loved ones. He'd gone with his friends to wander the Continent, seeking something; perhaps it was to try to forget.

And now she was about to give him news that would send his life spinning out of his control all over again. Yet, he did need to know, and he was as responsible as she was for this child they had created. She couldn't keep this from him, but she would wait until all the other guests admired the portraits, and then she must tell him that he would be a father by winter.

The other guests arrived and walked about admiring the portraits. His defeated expression pierced her heart. There was an air of melancholy about him that disturbed her very much. She walked around by herself, but the portraits were like a blur to her because of what she faced when the viewing ended. While Laura thought it an important step for Bell to share the portraits with close friends, she realized her timing was terrible. She tried to think of a reason to delay, because she didn't want to shock him with her news after the viewing. Even one more day would give him some respite from the sadness that clearly enveloped him now.

After everyone had viewed the portraits, Colin regarded Bell with an enigmatic expression. Then he'd taken Harry aside. The two of them challenged Justin and Lady Atherton to a game of whist in the drawing room.

Laura was on the verge of claiming tiredness, which was true for her most of the time, when the butler entered.

"My lord, a man by the name of Smyth is here on a business matter. He said that he had information for you."

"I'll meet him in my study," Bell said.

Laura looked at him. "Is it the investigator?"

"Yes, there's bound to be news."

"I want to be there," she said.

"Laura, it may prove to be disgusting. I don't want to expose you to that."

"It involves my son," she said. "I want to hear it first-hand. I don't want to be protected."

"Very well," he said, taking her arm. "If it is too vulgar, I may ask you to leave."

"I can bear it. I wish to know, because he threatened my son."

Soon after they settled in the study, a knock sounded. When the investigator entered, he looked a bit taken aback at Laura's presence, but Bell told him to proceed.

Smyth handed him a leather folder. "The details are inside. He covered his tracks well. That's the reason for the delay."

"Give me a brief summary of what you found."

"I detected no criminal activity, but he's deep in debt."

He'd figured as much. "Is that all?"

"No, my lord. He is hiding something—or rather persons—in a village fifteen miles from his property in Goatham Green."

Bell arched his brows. "A woman?"

"Yes, my lord. A woman and two bastards."

"How is he supporting them?"

"I wasn't sure at first. So I dressed as a worker and

went to the local tavern to order a pint. Then I struck up a conversation with two of the locals and inquired about the possibility of finding work at Goatham Green. The men at the tavern advised me to look elsewhere. We knew he was bleeding the tenants, but he raised their rent by another twenty percent."

Bell went to his desk and unlocked a drawer and handed a full purse to the investigator. "Thank you, Smyth."

Laura had covered her mouth throughout the entire report.

After the investigator left, Bell looked at Laura "Are you all right?"

She nodded. "Oh, those poor children."

"So now we know that Montclief is in debt because he's keeping a mistress."

"He has a wife and five boys," she said. "How could he treat his family in such a vulgar and awful manner?"

"His bad character is fixed, I suppose. Now you know the reason he did not perform his duties as Justin's guardian."

"Why would he threaten to take Justin when he was supporting two families?"

"He probably meant to remove you from the house so that he could steal valuables. We know he's capable since he ransacked your town house. I think it is time to expose him. He is keeping a mistress and a family at the same time. The Court of Chancery will consider that immoral conduct, which is grounds for removing him as guardian."

"But the courts move slowly, do they not?" Laura said. "And there is scandal to consider as well. Oh, his poor wife and children. What of the other family?"

"I don't know what will happen to the two families, but I believe I can avoid public scandal for the sake of the innocents. Montclief does not want the world to know about his two families. I will tell him he'd better be prepared to be ridiculed and shamed if he wants to fight this. The easiest way out for Montclief is to sign over papers giving me legal guardianship of Justin. I can bring pressure to bear on Montclief by asking a few of my allies to review the investigator's report. Montclief does not want anyone to know about his vulgar activities."

"It would be better for Mrs. Montclief and all of his children," she said. "I hope Montclief recognizes that."

Bell drew out a piece of paper. "Now, I'm writing a letter to Montclief telling him I have Justin."

Laura gasped.

"He will come, Laura, and then he will have to face all of us." He folded his hands on his desk. "Now, what did you have to tell me?"

"It can wait," she said, rising.

He stood. "Laura, you were adamant that you must speak to me."

"It can wait until after we resolve the issues with Montclief."

"Are you certain?"

"Yes," she said. There was no point in telling him now. It would only add more stress to an already stressful situation.

Chapter Eighteen

$\mathcal{T}$wo weeks later, Laura smiled as Lady Atherton attempted to try her hand at archery once more. "I may be ancient, but I am determined to hit the bull's-eye."

"Run for your life, Brutus," Bell called out.

"Careful or I'll take aim at your derriere," Lady Atherton said.

Justin pulled back his bow and hit the target dead center.

Bell walked over to Laura. She sat on a wrought-iron bench embroidering an infant gown. "Is that the same one you were working on during the journey?"

"No, this is a new one," she said.

"How many gowns does an infant require?" Bell asked.

"You have never been around infants, have you?"

"No," he said.

"They have the usual human needs, only they are unable to take care of them."

"What do you mean?" he said.

She regarded him without smiling. "They soil their clothing."

"Ah," he said. "That would explain why the infant needs more than one gown."

Justin shaded his eyes. "There's a coach coming."

"I suppose that would be Montclief," Bell said.

Montclief strutted onto the grounds of Thornhill Park, slapping his gloves on his fat thighs.

He strode over to Laura. "I demand an explanation. You ran away with my nephew without consulting me. You will hand him over at this moment along with your key to Hollwood Abbey. Do not think to fool me this time or I will haul you before the courts."

Harry looked at Colin. "I bet you five pounds Bellingham will kill him."

"You don't have five pounds," Colin said.

"That's why I made the wager," Harry said.

Bell threw his fist into Montclief's cheek.

Montclief fell to the ground, where he floundered, holding his hand to his cheek. "I'll have you brought up on charges for assault."

"I rather doubt it," Bell said. "You have abused a lady. You threatened her without just cause. You also stole valuables from her home. You are not a gentleman. I feel very sorry for your children, who will probably find out that their father has a secret family."

Montclief's face turned crimson as he struggled to his feet. "Your information is false. Where did you hear this?"

"I am more than happy to read the entire report from an investigator I hired before all my guests and the local magistrate as well. The way I see it, you have two choices. You can fight me in a nasty public battle in the Court of Chancery for guardianship of Justin. However, I have solid proof that you have two illegitimate children and that you are morally bankrupt. I do not believe the court will judge you fit to be Justin's guardian, especially since you have utterly failed in that capacity.

"On the other hand, you can spare both of your families and yourself scandal by giving up your guardianship. I have no doubt the courts will agree that I am a better guardian, given that I am the one who helped his mother look after him while you were dallying with a mistress."

Montclief blustered. "Lies, all lies. You paid someone to make up the story."

"All it would take is the investigator to produce the woman with whom you are living out of wedlock and the children," he said. "Do you really want to be publicly humiliated in all of the papers?"

Montclief clenched and unclenched his hands. "He is my nephew."

"I disavow all ties with you," Justin said. "You are a terrible, selfish person."

Bell took out his watch. "Montclief, you have ten minutes to vacate my property."

Montclief's nostrils flared, but he walked back to his carriage. Not long after, it departed.

Justin hugged his mother. "We're free of him forever."

Bell met Laura's gaze.

"Thank you," she said.

* * *

Late that evening

As everyone else drifted out of the drawing room, Bell asked Laura to stay behind. He sat beside her on the red sofa and took her hand. "Laura, you must be relieved knowing your son and his inheritance will be safe from Montclief."

"I am," she said. "Thank you for all that you have done for Justin and me. It turned out to be fortunate for me when you insisted upon bringing that flask."

"I care very much for you and Justin," he said. "But I've gone so long without caring about anyone except a few trusted friends. Yes, I am adept at politics and anything that requires logic and a cool head. It is easy to be bold when there is no one for whom you are responsible. I wanted it that way, and I lived a hedonistic life. I was cold and cynical. If not for my friends, I don't know what would have happened. And then I met you, and gradually, without my even noticing, a part of me that had gone away came back."

"I'm glad," she said.

"I think it was because of you. When I first saw you, I was struck by you," he said. "You have a sweet smile that is so rare. I just knew at that moment that I was intrigued. Then the next day I returned the flask, and you were clearly vexed by Montclief's appearance. When you said I was your fiancé, I was amused at first, but Montclief proved himself so disgusting, I couldn't deny your words."

"I will be honest," she said. "You turned my world upside down. I mean no disrespect to my late husband, but I was woefully ill-prepared for that wild kiss. Your head will no doubt swell when I tell you I relived that kiss for many nights."

"The thing is I just leaped from one day to another," he said. "I didn't stop to think beyond how to entice you to my bed, but then I encountered your wayward son. I felt that if I didn't step in, Montclief would surely take him. I never intended to become so involved in your lives. It was only very recently that I reflected over everything and re-alized I had...re-created a family."

She looked at him. "What happened all those years ago when your family passed away?"

"I told you part of it previously. The doctor's latest re-port sounded dire for the first time. Their previous ones had sounded serious but hopeful. Until that moment, I did not understand how bad it was. I was young and scared. All I wanted was oblivion. I went to the room of an ac-quaintance, and I drank a lot of gin. I was roaring drunk and passed out on a sofa." He drew in a breath. "At dawn, I practically crawled back to my room. I don't recall any-thing until I heard loud banging on my door. When I opened it, the officials at the university said they had been searching for me the night before and couldn't find me. A coach was waiting." He paused. "They said I must rush home, because my parents and my brother had taken a bad turn. I had not seen them for two years. When I got home, I saw the straw at the door."

He leaned forward and stared at the carpet. "I was too late."

She set her hand on his arm. "That is why you feel guilty."

"I fell on my knees on the straw. I must have shouted out, because the door opened. My father's friend led me inside. There were three doctors. They tried to give me laudanum. I threw it on the floor." He swallowed hard. "I was furious with the doctors for not telling me the truth earlier. I blamed them, because I had not seen my mother, father, and brother for two years." He gritted his teeth. "They said it was for the best, because I was the heir."

Laura's heart ached for him. Now she understood why he'd never wanted to marry and have a family. "You did not have a chance to say good-bye."

"I was so numb I didn't know what to do. I think I was in disbelief. Then the coroner came, and all of a sudden, I felt as if I were suffocating. The doctors feared that I had become ill, but it was a reaction to the sudden shock. That same evening, my friends Will and Fordham came to the town house. I had thrown everyone else out, save the servants. My friends knew I was in bad shape, so they took me to Fordham's rooms. They plied me with brandy, because they did not know what else to do. They sat with me and did not leave me. I have no idea how much time went by before all the grief welled up in me. I wept, horrible sobbing cries for so long that I lost my voice.

"By the time I returned to England, I was a shell of my former self. You know the rest. My raking and the women. I didn't want to feel anything. I hated it when people asked why I'd been gone so long. I despised the lurid curiosity. I especially hated the stupid things they would say, that it was God's will or it was their time. I refused to speak about any of it. Anyone who even dared to mention my family got the cut direct. I wanted to forget, but I can't. I have nightmares where I relive that day. I never know when they will strike." He sat back and looked at her. "I can never escape it."

"You had no time to prepare for their deaths," she said. "Losing all of your family was a cruel blow. The doctors probably thought they were doing the right thing by shielding you, but your anger was understandable. You had no family to surround you in your time of grief, but you had friends who cared and made sure you were not alone."

"I don't know how I would have gone on without them," he said.

"I will tell you from my own experience that even knowing that the end is near, there is still shock when a loved one passes. I, too, felt numb at first, and then I kept encountering reminders of Phillip. It was the mundane items—a comb, a quizzing glass, a shaving brush—that tore my heart to pieces. The hardest part for me isn't the memories. It's that the sound of his voice has faded."

She took his hand. "I understand your guilt. I felt guilty, too. More than once when Phillip was in pain and being obstinate, I cut up at him. After he died, I cried because I ought to have been more understanding." She took a deep breath and let it out. "I know you feel that you failed your family, but given the circumstances, you could not have known.

"I think the reason you feel there is no resolution is because you had no chance to see them again. I may be wrong, but I know this much, for I have observed it firsthand." She blinked back the tears. "A part of your father lives within you. From the beginning, you knew how to manage Justin. While I believe I could have nipped his rebellion on my own, I was always grateful for your advice and for the time you took to be the male role model he desperately needed."

He put his arms around her and hugged her hard. "Thank you."

When he released her, the clock struck midnight. "It is late," she said.

"Laura, you said there is something important you must tell me."

She hesitated. It would be so hard to tell him. One more day would make no difference. "We are both emotionally drained. Tomorrow would be better."

His brows drew together. "Why are you procrastinating?"

"It is not something you will welcome." She was afraid, but she could no longer delay.

"You are leaving," he said.

"There is no longer a reason to stay. I plan to take Justin home to Hampshire as soon as transportation can be arranged."

"I insist on taking you back to London."

"I appreciate your offer, but I need to go home."

"Come back to London with me," he said. "I never took you to the opera."

"I can't," she said.

"Of course you can. I want to spend as much time with you as possible before I leave on my journey."

Her heart beat hard. He had a right to know. "There is something else I have to tell you, but I'm not sure this is the right time."

"There usually is no right time. Something is wrong. You have not been yourself since the moment we arrived here. At first I thought it was Montclief, but obviously that is not what troubles you now."

Her nerves got the best of her, but she had to tell

him. She couldn't even imagine his reaction, but the longer she waited, the harder it would be. "I...I am not barren."

He frowned. "What?"

She'd said it all wrong, because she was nervous. "Do you remember the night I told you there was very little chance that I would c-conceive?"

His lips parted. He said nothing for a full minute.

Her heart drummed in her ears. *I'm so sorry. I know you don't want this.*

"What are you saying?"

"I'm with child," she whispered.

He stared at her as if he were in shock. "Are you certain? You have not seen a doctor. You didn't conceive during your marriage."

"I have all of the signs." She gripped her hands so he wouldn't see them tremble.

He shook his head slowly. "It was only the one time that I..."

"I could submit to an examination, but I...I am sure of it," she said.

"Laura, I will send for a doctor tomorrow."

"No, I don't want Justin to worry that I'm ill. He took it so hard when Phillip died."

"I will tell him that you were feeling nauseous, but it's nothing to worry about." He raked his hand through his hair. "God, I never expected this."

"Neither did I."

"Don't worry. If you are pregnant, I will get a special license."

Misery welled up in her chest. She thought about that bright sunny day when Phillip had taken her for a walk and got down on one knee. He'd told her that he loved her and couldn't live without her.

"Laura, if you are increasing, I will take care of you and our child."

She looked at her lap.

"I know it's not what either of us wanted," he said, "but let's not assume the worst. We will get the verdict from the doctor tomorrow."

He'd referred to their child as the worst possible outcome. She blinked back tears. He didn't even know that his words had cut her heart to pieces.

"Don't worry. I won't abandon you."

"You have plans to journey with your friends."

"Laura, I can see that you're overset, with good reason, but you could be worrying for nothing."

"You don't want to marry."

"I know you never planned on marriage, either, but try not to worry."

Her words had blown back in her face, and now she couldn't take them back.

"One step at a time," he said. "Tomorrow we will know one way or the other."

She didn't need a doctor to tell her what she already knew.

He squeezed her hand. "I suspect that your symptoms might well be the consequence of vexation. You've had ample reason to worry about Montclief, but your son is safe now."

She knew that wasn't the case, but he was denying the possibility because he didn't want to face the consequences. Neither did she.

* * *

Bell paced his study. He'd told Colin and Harry to take Justin fishing. His friends had looked at him curiously, but they'd asked no questions. They knew him well enough to understand that something was awry.

Half an hour ago, the young doctor had arrived. Bell told him he thought his wife was with child. Last night, he'd remained calm for her sake, but he'd tossed and turned for hours. He'd told himself that it was unlikely she was pregnant. After all, she'd never conceived during her marriage. But her husband had been elderly, and she'd confessed that he thought his health was returning when he'd proposed to her.

He'd told himself that it was unlikely she would conceive because of her irregular cycles and because he'd only come inside her once. But even if it wasn't probable, it was possible.

He knew nothing about the signs of pregnancy, but thinking back, he recalled Laura's ever-present fatigue. Damn it all to hell. No wonder Laura had been acting oddly. She'd probably been scared witless.

Someone knocked on the door, startling him. He took a deep breath. "Enter," he said.

The doctor walked inside, carrying a bag and smiling. "Congratulations, my lord. You will be a father by winter."

His heart thudded in his chest.

"The approximate date is uncertain. Your wife's cycles are irregular, so it's a bit hard to determine. It's early days yet as far as I can tell."

He was breathing a little too fast. "She is with child?"

"Yes, and all looks well. The morning sickness usually passes after three months. Plain toast and weak tea when she awakens usually helps."

"Thank you," he said in a hoarse voice.

After the doctor left, Bell slowly sat in one of the chairs before his desk. His heart kept thumping. He was going to be a father. His chest tightened. He had to do his duty by her and the child.

He remembered that tiny gown she'd been embroidering for her sister. He'd told her she seemed like the sort who liked infants. She'd looked a little sad when she'd told him she was barren.

Sheer terror gripped him. He recalled the brute force of the pain when he'd lost his family. He'd decided never to wed because he couldn't bear to love someone only to lose them again. God help him. He'd relived that horrific day countless times in nightmares.

But he couldn't abandon Laura and the child. He had to overcome the fear, because she needed him. The unborn child needed him. He had to do what was right, because he wasn't the only one who was scared.

A knock sounded. He walked over to the door as if he were in a fog. When he opened it, Laura stood there. Her face was pale. "Come in," he said.

He led her to one of the chairs and sat beside her. "Laura, the doctor confirmed your pregnancy."

She laced her fingers over her flat stomach. "All last night, I thought about what we should do."

He had to shake off the shock. "I will go to London and get a special license."

"It will be a marriage of convenience," she said.

"Laura, don't worry. I will do my duty by you and the child."

"How can we forge a happy marriage under these circumstances?"

"We will make the best of it," he said.

"You are only thinking of the immediate situation." She looked at him. "But what happens after three months or six months when reality sets in?"

Something hot sizzled inside him. "We don't have a choice."

"You would not even commit to a friendship beyond the season," she said.

His eyes blazed. "What happened to all your words about my being a good role model to your son? Do you think that I would not be a good father to our child?"

"I have thought about this a great deal, but to be fair, I've known longer than you what we were facing. And I remembered that you said there would never be a Lady Bellingham. You told me that you will never be a family man."

"Circumstances changed. I will live up to my responsibilities."

She looked at him. "Yes, I'm sure you will, and you will resent being tied down in a marriage you never wanted."

"Damn it, Laura. You never wanted to be tied down, either, but this isn't about us. It's about our child. This is not what we planned, but we have a responsibility. What are your real objections? Because I know you haven't told me what you're really afraid of."

"What happens after we marry?" she said. "What happens when you realize that you are trapped into a marriage you never wanted?"

He searched her eyes. "I'm not the one objecting. You are. Now tell me the truth. Why are you so hell-bent on making this more difficult? You know we must marry, and I have promised to do my duty by you and the child."

Her eyes welled. "I know we must marry. The problem is you view it as a duty."

"Laura, you know I care about you."

"I've been married, and I will tell you that it takes commitment. Both husband and wife have to be willing to work through the problems during the hard times."

"You have forgotten the commitment I made to you and Justin."

"No, but I also have not forgotten the week you stayed away because you were getting in a bit deep, to use your words."

"So you retract your forgiveness, Laura?"

She winced. "No."

"Then for God's sake, tell me why you are putting us through this misery?"

"Because I don't know how we can sustain a marriage when you don't love me."

He went to his room and ordered his valet to pack a valise. First thing tomorrow, he would take a carriage to London and procure the special license. Then he went downstairs for luncheon. Everyone else was already seated at the table. Laura met his gaze and then lowered her eyes.

He took his place at the head of the table. "I have an urgent business matter in London. I must leave early tomorrow. I will return soon. Please feel free to stay."

Harry and Colin exchanged glances. Then Colin cleared his throat. "We should probably return as well."

Bell shook his head. "Stay. When I return, I will share news with you."

No one said much during the meal. They hadn't missed the charged atmosphere.

After luncheon ended, Bell approached Laura. "I wish to speak to you in my study."

She nodded and took his arm.

He led her inside. "I will procure the license in London. When I return, we will marry. I imagine you wish to invite your family."

"I am to blame for all of this," she said. "I have burdened you with my problems and put you in an untenable position. You must regret that you ever met me."

"No, Laura. I only regret that I have said and done things that led to this impasse. We will be forever bound by the child we have created. When I return, we will discuss how we will go on. We can choose to live in animosity or we can choose to work through our differences. I hope it is the latter, because I only ever wanted to make you happy. Now I don't know if that is possible."

"We have lived in each other's pockets. I think the time apart will allow us both to reflect and gain perspective of all that has happened. I said things that were unfair, because I was frightened. But you are right. We are bound by our child, and we must find a way to create harmony between us."

Chapter Nineteen

Five days later

Laura sat in the drawing room with Lady Atherton, who was embroidering a tiny gown for Laura's baby. "Bellingham will return tomorrow with the special license. Have you decided what you will wear?"

She felt a pang in her heart. "Yes, I will wear the blue gown with the sheer overskirt and a bonnet with silk flowers."

"My dear, why are you so unhappy? He is a good man, and he adores you."

"I love him dearly, but I don't know how we can find happiness when he does not return my feelings. I will always feel the pain."

"Did you tell him that you love him?"

She hesitated. "I told him that I didn't know how we could sustain a marriage when he doesn't love me."

"Oh, dear heaven," Lady Atherton said. "He may not have said the words, but he has shown his love for you repeatedly. Look at everything he has done."

"Do not mistake me. I am grateful to him, but he has never declared tender feelings. The most he has offered is friendship—and now marriage because of the child."

Lady Atherton set her embroidery aside. "Men do not communicate with words. They demonstrate their feelings. When a woman lets her man know that he is the only one in the world she could ever want, he feels he can declare his feelings."

Laura frowned. "Phillip—"

"Is gone," Lady Atherton said. "You must not compare them. Can you imagine if Bellingham compared you to other women? How would you feel?"

"I never openly said it to him," Laura said. "But he did say in a jovial way that he worried that he couldn't compare to my quote 'sainted husband.'"

"Laura, you are pushing him away because you are afraid that he doesn't love you, and in doing so, you are undermining your marriage before it even starts. He is every bit as vulnerable as you are, but he's a man, and he won't admit it. I want you to promise me when he walks through the door that you will greet him with open arms. Tell him that you missed him terribly, because I know you have. And then take him upstairs and tell him you love him and cannot live without him. Trust me. He will reciprocate in kind."

"You are right as always," Laura said. "I have nothing to lose but my heart, and I already lost it to him."

"My dear, I am positive he lost his heart to you many weeks ago."

* * *

The next day

Bell stepped out of the carriage, wishing he hadn't been so blind. If he'd only listened to her, really listened in the first place, he would have seen how simple the answer was. But he'd been stubborn and thought she knew how he felt about her. He'd told her he cared about her, but he'd been an idiot. He'd fallen short of the mark.

But he'd done something that he hoped would help make up for all of it. God, he was weary, but he was glad to be home. And he hadn't felt that way in a very long time. He started up the steps when the door opened.

Laura ran right into his arms. "I missed you."

Something in his chest unfurled, and he hugged her hard. "I missed you, too."

"Come with me," she said. "I want you all to myself."

He laughed a little. "That's an invitation I cannot resist."

She gave him a sly smile. "Justin and your friends are fishing. Lady Atherton is taking her beauty nap."

"Is there a reason you are telling me this?" he said as they walked up the stairs.

"Be patient."

She led him inside her room, shut the door, and threw her arms around him. Then she kissed him deeply. His heart expanded, and all he knew was that he had to kiss her back. She opened for his tongue, and he was lost in the wondrous sensations that only she could excite in him.

Then she looked at him. "I want you—now."

"Laura, darling, there's something I want to tell you first."

She caressed his cock through his trousers.

He inhaled and exhaled slowly. Then he caught her hand. "There's something I forgot to do before I left."

She looked at him quizzically.

He knelt on one knee. "I love you desperately. Will you marry me?"

Her eyes teared up a little. "I love you with all my heart, and I will marry you."

"Thank goodness," he said. "I invited your entire family to attend the wedding."

She gasped. "Oh, you are so wonderful."

"Your father will marry us."

"Oh. Don't tell him that we anticipated the wedding."

He picked her up and set her on the edge of the mattress. "I amended one of the rules."

"Oh?" she said.

"Rule number one," he said. "Tell her you love her, because that's the only rule that matters."

Epilogue

Eight months later

*B*ell's stomach clenched. Laura had been in labor for six hours. He was scared witless that something would go wrong. He couldn't bear it if he lost her and the babe.

Lady Atherton took him by the arm and led him to the sideboard. She poured a small amount of brandy into a glass. "Drink this to calm your nerves."

Justin jiggled his leg. "How much longer?"

"Babies take their time," Lady Atherton said. "Your grandmother and Aunt Rachel are with your mother. She will be fine."

A horrible guttural cry sounded. It wasn't the first time, either. Bell was so worried his mouth dried and his heart raced.

She cried out again for so long he thought she would burst something.

Then silence. All was silent. "Oh my God. She's hurt."

Then an infant squalled. Bell paced faster. The babe kept crying.

"Don't worry," Lady Atherton said. "They are making Laura presentable."

"I don't care. I just want to see my wife."

Laura's sister Rachel appeared at the landing. "You may come in now."

He bounded up the stairs, and then he treaded into the room where his beautiful wife lay with a bundled up infant in her arms.

"We have a son," she said.

His eyes misted as he watched Laura put the infant to her breast. He kissed her cheek. "Thank you."

"He is perfect," she said.

"I wish to name him after my brother Steven."

"I think that is a wonderful idea," she said.

"If not for you, I would never have experienced such joy," he said. "One day, I will tell him that it all started with his elder brother's brandy flask."

"You will do no such thing," she said a bit faintly. "Do you want to hold him?"

"Yes."

Laura showed him how to support their son's head.

He walked about the room, grinning at Steven. "Once upon a time, there was a very wicked earl who fell in love with a very pretty lady. She lied through her teeth and said the wicked earl was her fiancé. He demanded a kiss, but the pretty lady put a magical spell on him. The wicked earl was no longer wicked, because he fell in love with the pretty lady."

Bell returned to his wife's side. "I love you, Laura. If not for you, I would be a very lonely man."

She smiled. "My love, we were meant to be together."

Colin Brockhurst, Earl of Ravenshire, and Lady Angeline Brenham will do anything to escape the betrothal their parents arranged for them—even devise a faux courtship and breakup to win their freedom. But one searing little kiss will change everything...

Please turn the page for a preview of

What a Reckless Rogue Needs.

Chapter 1

Colin Brockhurst, Earl of Ravenshire, did not give a rat's arse about the promise that his mother, the Duchess of Chadwick, had made twenty-eight years ago.

The clatter of the horses' hooves on the curving graveled drive signaled his imminent arrival for the annual house party given by the Duke and Duchess of Wycoff, his parents' dearest friends. Colin caught glimpses of Padua House, a sprawling mansion that owed its bizarre façade to too many centuries of architectural renovations. His mother said the house had character. That was the kind explanation.

When the carriage rolled to a halt before the grand mansion, there was no one to greet him. Colin shrugged as he walked up the horseshoe-shaped steps. He'd arrived a week later than his family, having made an excuse about illness—anything to delay the misery. After the butler took his greatcoat, hat, and gloves, he directed Colin to the drawing room.

Colin trudged up the stairs, preparing himself for one of Angeline's cutting remarks and vowing he would not respond. He'd literally spent a lifetime dealing with her rude behavior, but no more. When she attempted to goad him, and he knew she would, he would simply give her a blank stare.

The Duchess of Wycoff welcomed him. "Colin, dear boy, we have waited an age for you. I know Angeline has been on pins and needles." The duchess turned to her daughter, who was engaged in a tête-à-tête with a gentleman. "Angie, darling, do say hello to Colin."

"Tardy as usual, Colin," Angeline said in a bored tone.

He bowed and muttered, "My lady."

"What, no enthusiasm?" The gentleman sitting with her laughed and turned to Colin. "Sorry, Ravenshire. I cannot resist Lady Angeline's wit."

Colin narrowed his eyes at Gordon Crompton, Viscount Sturridge. He was perpetually in debt, due to his well-known gambling habit. How the devil had he gotten an invitation to the house party?

Angeline's twenty-one-year-old brother, Simon, the Earl of Wescott, tried to affect a bored expression. "I brought Sturridge along for entertainment in your absence, Colin."

Colin wondered exactly what sort of entertainment Sturridge had introduced to Simon. He intended to speak to Angie's brother and find out how he'd gotten involved with that ne'er-do-well.

"Ah, here it is," the Duchess of Wycoff cried as a footman brought in an ancient cradle and set it before the fireplace.

Bloody hell, he hated this ridiculous ritual. Colin's

mother, the Duchess of Chadwick, whipped out a hand-kerchief to blot her tears. His twin sisters, Bianca and Bernadette, giggled behind their hands. His father leveled a stern gaze at him as if to say, *Do not dare ruin this for your mother.*

Two bright red splotches marred Angeline's cheeks. "Mama, please, not the cradle."

Well, at least on that count, he and Angeline were in accord.

The Duchess of Wycoff hushed her daughter and invited the Duchess of Chadwick to join her. Colin folded his arms over his chest and scowled at Bianca, who was whispering to Bernadette. Both of their eyes were dancing with amusement.

The Duchess of Wycoff drew in a breath. "Twenty-eight years ago, I laid my daughter Angeline in the cradle next to Colin. On that day, the Duchess of Chadwick and I vowed that our beautiful babes would marry." The duchess smiled at Colin. "Of course, we had hoped that day would arrive a bit sooner, but we have not given up hope." She regarded Colin with a meaningful expression, one he had no trouble interpreting.

Oh, Lord. Colin slid his gaze at Angeline, whose complexion had grown ashen. There had been many blatant hints over the years, but he actually felt badly for Angeline, too. It couldn't be any easier for her than it was for him.

He'd sworn he wouldn't cave in to their ludicrous marriage arrangement, no matter how much pressure his family exerted upon him. Of course, his mother had lectured him for allowing Angeline to remain on the shelf, which was absolutely foolish. If Angie wanted to marry, she'd find some poor sod who had no idea of her real nature.

"Well, then," the Duchess of Wycoff said. "Let us all rest for a bit. Dinner will be served at seven as we keep country hours."

Colin couldn't wait to escape.

Angeline hated being an old maid. The only thing that stood between her and ridicule was her father's title. No one dared jeer at a duke's daughter. But unless she did something soon, she'd find herself hopelessly on the shelf.

She had a plan, but she needed Colin's help. Of course, she might wait until after dark to sneak into Colin's room, but then she would be far too likely to encounter his valet. The last thing she needed was for the servants to gossip. Mama's maid Marie knew everything that went on below-stairs and above as well. Angeline meant to conceal the details from everyone except Colin. Hopefully he would cooperate for a change. The sight of that cradle today ought to put the fear of the devil in him, but then he was a man and could wait a decade or more before he chose to marry. She, on the other hand, would become an embarrassment to her own family if she didn't find a husband soon.

Angeline gritted her teeth. She despised having to ask Colin's assistance, but she'd run out of options. After she padded down the corridor, she turned right. She knew which room Colin occupied since it had long ago been officially designated for his use during the summer house parties. When she stopped before his door, she almost knocked, but she didn't want to risk alerting Simon, whose room was at the end of the corridor. So she eased the door open and slowly closed it with a slight *click*.

When she turned around, she gasped.

Colin stood there sans shirt with a towel in his hand. There was a dusting of black hair on his chest, and oh, heaven, an arrow of black hair below his navel. For a moment, her mouth went dry. When she raised her gaze to him, he shook his head. "Have you lost your wits?" he said under his breath.

"I need your help," she whispered. "It's in your best interest."

"Nothing about you is in my best interest. You had better go now. If we're discovered, they'll have all the ammunition they need to march us to the altar. Now go."

She wouldn't tell him that she feared she'd already become the object of derision among the ton. Drat it all. She ought to have found a husband two years ago, but the reason she hadn't done so stood before her. "If we go on as before, they will find some way to make us marry," she said.

"Short of shackling our legs together, they can't force us to walk down the aisle." He cupped her elbow. "Now leave here before someone finds you."

She dug in her heels. "I need a husband."

"What? You loathe me."

"I need you to find me a husband," she said.

He snorted. "You want *me* to make a match for *you*?"

Her face grew hot. "I should have known you would poke fun at me."

He took her by the shoulders. Even though she'd known him all of her life, she felt more than a little disarmed by the intense expression in his dark eyes.

"Why are you asking me to find you a husband?" he said.

She tried to push him away, but he held her fast. "The truth, Angie. Has this got something to do with Sturridge?"

"Do you think I'm stupid? I know he's a fortune hunter," she said. "But consider this. If you find me a husband, we'll both be off the hook forever. Imagine a life with no more cradle rituals."

"We're out in the middle of the country. Where the devil do you think I'm going to find you a suitor, even if I wanted to help you?"

"Invite some of your friends," she said.

"No. None of my friends are suited for marriage anyway. Why are you so desperate?"

She scowled at him. "Because if I don't find one soon, I will be on the shelf—or married to you. And you know very well our parents can exert more than a little pressure on both of us. Your father can cut your allowance, and my parents can pile on the guilt about how I'm embarrassing them. Before you know it, we'll be wed in woe."

"Angeline, I'm not finding you a husband, and regardless of how much our parents try to pressure us, they cannot force us to marry."

A knock sounded on the door, startling Angeline. Colin put his finger over her mouth. "Who is it?"

"Your father."

"A moment, please." Then he grabbed Angeline's hand and strode over to the bed. Using hand motions, he indicated she should crawl underneath the mattress.

She shook her head.

He pointed at the door and gave her a furious look.

She lowered to the carpet and scooted beneath the bed. Immediately, she held her hand over her face because she feared she'd sneeze from the dust. She looked at Colin's boots and saw his father's shoes as well. This was the most ridiculous thing she'd ever done in her life. She might have laughed if the consequences weren't so dire.

"Colin, you've allowed this to go on too long. Angeline is in danger of becoming a laughingstock. It is past time you proposed."

Her eyes smarted. She'd been right after all. Everyone thought her an old maid, a woman no one wanted. The only man she'd ever wanted had treated her like a pariah from as far back as she could remember. She ought to hate him for it, and she'd done everything in her power to show that she didn't like him one bit. But something had happened between them a year ago, and everything had changed for her. Apparently, nothing had changed for him.

"Papa, believe me," Colin said. "Angeline doesn't want to marry me any more than I wish to marry her. I know this is Mama's particular wish, but it is medieval."

"Colin, hear me well. I know you do not want to give up sowing your wild oats, but I won't stand for it any longer. Either you do your duty by her or I will cut off your allowance. I've said my piece. You will come to terms with your duty before this house party ends."

Angeline waited for the door to shut. Then she managed to scoot out from under the bed. Colin took her hand and helped her to her feet. "I suppose you couldn't help overhearing my father."

"Just as I predicted," she said.

"I have an idea," he said. "It won't be pretty, but our

parents will cover it up to ensure there's not scandal."

She regarded him through narrowed eyes. "What is your idea?"

"We'll pretend to be engaged. Then you will break it," he said. "After that, they'll give up this foolish marriage plan once and for all."

"Wait a minute, you're making me call it off?" she said.

"Keep your voice down," he said under his breath. "Only the woman can call it off, as you well know."

"Very well, but we must pretend to be...in love," she said.

"Oh, Lord."

"If we don't, our parents will know we've invented a scheme."

He considered her with a grin. "Well, perhaps we should practice."

"All you have to do is look at me as if you cannot live without me," she said.

He snorted. "I'm no actor."

"You'd better learn fast," she said.

"Me? It wasn't so long ago that you tried to stab my leg with a fork beneath the table," he said.

She took a step closer. "You deserved it."

"You deserve to pay for that," he said.

"Oh, please, I'm shaking in my slippers," she said.

He pulled her up to his chest. "You don't believe me, do you?"

She caught her breath. When she started to speak, he lowered his head and captured her lips.

THE DISH

Where Authors Give You the Inside Scoop

♥ ♥ ♥ ♥ ♥ ♥ ♥ ♥ ♥ ♥ ♥ ♥ ♥ ♥ ♥ ♥

From the desk of Vicky Dreiling

Dear Reader,

Some characters demand center stage. Like Andrew Carrington, the Earl of Bellingham, known as Bell to his friends. Bellingham first walked on stage as a minor character in my third historical romance *How to Ravish a Rake*. I had not planned him, but from the moment he spoke, I knew he would have his own book because of his incredible charisma. He also had the starring role in the e-novella *A Season for Sin*. As I began to write the e-novella, I realized that it was almost effortless. Frankly, I was and still am infatuated with him. That makes me laugh, because he is a figment of my imagination, but from the beginning, I could not ignore his strong presence.

After *A Season for Sin* was published, I started writing the full-length book WHAT A WICKED EARL WANTS so that Bell could have the happily ever after he richly deserved. A chance encounter brings Bellingham and the heroine, Laura, together. Bellingham is a rake who hopes to make a conquest of her, but despite their attraction, there are major obstacles. Laura is a respectable widow, mother, and daughter of a vicar. Bellingham only wants a temporary liaison, but he finds himself rescuing the lovely lady. His offer of help leads him down a path he never could have imagined.

I've dreamed about my characters previously, but my dreams about Bell and Laura were so vivid that I woke up repeatedly during the writing of WHAT A WICKED EARL WANTS. Usually when I dream about my books in progress, I only see the characters momentarily. But when I dreamed about Bell and Laura, entire scenes played themselves in my head, DVD style, and sometimes a few of them in a night. While I didn't get up in the middle of the night to write those scenes down, thankfully I remembered them the next morning and some of those dreams have made their way into the book. I'll give you a hint of one dream I used in a scene. It involves some funny "rules."

This couple surprised me repeatedly when I was awake and writing, too. I was enthralled with Bellingham and Laura. Yes, I know the ideas come from me, but sometimes, it almost feels as if the characters really do leap off the page. That was certainly the case for Bell and Laura.

As the writing progressed, I often felt as if I were peeling off another layer of Bellingham's character. He is a man with deep wounds and very determined not to stir up the past. Yet I realized that subconsciously his actions were informed by all that had happened to him as a young man. I knew it would take a very special heroine to help him reconcile his past. Laura knows what he needs, and though he doesn't make it easy for her, she never gives up.

I confess I still have a bit of a crush on Bellingham. ☺
I hope you will, too.

Enjoy!

[signature: Vicky Dreiling]

VickyDreiling.com
Facebook.com
Twitter @vickydreiling

♥ ♥ ♥ ♥ ♥ ♥ ♥ ♥ ♥ ♥ ♥ ♥ ♥ ♥

From the desk of Stella Cameron

Frog Crossing
Out West

Dear Reader,

My dog, Millie, doesn't like salt water, or bath water, or
rain—but it is the sight of all seven pounds of her trying
to drink Puget Sound that stays with me. Urged to walk
into about half an inch of ripples bubbling over pebbles
on a beach, she slurped madly as if she could get rid of
anything wet that might touch her feet.

That picture just popped into my head once more,
just as I thought about what I might write to you about

the Chimney Rock books and how stories shape up for me.

We were standing at the water's edge on Whidbey Island, looking across Saratoga Passage toward Camano Island. *Darkness Bound*, the first book in the series, was finished and now it was time for DARKNESS BRED, on sale now.

Elin and Sean were already my heroine and hero. I knew that much before I finished the previous story, but there were so many other questions hanging around. And so many unfinished and important parts of lives I had already shown you. When we write books there's a balancing act between telling/showing too much, and the opposite. Every character clamors to climb in but only those important to the current story can have a ticket to enter. The trick is to weed out the loudest and least interesting from the ones we *have* to know about.

The hidden world on Whidbey Island is busy, and gets busier. Once you are inside it's not just colorful and varied, sometimes endearing and often scary, it is also addictive. Magic and mystery rub shoulders with what sometimes seems…just simply irresistible. How can I not want to explore every character's tale?

That's what makes me feel a bit like Millie draining Puget Sound of water—I have to clear away what I don't want until I find the best stuff. Only I'm more fortunate than my dog because I do get to make all the difference.

Now you have your ticket to ride along with me again—enjoy every inch!

All the best,

Stella Cameron

♥ ♥ ♥ ♥ ♥ ♥ ♥ ♥ ♥ ♥ ♥ ♥ ♥ ♥ ♥

From the desk of Rochelle Alers

Dear Reader,

How many of us had high school crushes, then years later come face-to-face with the boy who will always hold a special place in our hearts? This is what happens with Morgan Dane in HAVEN CREEK. At thirteen she'd believed herself in love with high school hunk, Nathaniel Shaw, but as a tall, skinny girl constantly teased for her prepubescent body, she can only worship him from afar.

I wanted HAVEN CREEK to become a modern-day fairy tale complete with a beautiful princess and a handsome prince, and, as in every fairy tale, there is something that will keep them apart before they're able to live happily ever after. The princess in HAVEN CREEK lives her life by a set of inflexible rules, while it is a family secret that makes it nearly impossible for the prince to trust anyone.

You will reunite with architect Morgan Dane, who has been commissioned to oversee the restoration of Angels Landing Plantation. As she begins the task of hiring local artisans for the project, she knows the perfect candidate to supervise the reconstruction of the slave village. He is master carpenter and prodigal son Nathaniel Shaw.

Although Nate has returned to his boyhood home, he has become a recluse while he concentrates on running his family's furniture-making business and keeping his younger brother out of trouble. But everything changes when Morgan asks him to become involved in her restoration project. It isn't what she's offering that presents a challenge to Nate, but it is Morgan herself. When he left the Creek she was a shy teenage girl. Now she is a confident, thirtysomething woman holding him completely enthralled with her brains *and* her beauty.

In HAVEN CREEK you will travel back to the Lowcountry with its magnificent sunsets; slow, meandering creeks and streams; primordial swamps teeming with indigenous wildlife; a pristine beach serving as a year-round recreational area; and the residents of the island with whom you've become familiar.

Church, community, and family—and not necessarily in that order—are an integral part of Lowcountry life, and never is that more apparent than on Cavanaugh Island. As soon as you read the first page of HAVEN CREEK you will be given an up-close and personal look into the Gullah culture with its island-wide celebrations, interactions at family Sunday dinners, and a quixotic young woman who has the gift of sight.

The gossipmongers are back along with the region's famous mouth-watering cuisine and a supporting cast of characters—young *and* old—who will keep you laughing throughout the novel.

Read, enjoy, and do let me hear from you!!!

Rochelle Alers

ralersbooks@aol.com
www.rochellealers.org

♥ ♥ ♥ ♥ ♥ ♥ ♥ ♥ ♥ ♥ ♥ ♥ ♥ ♥ ♥ ♥

From the desk of Laura Drake

Dear Readers,

Who can resist a cowboy?

Not me. Especially a bull rider, who has the courage to get on two thousand pounds of attitude that wants to throw him in the dirt and dance on his dangling parts. But you don't need to be familiar with rodeo to enjoy THE SWEET SPOT. It's an emotional story first, about two people dealing with real-life problems, and rediscovering love at the end of a long dirt road.

To introduce you to Charla Rae Denny, the heroine of THE SWEET SPOT, I thought I'd share with you her list of life lessons:

1. Before you throw your ex off your ranch, be sure you know how to run it.
2. A Goth-Dolly Parton lookalike *can* make a great friend. And Dumpster monkeys are helpful, too.
3. Next time, start a hardware store instead of a bucking bull business—the stock doesn't try to commit suicide every few minutes.
4. "Never trust a husband too far, nor a bachelor too near." —Helen Rowland
5. If you're the subject of the latest gossip-fest, stay away from the Clip-n-Curl.
6. Life is full of second chances, if you can get over yourself enough to grab them.

7. "To forgive is to set a prisoner free, and discover that the prisoner is you." —Louis B. Smede

I hope you'll enjoy THE SWEET SPOT, and look for JB and Charla in the next two books in the series!

Find out more about Forever Romance!

Visit us at
www.hachettebookgroup.com/publishing_forever.aspx

Find us on Facebook
http://www.facebook.com/ForeverRomance

Follow us on Twitter
http://twitter.com/ForeverRomance

NEW AND UPCOMING TITLES

Each month we feature our new titles
and reader favorites.

CONTESTS AND GIVEAWAYS

We give away galleys, autographed copies,
and all kinds of exclusive items.

AUTHOR INFO

You'll find bios, articles, and links to personal websites
for all your favorite authors—and so much more.

GET SOCIAL

Connect with your favorite authors, editors, and
other Forever fans, and share what's important to you.

THE BUZZ

Sign up for our monthly romance newsletter,
and be the first to read all about it.

VISIT US ONLINE AT

WWW.HACHETTEBOOKGROUP.COM

FEATURES:

**OPENBOOK BROWSE AND
SEARCH EXCERPTS**

•

AUDIOBOOK EXCERPTS AND PODCASTS

•

AUTHOR ARTICLES AND INTERVIEWS

•

**BESTSELLER AND PUBLISHING
GROUP NEWS**

•

SIGN UP FOR E-NEWSLETTERS

•

**AUTHOR APPEARANCES AND TOUR
INFORMATION**

•

SOCIAL MEDIA FEEDS AND WIDGETS

•

DOWNLOAD FREE APPS

BOOKMARK HACHETTE BOOK GROUP
@ WWW.HACHETTEBOOKGROUP.COM